by vanessa zian

Dog Tags & Lace Series

Midnight to December

Ruby in July

Mine after October

March becomes Dawn

Standalone

The Lifecycle of a Crush

mine after october

vanessa zian

Cover Design - Lori Jackson Designs
Design Concept - Willow Winters
Editing - Jacqui Muller
Proofreading - Catherine Elaine

To my sisters, Maya and Melanie.
The very best kind of wild.

content notice

My books weave in subplots of trauma and may be triggering to some, but there's good reason for it. I'm all about the happily ever after, so you will absolutely get that. But my aim is to leave the reader with the ultimate narrative full of truths, no matter what the trauma. We all have experienced some at some point, whether it be "small t" or the "Big T" kind.

We learn by sharing stories. We heal by tweaking the narrative. And we soar when we can join forces and journey together. It's what I'm here for, and I'm so glad you are too.

prologue

. . .

lucy

I RUN MY hand through his hair, sandy blond with early stages of a receding line, and I think about the war I've started by being here in the first place. Already I can feel the regret bubbling in my belly, my subconscious chastising me for allowing my ego to escalate an otherwise surmountable relationship crisis. I should have never let this happen, never have lost control, and with that realization comes a strange urge to squeeze and tug his hair as hard as I can.

I'm lying next to him on my side with one hand cradling my own head and the other hand exploring the curves of his, the blanket beneath us providing makeshift and temporary accommodations. A small glisten of sweat rolls down his face in front of his ear. This August heat is no match for the office air conditioning.

"What are you thinking about?" he asks me.

"Ripping the hair right out of your skull," I answer honestly. Maybe there's something about lying naked with a man that brings out the truth in you.

"Hmm, nice. Alright, want to know what I'm thinking about

then?" He's on his back, staring up at my office ceiling, the fluorescent lights turned off and offering up a ghost-like gray hue. I can see the dust motes floating within the eerie evening yellow of sunlight, coming through in slashes between the slats of horizontal blinds.

He darts his eyes my way in question. What did he say again? Oh right, do I want to know what he's thinking. *Not particularly.*

I pull my hand away from his hair and drape my forearm on the curve of my hip. "Sure. Let's hear it," I lie.

"Skinning you alive," he says through a grin. The crinkles of crows feet come to life as he laughs at his own joke.

"Sick."

He raises his hands in surrender and says, "Just following your lead."

"Fair enough. Alright, I'll try and contain my twisted thoughts, then."

"That'd be a nice change."

He's full of shit. He loves my sick thoughts. No, not my harmful joke ones about ripping out his hair, but the other things. The thoughts that landed us right here on the floor in the slip of real estate between my desk and dirty office window. Again. After I swore we wouldn't do this. There are too many people that can get hurt in this.

Yet I gave in, and here we are. I knew damn well what he was doing when he suggested a "pick your brain" meeting after work. When he fed me that drink. I knew damn well what I was doing when I took it all too eagerly.

Liquid courage makes you do stupid things.

Sometimes we want to be stupid. It's a nice change from always trying so hard to be smart. To be a sensible grown up. To be responsible and perfect. Trying so hard to get everything right all the time, controlling every little thing you possibly can to stay afloat. I am absolutely sick and tired of working so hard all the time to get everything right. It's why I played along and took the "meeting" and the drink.

But there's that nagging little feeling in the back of my mind that knows I will pay for this in a way that will absolutely not be worth it. It's inevitable.

Too bad the me of one hour ago, one week ago, one month ago —too bad she didn't give a shit. Too bad she started this battle, which ultimately means marital war.

one

. . .

lila

THERE ARE THREE things in life that I absolutely cannot live without, babes: mascara, mascara, and mascara. There, I said it. Call me vain, whatever. You can keep your coffee, your beach house, your tequila. Actually, on second thought—mascara, tequila, mascara. Yes, that feels right, don't you think?

Although, right this second I'm regretting that final drink last night. I really hope the holder of the mascara wand in front of me can't smell my breath. He's annoyingly quiet, this particular makeup artist, and I tense a little with the thought of his potential judgment. Not that his opinion matters anyway. If he smells tequila and is judging me? Well then fuck him. He's probably just jealous that I live a fun life and he's stuck at home, pouring over the latest Sephora finds like it's the best thing he's got going on. I dare him to say something. I can just imagine it—"God, you smell like shit. Is that tequila on your breath?" And then I'd go, "Yeah, and your point?" He'd roll his eyes and go, "Hope it was worth it," and I'd flip my hair and go, "Oh, it always is. Jealous much?"

Oh my God. I'm doing it again. I'm having a pretend argument in my head with someone.

I groan a little at the realization. I'm pretty good at that kind of thing. I can have an entire, epic fight with someone in my head that in all likelihood will never even happen in real life. But it feels so *real* to me, it's wild. There's a sick satisfaction I get in having these arguments. I get to call them out on their shit and slam them with my "I see right through you" remarks that make them retreat like little wounded babies. In these fake arguments, I always win and say all the right things.

I catch a glimpse of myself in the mirror and groan again at the obvious haze in my otherwise green eyes. *You look like shit.*

"You alright, did I poke you?" My faux enemy looks down at me, and I see nothing but sincerity in his kind, hazel eyes. There's a sprinkle of gray in his black hair, but otherwise I really can't tell if he's thirty or fifty-five. He's perfectly sculpted in a black tee and has that kind of luscious cocoa skin that screams of being nurtured with care. I feel a pang of jealousy, not just of his skin in and of itself, but of the obvious self-love of the package as a whole.

"No, just one too many last night," I admit to him. What was his name again? Samuel? No wait, that was the one from the runway gig last week. This guy here has a more catchy name, I've worked with him once or twice before. He's one of the only makeup artists I've worked with where I don't actually feel the need to fix anything after he's finished.

"Thought I smelled a little tequila on that gorgeous mouth of yours." *Yes. I'm still gorgeous, he said so himself.* "Enjoy it for all you can, love. It's what youth is all about." He puts down his latest makeup utensil and scours through another bag for something. I watch with hope and relief as he pulls out a pill bottle. "What's your poison, aspirin or ibuprofen?" he asks.

"Bless you, Adrian," I say with a dramatic blink. (I'm so grateful his name suddenly came to me.) "I'd love the ibuprofen."

He pops out two pills in the palm of his hand, pausing mid

pour to check in with me, his eyebrow raised in question. I mouth "three" with a nod of my head and he drops out one more. I feel a kind of fatherly warmth as he gingerly grabs my hand to deliver the pebbles of rehabilitation. He hands me a water bottle and I greedily down the meds. Next he reaches in his bag for something else. I see the oat bar snack pack (flapjacks, as they call them here in the UK), and watch as Adrian deftly tears it open. My stomach drops as it dawns on me what he's doing.

I wave my hand, "No thanks, I'm okay." How many calories is one of those bars? Too many, I'm sure. Pure carbs that will convert to sugar and make me fat. I'm downright *scared* of that snack bar. I can hear a voice in my head, *there should be no emotions elicited by food,* but I push it down. Today's photo shoot is a big deal for a newish model like me, and I can't be bloated.

Adrian gives me a firm head shake. "Oh no, Lila. You are far too smart, *I know,* to be turning down one measly little flapjack. Have you eaten today?"

I shake my head no. Usually I would lie about that, but he seems to bring out strange truths in me.

"Thought so," he continues. "A small piece. Eat. It helps with the medication."

I sigh in defeat and take the oat bar piece he hands me. I bite in and try to ignore how delicious the tickles of caramel-sugar taste on my tongue. If I enjoy this too much, I'll be at war with myself all day, thinking about that goddamn flapjack and how I want another one, then another. Nope, absolutely not, I cannot do that.

I wash down the oat jumble in my mouth with some more water. I wait for a wave of nausea, but none hits. If I'm not mistaken, I do actually feel a bit better. Maybe Adrian's used to this kind of thing. Maybe I'm not a complete fuckup if he so accurately knew exactly what the model sitting before him needed.

"How long have you been in London for?" Adrian asks.

"Not too long. A few weeks." I'm underestimating that time

frame, but for some reason it sounds better to me to still be playing the "brand new" card.

It was three months ago that I up and packed my room in my apartment, stashed what I could in my parents' basement storage, shipped a few things overseas and jumped on a plane. One way ticket to London. New country, new opportunities, new life. I booked an appointment with an insanely expensive hair salon, chopped my platinum locks in exchange for a chic, pearl bob with the perfect full bangs ("fringe," as they call bangs here) to frame my jade cat-eyes that I'm famous for. Or trying to be, anyways. I had beamed when the stylist told me few had the cheekbones and overall look to pull off the cut. I remember looking in the mirror and noting that my nose didn't look quite so big with the bangs—I mean fringe. I had said so to the girl and she laughed, telling me my nose was far from big. I smiled politely, happy to have confirmation that she didn't think so, even if I do still feel I'd look better if my nose was just a teeny bit more upturned.

Alright, I realize I sound a little obsessed with looks, and I swear I really am not usually like this. It's just that I'm paving my way, painfully slowly, in the modeling world. What else are you going to do when you were born with sticks for limbs that tower over every other woman, and some men, at just shy of six feet tall? And don't even suggest basketball. No, baby cakes. Not for me. Not an athletic bone in my body. Yet I've been told my whole life that I should either play basketball or volleyball (I'm sure you know by now that's also a no for me), or that I should model. And with my mom being the famous L. Delphi-Ray, indie fashion designer extraordinaire, it seemed like a great plan.

Only modeling isn't quite so easy and glamorous as you'd think. I'm learning that the hard way. My mom tried to warn me, and the rebel in me is hell bent on proving her wrong.

My confidence is fading with each passing day.

Let me break it down for you. Unless you're Kendall, the pay is shit. Runway brings in maybe $300, max, but I did more than my share completely for free in the beginning. I tried to look at it as an opportunity to perfect my walk and get my name out there. Not my mom's name, not "Lilith's daughter," but me on my own. It worked, but fuck, I had to pay my dues. I have a decent portfolio, but each casting call is still hit or miss. I'm far from being requested on a regular basis, being the one in charge, or being the face of some top perfume for their latest campaign. I'm still waiting on that coveted *Vogue* cover.

I do get some photo shoot opportunities that are steadily getting me more and more exposure. Today is an editorial shoot for an online magazine so I'm bringing in a pretty decent amount. But it's not like I'm booking these things daily. Lingerie can pay great, but I don't have the tits for that. Great bubble ass, no tits. And no, that's not my own judgmental self-talk, I've actually *heard* that straight out of the mouths of casting and art directors at a few casting calls. Do they even realize I can hear them? My sister Lucy got the great rack, and far more comfortable height of five foot eight. We're both gifted with a natural year-long tan thanks to our mom's Columbian heritage, but Lucy got the glossy, caramel hair as opposed to my mousy brown. Oh, and she's good at everything. The perfect big sister, right along with our perfect mother. I'm the little fuckup, just a heads up, the one getting in trouble for being too impulsive, not having the good grades (sorry to disappoint you, Adrian, but I'm not as smart as you think!). I'm the little sister by eight years, and I have the feeling I'll never be seen as an actual adult by my family. At least not if I were to stay in Pennsylvania, where I was born and raised, quaint suburb outside of Philly.

So here I am, twenty-five and "old" by industry standards, navigating the tube and horrible commute times to any job I'm fortunate enough to get.

But it's a start. And it's mine.

Why London, you ask? Because it's old and beautiful, glamorous enough to be on another continent, but I can still speak the language. If I were Lucy, I'd be nearly fluent in Spanish and would have had more options. But my Spanish is painfully far behind hers, to the point where I'd rather keep it to myself.

Adrian feathers a brush on my neck and collar bone, and with each light stroke to my skin I feel myself falling more and more into relief. This is good, painting my skin brings the perfection I need. And Adrian is absolutely one of the better artists.

"Are you finding success so far?" he asks me.

Ordinarily I'd lie and overemphasize my so-called "success," but I'm drawn to his fatherly air of wisdom. "Not quite as much as I'd like, but I'm getting some consistent work, at least. I wish it'd pay a bit more, but it's better than nothing."

"You have a beautiful, angular look and eyes that are a dream to paint and play up."

"Why Adrian, I think I'm blushing now."

"No, that's just my Chanel rouge on the apples of your cheeks," he teases with a wink. "Where are you staying?" he asks as he rifles through his plethora of compacts and cases.

"An acquaintance of mine hooked me up with a girlfriend and we share a flat." I'm tempted to brag and say that the "acquaintance" in question is famous Grammy winning musician Grayson Atkinson. Friend and colleague of Ruby Francesca, also a Grammy winning artist. But to mention that would then lead to further questions, which might lead to conversations of Ruby's fiancé, the charming Joey Conti, and my heart might break a little at that. "It's fine for now," I continue, "but I'm not sure I'm the type to share a tiny bathroom with someone forever."

"Ah, yes. You Americans are used to supersized everything, bathrooms included, I imagine."

"Oh I'm absolutely fine without supersize, believe me. Just not when it comes to bathrooms. And closets," I add with a little laugh. "Your idea of 'closets' around here is quite the adjustment I've had to contend with."

Adrian dabs his ring finger in a circle of hot pink powder before moving to my eye. I close my eyes and feel the delicate pressure of his finger on my lid. "You and my daughter would get along great," he says. "She's currently obsessed with clothing and complains about her tiny wardrobe on a regular basis. My wife and I used to joke that we'd ship her off to Texas, but I have a feeling she actually wouldn't mind that."

"You have a wife?" I blurt out in surprise. "A straight make-up artist? That's gotta be a first."

"Late wife, she passed away four years ago."

"Oh my gosh. I'm so sorry." I gulp. I'm highly awkward in situations like this.

"It's alright. But love," Adrian says with a playful tap on the tip of my nose. "You must learn to shed those outdated, ill-fitting concepts of people. Humans don't all fit into neat and tidy boxes, and the more you try to shove them there, the less you're able to see and accept the truth and beauty of others." He looks pointedly at me. "And of yourself, especially. A terrifyingly dark place to live," he says with a mock shudder.

I scrunch my nose in shame. Apparently I'm a fuckup in London too. "Sorry, you're just..." I attempt something clever to recover, "...too pretty to be straight, that's all."

"Flattery will get you everywhere."

I relax a little, relieved I haven't offended too badly. "How old is she? Your daughter?"

"Thirteen." Adrian shifts over to my other eye. "And I have an eleven-year-old daughter as well, but she's not quite been bitten by the fashion bug just yet. It's coming though, I can see signs of it already. Extra long looks in the mirror and changing outfits twice in a day. A shopping trip request is next, I'm sure of it."

I smile politely, thankful for Adrian's small talk. It calms my nerves, which I need today because according to my agency, the photographer on today's shoot is an "industry genius." In fact I was told I should be thrilled he chose me for one of the looks. Apparently he's the main reason I landed this assignment, and it'll be my biggest one yet, offering more exposure than I've had for any other job so far.

I can hear the chatter and planning of the team getting set up in the sterile white of the studio area. I steal a peek over to the space and notice what I'm guessing to be the photographer, given the camera in his hand.

He's dressed in all black, tall and lean with broad shoulders. Sheer body language and exuded confidence scream "I know what I want, and you better make it happen." There's something intimidating about him.

My heart starts doing a little gallop. Everyone around him seems a bit fidgety, mirroring my nervousness. Everyone except the stylist, anyhow.

And then the photographer turns his head slightly, and my heart really starts to pick up. I squint, realizing that I've met him before. Just recently, actually. Last weekend. *Oh, shit.*

"Quit squinting, Lila. We can't have wrinkles, now, can we?"

I look back up at Adrian and murmur, "No, we cannot." I close my eyes again, let him continue his work as I think back to the photographer. I'm trying to marry my recollection of him from this weekend to the figure about to be staring at me through a lens. Because I had pegged him that night we met as someone I had high hopes to get to know better.

In fact, I pegged him as my Hot Nerd.

I get a little flutter of excitement as I calculate the odds of him being today's photographer. Would he remember me? When I say we "sorta" met, it's because I think there may have been a communication gap of sorts.

We were both at this party, and I was looking exquisite in black sequined shorts, a sleeveless burgundy v-neck blouse, cut low, and an oversize suit-style black blazer. I've been learning some go-to looks, because you just never know how to dress when you're outside of your usual comfort zone, but I was feeling confident that night as I compared myself to the other guests.

Yes, I was feeling hot, loving my chic new bob, fringe tickling my lashes, and so I made my move on Hot Nerd. Except in the entire course of the brief interaction, he said not so much as a single word to me in response.

To clarify—that's not exactly the norm for me.

It was in the dark basement, or rather "lower ground level," of some affluent composer's house (mansion, really). Grayson had hooked me up with the invite as his plus one. Having famous friends is nice, right up until they ditch you for their own adventures. I guess Grayson figured I could handle my own, and he's right, I can. Plus I was grateful for the in, seeing as networking and meeting the right people is basically my full time job at this point. I'm scraping by, and late nights and my medicinal crutches are burning holes in my pockets. This lifestyle isn't sustainable unless I start making some real money.

Back to this party, though, and the run-in with my guy. Actually, let me first tell you about the *house* where this party was hosted. A sprawling estate, ancient gray stone and spread out in such a way that there was an actual courtyard nestled between long stretches of wings. Right here in London. As I walked in I was more than a little thankful to be on the arm of Grayson, who in his usual way walked in like he owned the place. He was looking gorgeous as always in navy slacks and a paisley button down, and we wandered straight into the Wine Lounge. Yes, a lounge, not a cellar. A room specifically for wine—the walls decked out with a grid pattern of bottles on display. The wallpaper was this iridescent black and white, called "oyster shell" and textured to the point of being art in and of itself. I had been commenting on the beautiful elegance of it when a velvety American female voice said, "Thank you," and introductions were made with the very tall, dark, and stunning Beth Diana Smith, interior design extraordinaire.

The name rang a bell—I remember my mom gushing over an article about her a year or two ago. "Are you usually based out of New Jersey?" I asked.

"Yes!"

"Recently in House Beautiful?" I already knew the answer, but I was trying to be chill and casual.

"A time or two, yes," she said in the kind of humble way that awakens my envy. You can't be a creative genius *and* very cool about it. "Let's see, there I most recently I wrote an article on Black designers. Maybe that's what you're thinking of?"

I nodded, feeling very out of my element. This woman is not only creative, but smart to the point of contributing to respected magazines. My insecurities were bubbling in a most unwelcome way that evening.

"My flat has been completely elevated to the next level, thanks to this one," Grayson boasted, grandiose as always, with air kisses to each of the dazzling Beth Diana Smith's cheeks.

"You designed Grayson's place too?" I asked, impressed. Beth nodded and I tried to act knowledgeable on interior design, saying I love how every corner of this space as well as Grayson's has something bold and unique, internally thinking how completely incapable I would be of executing looks so exquisite on my own.

So basically, I had been feeling a little small that night.

And as I said, Grayson's company wasn't long kept, and Beth Diana Smith was quickly scooped up by another party guest—an actor I recognized—eager to pick her brain on her country estate.

"Don't get into too much trouble now, love," Grayson had said to me before scurrying off to a group of very fancy people, leaving me alone and feeling out of place. With my mom being who she is, I'm used to a certain amount of opulence and high society, but it still isn't *my* name that has earned anything.

So look, when you're in a situation like that, a home of someone obviously wealthy beyond imagination, and surrounded by the best of the best in a city like London, the last thing you do is look intimidated. So I popped my chin up in the air, grabbed a champagne flute from a wandering caterer's tray, and swept my eyes across the place to assess my plan of attack. I had noticed a half-circle staircase offset from the cream marble floors of the entry hall, with an enticing pulse of music calling from down below. I had followed the sound, carefully clacking my heels on the steps, and rounded a corner to a space that looked like its own private night club. A sleek bar, bathed in black granite sat nestled in the corner. The black was echoed on the walls, broken up by massive canvases of modern art and an aurora light display of color waves from some unknown source. Whiffs of expensive perfumes and cologne hit my nostrils, and I was glad I had dabbed on my YSL before walking in.

While it was dark and crowded in there, a mix of beautiful people all stylish and probably snobs, I still felt oddly on display, The American Girl Nobody, drowning in a sea of glamour and ease, the laughter floating around me but never quite reaching my bubble.

It was right as waves of social anxiety were about to hit when I saw him. This one guy by the bar. *Oh yes, yes please.* He was delicious, a beautiful nerd, from what I could tell, leaning on the bar but talking to no one. He wore a blank and maybe bored expression on his face, clearly out of place in the swarms of stylish people around us.

Hear me out—he had on a pale blue, button-down shirt, an actual scarf, and a navy sweater vest. I know, adorable, right? Simple jeans, glasses, shaggy pitch black hair. He looked like he had been an extra on a different film and accidentally wandered onto the wrong set. I remember thinking I could eat him right up, he was so yummy. Sparkling emerald eyes, if I remember correctly? I'm kidding. I absolutely remember. They were fucking gorgeous.

I had glided my way up next to him, and leaned an elbow on the bar, noting he was tall too, probably six-four. Even in my heels I was still not taller than him, which is rare for me. Slim build, but the right amount of broad shoulder width to not be scrawny. His sleeves were pushed up the slightest bit on his forearm. *Wait, now, I* had thought, *is that a peek of a tattoo?* I registered how sweet it was, that my hot little nerd had a hot little tattoo. All I could see was a bit of black ink, the rest hidden beyond the sleeve. He had looked over to me, and I took my shot.

"You look like you might be my next boy toy," I purred and gave him my best "fuck me" eyes, kind of heavy-hooded and full of promise. The weight of my lashes had me thankful I just had them done.

I watched to see when realization would dawn for him. It's a fun moment for me, when my conquests stammer upon realizing I've chosen *them* to flirt with. I waited for the same look from Hot Nerd—that the gorgeous blonde next to him was actually hitting on little old him. He'd had on these tortoiseshell glasses that night. They look to be the same ones that I'm noticing on him here in the studio now as I watch him fiddle with some lighting setup. My God, glasses and tinkering with the lighting, I can't even with this cuteness. Hot nerd vibes all the way.

But last weekend at the party, he had only stared at me as I made my move and said my line. His face was unreadable. He had reached in his pocket and pulled out a small, silver case. As he opened it I watched in disbelief as he revealed cigarettes, and hand rolled ones by the look of it. *Maybe joints?* I had thought. I wasn't sure, I just remember being surprised. I was mesmerized by his long fingers, seductive-like, as he grabbed a slim, white stick. He gestured to me, silently offering me one, and I shook my head no.

Did he not hear my pickup line? I had wondered. Maybe I should have spoken louder, but I seriously doubted he didn't hear me. I thought that maybe he didn't speak English.

I blink away the memory and look back up to Adrian as he sprays some solution on a brush. "The photographer, is he from around here?" I ask.

Adrian glances over his shoulder, tipping slightly at the waist to peer around the corner. "Simon Sharp, mastermind," he says, returning his attention to me. "You mean is he from London?"

"Yeah. I think I met him last weekend at a party, but I wasn't sure if he spoke English."

A suspicious smile snakes its way across Adrian's face. "He speaks English. When he wants to."

I nod, having no idea what that's supposed to mean, but I file away the info. My mind is officially intrigued and floats back to my interaction with what I now know to be Photographer Simon Sharp and his surprising smoking habit that contradicts his nerd-like self. Guess we all have a secret vice or two.

Simon Sharp had raised the cigarette to his lips, reached back in his pocket for a lighter, and once again my eyes were glued to him. I watched the flame of the elegant silver lighter as it met the tip of his smoke, igniting a round glow of burn at the end. As the clouds of smoke curled their way over to me, I inhaled. Definitely tobacco, not a joint.

"You don't strike me as someone that would have such a naughty little habit," I had said. His fingers pinched the cigarette, grabbing it out of his mouth and he exhaled silently, still saying nothing. So far the only indication he'd given me of even registering my presence was the small gesture to offer me a cigarette. A *fag*, I remind myself. I hate to sound so painfully American.

I remember crossing my arms over my chest, hoping my pushup bra was doing the impossible and creating a little cleavage in the V of my blouse. What I wouldn't give to have been gifted with Lucy's tits.

"Don't be shy, now," I said into his ear as intimately as I could manage over the music. "Did you hear me, handsome?" Once again I felt like I was failing to get his attention. He wasn't even looking at me at that point, just staring straight ahead like I wasn't even there, the profile of his face his only offering. I figured I was making him really uncomfortable. My new haircut *did* seem to have an intimidating effect. I grazed my fingertips on his chest, ever so slightly, the soft brush of his sweater vest revealing quality cashmere. "I said, 'you look like you're going to be my next boy toy.' Doesn't that sound fun?"

At that I did in fact get the tiniest side glance out of him. But to my disappointment it was a blank stare at me, and then his eyes darted down to my hand on his chest, before lazily pulling right back away from me again.

I dropped my hand from the beckoning softness of his sweater vest, and he raised the cigarette to his lips again, cheeks sucking in slightly as he inhaled. Call me crazy, but all I could think was that my hot and shy nerd was looking so sexy with that smoke. Why is it that in Europe, everything looks better? Eating bread and cheese in the U.S. makes you look like a cow. But in France? You look seductive. Drinking beer in the U.S. conjures images of frat boys, or worse—a beer bellied, red-nosed middle-aged drunk. But in Germany? Merely fun drenched in tradition, the smell of yeast a perfect compliment to charming beer garden halls.

And here in the UK, smoking a cigarette (indoors, no less) looks sensual as fuck.

I blink away the memory, realizing I'm a bit flushed under the warmth of the studio lights as I watch my Hot Nerd now, prepping the shoot. Today he's dressed simply and professionally in black slacks and a slim-fitting black turtleneck, (only in Europe could a turtleneck on a man look hot), and I'm wondering if he's got that cigarette case on him now. He moves with ease around the setup, his dark hair shaggy like proper haircuts are the least of his concerns. His face sports the slightest of beards, just as it had a few days ago, and I wonder what scratching my nails through it would feel like. He's chatting with someone, an assistant, probably, gesturing this way and that. I notice with curiosity the young girl with pink hair nodding nervously at him, fidgeting and looking eager to get out of his presence. Poor little thing. Maybe she, too, has a thing for our guy.

Oh he's mine though, babe. Sorry, buttercup. Feels like destiny that we've been thrown together twice in one week.

Besides, those two wouldn't know what to do with one another anyway. I bet it would be all awkward fumbles and lots of, "Sorry, yep, sorry. This okay?" Hot Nerd clearly needs a strong woman like me to pull him out of his shell.

"Mastermind," that's what Adrian had called him, confirming the genius that my agency has touted. I can picture the studious and quiet kid young Simon must have been, the awkward little artist in school, excelling when the other kids were focused on rugby and whatever else little British boys do.

I straighten in my seat as I watch Simon scanning around the area. He glances over my way, green eyes behind those tortoiseshell glasses meeting mine, and he catches me staring. I want to ease his mind, so I slowly lick my lips and smile, shimmy my shoulders a little and wink.

But to my complete and utter shock, Simon furrows his brow in a scowl, slowly shakes his head and *rolls his eyes*.

Wait, what? Did I see that right? That was not at all the awkward Hot Nerd demeanor I expected. If I didn't know better I'd think he just looked at me with irritation or something.

"Mouth open," Adrian says, with a gentle hand on my jaw to face back toward him. I do as he says, parting my lips so he can complete his magic, and I think back to the party and how my brief interaction with Simon ended.

He had maintained his silence and after a few heavy moments of nothingness, popped up from his lean on the bar before turning away. He then headed toward the massive floor to ceiling sliding doors, open to the patio beyond, and stepped out into the night. I was left staring at the back of his sweater vest, a smidge guilty at having scared him off. I had watched as he flicked his cigarette into a fire pit, then headed up a small set of wide, stone steps and out of sight, the black night swallowing him up. I was tempted to follow after him, tap him on the shoulder for one last communication attempt, but I don't do that. I don't chase after boys, they chase after me.

At least, they usually do.

I push away the disgusting drip of self doubt that just threatened to take up space in my head. And then it dawns on me—he's a photographer, of course! An artsy photographer, which means he's probably gay! Gay, and also just really, really shy. Nerd types never do know how to talk to me without stammering. Hopefully he'll be able to push past that as he's working with me today. Poor guy must struggle given that he's surrounded by beautiful women on a regular basis. Maybe behind a lens he finds more confidence, or maybe his awkwardness adds to his genius somehow.

A hairstylist comes up to make a few adjustments, and I'm directed to the rack where a dress with an attached dark hood awaits me. I step in, let the stylist Meg adjust the hood just right around my head.

"Oh, your fringe is perfect with this," she gushes, and I beam. I look incredible, I'm sure of it. I prepare to make my way to Simon and the set. Oh well, he may be gay, but at least I'll have some eye candy for my shoot. I grin and offer out my hand to him.

"Lila Ray, it's nice to *formally* meet you. I hear your work is exceptional, and I have some great ideas for this look. Let's have some fun, right?"

I wait for his response, knowing I finally get to hear my Hot Nerd's voice. I'm a little tingly at the thought.

Only the words in his gravelly voice are not at all expected, because instead of a return of my greeting, he simply scratches out, "No."

The room is momentarily silent, other than the subtle tones of Supertramp's "Bloody Well Right" playing as our background music. The pink-haired assistant says, "No? No to what?"

And Simon nods his head toward me. "No to her."

My cheeks feel hot and I'm thankful for the layers of foundation, a mask of my embarrassment. Surely he didn't just say "no to her," meaning no to me, right?

But apparently he did, because to drive home his point, he says, "She's absolutely all wrong, this won't do." He then turns to walk away, and I'm left stunned and silent in his wake.

two

. . .

simon

SIMON KNOWS HE'S being rude, but that's really none of his concern. This is not someone he would like attached to his name, as he knows there are plenty of other models out there. He has no problem turning away one desperate, yet hopelessly spoiled American.

He's done it before, and he'll do it again.

Cherry, his assistant, coughs uncomfortably, following him. "Are you sure, Si?" she asks.

He stops walking and turns to her. "Not her. She's not right for this."

"Right. Well our next model is Carly, and she isn't due to arrive for another twenty minutes. She'll still need hair and makeup."

Behind him he hears the art director whisper, "Hang on, let me see what's going on." Then an American accent responds, "Actually I'll handle it, I think I know what the problem is."

Footsteps shuffle up to him and he feels a tap on the shoulder. Reluctantly, he turns to face the blonde. He offers her no smile, only clenches his jaw and keeps his lips in a stern, straight line. He says nothing, eager to see her squirm.

But she grins, to his annoyance. "Hi," she leans in with a whisper like they are old friends sharing a secret. "I think you and I both know what this is about. And look, I apologize for the other night if I made you uncomfortable. I by no means meant to. Start again?" she asks, holding her hand out once more for an attempt to shake.

Simon remains silent, hands held in his pockets.

The blonde drops her hand. He watches with amusement as her face shifts from sweet and what he is sure is faux innocence, to the tempers of rage he has a feeling boil just below her surface. Her voice clipped, she attempts to speak again. "Okay, look, am I missing something here?"

"Yes. That you're no longer needed," he says.

And he delights in watching her eyes narrow, steam nearly escaping from her ears under the caped hood. "Excuse me, but what the fuck is the problem here? I mean I can do it all, whatever you need, I'll make it happen. The agency did say *you selected* me."

He clenches his jaw tighter, remembering her portfolio. He had been rifling through an endless charade of beautiful faces, nearly bored and ready to take a break, until this one had caught his eye. A blonde with a stunning look. Not girl-next-door in the way that can make many blondes come across as generic. No, this one had an air of mystery to her. The cheekbones, the pointed chin, the cat eyes, just a bit too small, but wide and set in such a way that instantly captivated. Simon had poured over this mystery girl's photos with admiration. Her movements held an intensity to them. She was most certainly new to the fashion scene, some angles off, elbow positioning or hand placements not quite right, but that could all be tweaked with the proper direction. It was her eyes there were impossible to ignore.

He had in fact been eager to work with her, help her unleash her full potential. Simon was a professional, first and foremost, but he had to admit he was eager to have an excuse to touch her skin, maybe shift a stray strand of hair from her face.

His intrigue quickly evaporated though when she had approached him at that ridiculous party, stating her claim on him as her next boy toy.

He was instantly repulsed. Simon was not the man for that kind of job. He had been so disappointed when those words slipped from her beautiful mouth. Disappointed, and surprised when he heard her American accent. Her look did not match the California "vibe" as they say one bit. And yet, American she clearly was. He had hoped that night that she was just tipsy and embarrassing herself, that while her personality was not what he had imagined, at least he could still work with this new talent and see what he might pull out of her.

But then here today she had done it again—another forward move when she'd given him a look when they locked eyes. She licked her lips in a ridiculous way that he knew was meant to be sexy, but only further added to the bitter taste in his mouth about this girl. She was revealing herself to be nothing like what he had hoped when he first saw her portfolio.

And then the way she marched up to the set as though she were the one in charge. Absolutely not. It was the final straw. At that moment he refused to work with her.

He glances back down to Cherry's pink ponytail, avoiding eye contact with the room as a whole. "I've changed my mind. She's not right. Different in person. The back highlight won't spill on her face in the right way, and the blue gel will be wrong with her hair. I need a brunette. Full cheeks. Next is Carly, correct?" Actually Simon had thought the peek of ash blonde under the hood would look fantastic when picking up the subtle blue of the light, but no matter. He was a skilled master and would find other ways to draw in the eye.

Cherry nods her head and peers down at her call sheet. "Carly, yes."

"Good. We'll wait." Time is money, he knows, but he doesn't care. His professional relationship with this particular client is one that can afford him some creative demands.

Hands in his pockets, he walks out of the illuminated space of the studio, and back towards the monitor to rifle through the earlier photos of the day, ignoring the clack of heels rushing behind him.

An obnoxious pressure on his shoulder has him growling. "Simon. Look, please." He raises an eyebrow, surprised the word "please" was able to escape the American's mouth. He turns to face her.

"Lulu, was it?" he says as he narrows his eyes to get a better look at hers. Cool green with specks of gold. Like smoky emeralds and gold doubloon in a treasure chest. Hazel-sage.

"Lila," she says with exaggerated emphasis. He smirks, enjoying the agitation evident in her shoulders. He's confident she's holding back wanting to say a few other choice words. It's a rare perk of the job to watch models when their tempers explode. Beautiful people are wonderfully entertaining when angry.

"Fine. Lila. Yes?"

"Please." There it is again. She said a word he's far more accepting of. "I'm all ready," she says with a swoop of her arm down her body. "What's the harm in a few shots to sample?"

On second thought, he might enjoy having a little fun with this sly little fox. He could make her bend to his demands until she was miserable and storming out in a huff. "Fine, little fox."

"What did you call me—"

He raises a finger at her in interruption. "But you play by my rules. And those shit brown eyes better know how to captivate on camera." His comment was a jab he knows is making her skin crawl. But there's something rather wonderful about being in a position where she wants this so badly that she has no choice but to bite her tongue. Let's see if she can keep her cool when he really shifts his directing magic into gear.

"My eyes are green, you know," she says to his back as he walks towards his camera.

Simon stops. Slowly turns to face her. Removes his glasses. "Oh no, little fox. *My* eyes are green." He places his glasses back on. "See the difference?" And he resumes his walk, this time, to his satisfaction, without the sound of Lila's heels behind him. Which means he's successfully shut her up and frozen her in her place.

"I'M SO SORRY," HE HEARS Meg the stylist whisper to Lila. "He's not known for his manners, but he's a genius, you'll see."

"So I hear," Lila mutters, and Simon can't help but smile.

"We tethered in?" he asks Cherry. She checks that the cord from the camera is connected to the monitor and tells him "yes." He nods. "Good. Then let's begin." He makes his adjustments to the lens before addressing Lila. "Alright, now take two small steps back. Nope, not three, that's too far. I said two, did you hear me?"

He peers through the lens and smiles to himself, watching her through the tunnel as she awkwardly takes a step forward. "Here?" she asks. Her tone is laced with restrained agitation.

"Fine. Now lean forward a bit. For fuck's sake, not like that, you're not the hunchback." Simon drops the camera from his face and glares at Lila. "Lean forward. With *elegance*. Think you can do that? Shoulders stay back. *Collar bone* forward. Let's see if we can find a neck in there, with any luck."

To Simon's surprise, Lila does as he asks. It's as if his commands spark more fire in her, and suddenly she comes to life, moving her arms with fluidity, and he snaps a few starter shots. "Fine, that's fine," he mutters. She's even more stunning to watch through the lens. Even now in these early moments before she's warmed up, she's a pleasure to watch move.

Reluctantly he pauses, moves to the monitor to flip through and check on lighting. "Let's angle the front lights a bit more this way," he says, and Cherry scurries to make the adjustments. "Good." He returns to his position in front of Lila, and raises the camera to start again. "Right leg forward. Nope, not like that, I said *right* leg, do you know the difference between left and right, Lila?" A few more snaps. "Better, that's fine. So you *can* hear at least." Snap snap. Snap. He pauses again for another glance at the monitor. The angle of the lights wrap around Lila in a luminous way, the effect soft in the highlights, the shadows on her neck creating just the air of mystery needed for this setup. He can't deny, she has a stunning look that makes it difficult to tear your eyes away.

Perhaps there's a little hope. Perhaps he can break her.

Lila continues her movements and Simon unleashes on the shutter button, already loving the way she transforms herself through the honed in laser focus view in the camera. Despite himself, he watches with admiration as Lila raises an arm over her head, her chin pointing downward and the glow of light sloping down her nose.

"Watch the fingers. Close them in more," Simon directs, and Lila does so perfectly. He can't help but be pleased with her surprisingly easy submission to his commands, though he can sense her frustration with him. There's a temper brewing beneath the surface, clearly, yet it would appear the girl's desperation for her modeling career is superseding her desire to explode and give Simon a piece of her mind.

This further ignites his need to make it clear exactly who is in charge. "What's that other arm doing, nobody wants *dangling spaghetti* for fuck's sake. Where are all those great ideas you bragged about?" Lila bends her other arm at the elbow and makes a gentle caress of her collarbone with her fingertips. "Good," is all he says.

After several more standing poses, he tells her to kneel down.

Lila drops to the floor, and Simon squats down too, feeling the intimacy of the two of them in this lower space in the room. "Now fold over, but turn your head and face up. Not too much, no, not that. Here," he says, rising and making his way over to her.

Simon looks down at the girl in front of him, this fiery wannabe vixen, and he notes how suddenly small and vulnerable she looks. It's as if she's frightened, if he's not mistaken. There's the slightest glimmer of it in her eye, a possible fear. It takes Simon by surprise, and he wonders for the first time what this girl's story is.

But just as quickly as that hint of trepidation came, it's gone, replaced by her narrowed eyes. "Yes?" she grits out beneath him through clenched teeth.

He squats down in front of her to grab her chin, and is met with a tiny flinch, the slightest act of startle just as his fingers are about to meet her skin.

He knows a flinch like that. His mind flashes back to another woman in his life, when that woman was really still just a girl in many ways, and she had flinched when Simon tried to wipe a smudge from her cheek. And that girl's flinch told Simon everything he had suspected, everything she could no longer deny. It was the moment when everything changed. The moment when Simon himself changed.

Lila's body is tense, and Simon pulls his hand back. "May I?" he asks, his voice softer. Head still, Lila moves her eyes to briefly meet his before dropping down to the floor. But she nods her head, just a little.

He once again reaches his hand out to her chin, softly cupping it, and pulls it down to the angle he wants. She huffs out a small sigh, and he smells a mix of coffee and something else on her breath. He runs his fingers along the high curve of her cheek bone, wanting to continue touching her, using this as an excuse to do so. "Here," he tells her. "We want the light to fall just here, yeah?" She blinks with another subtle head nod in acknowledgement. "Good girl," he says before rising to resume his place. "Cherry, the 70-200 lens, please. Let's get some close-ups."

As Cherry swaps out the lens, Simon watches Lila carefully as she holds her position. Cherry hands Simon the camera, and he raises it to his eye, tightening in on Lila's face, the bridge of her nose, her eyes.

He sees the unmistakable glisten beneath Lila's lashes. A tear wanting to fall. Mindlessly he holds his breath. And then Lila looks up, inhales deeply, blinks away the dampness in her eyes. He watches as her mask is placed right back on again, and her eyes dart back directly into the camera with fierce intensity, composure regained. "Like this," she asks, "master oh master?" She accompanies the question with several innocent blinks and flutters of her plump lashes.

"That's fine," is all he replies.

***

HE WAS TEMPTED TO CUT the shoot early and hold firm on his stance that she wasn't right for this, but an hour flew by and before he knew it, Cherry was telling him Carly, the next model, was nearly ready. He was annoyed with himself for getting swept up in photographing Lila. The spoiled American.

The team breaks for a pause and Simon reaches for his water. Lila appears beside him, dressed in her regular clothes now, navy shorts and a white tank, the straps draped over her collar bone loosely. Invitingly. Simon attempts to ignore the temptation to slip a strap down her shoulder, instead choosing to look her square in the eye.

Her arms are folded across her chest and she juts out a leg, tapping her foot with impatience. "Well?" she asks.

"Well what?" He gathers she's looking for feedback, but he's not going to indulge her with unfettered praise just for showing up to do her job.

"The shoot." Her voice is clipped, the words slow and emphasized with frustration. "Was it to your liking? Master?"

Simon removes his glasses and reaches for a cloth in his pocket. He proceeds to remove invisible smudges from his lenses before responding to Lila. "I can appreciate that you think you are some tough hot shot American that is entitled to be here. Fine."

"What the fuck is your—"

"Wait," Simon says, one finger raised to silence her. "Wait a moment. I'm not finished."

"This should be good." She unwinds her arms and places them on her hips. "I'll listen only because I'm for real downright curious," she says with a sardonic laugh. "Go ahead, you've obviously made your assumptions about me. Let's hear it. Tell me. Just how God awful was the American model?"

Simon finishes cleaning his lenses and returns the glasses back to his face. "It's not your modeling that's the problem. Your modeling is fine." *More than fine.* But he isn't going to tell her that.

"Gee, simmer down. Nothing quite blows up an ego like hearing that your work is 'fine.' Why not just call me average?"

"It's your attitude, Lila. *That* is why I didn't want to work with you. As I said, entitled. Wanting to barge in and take charge—that attitude wrapped up in some prissy sex kitten facade, and it's unappealing, unattractive, and downright distasteful. So, a word of advice." He pauses and looks her directly in the eye, aware of the hushed voices around them, the crew attempting to be stealth spectators of the exchange before them. "Think twice before you open your mouth to speak. You just might save yourself some trouble that way."

He starts to walk away, out of the room and down a small hallway, but Lila follows after him.

"You really are some fucking piece of shit asshole, aren't you?"

"Did you not just hear my advice about thinking before you speak?" he says over his shoulder, still walking down the dark hall, toward the exit. He's in need of a smoke, but it would appear his present company is not giving up so easily.

"I just don't understand. You barely know me, how can you make any assumptions? What gives you the right?"

Simon stops abruptly, and slowly turns to face Lila. "The right?"

"Uh-huh. Yeah. The right. As if you have any right to act like you know me."

"If we're talking about who has 'the right' as you say, then what gave you the right to attempt to claim me as your boy toy?" With this he smirks, enjoying her reaction, her obvious embarrassment at having been rejected when she clearly was used to the opposite. To men fawning over her like lust-sick fools.

Lila raises her hands to cover her face. "In my defense, I didn't know I'd be working with you," she says, dropping her hands from her face to throw them in the air in frustration.

"So you don't have any interest in having me as your boy toy then, is that it?" With a hand in his pocket, Simon leans a shoulder against the wall, enjoying watching her squirm as she attempts to explain herself.

"Oh my God, you are loving this, aren't you?"

"Answer the question. Where's all that confidence gone to, then?"

"Fine. I saw you at the party, I thought you looked...fun."

"How wrong you were."

"Obviously," she says, letting out a huff of breath. The loose strap of her tank that had been teasing him eventually slips down her shoulder. "Had I known I would have a professional relation-ship with you, I might have chosen my words more carefully. Alright? Satisfied?"

Simon steps forward, closer to Lila. He hooks a finger under the strap, slowly bringing it back up her arm, rounding over her shoulder. He can't help but appreciate her smooth skin, the ripples of tan and toned muscle in her shoulders, the slope of her collar bone. Lila glances down at his hand, now at the base of her neck, then back up to meet his eyes. She sucks in a breath before breathing out a quiet "thank you."

He keeps his hand there a moment, but then continues the movement up her neck, around the back before threading his fingers through her hair. He leans forward to press his lips to hers, but pauses. "What words would you have chosen? Instead?" he asks, eyes not meeting hers but instead held firmly on her mouth. He feels as her hand grips his shirt on his stomach, but she remains quiet.

"Well, Lila?"

"My boy toy photographer?" she retorts.

With a squeeze of her hair at the nape of her neck he presses his body against her, pinning her to the wall. "Wrong," he whispers, and she lets out a little gasp. "Try again." He smells her perfume, obnoxiously feminine and floral.

"My..." She squeezes tighter on his shirt.

"What, can't you find something better, Lila? Or must you always demand the upper hand?"

"I hardly had the upper hand back there, did I?" she says softly, eyes darting down the hall, back toward the studio.

"And yet, here you are. Chasing after me." This pisses her off, to his delicious delight. He sees the fury in her eyes.

"I don't chase after anyone." The words fall flat as her body makes no attempt to move, betraying her.

"Wrong again."

Lila licks her lips and pulls him closer with her hand wrapped in his shirt. She leans forward to kiss him, but Simon pulls his head back, keeping his hand tugging at her hair.

"You want me to kiss you?" he asks with a smirk.

"Why are you doing this?" she whispers, confusion etched all over her face. "You humiliate me back there, now you're looking like you're ready to devour me. I try and kiss you and you pull away?"

"I simply want to know what else you might have said that night if you knew I'd be your photographer." His voice is calm. Slow. Clear. "Giving you my commands." His eyes drop down to her mouth. "Anything but a stupid, shameful *boy toy*," he says, mockery dripping out of the last two words.

"I don't know," she finally whispers.

He smiles. "Hmm. Imagine that."

She keeps her lips parted and Simon goes in, unable to stop himself from tasting her. She smells like jasmine mixed with something sweet, but tastes like coffee and vanilla. He presses her more firmly against the wall as he explores her mouth, their kiss a fiery burst of energy he knows he'll regret later. It's too impulsive, too stupid of a move, and he knows better.

But for now, he's choosing to ignore reasoning, finding that the only thing he cares about is placing his mouth on Lila Ray and shutting her up. He's simultaneously tasting her and silencing her while he deepens their kiss. He's greedy with it, but she's a willing participant clawing at him, her hands wrapping around him and pressing into his back. He takes his other hand and glides over her breast, the thin fabric of her tank revealing her hardened nipple, and he groans into her mouth.

This was not the plan, he is not supposed to be kissing the arrogant American, and yet, here he is doing exactly that. There's something intoxicating about her despite her being all wrong for him. She's nothing like the girls he usually goes for, this bratty spitfire, and yet kissing her seemed to be a thought clouding his mind from the moment he zoomed in on her, her enchanting eyes captured in the intimate frame of his lens. He's no stranger to models, no stranger to the beauty and grace he sees on a regular basis, but with Lila something stirred in him. Something surprising and luring, despite every cell in his body telling him to keep her at arm's length.

With one final press of his hips into her, he stops, pulling back slightly to catch his breath. The buzz of energy lingers in the air around them, but he's determined to get ahold of himself and regain his control. He releases his hand from her hair and takes two slow steps backward, leaving her panting against the wall, her lips a guilty red that he assumes mirror his own.

He reaches a hand in his pocket for his cigarette case. He opens it and grabs one, placing it in his lips more as a distraction than anything else. Lila silently watches him, and he steps to his left before turning and walking out the door, leaving her.

three

. . .

lucy

"HE'S A COMPLETE and total fucking asshole," Lila says through my phone screen, and I grab my temple in annoyance, trying my best to find patience and serenity.

"What makes you say that? I thought he was the best of the best in the photography world," I counter. You should be forewarned that my sister has a tendency to shift from hot to cold pretty quickly, so it can be difficult to keep up. You have to take everything with a grain of salt.

Lila shakes her head. "He might be the best, but he's a fucking nightmare to work with. He's *mean*, Lucy. Like, for real mean. An arrogant asshole."

I sigh. "Well it's not like you share a nine to five office with him or anything. You don't have to see him each and every day like I do with some of the jackasses I work with. I think you can handle a few interactions with him now and then."

She rolls her eyes. "Thanks for all the validation."

I'd like to take this opportunity to explain—my little sister is a brat. In fact I'm sure this little tantrum of hers isn't quite warranted. I love her, believe you me, I do. But I also know her all too well.

I drop my hand and grab the pen from my desk to resume my doodling. She may be frustrating me, but I don't want her to see it. "Lila, if this guy is the genius everyone says he is, then you should be lucky to have had the opportunity to work with him. I hope you put your game face on, at least." See, what Lila doesn't realize is that people won't all cater to her every whim. I can see it now, she'd have the opportunity to work with this guy, giving her a leg up in the world she claims to so desperately want to be a part of, and then she blows it all up by being her spoiled self. She never could handle criticism or conflict very well.

I adore my little sister, but it's true. Her whole life has been all of us swooping in to save her from her rash and reckless habits. She has no idea all we do for her. No idea what I myself have done for her, a secondary mother to her in many ways.

"My God, don't you know me at all? Of course I put my game face on," Lila says with another eye roll. With the video chat, there's a bit of a lag and so her eye roll has this exaggerated comet's tail across the screen. "I crushed the photo shoot. Everyone said so. I even got a sympathy invite from the makeup artist to his house tonight for family dinner."

My ears perk up at this. I want support for my little sister, and a family dinner feels like a smart idea. She needs some good influences in her life overseas. "Good. That's great! Does he seem like a decent guy? Not like a ploy to lure you to his house for sex?"

"No. Definitely not, he's decent."

"Then you should go! Are you going?"

"What? No! Oh my God. *No*," Lila says with a firm shake of her head. "I told him 'maybe' just to be nice, but I can't go to some quaint little family dinner. It was sweet of him to offer, that's all. And it proves that this photographer really was an ass, so much so that the damn makeup artist took pity on me, which is pretty telling."

"Why not? Why not just go to a dinner?"

"Because that's weird! I'm twenty-five, not forty-five. I go out. I dance. I dress to the nines and I'm *seen* and maybe even photographed. I'm not doing family dinner with people I don't even know."

"Lila, you're looking at it all wrong." I try for another angle, one that I think will get through to her. "If he's a successful makeup artist, dinner at his family home is networking." I wait and watch as she chews her lower lip. I see her wheels turning. "Plus you might get free makeup samples or something out of it," I add.

"That is a good point."

"I have lots of good points." She huffs a little, but smiles, at least.

"How's Justin?" she asks, and I shift a little in my desk chair. Figures. Lila hardly ever thinks to ask about my husband, but she chooses now to do so.

"He's fine, busy with work and the launch of this new app, but good."

"Well tell him hi."

"I will," I say. Eager to change the subject, I raise my wrist to look at my watch. "What time is it there, you said your dinner invite is for tonight? Shouldn't you be getting ready?"

Lila raises an eyebrow. "You're awfully excited about this dinner for me. Maybe *you* should be the one going."

"Hmmm. Think I could grab a flight that time travels backwards and I'd make it in time?" *Oh how I wish that were possible.*

"Tell Justin he should work on the technology for that next."

"And how about you, dear sister? Where would you time travel to if you could?"

She taps a slim, perfectly manicured finger to her pursed upper lip. "Easy. I'd go back in time to when our parents conceived so I could be reborn as *you*," she says with a dramatic pop open of her eyes to me on screen. "Perfect Lucy, it might be nice."

"Funny. I'd go back in time to be you."

"Like hell you would."

"I would!" I insist. "The cute little sister that gets away with murder because everyone finds her so adorable and innocent?" I snort. "If they only knew."

"Why Lucy," Lila says with a dramatic tsk. "And leave your post as master in command to all? I hardly think you could stand that lack of power."

I shake my head. "You're such a..." I don't finish the sentence.

She smiles though. "See? Called your bluff."

"Whatever. Just go to your dinner."

"It's six already. I can't, it's too late."

"Then reach out and thank him and ask for another time. Please? You need good people in your world, your roommate doesn't seem too available."

Lila groans. "Fine. Only for the potential make up samples though."

"Good," I say, satisfied. We hang up and I lean back in my chair with a sigh. I glance at the clock and groan.

Thirty minutes. Thirty minutes until a meeting that I'm dreading, but there's no way I can get out of it. I lean my elbows on my desk and rub my temples. What has my life become, how did I get here? I need to get my game face on and remain professional for this meeting. No more fucking around. And definitely no more fucking *him*.

An idea pops in my head. The other day I had pulled out old journals from a stash in my cedar trunk. I guess I was feeling nostalgic. Lila's old childhood notes to me were in there, pulling at my heart strings. I forget how interdependent we once were, but in such a different way than we are now. She was like my little kid and I was her other mom.

I miss her. Maybe a quick escape overseas to visit my little sister is just what I need. A mini adventure, an opportunity to hit reset and find my bearings.

If nothing else, I'll pretend that I can magically fix everything.

before

. . .

To Simon

~~I am sorry for your loss.~~

It is me, Elsie. I am very sorry your mum died. At least you can live nearby becuze my Aunt Victoria will be taking care of you. She is sad ~~two~~. too. Your mum was her best friend. I can share all my sweets with you to make you feel better. I am happy you will go to my school. Our playground is nice. I will show you around. You can meet my friends.

From Elsie.

four

. . .

simon

HE RUBS HIS hand down the side of his face, locked into the hypnotizing eyes on the screen in front of him. Lila Ray. The model he can't seem to get out of his mind these past few days, a confusing little fox that had him momentarily lose his self control. He was cursing himself for his moment of weakness there in that hallway with her. Never before had he so much as had a flirtatious exchange with a model, let alone completely lose his mind and actually *kiss* one. It was beyond his own code of professionalism, and he was dumbfounded as to what exactly had happened that caused him to act on such stupid impulse.

Simon's tuxedo cat lurches up onto the desk, and he absently scratches the cat's neck before realizing the cat's crime of jumping up in the first place.

"Oh, no, Basil. You know better." He lifts the cat and places him back onto the floor by the wheels of his desk chair. "Nice try," he says, staring down at the defeated Basil. The cat tilts his head at Simon, calculating his next move. Eventually Basil gives up and walks toward the window, finding a pool of sunlight glowing on the wood flooring. He stretches himself out, drenched in the warmth of the sunshine.

Simon returns his attention back to his screen, determined to focus on his edits, but he keeps replaying the scene that day. Each photo offers up a memory of what was going through Simon's mind as he was photographing Lila Ray.

She had taken him by surprise with that moment of vulnerability. He's certain he had not been mistaken—Lila had been frightened. While not known for any sort of coddling in his approach, Simon was not necessarily one to strive for fear either. It had splintered his frame of mind when she had flinched at his touch, and he found himself softening to her.

The rest of the shoot he pulled back, ever so slightly, making commands that leaned more gentle. Lila had slipped deeper into her role and transformed herself right in front of him through his lens. He had been disappointed when her time was up, though simultaneously relieved as well.

But she had to follow him, didn't she? She couldn't quietly slip out and leave him be. No. She had to confront him, all while standing there in front of him in that joke of an excuse for a shirt. The thin white tank exposing her skin and calling to him, distracting him. And when he tried to walk away, she followed, and in that secluded space with no one there to offer accountability, he had given in to his basic lust.

As he studies his screen, flipping through the hundred or so shots of Lila, Simon has a feeling of regret that he hadn't been able to work with her even longer. It's a feeling that surprises him, given his own feelings regarding fashion photography.

It was the industry that had found his talents most intriguing, and therefore the greatest source of his income. Yet when he first launched his business, it was architecture that was, and still remains, his first passion. Ancient structures and jobs with historical organizations had been his plan and his dream, until someone discovered his unique talents in capturing not just the landscape and structures themselves, but the *people* within those structures. From that point on, his career in the fashion industry took off.

Ironically, the more elusive he tried to be within the fashion world, the more sought after he suddenly became. The money had been impossible to turn down, so he'd withheld his innermost cringes and jumped on board with creating elaborate mood boards and pretending to give a damn about emphasizing the drape of the fabric or the current styles that are all the rage. Nowadays when he can manage a location off studio and into the real world, he does. One of his first sites which he had convinced a client to try ended up earning him the Visionary of the Year award, thus further propelling him into the spotlight. Now he's the photographer every designer, magazine, show, and artist wants to work with.

All despite his own distaste for the industry, and the people within it. People that find obsession with the "it" factor, whatever that means. People committed to making regular humans feel badly about themselves, never beautiful enough. He pities the industry as a whole for that very reason.

And here he is, a complete and utter hypocrite falling in line, grinding the gears of it himself.

But then there's the blonde, Lila. He had regretfully pegged her to be just as lifeless as the rest of them, until he saw that look cross her eye. The flinch at his touch, when she had only moments ago been fuming with barely contained fury. It was then that he realized he had misread something in her. As he looks at her now, her expression draws him in. It's easy to look at the images as a whole, to see the beautiful face and the elegant grace of her movements in each pose. It's her eyes, though, that Simon feels a pull toward. There's a blankness to them, and he wonders what she's masking, this Lila Ray.

What happened to you? he thinks. And then guilt consumes him as he thinks about his reckless kiss. He should never have made a move on someone who is clearly vulnerable, clearly been hurt but trying so hard to hide it.

"Oh, well she's rather lovely, isn't she?" his aunt asks as she hands Simon a cup of tea. Victoria places a hand on Simon's shoulder and leans over to peer closer at the screen. "Where is she from?"

"She's American, believe it or not."

"American? Interesting. You ever work with her before?" Victoria steps away and resumes her work, grabbing the duster and busying herself with the surfaces of Simon's office.

"No, first time. She's new to London, I believe."

"I have no doubt she'll make it straight to the top, especially if she managed a job working with you," Victoria says with a scraggly-tooth grin, and Simon winces at the state of her dental health. He makes a mental note to himself to find a creative way to fund some cosmetic dental procedures for her. "Am I bothering you in here, need me to stop?"

"It's fine, Victoria. I can manage this room."

"No, no. I insist, how much longer will you be? I'll just get straight to the vacuuming and come back in a bit to tidy in here."

Simon rises, unplugging his laptop and folding it into its case. "It's fine," he says. "I'll step out of your way to let you work in peace. I'm going for a quick ride, then off to the gym."

"Don't let me run you out, now," she says, though she scurries over to dust his desktop, seeming to have no problem with the arrangement.

"You're not," Simon assures her, and he grabs his bag, eager to get out from under his aunt's nosy presence. He's happy to be able to offer her some income by way of housekeeping, but her attempts at chit-chat are something he'd rather avoid.

AFTER A BIKE RIDE, SIMON makes his way down the stairs to the hidden cave that houses the small gym. He swings open the door and is immediately filled with calm from the stale, yet comforting scents of rubber and cleaning supplies. The room is dark and warm, with a small variety of stationary bikes, treadmills, weight machines and a solitary television that is permanently stuck on one channel. Simon notes with satisfaction that Roger's Gym is nearly empty, only two other members in now—a small and sturdy woman with gray hair and faded tattoos lifting weights, and a man about his age on a treadmill. Nice and quiet.

The gym is a tiny fitness center with weights nearly as old as Simon's own twenty-seven years, but it's a quiet, hidden gem. The owner, Roger, is an old American, retired from the military. Simon learned a few years ago after just moving into the neighborhood that Roger had moved to England as soon as he retired. London had been his favorite city. While searching for a location for an athletic wear client, Simon had discovered the gym and its robust owner Roger, and he and Simon had become unlikely friends.

Simon scans the space and takes his spot on his favorite treadmill, one in a dark and dust-filled corner. He settles his water bottle, pulls out his earbuds and finds a podcast to listen to during his run.

Several minutes into his run, Simon is met with annoyance at the sound of an American voice speaking entirely too loudly into her cell phone, breaking past his own earbuds and distractedly interrupting his podcast. He nearly trips as he glances in the mirror to find none other than Lila to be the owner of the voice, though she seems blissfully unaware of Simon. She's in an olive green sports bra and shorts ensemble, though it's not much more than a bathing suit. She wears no makeup, and her short hair and fringe are pulled back in a wide headband. If it weren't for her unmistakable eyes, he'd barely recognize her.

"Mom, did you try...no, not that," Lila says with obvious frustration. Simon's not trying to eavesdrop, but she's perched on the edges of the machine two over from him, and is impossible to ignore. "It's *not* hard. You *can* do this." She sighs and closes her eyes, and Simon notes the smile of amusement on the guy on the treadmill next to her.

"Let's start over," she says, her voice edgy. "Turn it on and off again. Wait a hot sec, then when the system's back on, press the input button." With a hand on her hip, she bites her lip as she waits for a response. "Perfect, see? Almost there. Now, take the blue remote, and move over to the left. Yes! There you go. Now press the little button with the house on it, and you'll be at the main menu, kay?" He watches through the mirror as Lila smiles with faux brightness and nods her head. "Awesome! You should be good now. I'll text you how to turn it off...yes, mom, it's fine! I'm hanging up now, bye, bye..." and she lets out a dramatic groan before dropping her phone in the cupholder of her treadmill.

The man next to her presses a button, slowing his speed, and turns to Lila. "What would they do without us, right?"

She throws her head back in a genuine laugh. "Parents? Yeah. Sure. I sincerely doubt my parents feel they'd be lost without me. More just 'Hey, at least she's good at fixing the TV for us,' I'd say is their attitude."

"You're joking. A daughter with beauty and TV fixing skills? Seems like a pretty good win, if you ask me. They should feel lucky to have you."

He's flirting with her. Not that Simon cares. The kiss was merely a strange impulse. A one time thing. So fine, let this bloke deal with the bratty American.

Still unrecognized, Simon tries to return his attention to his own podcast on ancient Egypt, turning up the volume to avoid hearing their conversation. He tries even harder to not notice the arm touch Lila gives the man, then the laugh they share at how doing so causes her to stumble on her treadmill slightly, or how the bloke tries to help steady her, touching *her* arm now and clearly scanning his eyes up and down her body.

Ignore it, he tells himself. Eventually they both shut the hell up and continue on with their runs. But by then Simon's fully distracted by Lila's presence as she runs along at what looks to be a steadily increasing pace, her machine shifting up the inclines on a stored program. He watches as her breathing becomes heavier, sweat quickly streaming down her face, until she finally curses and slows down the machine to a more moderate pace, looking defeated.

She looks young. Innocent, even—a contradiction to the look he assumes she prefers to convey. This version of her here, this air of underdog innocence feels like what Simon caught a glimpse of when she flinched at his touch. And again, when she had no response when he asked how she would have expressed interest if she knew they would have a professional relationship. He gets the sense that he's had a rare opportunity to see the real Lila, and here she is again, right here, right now. She's out in the open and exposed without her usual mask. He wonders if she too, chose this gym for its obscurity? Or perhaps she knows Roger somehow, a clandestine American watering hole.

Simon shakes his head to himself, willing his unwelcome thoughts of Lila out of his mind. She's an American model snob, nothing else. No need to make her out to be anything more than she is. Why he's trying to see her as some vulnerable soul needing to be rescued, he's not sure. But it's foolish and he's committed to putting an end to it.

After his ten kilometers is finally met, Simon slows the belt down to a walk, grabbing his towel to wipe the sweat from his face and chest. He swaps out the towel for his water, and steals another glance over to Lila.

Her eyes appear glazed over, like a lifeless ghost in the shell of a human body. After a moment she begins to blink rapidly and quickly shakes her head as if to shake away a thought. She reaches for her water, but thinks twice and retreats. Simon watches as she takes hold of the railing to steady herself, hitting pause on her machine to stop the belt. Once again she reaches for her water, her hand trembling unmistakably. Simon looks and sees her skin turning nearly as green as her clothing and he stops his machine.

"Hey there, you alright?" he asks her, his first time acknowledging her directly.

"I just need…" Lila starts. But then the upper half of her body folds over, as if to lean down on the side rail of the machine like a child in class looking to lay their head on the desk for a quick snooze.

And instantly, Simon knows what's about to happen.

He leaps over the empty machine between them and darts to her just in time to catch her lifeless body in his sweaty, waiting arms.

He catches her before her previous flirting partner even registers what's happening.

"LILA, LILA, HONEY, WHATCHA DOIN' dropping like a fly on my gym floor?" Roger asks. Lila still remains in Simon's arms, her head laying on his outstretched leg, both of them on the floor beside her abandoned treadmill. She opens her eyes briefly before squeezing her brows and pinching her eyes closed again.

"I'm fine," Lila mumbles, raising an arm over her eyes to block out the light. "I don't feel well."

The other runner (who took far too long for his idiot self to realize the new apple of his eye was fainting), chimes in. "What happened, you alright?" He lowers himself down, reaches out a hand to Lila's forehead, and Simon tenses.

"We've got this," Simon snaps at him.

"I'm seeing if she's feverish."

"Your hand's a thermometer, then?"

"Easy, now. What's your problem?" the man says, a startled look on his face. But he pulls back and rises to a stand.

"Alright, fellas, too many heroes in the kitchen. John, I think we got this, let's not crowd the poor lady," Roger says.

Simon internally smiles in victory, and the man steps back,

shifting his weight uncomfortably before finally deciding to lean on a rail to stare at them uselessly.

"You going to be sick?" Simon asks Lila.

"I dunno. I don't think so. Maybe."

Roger crouches down next to Lila, a giant teddy bear hovering over a delicate doll. "Just stay there, get your bearings. Do you pass out often?" His blonde beard and red nose have a way of creating a comical surfer Father Christmas kind of look.

"No, not in years. And usually only when getting bloodwork done."

"Have you eaten, Lila?" Simon asks.

"Um..."

"I'll take that as a no. Roger, you have any biscuits or something? Crackers, maybe?" He reaches in his pocket for his wallet and hands it to Roger. "Here, mate. Grab something from the vending machine for her."

Roger waves off Simon's wallet and rises. "Keep your money, I'll get something for her. Keep her talking." He walks to the back and Simon returns his attention to the head in his lap, aware of the lingering presence standing there like a nosy neighbor.

"Who are you?" Lila asks Simon, peering through one eye under her forearm.

"It's me, Si."

"Sigh? What? What the hell is a sigh?"

"*Si*. As in, Simon. Simon Sharp. The photographer."

"Asshole hot nerd?" She drops her arm and presses down into Simon's leg to lift up her torso slightly, then scans her eyes up and down Simon's bare arms, exposed in his gray sleeveless gym shirt. "No. You have tattoos. Like, everywhere. Hot Nerd doesn't have tattoos." At the sound of her calling Simon "Hot Nerd," the leering idiot John finally gives up and retreats back to his treadmill, placing earbuds in and resuming his run.

"You really are a piece of work, aren't you?" Simon asks with irritation.

"Where are your glasses? You can't be him. Si? Is that what you said?"

"For fuck's sake, Lila. Yes. It's me. Your *photographer* from the other day. Look, are you feeling alright?" Simon's all too aware of her skin beneath his palm, his hand draped around her exposed torso. "When...did...you...last...eat?" he asks again, annunciating every word as if speaking to a child.

Roger returns with a pack of crisps and a chocolate bar. His burly hands rip open the bag and he passes it to Lila. "Eat, Lila."

Slowly, she leans fully forward out of Simon's lap, bringing in her legs to her chest and resting her elbows on her knees. The men watch her carefully as she extends a long slim arm to the bag. Wordlessly, she grabs a crisp and takes the tiniest of bites, the entire action looking as if it requires every ounce of energy she has. Simon reaches his hand to her curved back, gliding it up and down the ridges of her spine in an awkward attempt at comfort.

"Thank you. This is embarrassing," she whispers down to the floor. Simon and Roger pass a knowing glance at one another.

"Is it money or vanity causing you to make the stupid decision to skip meals?" Simon asks.

Roger shoots him an alarmed look before returning his attention back to Lila. "What he means is, I think..." he stammers, but he struggles to form a proper sentence.

"I know what he means," Lila spits out. "Asshole."

"Right," Simon says as he hops up to a stand. "Well, glad you're better. Alright then. You good to get home on your own?" He glances over to the other runner and is relieved to see he's no longer paying any mind to the three of them.

Roger leans forward to subtly get Simon's attention. "Hey, maybe uh, you make sure she gets home okay?"

"I'd say she's fine. It's clearly self-induced."

Lila nibbles at another crisp, a little more natural color returning to her face. "What is it with people in this industry thinking that we can't hear them? *I can hear you*, you know."

"I can't just close up shop here, Simon. Get the girl home safely."

"You're not exactly busy," Simon says with a swoop of his hand gesturing to the nearly empty space, save the other two occupants.

Roger grins. "Aren't Brits supposed to be jovial? I mean maybe I can ask John to escort Lila home."

On second thought, perhaps he should keep an eye on her. "Fine. Lila, where do you live?"

Lila sighs and rises to her feet, wiping the remnants of her snack on her shorts. "It's like a ten minute walk that way," she says, one graceful finger indicating the direction. Typical. Of course she lives in his neighborhood. "Are you really Simon the photographer? Si?" She looks to Roger for confirmation. "Is he for real?"

Roger shrugs. "That's all I've known him as." He places a hand in his pocket. "Let him walk you home, Lila. I can't have you passing out again leaving my gym, you'll set a bad example."

"Might be a great one, depending on what people are looking for," she says, her voice despondent. She appears defeated, her feisty facade attempting to creep in, but not quite within reach. She grabs her things from the treadmill cupholder and looks at Roger. "Sorry for scaring you."

"Good. I accept. Now go eat something, for the love of God. Haven't you heard? Nutrition is in."

"Yeah, alright, old man," she says with a lifeless pat to his shoulder. "I really am fine. I just got busy today and rushed out of the house, that's all."

"If you say so."

Lila starts to walk towards the door with Simon following closely behind, but then she pauses and turns around. "Hey, Roger, can this not be...you know. Don't go all high and mighty and make this a thing you tease me about. Too easy, too cheap a shot to make fun of the girl that passed out in your gym. You're better than that, right?" Her tone is meant to be sarcastic, but the sincerity in Lila's eyes reminds Simon of a shamed rescue puppy.

Roger seems to contemplate the appropriate response, and Simon too finds himself curious what he'll say. Finally, Roger folds his arms across his burly chest. "Honey, look. I don't need the money for a gym, I just have it because it's something to do and I like offering up a comfortable spot for people to come and get a workout in. Bottom line for me. That's what it's about, being strong. Healthy. Sure I give people a hard time now and then, but taking care of yourself is something to take seriously. You get what I'm saying?"

Lila's corner of her lip raises in a slight smile. "Figures. I come all the way to London to get away, yet still the parental forces in the world seem to find me." She shakes her head, but smiles fully now. "Thanks for the chips. Crisps."

"You're welcome." And Simon and Lila walk out of the gym and into the light of what feels like a brand new day.

five

. . .

lila

OH MY GOD. I'm walking out of the gym after that fiasco, and I am so utterly mortified I could pretty much die. I cannot believe that just happened.

Did that really just happen?

Let this be a bad dream. Please, please, let me wake up and have that be a bad dream. Because I cannot believe I passed out in the goddamn gym. Like a pathetic idiot. I should go on my socials and read the nastiest comments I can find, just so that *that* can take the focus off and send me in my downward spiral—one that isn't solely based on this incident. *You're so stupid, such an idiot.*

I need to get my shit together, the shame is quickly getting out of control. That had to happen in front of the photographer of all people, why does the universe hate me? *The damn photographer?!* The one who kissed me before up and walking out, his face filled with regret like he just made world's biggest mistake.

I can feel tears coming, I just want to hide away in a dark corner and erase the memory all together like it never happened. They all knew it too, knew I passed out from not eating. I should have just said I have a weird condition or something, some medical thing that makes me pass out sometimes. But no. Didn't think fast enough. "Self-induced," Simon had said, that fucking beautiful asshole.

Fine. Food and me have not always been friends, but I promise you, we've come a long way. I'm not anorexic or anything, and maybe as a kid I was more extreme, but I'm far better now. I just like to keep to the very bottom of a healthy BMI. Emphasis on healthy. It's part of my job. It's really not a big deal, and it's more easily achieved when I space out my meals. But it's less than fun sharing a small flat with someone, and I'm not really into having an audience when I eat, so that's been a bit of a struggle. I probably need a therapy session. I can admit that. Work through this shame. I can do Telehealth. Everything's going to be fine.

All this is stirring up the younger version of me that would get caught in the throes of my depression. Those were some dark years that I have no intention of revisiting.

No. Today was different. Today was just an ill-timed mistake. I went a little too hard on an empty stomach. I know that. But Roger and Simon—Si. I hate so much that they were there for it. It's like having your biggest demon out there on display for everyone to mock and judge and see just how weak you are, and I hate, hate, hate so much that that's what just happened. *Oh my God, oh my God, oh my God.* I try and hold back the regretful groan that's locked and loaded in my throat. My head is in a spin, my thoughts feel disjointed.

And now here I am, trying not to cry. It's so stupid. I sniffle and blink back the tears that are threatening to fall, aware that I still have an audience as I'm stepping out onto the street in front of the gym. I turn right with a "See ya around" to Simon, hoping he can't hear the catch in my voice.

Please, please, please, just leave me alone. I want to go crawl into bed and forget everything that just happened. "I'm fine, thanks for your help," I say, quickening my steps.

But Simon runs up in front of me, blocking my path. "Stop, Lila."

I don't even want to look up at him, knowing the tears are just about beyond my control. He's the last person I want to have as witness to a humiliating crumble. Fuck him.

I can't believe he's even the same person. I tentatively take a look at him and note the plethora of tattoos encasing each arm, creeping out from beyond the rounded collar of his shirt and up his neck. I try and focus on his features as a way to distract myself from my tears. His glasses are gone, and his thick eyebrows host one small bare spot where a scar slices through above his left eye. His nose has a tiny ridge in the middle that widens out slightly. Lips that look horribly inviting, even now, and house yet another slash scar on the left upper lip. I wonder if he's seen abuse in his childhood, judging by the looks of these strange scars. If it weren't for his startling green eyes and wispy dark hair, I'd hardly believe it was the same guy as Hot Nerd.

I'm also thinking I need a new name for him.

A car horn beeps up ahead of us, and I startle at the sound, the world around me coming back to life as I get my bearings. A whiff of some nearby restaurant hits my nostrils, and I'm nauseated by the smell of charcoal or burning meat mixed with car fumes from the traffic. I grab my stomach and grimace. "The smell," I manage to say, and a few tears escape past my lashes. I'm hoping they can pass for general disgust instead of the actual emotion behind them. I raise my other hand and quickly wipe them away. "I can't stand the smell out here, it's awful," I say with an attempted chuckle. "So gross."

"Fuck," Simon says, looking down to the sidewalk, then behind his shoulder and around us, as if trying to decide what to do. I see the tattoo from the front of his neck wrapping around the back as well, some maze type thing. He places his hands on his hips, and I can't help but stare curiously at the tattoos wrapped around his biceps. He's like a human canvas. The work on the left arm has scales and what I'm now seeing to be a dragon etched in the design, slashes of negative space slicing through. His right arm has some other creature I can't quite make out without staring longer than I should. An owl, maybe, with feathers that appear nearly life-like. I wonder if there's more under his shirt. "Alright," he says. "Think you could get on a bike?"

"Huh?" I blink in confusion, tearing my eyes from his ink and into his eyes. He's looking at me with more kindness than I thought he was capable of. "Could I get on a bike? Like a bicycle?"

"No," he says with amusement. "Not a bicycle. A *motorcycle*." He crosses his arms over his chest to await my response, and I watch as the scales of his dragon tattoo stretch out slightly.

"Oh," is all I say, like a tongue tied moron.

"Could you get on one? You know, without passing out?" There's agitation in his tone, but he's giving me this look that feels like concern and disappointment. It's confusing. Like he wants more for me and I let him down.

I gesture up ahead of me, not wanting his pity. "I'm not far from home, just a quick walk. Really, it's fine. I promise to lie and tell Roger you walked me home. No need to continue this whole charade like you actually give a shit, 'kay?"

But instead of walking off, he unwinds his arms and grabs my elbow in a quick, jerky movement. He manhandles me backwards, and I stumble over my own feet. I trip slightly, and he switches the hand that's holding my elbow, replacing it with his other so that he can take his arm and snake it around my waist, steadying me. "Come on," he says, and he walks us up toward a motorcycle parked on the street. I'm sure I look like I'm being kidnapped, but as I glance around to the people on the streets, no one seems to even register our presence.

I'm annoyed and embarrassed, yes, but it's outweighed by intrigue, so I keep quiet. If he wants to manhandle me and get me on his bike, I'm honestly not too up for arguing about it. Fine, let him. It feels kind of nice to let go for a minute and be led in this way. I'm so tired, suddenly. So, so tired. Too tired to argue.

We get to his bike and he releases me, handing me a helmet. When I blink and only stare at it, he sighs and puts it back down. He grabs my sweatshirt and phone and water bottle out of my hands. I silently watch as he puts them in a small bag attached to the bike, then grabs the helmet to put it on me. It feels singularly heavy on my head, and I wonder briefly how ridiculous I look. Simon takes his own helmet, puts it in place, then swings his leg over with ease to straddle the bike. A nod of his head indicates for me to join, and I awkwardly swing my leg over behind him.

For a moment I just perch there, hesitant. I know I'm supposed to wrap my arms around him, but it all feels so intimate, and I'm filled with this feeling of floating along, mindless in my actions. What am I even doing here?

I see the turn of Simon's helmet in front of me, and he says, "Well? You ready?" and I nod like a mute idiot and wrap my arms around him tightly, hanging on for dear life. With a kick he roars the bike to life, and I grab his shirt in my fists, feeling the firmness of his abs beneath my knuckles.

Off we go.

THERE'S A FEW THINGS THAT I really love about London. I love the tidiness of the streets, the quaint brick and stone that feels mature, in a way. Everything here looks like it has a story, as though any snapshot could be the graphic for a beautiful fairytale. I think that's why I like Europe so much in general. The history of it makes today's problems feel so incredibly small. It's a nice reminder.

But rolling along the streets, watching through the window of Simon's helmet like this, I'm having a whole new appreciation for this place I'm trying to make my home. In so many ways I feel like I haven't been able to relax at all since being here. I'm always on edge, always rushing or worrying or anxious about where I'm going or if I'm doing things right. Doing what right, exactly? I don't even know. I guess that's the strangeness of being a foreigner. Here I am, trying to make a new home for myself, make a name for myself, which I thought would be easier with a fresh start, yet it's only left me feeling more out of place. It feels like the world exists in this tunnel, and I'm pulled further and further back, visuals around me getting stretched out and distorted, and I'm standing at the opening of the tunnel, unsure of how to immerse myself.

As surreal as it is cruising here now with Simon, wind chilly on my skin, I feel kind of alright. I think I'm just so exhausted from *trying* so hard in this strange land these past couple months that I've got nothing left in me but to just ride along and let him take the reins. It's nice.

The city passes us by and gets less and less chaotic. We pull onto a tree-lined street, one side a strip of shops, the other a sidewalk and small half wall, stone on the bottom and white rails like bowling pins on top. Simon pulls us up along a curb and parks, and I unravel my arms from his waist, aware of the dampness on my arms from both our skin and sweat in the early September heat. We remove our helmets, he hands me my things from the case, and he leads us into a small grocery store.

A quiet ding of small bells ring out as he opens the door for me, we step in. The space is inviting with a quaint and upscale feel to it. There are shiny bins of produce in a rainbow of colors, small packaged goodies and the smell of fine cheeses envelope me in a comforting embrace. My stomach growls and my ears perk up at the sound, but Simon has the graciousness to either pretend to ignore it out of politeness, or maybe ignore it simply because he's over the topic of my obvious hunger.

He picks out a few things, never once asking my thoughts which annoys me a little, but I remain quiet, energy zapped with no fight in me. I figure it's easier to just let him take the lead here and enjoy the change of plans from what was otherwise going to be another boring night of me drowning in some tequila, alone while my roommate Penny is off doing her thing. We haven't exactly clicked, me and her. She has a fiancé and steady work schedule which means she's gone all day, and I have the feeling she accepted me as a roommate more as a favor to Grayson than anything else.

Simon checks out, popping the items in the canvas tote he brought in with him, and we head back outdoors into the late afternoon sun. I'm getting a little chilly, so I stop and put on my sweatshirt, self conscious suddenly of how scantily clad I had been up until now. On the bike wrapped around Simon I was amazingly comfortable, but the sun is dropping and the leaves are rustling, and I'm grateful to have the extra layer.

I finally break our silence as I follow Simon past his bike and across the street. "Where are we going?"

"You're going to eat."

"No, really? So that's what the food is for? You're kidding." I swear I'm usually more clever than this. I hate that I sound so dumb and generic.

I get nothing but silence from him. I try again. "Fine, yeah…I gathered as much. But where?"

He raises his arm up ahead. "Not much further. Holland Park, have you been?"

I shake my head no, feeling a kind of embarrassment in admitting it. Which is stupid, obviously. London is huge, it's not like I'd be expected to know each and every spot, but I still feel like a basic tourist at being completely unaware of the place he's headed to. Which clearly is a piece of the city that was a quick and easy decision for Simon to make on where to take me.

Where to take me. It has a strange sound to it. Why is he doing this? Is this him being nice? Might he feel bad for being such an ass to me during the photo shoot? Or maybe that's why he kissed me, because he felt bad, is that possible? Or maybe I just imagined the whole thing because being here with him now it feels like he's a perfect stranger, a mere city tour guide leading me along.

We turn on the sidewalk, enter in through a small archway and down a path, and the space opens up to an expansive scenery of garden bliss. It's not too crowded, maybe thanks to the fact that it's a Wednesday, and I'm immediately at ease within the peace of this place. There're the pockets of gardens as far as the eye can see, bubbling water fountains, meandering paths and stretches of lush green carpets of grass. It's a little oasis right here in the city, and I realize I haven't gotten out to explore nearly enough.

We walk deeper into the park, the smell of flowers and moss soothing me. We have no blanket or anything, so Simon finds a bench nestled in a small sectioned off area, and I laugh. "Is that a peacock?" The bird is pitter-pattering around nonchalantly, feathers down and dragging behind him on the pebbles of the path.

Simon smiles too, and I realize that it might be the first time I've seen a real smile on his face. "What, you've never seen a peacock before?" He's making quick work of ham and cheese on a fresh roll, and he finishes and hands it to me. I gratefully grab the sandwich with zero plans to try and fight him.

"Well obviously I have, I just wasn't expecting a peacock to be roaming around, that's all." I take a bite and groan at the mix of salt from the ham, the creaminess of the cheese, the spongy spring of the roll. So simple, yet so satisfying. My granola bars and salads I've been living off of lately suddenly seem like I've been in a land of cardboard and bamboo, and this small indulgence is heaven.

You can eat this and enjoy it. Just for today, it's no big deal, I remind myself. While my diet is definitely a part of my job, it's a little easier to be less concerned with it here now when surrounded by so much natural beauty and serenity. I cross my legs and lean back in my bench, the slats of wood digging into my spine, but I don't even care. I'm going to try and relax and enjoy this. I can do this.

"This is nice," I say, and dive into another bite of my sandwich, willing myself to not think about the fact that I'm eating with an audience. I try to quiet my eating anxiety by making a note that

Simon's not even looking in my direction. My teeth get stuck on an unsuccessful attempt to bite through the ham, and I try and block the site with my hand, willing the damn piece to hurry up and tear. It does, thankfully, and Simon's still staring straight ahead. Thank God we're sitting next to each other and not facing one another.

My therapist would probably love all this good exposure therapy for me. I'm eating with another human. And one I'm way too attracted to at that.

We sit and eat in silence, my nerves thankfully quieting with each bite, (smaller and more careful now). I finish the whole sandwich, determined to prove to Simon that I don't starve myself. Plus I have to admit, that shit was delicious.

I get the feeling that Simon's not sure what to do with me anymore. As if he had a plan to get me fed, get me out of my woozy state, and now he's thinking "Now what?" With a little energy regained from my food, it feels like my chance to gain back the upper hand.

"So, photographer Simon with the secret tattoos. Now that you've fulfilled your duty and can solidly tell Roger you didn't let me out of your sights until you were sure I was safe from the risk of passing out again, what will you do with me?" I lean my elbow on the back of the bench, facing him, and raise a questioning eyebrow. I remember the last time I faced him like this, the night we "met," if you could call it that. I cringe a little at the memory of me telling him he'd be my next boy toy. Wrong. Audience. I can see that now. When he called me out on it the day of the shoot, I just about died of embarrassment.

He looks at me, studying me, maybe. There's hunger in his eyes though, I definitely think he's attracted to me. He's so alarmingly good looking in a whole new way that's polar opposite from my Hot Nerd impression that I find myself struggling to feel my usual confidence. I much preferred the initial impression I had of him. It's completely obliterated now.

Simon ignores my question. "Why did you become a model?"

"What?"

"Modeling, why?"

"Why did you become a photographer?"

He smirks. "Right. Fine. Let's see, well, I've never been one for the art of sales or disingenuous conversation—"

"Shocking."

"Must you interrupt?"

"I must," I say. Then I feel a tiny bit guilty. He's actually been nice to me today. "Sorry, couldn't help myself. Go ahead. No sales, you like authentic conversation."

"Something you're unaccustomed to, I imagine."

"Ouch," I pout. "You feed me, then insult me."

"Have you given me much else to work with, Lila?" I watch the rise and fall of his chest, a blip of his pulse beneath the black ink on his neck. "I think I liked you better when you were hungry. You were at least quiet, then. It's as though I fed the beast."

"Fed the beast? Really? My God, and here I thought for a sec you were actually being kind of nice. But being kind really is hard for you, isn't it?" I huff a little in disbelief. Something just doesn't sit right with me with that comment. "I've been called a lot of things, but 'beast' might just be brand new for me. Hope you're proud."

"What else have you been called?" He reaches in the bag and pulls out a peach, takes a bite. I wonder how someone can look so sexy while eating.

"Um, no," I say firmly. "I don't need to sit here and list out the terrible things I've been called."

"Why not? It might be freeing to let it out."

"And give you more fuel for your fire? No thanks. Let's get back to you. Photography. What you like about it. I'm all ears."

I see a flicker of something cross his eyes, but then his dark lashes close on them and he faces forward again.

"Alright. Well, there's a quietness when viewing the world

through a lens. I can crop out what I don't like, zoom in on what I do. Discard and collect as I see fit."

I nod, not really sure what to say.

"And now you. Why modeling?"

I sigh and watch a couple of kids up ahead, chasing after a small bird. They look so carefree and enthralled with the little game, and I'm jealous of their ability to be enraptured so easily. Then I see the mom, on a bench, staring at her phone. I'm instantly mad at her for missing this adorable moment of her kids.

I pull myself away from the young family and try to return my attention to Simon's question. "Umm, so my mom is a fashion designer. L. Delphi-Ray?" I peer over to him to watch for that look of being impressed, but thankfully his face remains still, just quietly listening. He lifts the peach to his mouth and bites and I smile at the simple human-ness of the act. He licks a little juice from the corner of his mouth.

I continue. "Fashion has always been in my world, obviously. Not that my mom condoned my sister or me to get into modeling. Lucy, my sister, has always had a perfect and clear career path, destined to change the world, but not me."

"What's your sister's career?"

I nod, unsurprised. Of course he wants to know her career. "She runs a non-profit that links kids in foster care with professionals all across the world in jobs the kids might be interested in. Social workers facilitate their video sessions, it's gained all kinds of traction, thanks to Lucy." I may be jealous of my sister, but I can't help but feel pride as well.

"Sounds like she simply got lucky, found something that works for her. It takes more time for others," he offers, and it's actually kind of sweet. I expected him to want to know more, people usually do, but instead he's offering me encouragement.

"Yeah, well she's all brains and beauty. And I've just..." My voice trails off, unsure where I'm going with this.

"Yes?" Simon prompts, and he licks a little juice from his lips.

My eyes drop to the peach in his hand, fuzzy flesh and the shine of the glistening coral meat inside, and he offers it to me. I take the peach from him, bite into it and slurp up the surprising explosion of juice. It's sweet and tangy and so strangely sensual, sharing a peach with Simon the photographer.

I chew and dab my finger at the corner of my lip to wipe up some juice. I actually feel almost comfortable with doing so in front of someone else, I realize with surprise. I look up at Simon as if it just occurred to me where we are and what we're doing. "Why am I sharing a peach with you?"

He shrugs, casually wipes his hand on the fabric of his stomach and leans back on the bench, elbows perched. "Because you're hungry," he says, staring ahead of us at the peacock gliding along carelessly a mere yard away from our feet. "You were saying?" My eyes move down his body and I try not to stare at the thin material of his shorts, because I'm pretty sure if I look close enough I could make out the details of his penis. It happens anyway, my eyes have a mind of their own. Yup, I can absolutely see the perfect cylinder of his dick.

I clear my throat and try and focus back on the roaming peacock and the sound of laughter from the two kids ahead. "Yeah. So I went to college for business at my mom's insistence. Squeezed in some psych and history classes which I *loved*, but after graduation I had no idea what to do with the degree. I would work for my mom now and then more just if she needed someone last minute, so I finally decided to just give modeling a real try. And now here I am."

"It's not your passion, though. You don't really love it."

"Yes I do, what makes you say that?"

"You're good at it, everyone tells you you're beautiful and you move like a ballerina, but there's something missing in it for you. I can tell. It's not what you're meant to be doing." He's matter of fact when he says this.

"How can you tell, what do you mean?"

"You don't have the fire."

I should be insulted, he has absolutely zero hint of humor or sarcasm in his tone. It's all steely seriousness, but my only reaction is a little flip of my belly. "You're so mean," I say, a tad frustrated at how that's literally all I could come up with. Why do I lose all my cleverness around him? He's got me off my game.

"It wasn't meant to be mean. But no matter, I think you like someone finally not fawning over your looks and actually talking seriously with you."

I consider his observation. Is he right? Do I like the way he's so brusque with me? Then I remember his comment about my shit-brown eyes. *That*, I did not like.

"My eyes are green," I blurt out. I stare at him, unblinking. The corner of his mouth with the scar raises in a smirk. I'm tempted to reach out and touch it.

"If your eyes are green, then what are mine?"

I huff out a breath in disbelief, trying not to be transfixed by the black lashes surrounding his admittedly startling green eyes. He inches his elbow up to the bench a little closer to mine, his skin grazing my skin. "Well, Lila?"

"Arsenic green," I shrug. "You know, that dye that used to kill people in the Victorian ages." I'm pretty proud I just pulled out that reference. I had always liked old timey facts and hearing old stories, learning about the past. I'm a junkie for a good documentary to escape into, it's a nice way to hide from the exhausting competitiveness necessary for today's survival. It's all useless info, though, so when I get a chance to use it, it's fun. Especially now with Simon.

"You mean Scheele's Green? When people were more concerned with looks than danger caused by a dye?"

"Yes, exactly," I say in surprise. "How do you know that?"

"I'm a fashion photographer, though not necessarily by choice. It helps to look into the history and feel a bit more connection to the work."

I nod, losing myself momentarily at the maze pattern on his neck. I can't believe how utterly wrong I was in my initial impression of him. Definitely never thought he would be hiding tattoos under all his professor layers. "Maybe absinthe green is more accurate," I say quietly. "For your eyes."

He lifts a hand and reaches for the collar of my sweatshirt. His fingertips graze my collarbone as he pulls aside the neckline, exposing the strap of my sports bra. "And what color is this?" he asks.

I open my mouth in surprise at the contact. "Oh. Um, sage green maybe?" I narrow my eyes. "Why?"

I feel as he pushes underneath my strap, dragging his finger down a bit along my skin before retreating and dropping his hand. My collarbone and skin immediately mourn in the loss of the contact.

"That's your eyes then. Sage."

"So not shit brown?" I challenge, but he only holds his gaze, saying nothing. I turn to face forward again and cross my arms over my chest. "You could have just pointed to my shorts, you know."

And I'm stunned when I hear him say, "I wanted to touch you." I nearly do a double take, his admission is so unexpected and random. "I have wanted to touch you since I first saw your photos, Lila. Prior to meeting you."

First a surprise kiss in a random hallway, now this random statement. My heartbeat quickens, and I resolve to not react as eagerly as I'd like. What do you say to that? I bite my lip, contemplating how to respond. Did I hear that correctly? He wanted to touch me? What happened to hating me, refusing to work with me, all but yelling at me in his directing attempts during the shoot? Then a sudden kiss, followed by a sudden stop and him deserting me. He's been cold then hot, then cold until after my humiliating gym situation, out on the street where he softened.

He's not exactly shy like I thought, but...distant, in a way.

And now here he is saying he wants to touch me? I want to be mad at his mind-fuck unreadability, but my attraction to him has held firm, despite it all. Does he hate me but want to fuck me? Is that what's happening? Or maybe he hates that he *wants* to fuck me.

Eventually I simply nod. And then my nod turns to a grin. I'm unable to stop the smile from giving myself away. This is what I wanted, right? Hot Nerd. Hot...whatever he is.

I can handle him. If he wants to touch me, then that's fine by me. More than fine. "Good," I say.

"Good," he repeats.

I have the overwhelming need to have him take me home with him. Normally that wouldn't be a problem. I'd give a guy the look, maybe a "Your place or mine?" line and off we'd go. Sex is a such a fun pastime, and I'm rarely hard pressed to find willing participants.

But it's different in the light of day as opposed to the dark shadows of a hot and sticky bar.

It's different in the sober air of a floral scented park as opposed to the drunken whispers of alcohol infused breath.

But it's there. The desire is there, thick and damn near torturous.

"Why do you want to touch me?" I finally ask. I can't help it, I have to know.

"Lila, I want to do a lot more than touch you." His eyes hold firm on mine as he says this. So serious. My heart flutters a bit. "When I kissed you I wasn't thinking. But I couldn't stop myself." He makes it sound like a sinful confession.

"Did you regret it? The kiss?"

"I told myself I did. But no."

"So you're attracted to me?" It's stupid to ask, I know. I think I just want to hear him say it.

Slowly he reaches out to me, places a hand on my thigh, pulling me closer to him. I tense a little at his touch, wondering what he's about to do. He leans towards me, turning his head as if he's looking behind me, but his mouth is by my ear. I can feel his breath on my neck, smell the intoxicatingly masculine mix of spice and salty sweat. "I'm so fucking attracted to you," he whispers, "all of my rational thoughts go out the window when I'm near you." He glides his hand up from my thigh to under my sweatshirt and onto the bare skin on the side of my stomach. I want him to keep going, to feel his hands everywhere on me, but of course we're out in public in broad daylight. Still, I'm covered in lust filled chills.

His accent. His quiet and serious facade. His bike, his tattoos, the way he looks at me, touches me, his apparent genius photography talent.

And he wants *me*? Of course he wants me, what am I talking about—everyone does.

I only hope I can handle him.

six

. . .

lucy

WHAT IS IT about airplanes that make you live in this constant state of heightened everything? The smells, all the same on every plane, a tad clinical until the food service starts. That's when the smell turns into something that's more dorm room cooking meets remnants of attempted fine dining. The efforts of good meal prep are there, but ultimately there's no masking the fact that the shit was prepped eons ago and reheated in a microwave. And then you get the sweet and sour musk of the burly man with the friendly smile. You look and you know from his eyes that he's kind, but you're not remotely interested in talking, and still you can't escape the smell of his sweat and Old Spice. Or the smell of the old lady's perfume and slight tuna breath underneath. It should be illegal to serve seafood in airports or flights, in my opinion.

I lift the metal plate of the buckle in my lap to free myself and get up to walk down the little runway to the bathroom. All these smells seem to be absolutely everywhere. At the same time, the floor under my navy ballet flats seems to be harder and more brittle with each passing step. And is it my imagination or is the floor coming up towards me?

Finally, finally, I get to my unglamorous destination, fumble with the knob and folding door, and spill my way into the tiny box serving as a wasteland for the passengers of the plane. One quick view of the steel and streaks of blue of the toilet, and I'm done for. I keel over, grabbing my hair off my neck in a desperate fist just in time to convulse with the release of my meager dinner. Maybe I should have eaten more prior to the flight. Maybe the glass of wine (okay, two glasses) at the airport bar were a mistake.

Maybe I'm pregnant.

No. No. That can't be.

Actually yes, it very much can be, though the thought of that might just make me sick again, ready to toss up the remaining bile in my body, and I'm really not interested in continuing.

I should have thought things through a little better before deciding on impulse to purchase a ticket, jump on a plane and surprise my sister.

I'm trying to calculate when I'm due for my next period. I'm one of those lucky ones that really only suffers the crimson tide for a couple days at a time, and I get a pretty friendly five or six weeks in between. Periods just never were a big deal to me, I never knew what the drama was about, other than being unlucky in having had my first one at the young age of ten. It was just shy of my eleventh birthday. I was prepared for that kind of thing, having diligently taken notes in my fifth grade "Reveal All" assembly we had been cattle called to. The lady presenting was one of those motherly hippie types, with natural, long gray hair in thick dreads, and a glimmer in her eye that matched the glimmer of her sequins adorned chiffon kimono. She made periods and puberty seem like a special club we girls should all be proud to be a part of. And we all were excited to join, secretly.

Except that I was the first of my friends to join that club, and let me tell you, it wasn't a club that felt very exciting when you realized it was just another indicator of the very Adult Self that had always seemed to be thrust upon you. Look, I was the natural one to pave the way for that kind of thing. (I can't even count how many pads I've handed out to blushing, unprepared girls, reassuring them that it's all good, welcome to the club.) But I find it odd and slightly annoying that I'm always the one to trail blaze anything adult-like. There's a sense of diplomacy I have to adhere to, and I never even ran for election. Why can't I ever be the one to throw caution to the wind? Why can't I let down my hair a little now and then?

Well, actually I had recently. The thought sits bitter in my mouth like the bitterness of the vomit remnants sitting unwelcome on my tongue and lingering in my throat.

I scour through my bag, find the mini mouthwash nestled in its clear Zip-Lock baggie of other liquids, and damn near orgasm at the whip of alcohol and mint in my mouth as I swish. Dear God, Listerine never tasted so good.

I make my way back out, consumed by thoughts of a potential life force growing within me. How I wish, I wish, I had a pregnancy test with me. How absurd would that be, taking a test on a plane and finding out whether or not your life would forever be changed? As I step out, the plump flight attendant asks me if I'm okay as I fumble with the door behind me, and I find myself blurting out my pregnancy concern. She startles, her cheeks pink, but quickly recovers with a bright smile. Why I shared my thought with her, I'm not really sure. Maybe I just needed to say it out loud.

"You think you might be? Or you know?" she asks. Judy, that's what her name tag says. An image of Judy Jetson pops in my head.

I nod my head at the lavatory behind me. "Well, I just refunded my overpriced red wine from the airport bar, which is not like me. So I think, but have no way to know for sure."

"You need a test?" Her voice is a whisper, or as close to a whisper as she can manage with the rumble of the engines as our constant soundtrack. But her tone, if I'm not mistaken, is conveying an offer. As in, she can find me a test if I want one.

Do I want to know? Here? Is that pathetic?

But I realize now I want to get my hands on a test no matter what, and if she's got one to give, I'm taking it.

I nod my head numbly, and she opens a gray cabinet door, the squeak of sound from the hinge making my skin crawl. I watch as she grabs a small cardboard box. She hands it over to me, looking all too excited. "I hardly ever get to pass these out, actually this is only my second time doing so," she says.

"And? The results the first time?" I ask.

Her face falls. "It was negative. But still exciting for a small minute. You have a glow, though. I have higher hopes."

I ignore the fact that she assumes this would be good news. I see her eyes drop to my ring finger and the sizable rock and glittery band, and realize that sure, on the outside a pregnancy from a clearly married and well established woman would probably seem like a good thing. I plaster on a decent smile, committed to letting this poor thing feel some semblance of victory.

"Well, fingers crossed we can make a little Airplane Tales history for you then," I jest. At least someone will be happy if this thing has two lines instead of just one.

Back in the torture chamber of the small box of hidden mysteries of the world, I tear open the box. A jolt of turbulence hits and I damn near drop the thing right back in the steel bowl that just welcomed my wine. I eke out some pee, cursing the decision to take the flight attendant up on her offer as this box of a room is feeling like the last place I want to be hovering over a stick, aiming my pee at it like a drunken barfly aiming a fist at an unassuming and swaying subject. I manage though, and hope that the drops hitting the receiving fortune teller in my hand are enough.

I stand, jolt with another shot of turbulence and nearly drop the stick, laughing a little at the absurdity of the whole situation. I clean myself up and wonder what to do next. Do I wait in here for the next couple minutes until my results appear? Is it rude to commandeer the bathroom for this long? But how do I discreetly walk out with this thing, especially since it's supposed to be laying flat?

Turns out, I don't really need to consider these options, because the answer is already there, just like that.

At least Judy will be happy.

before

. . .

Dear Simon,

Mum told me what happened. Is it true? You were kicked out of school after that fight? The headmaster has always been a Fuckwit, hasn't he? Pay him no mind, you will rise to the top one day and be rubbing his nose in it, I know it. I can feel it.

I love you so very much, Simon, as I'm sure you know by now from all these darling love notes I keep writing you. I spent way too much money buying all the fancy pens I could get, just for you. I get a kick out of watching you grumble each time I hand one to you, even though I know you secretly love them. Maybe one day you'll actually be a gentleman and write one for me.

Sorry, that's never going to happen. That's what you would say to that, am I right? It's okay, I forgive you.

Don't let what happened get to you though, alright? You have a temper, so what?! A little fight now and then between boys is hardly alarming, everyone seems very extreme in their reactions. I bet you had good reason for it, I can't wait to hear your side of the story.

Okay. I better get back to paying attention here in class. The teacher thinks I'm very invested in writing good notes. I've got her fooled, ha!

Kissey face and yum yums.
X
Elsie

seven

. . .

simon

THE DECISION HAD come easily for him—he was going to take Lila back to his place. He told himself that it was to keep an eye on her to make sure she kept her food down and her head steady, but it was more than that.

His attraction to her is consuming and steady in its growth. He wants to touch her again and see what's beneath her mask of wicked fury. Perhaps it's the brief glimpses of the softer side of her that's drawing him in—he gathers it's one she is not used to exposing. Though he must admit, the contrast of her temper with the times she appears uncertain leave him wanting to know who she really is. In fact, he wants Lila to see for herself who she really is. And he wants to be the one to get her there. All of which is ridiculous and unnerving for him as he generally has little patience for that kind of thing. Nonetheless his interest and intrigue for Lila is there, and he is not one to deny himself of the things that he wants. There's no sense in continuing to deny this pull.

Not surprisingly, Lila didn't put up a fight when he made his intentions clear. But as they walk into his flat, the space mostly pristine thanks to his aunt's efforts, Simon is hesitant to make any move just yet.

He watches as Lila looks around, taking in the pale wood flooring, the dark cabinets of the kitchen, shining with a hint of lemon scent. She nods approvingly, which he finds amusing. It's as though she needs to vet the space. Some women walk into a space and comment on the artwork or the overall decor, making small talk and polite praises. Not Lila. She walks in as though ready to critique, which Simon imagines is more insecurity than genuine criticism.

Finally she moves to the couch and takes a seat, but Simon remains standing in the entryway. He debates what to do next, enjoying watching her as she sets down her things on the table in front of her. Even in gym clothing, her body moves with grace and fluidity, which Simon finds irresistibly feminine and naturally sensual. Lila sees a photo book in front of her, a collection of some of Simon's work, and she picks it up, delicately brushing a hand across as though to wipe away an imaginary speck of dust. She peers up at him with a question in her eyes, and he nods once. "Go ahead," he says. "My Aunt Victoria made it for me."

"A sweet aunt," she responds, her eyes held on the cover.

The cover image is one of a massive pile of stone, the remains of an ancient mausoleum, with Simon himself standing small in one corner. He rarely does self portraits, but that day he had felt an unexpected connection to the mausoleum, and on a whim had decided to stand beside one of the openings, his camera set on the ground angled up with a small stone in such a way that allowed the captured image a distorted angle where the foreground was exaggerated in size.

"Where is this?" Lila asks, still staring down at the photo.

"France. Cairn de Barnenez, considered one of the oldest buildings in the world."

"Tombs?" she asks, flipping through the first few photos with more of the structure.

"Yes."

"These are beautiful." Her tone holds reverence. "There's just something profound in a way with old buildings, isn't there? Like they hold an ability of some sort."

"What kind of ability?" he asks, surprised and curious with her obvious appreciation.

She shakes her head slightly. "I don't know, it's hard to explain. I guess in the way life can be silently narrated within the stillness of a prehistoric structure."

"I couldn't have said it better myself."

"It's funny," she says as she continues to flip through the pages. "You say you prefer this work as opposed to fashion, but I think your best photos here are the ones with people in them."

"So I've been told," he mutters.

"I mean that's where the real story is. In the relationship between the structure and environment and the people wandering through, taking it all in. I'm guessing that's why people love your work so much in the industry. You have a gift for giving significance to inanimate things. What designer wouldn't want that as a way to showcase their creations?" she asks, looking up at him with a smirk as if to say "like it or not, the job suits you."

But Simon only nods, walking into the kitchen in search of some wine. It seems with every passing minute with Lila he feels more intensely hungry for her, and in more ways than the simple lust he had initially felt.

He finds a bottle of red and pours them each a glass. He walks into the living area and sets her glass on the table before moving to a chair adjacent to the couch.

"You're not going to sit next to me?" she asks as she takes her wine.

"No." Simon lifts his glass in a salute and takes a sip, enjoying the velvety warmth of the liquid.

Lila sips as well and licks her lips in appreciation. Eventually she leans back, the photo book still in her lap. He watches as she scans the room, taking note of the minimal decor save for a few blown up photos adorning the walls, all of various prehistoric buildings.

"I can't figure you out," she says finally. He remains quiet, curious to what she'll say next. "You don't talk much, do you?"

He shrugs. "I find that people like to jammer on only to fill silence to ease their own discomfort."

"And what, you get a thrill out of discomfort? Or watching other people struggle in it?"

"My intention is never to cause outright harm, Lila."

"It was a joke," she says with another sip of her wine, this one much bigger, and he realizes he's making her nervous. "So now what? You're sitting all the way over there, I'm over here. You kissed me out of nowhere the other day, and then today ask me to come home with you, so..."

"So you thought we'd be removing clothing by now?"

"Well yes, Perceptive Simon. Exactly. I thought we'd be removing clothing by now." Her expression is mischievous. Flirtatious. Arousing. He could watch the ever changing kaleidoscope of her moods and expressions and never be bored.

He rests his chin in his hand, elbow perched on his armrest. "I'm not going to fuck you tonight, Lila," he says, and watches with amusement as her mouth gapes open in a small *O* shape. "Though I'd like to," he adds. He shifts ever so slightly in his seat, aware that even this very conversation has him aroused.

"So what's stopping you?"

Simon opens his mouth, ready to explain the value in patience, but Lila's eyes float over to a table in the corner where a small framed photo rests. She squints and leans forward for a better look. "Wait a sec, is that *Grayson*?"

Simon looks to the photo in question, one of him and Grayson as teenagers, Simon seventeen, Grayson about thirteen. "Yes, the musician. You know of him I gather?"

Lila rises from her seat to snatch up the photo. "Look at you two...babies! Grayson's my friend!" Simon's face must look surprised because Lila rushes on to explain. "I'm serious, he really is. He works with Ruby, who is dating, I mean engaged to actually," she says with rapid blinks, "my sister's longtime childhood friend Joey Conti. So yes, I like for real actually know Grayson. How do you know him?"

"He's a distant cousin, of sorts."

Lila's eyes roam around as if absorbing this. She nods and places the frame back in its spot before returning to the couch. "Well at least now I don't need to feel worried that you took me up here just to kidnap me. I remember Grayson saying he had a cousin that did photography in the industry. Guess I just can't believe it's *you*."

"The world is full of surprises," he says with little inflection. Simon feels somewhat disappointed by this connection, perhaps because of the fact that he and Grayson are no longer on good terms. Thankfully Lila doesn't appear to have any indication of that.

He tries to steer the conversation away from Grayson and back to her. He leans forward in his seat, resting his forearms on his thighs. "I'd like to get to know you better, Lila."

He watches as a smile spreads across her face. "Oh, I'd very much like you to get to know me too, Si." She places her glass down and once again rises from her seat. Simon gets the sense Lila doesn't like to sit still, but he watches with admiration as her body glides towards him. She lifts a leg, placing a knee next to his hip in preparation to straddle him, but he stops her.

"No, Lila." The smooth skin of her leg has him tense with his own desire, but he's committed to holding firm on waiting before doing anything physical just yet.

With a scoff Lila drops her leg and stands before Simon, hands on her hips. He sees her face change from mischief to angry heat. "Okay, what the fuck is with you? Do you want this or not?"

Simon leans back again and rests his elbow on the arm of the chair, amused by the fire in her eyes. "How many relationships have you had?" he asks.

"You wanna know my number? My body count?" With the look on her face one might think he'd asked her bank account balance.

"No, not how many people you've slept with. It's an arbitrary number. Sex can range from mindless and empty to intimate and meaningful, and the number of people you've shared a bed with hardly captures a relevant quantity of true connection one may have experienced."

"Oh my God, no you are not giving me a damn lesson right now. Who talks like that?"

Simon shrugs, remaining silent.

Lila sighs dramatically in defeat. "Whatever. That's just my life. Go on, you were saying?" she prompts with an agitated hand wave back to him. She turns and strolls around the room languidly, running a finger along the bookshelf adjacent to his chair. The movement is sensual and Simon once again has to rearrange himself to keep focused on the conversation he's attempting to have. He allows his eyes to drop momentarily to admire the roll of her ass as she takes each slow step, then returns his gaze to her profile.

"What I want to know is," he says, closing his eyes briefly to refocus, "how many significant relationships have you had? True partners? Not just sex."

"Why? How many have you had?" she asks. She drops her hand from the bookshelf and walks back to her seat on the couch, dropping down with a heavy sigh. She crosses her legs and arms and tilts her head to him, eyes narrowed as though challenging him with the question.

"Three."

"And where are these three now?"

Simon thinks about this, the three women he's considered to be real relationships. It's been years since the most recent one. "I'm not sure," he answers honestly.

Lila nods. "Alright."

"So? How many for you?"

She bites her lip momentarily before answering. "Just one, I guess," she says with a shrug. She reaches forward for her wine and Simon notes the shift in her expression. Hurt crossing her face, perhaps, and he decides not to press further. She straightens her spine and adds, "I'm more into casual than relationships."

There it is. Lila's been hurt before, Simon can see that now. There's small drops of it that seep out in brief moments before getting swept up by her mask of coy and casual. Simon lets her comment sit for a moment, the sound of outside traffic filling the silence of the room. He considers her statement and how to respond, now understanding better that Lila uses casual as more of a safety barrier than an actual internal want.

Perhaps he's wrong. Perhaps she's career focused and therefore serious isn't on the agenda for her. He wants to believe that for her own sake.

But Simon knows better. He can see that there's more to it than that and he further resolves to be patient with Lila, cursing himself for impulsively kissing her the day of the shoot. She deserves better than such self-serving impulses, better than giving into reckless lust, something he imagines Lila has come to expect from men based on previous experience. His jaw and fists instinctively clench at the idea.

"Lila, I don't want casual with you." As soon as the words exit his mouth, Simon realizes just how accurate they are. Otherwise they would have already been rolling around naked and he'd be kicking her out the door by now. It's what he half expected when he asked her to come home with him. He could keep an eye on her, ensure she was alright, given into his temptation and then have Lila Ray out of his system.

But he didn't.

The side of Lila he's seen this afternoon was unexpected. It's as though she was feeling too unwell to unleash her cocky and spoiled facade, though truth be told the more time he spends with her, the less bothered by that facade he gets.

If he's honest with himself, her cocky and spoiled demeanor turns him on.

"So let me get this straight," she starts. "You…like me? As in, let's hold hands and do dinner dates and, I don't know, you buy me flowers and all that?" Her face is filled with confusion as if there's a mathematical equation in her mind she's struggling to solve.

Simon allows a slow smile to spread across his face. "I like you very much, yes. And Lila," he says, leaning forward, "you say you prefer casual, but I can assure you. You are far too brilliant a woman for me to casually take and then discard. And besides, I haven't been able to stop thinking about you."

"That sounds problematic," she says, but there's more softness in her voice than sarcasm.

"Quite the contrary. I've actually very much enjoyed having you in my thoughts. Problem is, I'm far too selfish for that to be where you remain."

Lila gapes at him in surprise, and Simon knows he's got her.

eight

. . .

lila

H E'S GIVING ME this look that screams intensity and my breath catches in my throat. I'm determined to look calm and collected, but he's so fucking *sexy* sitting there like that, I can't stand it. This inked up masterpiece, telling me he can't stop thinking about me, he wants to for real date me.

Why is it freaking me out so much?

I swallow and take a deep breath, attempting to not let my racing heart betray me in my voice. "You sure...you sure you don't just want to fuck, baby cakes?" I ask. "Seems easier. Probably better for you since you know, I'm an entitled American and everything." There. That should get to him.

Simon rises from his seat and walks over to me, his face full of pure determination. His lips look so kissable, why can't he just kiss me and we'll do this and call it a day?

"Maybe I'd like to be proven wrong," he says as he stands in front of me.

I look up at him and narrow my eyes. "I shouldn't have to prove anything to you."

"Alright," he says and I feel a little satisfaction at having made that point. He places his hands in his pockets. "I can admit when I've made a mistake, and my first impressions of you were —incomplete."

"My oh my...you think? Indulge me then, how so?" I tilt my chin towards him.

"You come off entitled and spoiled and haughty, but it's all a ruse, isn't it?"

I lean back and cross my arms to let out a little incredulous huff. "Do I start with arguing about how I'm not entitled and spoiled, or how it's not all a ruse? Hmm, I'm just not sure," I joke. How is it that he can stand there like that, insult me yet it drives me freakin' wild? Any other guy and I'd be storming out of here by now. It's like he's got a chokehold on me.

"That temper of yours drives me mad," he says with a little smirk on his beautiful and infuriating face. His green eyes I swear are piercing into my soul and scrambling my brain.

He's enjoying this, I can tell. He loves keeping me on my toes, never sure where exactly he stands. He wants me, sure, he's made that clear. But then he says shit like how I'm spoiled and haughty.

Simon takes a step back, looks down at the floor for a sec, then back up and to the side. I follow his line of vision to the window and the view of the building next to his, this one a white structure with charming black shutters flanking the window panes. I glance back to find him staring at me again. I have an urge to reach up to him, touch him and feel him, soak in his tobacco and pine scent.

But I don't. In fact, I resolve to remain defiantly quiet and still.

"So then, what do you say, Lila?" he asks and for a moment I'm confused. But then I remember his intentions.

"Are you asking me to be your girlfriend?" I ask. It sounds juvenile, but I can't think of how else to phrase it.

"I'm asking to get to know you better. Yes, maybe go out for dinner. Not jump straight to sex, because I have a feeling you prefer to use sex as a form of avoidance from real relationships." I gape at him, but he keeps going. "And I have a feeling it's better to make you wait. Which is why I asked you how many relationships you've had."

This guy. *He sees right through you,* a small voice in the back of my mind cries, and I try and shove it down. Simon finally moves and sits down beside me, draping an arm on the back of the couch behind me. I feel the urge to curl up into his chest and feel his arms wrap around me, but I remain still and painfully stiff in my position.

I try and think about how to answer. "I just..." I trail off and bite my lip in concentration. "Who exactly are you, Simon Sharp, Hot Nerd that I think I need a new nickname for?"

I watch as he lifts the hand that had been resting in his lap toward me. He grabs my right hand. I let him explore the ring on my middle finger, a simple silver band and a cluster of green gems in the shape of a flower. He kisses the knuckle beneath it and every cell in my body is screaming at the contact with his lips. He smiles, keeping my hand near his lips. "I'm more than okay with Hot Nerd. It's fitting."

I laugh. "How bout sexy mastermind? That's what Adrian called you."

"He called me sexy?" he jokes. I'm not sure I've heard him joke yet.

"Mastermind, you dummy. But yes," I say, pulling back my hand. I start fidgeting my leg as all kinds of restless energy floods me.

"My work is highly subjective, Lila. All creative endeavors are. For whatever reason the world seems to like my photos," he says with a shrug. "Adrian is kind, but I don't for one second believe I am gifted with anything more than a decent eye and a propensity for details."

"Well. Maybe that's just it."

"What?"

"It's your gift for recognizing the details that countless others fail to see even exist. Maybe that really does make you a master-mind." I hate to feed him this compliment and stroke his ego, but there it is, just blurting on out of me beyond my control. I glance over to him, then twist my body to perch my elbow on the back of the couch, next to his arm, determined to keep my gaze on his eyes despite how unsteady I feel around him.

"And you? What does the captivating and spoiled Lila Ray have that makes her a mastermind?" The eyebrow with the scar raises in question.

"I'll let you know when I figure it out."

"Don't do that, Lila. Don't joke down your talents or quality."

I shake my head at him and close my eyes momentarily. "Fine. You win." I lift my hand with the ring and look down at it, willing it to help center me. I try and change the subject. "Say, Si...what color are the gems of my ring?"

I'm still staring down at the small flower, but I think I can see the corner of his mouth twitch. "Is this a test?" he asks. I don't answer. "Fine," he says, reaching for my hand again to examine the ring. "I'd say they are sea glass green, with an iridescent hue that can lean almost purple in certain lights." He releases my hand, removes the arm that had been draped behind me and crosses his arms. "Do I pass?"

God I wish he would kiss me again. Why won't he just kiss me?

I shake my head and rise to a stand, gathering my things because I can't stand another minute of this tension-filled dance we're doing. He's fucking with my head it feels like. "Shit brown eyes," I say, walking towards his front door. "That was fucked up, you know that?"

"We've established that, yes. Why did you let me kiss you, then?" he challenges, the beautiful little devil. He's still sitting on the couch and looking all kinds of smug. "Unless you secretly crave a little humiliation." *What?!*

I drop my jaw in surprise and irritation. "I do not. I don't even...what does that even mean?" The tips of my ears feel hot. I need to get out of here.

Simon stands and walks towards me, stopping mere inches in front of me. I tense as he glides a knuckle down my throat. I'm tingly at the touch. "I think you very much do, and that scares you," he finally says. He leans down to kiss me, pausing briefly before pressing his lips to mine and I give the slightest of nods, eager to feel his lips on mine, even if my heart is racing with how off kilter I feel in his presence. He slips in the slightest bit of tongue, then abruptly pulls back, clearing his throat.

I raise a hand to my lips. "You don't scare me," I whisper, though even I can hear how little conviction is in my voice.

The corner of his mouth lifts slightly. "Not yet. But hopefully soon," he says, walking around me to open his door. "I take it you're ready?" he asks, and I nod, immobile at first but then eventually I follow behind.

I feel almost numb as we ride back to my flat. I tell him I'll walk up alone, insisting I don't want to be bombarded with questions from my flatmate.

But really I've decided that I have zero intention of ever contacting Simon Sharp, Hot Nerd Photographer ever again.

nine

. . .

lila

GOD, HE LOOKS hot cruising away down the street on that bike, tattoos all on display. My Hot Nerd Genius Mastermind. Such a shame, he's so beautiful.

But this whole afternoon was weird, so naturally I have to drop the guy. I mean he looks at me with such intense desire, it's wild. Don't get me wrong, I'm a little high off that look, but I think it's best we just leave it right there, because a fucking relationship with Simon is absolutely laughable. I mean, really? I thought it was pretty clear that we had an attraction to one another, so let's fuck and blow each other's minds, then call it a day, right? Why ruin it with a whole song and dance of messy emotions? I'm not commitment phobic or anything, I'm just not trying to commit with a guy like that. There's definite red flags there.

I'm stepping into my apartment building, glad that he bought my excuse of not wanting to have to explain him to my roommate (truth be told, that wasn't really a lie considering I really *don't* want to explain him), but honestly I just didn't want the guy to know where I live. Good riddance to him. What a freak my Hot Nerd turned out to be, such a bummer.

Not gonna lie, at one point I really thought he might be trying to kill me, or lock me up in a closet or something. It was weird. Why did he wait until the very last minute to so much as kiss me again? Sitting and *talking* was not at all what I expected when he asked if I wanted to go back to his place.

I did feel the tiniest bit more relaxed after seeing the picture with Grayson—right up until I remembered that Grayson told me to stay the hell away from Simon if I ever crossed paths with him in the field.

That's when it all clicked. I'm laughing at my luck, that the first London crush I've had turns out to be some ass that apparently likes playing mind games and has a dangerous side. Typical. We didn't trade numbers or anything, and I can just block him from my socials so I think I should be safe. Although, I am curious what I'll do if I have to work with him again. Or see him at the gym? I didn't think about that. I'll have to try and pester Roger about his usual schedule so I can avoid that.

"Hiya!" my roommate Penny says as I pull my key from the door and step into the living room. Penny is a pretty brunette with full lips, adorable dimples, and hair that I swear falls exactly how she wants it to, no matter what. And she's always in a good mood. I hate her. "You have someone waiting for you in your room."

For a split second my mind flashes to an image of Simon being in my room, on my peach duvet cover, tattooed arms perched on my eighty-seven crisp white pillows. But that's impossible, of course. I literally just watched him roar down the street, away from me.

"My room?" I ask Penny. "Who?"

Penny rises from her lazy drape on the couch and grins. "Your sister! How lovely for her to surprise you! Although when I popped in to ask if she wanted a drink," Penny says, lifting her own glass of something unnaturally pink and fruity looking, "she was asleep on your bed. Exhausted from her travels, I imagine, little darling thing." She says this last part in a whisper, as if she hadn't just a second ago been speaking at full volume.

"Huh? Are you sure? Lucy?" I mean, it's not crazy absurd that Lucy decided to surprise me, she's known to throw us all off and get a wild hair now and then. And once she gets an idea in her mind, you'd be hard pressed to stand in the way of her determination. I just didn't expect her to do something like make the trek all the way over here as a surprise. Unless she told me she was coming and I forgot? Is that possible?

"Lucy, yes! Gorgeous thing, she is. Great genes you two have. Wouldn't happen to have any brothers, now then, would ya?" Penny's all cheeky grin as she says this, despite the glittering rock on her own ring finger, betrothed as she is to her equally adorable and sweet fiancé.

"Ha, ha. Very funny. But no." I peer around the corner into my room and sure enough, there's my perfect sister, passed out like a sleeping beauty on my bed. I walk over and close the door for her before returning my attention back to Penny. "I will, however, join you in that drink, though."

"Brilliant! Follow me," she says like the four-and-a-half steps to the kitchen are an adventure. She retrieves a pitcher from the small fridge, and I grab a glass from the cabinet. I watch with amused curiosity as she pours and the flamingo pink waterfall fills up my glass.

"Do I dare ask what this is?"

"Let's see," Penny says with a flutter of her eyelashes as her eyes dart to the ceiling in thought. "Prosecco, rhubarb flavored gin, grapefruit juice, some raspberries, a bit of grenadine for fun."

I sip with caution, aware of all too many calories consumed today, but decide I'll just fast to hit reset tomorrow. Penny's watching me with excitement and I feel annoyed at the audience. I turn away from her prying eyes, but as the cool and tart drink slithers its way across my tongue, I'm pleasantly surprised. "Fuck, that's actually really good."

"Knew you'd like it."

I pull the glass back to eye it curiously. It's so pretty and pink it makes me feel instantly girlish. I feel kinda bad, I haven't really attempted to make friends with Penny since moving here, we both just seem so completely opposite. But if she makes drinks like this, and kindly welcomes my wildly unexpected sister like it's no big deal, then I guess I can't really be too annoyed with her.

"We should celebrate tonight! The sisters reunited, let's do something terribly British and fun!"

Right. That's why Penny drives me crazy, now I remember.

"Oh, you're a doll, Pen, but I think Lucy is probably content to just hang low and get settled for tonight."

"Yes, of course. Right. Well then, she said she wasn't sure how long she'd be, so hopefully we'll have many more opportunities for some fun, finally." She sips her drink, eyeing me over her glass like she's got more to say. "You're always so busy. Or studying."

And there it is.

By "studying," Penny is really referring to my little habit of hiding away in my room when I'm home. It's just easier to say I'm studying so that I can be left alone. Penny's exhausting.

But then I pick up on what she just said. "Wait, Lucy said she didn't know how long she'd be? Like, no return flight scheduled?" I clarify.

Penny shrugs and steps backwards out of the tiny nook of a kitchen and towards the couch. "I'm quite sure she said she didn't have a return flight booked, yeah. She's just here to go day by day and explore! I love that, really. The more the merrier, she's welcome to stay with us as long as she needs."

"Oh, I doubt she'll be too long, don't worry. She has a husband and very important job at home waiting for her," I say with mock enthusiasm, but Penny only nods with serious understanding.

"Of course."

I thank her for the drink and excuse myself, already exhausted from Penny's giddy energy. I creep quietly into my room to grab things for the shower I very badly need. I stare down at Lucy, olive limbs curled up like a cat, pouty lips parted slightly. The urge to jump up on the bed and obnoxiously wake her up hits me, but I think I want a shower more so I leave her be. I'll wake her later and grill her on what she's doing here.

For now, it's time to get cleaned up.

And then maybe do some online stalking of creepy Simon Sharp. Just a little.

ten

. . .

lucy

FUCK, YES. FUCK. The sex is so so good with him, though it absolutely shouldn't be. Is it because it's wrong? Or because I don't give two shits about him so I just demand exactly what I want? Who knows, but I'm down for the ride.

We're in my car, I'm straddling him and staring at his perfectly white teeth and surfer grin. I love his cropped blond hair and his hands that are on my hips, pushing me up and down on top of him, faster and harder. I love the stickiness of the leather under my shins, and how I'm trying to keep my head from hitting the roof of the car while simultaneously scanning around the parking lot, hoping not to get caught. I love the way we kept meeting eyes over the conference table at that meeting, both of us knowing what the other was thinking. Me feeling the vibrating ping of a text, sneaking a glance down to see his words telling me he liked my dress, and couldn't wait to inch his fingers up and between my legs to finger fuck my pussy to high hell. I had been struggling to keep my concentration in the meeting. Carter was looking away from me but doing that thing where he slowly dragged two fingers down along the side of his face, just in front of his ear. He told me before he would do that as a sign to let me know he was imagining me naked. I had laughed when he said it, playfully slapped his shoulder and told him to stop messing around, me being a properly married woman and all.

Of course he teased me and did it anyways, in the middle of a meeting, and fuck if I didn't need to uncross my legs, switching from left over right to right over left, getting hot at the sight. Carter thrives on flirtatious teasing and fun and games. And now I'm right back where the first line was crossed, in my car, fucking him in the passenger seat like my life depends on the climax I'm about to reach. The adrenaline has me a little tipsy. Just enough that I stepped right into his challenge of public car sex.

Except now the scene switches, and I hear a baby crying. I look down at Carter's face, but suddenly I'm no longer riding him. Instead I'm on the hard concrete floor of a basement and a baby is crying somewhere in the distance. I'm trying to peel myself off the floor, but my limbs feel about a million pounds, and I just can't work up the energy to get up. But I can feel the pull and need to, the need to get up and go get that baby. She's crying with such intensity, there's a plead in the cry and I'm completely helpless and incapable to get to her, to help her.

And then Justin, my husband— appearing in front of me. He's towering above me, an angelic glow around him and I'm cowering on the floor in shame. He reaches out a hand to help me up, his auburn hair falling in front of his face with the gesture, but when I reach for his hand, it turns to sand. The transformation from flesh and bone to the fine dusting of sand travels up his arm, across his shoulders and chest and eventually his whole body drops to the floor in one pile of beige dust cluttered with broken seashells. I go to reach for it, and am suddenly flung up from the floor and up to the ceiling in a weightless flight. I drop back down, then fly up again, jolted.

"Up, up, up! Time to get up!"

I pry my eyes open to see my incredibly evil sister jumping up and down on her bed beside me, my body and skull jostling up and down with her.

"Stop, for the love of God, please stop, Lila."

"Not until you tell me what you're doing here, baby cakes."

I raise a desperate arm out to whatever limb of hers is closest and yank her down. She crashes into me with a whine, but at least the dizzying bouncing has stopped.

"You are the worst," I grumble out, trying to sit up and get my bearings.

"You," she flips over and looks at me, adjusting herself up so that we're both sitting against the pillows and headboard, "have some explaining to do. Do mom and dad know you're here? Let me guess, they sent you to keep tabs on me."

I shake my head no. Explain to her that I only told Justin and also Grayson, so that Grayson could arrange for someone to pick me up from the airport and take me here. I'm worried she'll grill me with more questions, questions I don't really have answers to, but thankfully she seems satisfied with my explanation and minimal details.

"Penny said you had no return flight?" She's staring at her phone with intensity, not even really seeming interested in this fact. Her blonde bob is styled perfectly, smokey eyed makeup done and a tiny tube dress barely covering her body like she's ready to go out.

"I had some vacation time so figured I'd just see what your schedule's like and then go from there." I take a peek out the window and see that it's dark. "What time is it?"

"Happy hour time, that's what. The perfect time to get some drinks, though we'll have to sneak past Penny or she might try to tag along."

I groan realizing hiding my recently discovered pregnancy is going to be pretty hard with my sister the party animal. Wish I had thought this through a little better. Looks like I'm full of surprisingly bad decisions these days and I'm once again wondering if this is what it feels like when your life is about to fall apart. I wouldn't know, I'm usually prepped and planned down to a T. With how shitty my world feels right now, I can see why I'm rarely one to screw up. It's a shitty feeling when you have. Icky.

I climb out of Lila's bed and a wave of nausea hits. I clutch my stomach and look around for the water I remember bringing in here. "I feel like shit. Do you have pretzels or something?"

Lila briefly looks up from her phone quizzically. "Pretzels? Um, no I don't think so." She looks right back down at her phone, but swings her legs over the side of her bed to stand up, mindlessly wandering across the room and out the door towards her kitchen, her eyes still glued to her screen.

I go use the bathroom, wash my hands and stare in the mirror. My lips are chapped, but other than that I don't *look* pregnant. I rummage around and find Lila's brush, I know it's hers based on the silverly blonde locks in it, and run it through my hair. A swipe of some lipstick and I think I look halfway decent, even if inside I feel like I'm stuck on a sailboat in a hurricane.

Once outside the bathroom I take a quick look around Lila and Penny's place. It's small but tidy with pale gray walls and a modern L-shaped kitchen counter and white cabinets. There's a low sitting navy blue couch in the living room and two matching chairs on either side, all facing the TV. A high top rectangular table and two chairs separate the kitchen and living room spaces. A quick glance to my left and I see what I assume to be Penny's bedroom. The whole place can't be more than 600 square feet, but it's clean and comforting, somehow. I'm jealous of the beautiful simplicity of it in comparison to the monstrosity of a house Justin and I bought two years ago simply because we could.

I walk into the kitchen to where Lila is half staring at her phone, half rummaging through a cabinet.

"You want a digestive?" she asks me, handing me a cylinder snack package. "It's kind of like a cookie."

I gratefully grab the package and pull out a chocolate frosted circle, greedily biting in. It's surprisingly delicious and comforting, and I can already tell that with this nausea, having snacks on hand is going to be a necessity. I lean against the counter and let myself relax a little.

"So, what's on that phone that's got you so glued when your favorite sister has flown all the way across an ocean to be here, and you've barely even looked at me?" I finish the rest of my snack and walk next to her to return the package to the cabinet.

"Nothing," she says dismissively. "Just work research." She clicks one last thing and puts her phone face down on the counter. I feel like I'm still in a daze watching her, the jet lag and my current state catching up to me. She's pouring some pink juice into a cup and hands it to me, then takes her own juice and clinks my glass. "Cheers. To running away."

I startle at her toast, amazed she just called me out like that. But then she adds, "Only to have my sister sent over to come watch over me."

I laugh a little at how closely she almost landed on the truth, but true to Lila form, went straight back to herself and how the world revolves around her. "Your family loves you, what can we say? We just want to make sure you're doing alright, that's all. It's what big sisters are for, right?" I take a sip of my juice and realize too late that there's alcohol in it. I gulp with a twinge of guilt and stare at her wide-eyed. "What is this?"

"Isn't it delicious?" beams Lila's roommate Penny with a bounce into the kitchen to join us, sipping her own drink. We're all practically touching shoulders now with the addition of her. "Did you get a good nap in?"

I nod my head, pretending to sip while wondering how stealthy I can be in slowly pouring this thing out when no one's looking. "Much needed, yes."

"Good! Maybe we can all do drinks, then? Lila here is always very posh and busy-like, our schedules never seem to align, but I happen to be free and by the looks of it, you two are headed out. Mind if I join?"

"It's really more of a sisters catching up kind of night—" Lila starts, right as I say, "Of course, we'd love if you joined." Lila glares at me and I feign innocence. I know from our calls that Lila has been rebuffing Penny's attempts at basic friendship, and I suppose while I'm here I might as well step in and actually play good big sister to help make sure Lila surrounds herself with decent people. But also, Penny can help take the attention off me pretending to drink while not actually drinking all night.

I clear my throat loudly. "Penny, you surely know your way around better than us, so absolutely join us. Am I dressed okay?" I ask, looking down at my simple navy pants and white tank top undershirt. I had on a long sleeved top earlier, but abandoned it before collapsing on Lila's bed.

"Of course you are! As long as you're comfortable, there's no dress code at the pub."

"Wonderful!" I say with a smile and a look at Lila. She flashes me a look of anger but eventually plasters a fake smile on her face.

We get ourselves ready, prepping to have a night on the town, all while I figure out whether or not I can get the bartender alone for a minute to be in cahoots on a "vodka soda" that's actually a club soda, and how much longer until I can collapse on Lila's bed, because all I want to do is sleep away my current nightmare.

"SO HOW'S JUSTIN," LILA ASKS me with a suspicious smirk, "and all the hot, wild, so in love sex you're having?"

"Lila! Jesus, don't be inappropriate," I scold. I look at Penny and she looks momentarily startled, but then just shrugs and sips her drink.

A man by the bar with a sweaty collar and thick hands wrapped around a beer gives us a grin, and Lila rolls her eyes and says, "Do you mind?"

"I don't at all, actually, no. So she's married," he says, nodding toward me with a glance at my ring. "How about you, pretty one?"

"Dream. On," Lila says, and Penny is all wild eyed with amusement at the whole thing.

"Oh I will, don't you worry," he says with a grin that I have to admit, makes even me shudder and want to say something smart.

"Ugh. Penny, really? Is this pub the best place you could come up with?" Lila's face is tortured like she's sucking on an ice cube in a snow storm as she roams her eyes around to scan.

Poor Penny squeezes her eyebrows together in hurt. "Half the fun of this place *is* the local creeps like him. At least you get free drinks when you're nice to them. Guess that's out the window then."

I laugh, because Penny has something so sweet and unfiltered about her. I really think she'd be good for Lila as a friend, if Lila just got her head out of her own ass.

Lila's determined to zero in on my sex life though, because she repeats her question. "So, the wild sex? Old Justin making my sister swing from the chandeliers?" Her eyes have such a mischievous little spark in them that I kind of want to throw my drink on to splash the spark away with a fizzled out simmer.

"What is your deal with asking about me and your *brother-in-law*, freak?"

She snorts. "Oh but babydoll, *you* were the one moaning enthusiastically as fuck while taking your little nap earlier."

I fiddle with a strand of my necklace, thrown off at having been called out like that. That's right. My little sex dream. The one that was definitely not with my husband. So that's why she's prying like this. I shake my hair back in a way I hope looks calm and collected. "Maybe if you settled down you'd know what that kind of intimacy could feel like." God, I'm such a fucking hypocrite liar.

"Actually, you'd never believe it. I in fact did get the strangest invite earlier today." Lila looks a bit maniacal as she says this, even looking down to Penny like she wants her to be part of the inner circle about to hear whatever she's going to say.

"Yeah? What kind of invite?" Penny asks.

"That crazy photographer guy? The mean one?"

I nod. "I remember."

"Well I ran into him today at the gym. He invited me to a picnic to apologize, and so I went."

"Oh how sweet!" Penny gushes.

"And then he asks me to be in a relationship!" Lila juts out a slender shoulder and shakes her head in disgust. "So fucking weird."

"Wait, hold on a sec. This guy randomly just says, 'Sorry I was rude, let's have a picnic and be my girlfriend?'" I ask with disbelief.

"More or less, but yeah. I was pretty freaked out. I mean I don't even know the guy. Although you might, Penny. He's a cousin of Grayson's? Name is Simon Sharp?"

Penny shakes her head. "I know of him, but I moved away before he came around." Her back gets bumped by a drunken patron passing by and she spills her drink on herself. "Oh fudge, that's not what I wanted," she says with a wrinkle of her nose.

"Hey, you!" Lila yells out, stretching her arm behind Penny and poking the guy. "Hey!"

The guy stops, looking annoyed, before landing his eyes on Lila and grinning like his night has just been made. "Yes, gorgeous. Is this my lucky night?"

I lean down to Penny and whisper, "He's about to really regret that." I can't help but smile though. Lila's intensity can be entertaining.

"Depends on your definition of lucky, I'd say." She nods down to Penny. "You need to apologize to my friend. You bumped her with your barbaric self and caused her to spill her drink."

He places a hand on his heart and begins to apologize, then

does a double take when he gets a closer look at Penny. "Wait just a minute here. Penny...is that you?"

Penny looks up at the man and smiles sheepishly. "Hi, Tony." She sends Lila and I a nervous glance, and we look at each other in confusion.

The man has stars in his eyes, and no longer for Lila, but for Penny instead. "You look...beautiful," he gushes.

"Right. Thank you," she says. She turns to us and explains, "Tony used to work with me back when we were in university."

"I always had the biggest thing for you," he says with such earnestness in his face it's actually a little heartwarming.

Penny tucks some hair behind her ear. "Yeah, I kinda figured."

Lila reaches out for Penny's left hand and lifts it. "Missed your chance, Tony boy. Our Penny here is taken."

I roll my eyes, knowing my dear sister is delighting in delivering this bad news to poor Tony. She's wicked like that. Penny looks a tiny bit mortified, but then concedes with a chuckle and a twist of her engagement ring.

"Move along, Tony. Bye-bye," Lila says, waving the poor guy off.

Penny gives a small wave and the guy backs away with a sad last pitch to Penny, asking her to find him on Facebook if things don't work out with her and the fiancé. She nods with about as much enthusiasm as a palace guard before turning back to us.

"Oh my gosh that was utterly fantastic, Lila. He used to be so creepy to me, finding weird little excuses to touch my hair or remove imaginary lint from my shirt, but I never knew how to wave him off."

Lila reaches an arm around Penny's shoulder. "Stick with me, I've got you covered."

I smile, enjoying the interaction between the two of them. This is good for Lila, Penny seems like she has a good head on her shoulders.

My phone buzzes and I place my sparkling water down to grab

the phone from my bag. My heart sinks as I see it's Justin calling. I wave the phone up to Lila to show her. "Let me step out to talk to him," I say, and I make my way through the crowd and out onto the street.

With a gust of fresh outdoor air and a deep breath, I answer. "Hi, babe."

"Lucy, hi." Quiet silence. "You called me babe," he notes.

"Oh, habit," I laugh nervously. We're both silent for a moment and I shift my weight from one foot to the other. I glance around the bustling street, the glow of the shops and the clusters of people wandering around enjoying their evening. Just a normal night on the town.

"I know you just left, but I miss you already," he finally says.

"I miss you too," I say honestly. I actually do, I realize. Not just in the physical sense, but in so many other ways too.

"Lucy, I hope you didn't leave because of me. Because I'm sorry, please know that."

"I know you are," I attempt to reassure him. I hate hearing his apologies.

"And I want you to know I've had Sam step in to do the consulting with her, so I don't have to anymore. I barely even see her."

I sigh. "That wasn't necessary, Justin."

"You still seemed so mad at me, though. And I get it, I really do," he rushes to add.

"I'm not mad anymore, I'm just here for a little breather to check up on Lila, that's all." Even I can hear how flat my tone is.

"Okay." A pause. Laughter from inside the pub. A passing of a car. "I love you," he eventually adds. "Talk tomorrow?"

"Yes, sure. I love you too," I say and we hang up, me feeling like that was the most empty and sad little phone call between a husband and wife of just a few years.

I think back to that night a couple months ago—a harmless dinner out, just the two of us, me and Justin. A quiet date night at a nice restaurant, him in a nice suit and me in a nice dress. All so nice and pleasant.

He had excused himself to use the restroom and had left his phone out on the table. A text came through. I glanced, a little curious. He had been staring at his phone an awful lot lately, saying it was work stuff. But you know when something's off, don't you? As a wife, you just know that when your husband is telling you it's a work text, but he has this tell-tale smile on his face that is *warm* and kind and downright adorable, you just know something's not quite right. No one smiles with such affection at a work text. You notice when he starts putting a little more effort into which shirt matches which belt and which shoes. You know when he seems far more giddy than usual about the day up ahead of him, rushing out the door with a bit more energy like a kid gearing up for a field trip. Before you know it, he's coming home all big smiles and light-hearted laughs like suddenly adulting isn't as stressful anymore. That is, until you ask him about that domestic task he was supposed to complete and now you're enemy number one, his mood shifting like you asked for him to put a drill into his skull.

Listen, my husband worships me, I know he does. And I really don't think he has it in him to truly cheat. I still don't—even with my own sins now firmly under my belt. But fuck if he wasn't emotionally cheating with someone. I just knew it, *knew* it in my bones.

So yeah, I looked at his incoming text while at that dinner. Because it wasn't just one ping of a text. Maybe just one I would have ignored. But it was another, then another, and by the fourth I twisted that phone on that nice tablecloth right around to face me, and imagine the sinking of my heart when I saw the name, "Dr. Gabby," and her sweet little texts thanking him for some thing or another and then a picture of what looked to be her fireplace mantle. It was too hard to see in the little preview, and I didn't want to oust myself by opening the phone, but I knew right then and there that my man was having an emotional affair with a woman he met through work.

That's when my heart dropped into my stomach, and my pulse started beating in my ears.

Here's what's really funny—really fucking funny and ironic. We were out to dinner at *his* insistence. That's right. He was begging me for that nice dinner out, just the two of us, saying we hadn't been connecting lately, saying his dear wife had been so busy with work lately and that we needed to do something fun.

I knew he had been unhappy. I'd hit my work stride, getting the director position at my job, one that I had been working my ass off for, schmoozing all the right people, making sure our non-profit name and its work was known by anyone deemed worthy, and forming connections to enlist the right politicians no one else had bothered with. I was good at the job, and it was paying off.

That is, it *was* paying off up until Justin cracked one too many jokes about me being married to my work, never home, how I give all the love to everyone else so that there's none left for him. Fine. Whatever. He knew I was a go-getter when I married him, I thought it's what he loved about me.

"It was what I loved about you," he had said when I presented that point in the middle of an argument. Yet another fight. "I just didn't know you'd eventually run out of go-getter love for me."

So no, things hadn't been exactly perfect between us. And I wanted that to change, I really did. I could feel him pulling away. There had been a shift, a subtle little shift that might be imperceptible to the outside eye, but one can feel it like the change in the wind on an otherwise sunny day. That moment of a strange shadow from a cloud creeping past the sun. Whereas at one point in time I'd come home from work and feel annoyed when Justin would immediately be all over me for a hug and kiss, there came a day when he stayed put on the couch. Phone in hand. Barely acknowledging my presence.

Smiling warmly at his screen.

eleven

. . .

simon

I T HAD TAKEN Simon two whole days to realize Lila Ray had blocked him. He had been busy with edits, client meetings, the dreaded mood board compilations and hadn't given much thought to Lila.

Until the day that he did, when he looked to message her and realized she was nowhere to be found.

And for some reason, this stirred an anger in Simon that he was unable to let go of. It took him two more days to realize just how angry he was, finding himself slamming around cabinet doors in his kitchen while in the midst of ordinary food prep, or grumbling rudely to his aunt whenever Victoria was there cooking or cleaning and trying to make small talk.

"Something wrong, love?" she had asked with concern after hearing a loud "Fuck!" come out of his office followed by the startling sound of yet another forceful crash of innocent objects.

"I'm fine," was all he said, and he feared he was putting his poor aunt into a fit of worry that the old temper Simon was rather famous for was resurrecting itself. He had cracked his neck and attempted to collect himself, not wanting to deal with a potential subdued lecture wrapped in maniacal baking from his aunt. Her scones were delicious, yes, but not always worth the price. She often accompanied notes with them. A "You are kind at heart, never forget that, x -V" or worse, whatever little cryptic poem she had stumbled across with a "Read this and thought of you. I remember when you too were that little scared frog, lost in a pond."

He's back at the gym today, the second time today in fact, and he's telling himself it's because he didn't have quite enough time earlier to complete his workout before a client meeting. Certainly he's not back again in hopes of seeing Lila.

Roger, unfortunately, is onto him. "You missed her. She was here about an hour ago."

Simon debates feigning innocence, but looks at Roger's raised eyebrow and decides against it.

"Fuck," is all he says before moving to some weights. Roger follows after him, rearranging some misplaced dumbbells and busying himself with tidying.

"She was here with her sister. Nice girl, Lucy was the name. Maybe she's been busy entertaining her while her sister's in town?" he offers.

Simon's interest is piqued. Lila has a sister, that's right. He briefly remembers her mentioning that while also discussing their mom, the fashion designer. He takes a seat on a bench to prep for bicep curls, and decides to confide in Roger. "She's blocked me. I have no way to reach her."

Roger laughs and looks at him with surprise. "Really? Well what the hell did you do? Seemed like you two had some..."

"What?" Simon spits out with impatience.

Roger only shakes his head and returns to his dumbbell arrangements. "Don't know. A charge of sorts. So what'd you do that made her write you off?"

"I asked to get to know her better."

"Whoa, shots fired." Another laugh, and Simon sits with bitterness, regretting opening up to Roger. "You know a woman like that, all darts and daggers, she needs a little more finesse."

"I don't have time for finesse. Or games. High maintenance doesn't suit me."

"And yet, you asked to get to know her better."

"I didn't know she was high maintenance when I made that poor decision," Simon spits out, death stare held firm.

"Bullshit. Sure you did. And you liked it, she pulled you in." Simon ignores Roger. He doesn't want to blow his temper on him, but Simon's getting increasingly irritated.

Roger doesn't quit. "Let me ask you this—what don't you like exactly? That she hooked her talons into you, but you couldn't hold on? The temptress was overly tempting? You got wrapped up, lots to like there, but are now sore that she backed off?"

Simon rises up abruptly with a finger into Roger's chest. "Don't you fucking tell me what I like or don't like."

"Simon!" shrieks the motherly voice of what Simon is suddenly certain is his Aunt Victoria. "My God, what's gotten into you?"

Simon keeps his finger to Roger's chest but turns to look at the unexpected and horrified face of his aunt, wondering what the hell she's doing here. He turns back around to face Roger, whose hands are held out to his side in defeat, though based on sheer size and muscles, Roger could break Simon in half, even with Roger's slightly shorter stature.

Roger, ever the mild mannered gentle giant, laughs and backs away. "Seems I hit a soft spot?"

Victoria rushes over to Simon and hands him a device in an abrupt toss, which he barely catches. "Here. You forgot your phone, you...you...reckless idiot. What is *with* you lately? You're smashing around your flat leaving me to pick up the pieces, you've barely spoken a word, which I can hardly believe you could be any quieter in the first place. It's all grumbles and grunts and no "thank you for my lovely dinner you left for me, sweet Victoria," but instead the only evidence I get that you even ate was the dirty dish in the sink, which is also most unlike you. What is going on?" His usually soft and sweet aunt is looking at him like she's through with patience, as if she's been biting her tongue for longer than she'd care to admit. Simon drops his head slightly. Not in shame, no. Just in wanting to end her lecture.

"Oh it's just a girl," says a smiling Roger. He steps forward to offer Victoria a hand. "You ladies do know how to get under our skin. Hi, you must be Simon's gorgeous sister."

Simon watches with horror as Victoria blushes. "No, not sister, though we are only twenty years apart." *Is she batting her eyelashes?*

"Mother then?"

"No. Not by birth, anyhow, though I did raise the little hellion since he was nine years old. I'm his aunt. Victoria, pleasure to meet you."

Roger's eyes are smiling down at Victoria, holding a steady gaze, though he says, "Simon, why didn't you tell me about this lovely lady in your life?" He raises her hand to his lips, then pauses momentarily. "May I?" and Simon nearly gags as she gives a subtle head nod yes, and Roger kisses the back of her hand. "Please tell me you're single and free for dinner tonight."

"As a matter of fact, I'm not. But that can certainly be changed and I will be."

"Christ, what the fuck is going on?" a weary Simon asks. "Awfully forward, aren't we, Jolly Roger?"

Roger gently drops the starstruck Victoria's hand and faces Simon. "At my age, you waste no time. So when a beautiful woman comes in to yell at you," he says, nodding to Simon, "bringing you a look of shame, what can I say. I'm instantly in need of...getting to know her better." The look on Roger's face tells Simon all he needs to know that that last line was no coincidence.

In a flash, Simon grabs his things and walks past Roger with one hard shove to his chest. Roger obliges and takes a courtesy stumble backwards, as if Simon truly had any impact on the man, and Victoria once again cries out her nephew's name in a scolding.

But Simon doesn't stick around to listen, instead choosing to walk right out the door.

Which is too bad, really, since a mere ten minutes later, Lucy and Lila return to the gym, Lucy having forgotten something as well, and the sisters returning to retrieve it.

Thankfully, Roger makes it a point to introduce the two to Victoria, who was still there chatting with Roger when they waltzed in. A tiny maneuver, but better than nothing.

WHEN VICTORIA WALKS BACK IN the door to Simon's flat half an hour later, he tries to soften for his aunt's sake.

Victoria had been nothing but saint-like to Simon for all his life. The best friend of Simon's mum, it was Victoria that stepped in to raise Simon when his mum died, and his dad had already been long out of the picture by then. It was Victoria that saw Simon's creative talents and bought him his first camera, broke as she was with barely a pence to spare. Victoria understood Simon's temper not as the curse of a "problem child" as school teachers would say, but as a symptom of being lonely and misunderstood, abandoned by his father and with mistrust as his shield of armor. Victoria would fight battles for him with words to defend the battles he had fought with fists. She ensured he was accepted within her family, made to feel as if he were one of them. As the less successful sister in her own family (her sister Daisy, Grayson's mum, owned a successful music shop, in contrast to Victoria's housekeeping busi-ness), Simon had a feeling that raising him gave Victoria a new sense of purpose and value. A seat at the table no longer as the single and without child spinster, but as the surrogate single mum.

Still, he saw her struggle over the years. The extra jobs she took on, the dates she refused, and the drab clothing she wore so he could go to school dressed with the best high street could offer.

Simon's in the kitchen when Victoria walks in, and he looks up from his plate of eggs in quiet welcome.

She raises a hand up. "I'm not here to berate you, though you likely deserve it."

He leans back in his chair and stretches out his legs, dropping his fork to listen.

"You've had a quiet couple of years, focused on your work. Single as far as I know, I believe?" She drops off, not quite finishing her thought, but Simon nods in acknowledgement to save her from the discomfort. "Roger says you met a girl."

He scoffs, rising from his seat and taking his plate to the sink. "Did he mention that she blocked me?"

He sees a smile slither across Victoria's face. "Oh yes. Funny thing, though. I happened to meet her. And wouldn't you know, it's your blonde that I've seen you spend hours over 'editing' her photos. She's quite captivating, isn't she?"

"What? What do you mean you've met her?"

Victoria looks all together proud as she says, "Just moments ago, she and her sister walked into the gym to collect something they had forgotten. Roger made introductions." She hands him a paper. "And I collected her number."

"How?"

"I explained that you were simply distraught at having upset her, you wanted to apologize but had no way to reach her, could I please have her number so you could make things right?"

"Apologies for what?" Simon asks with alarm.

Victoria waves him off. "Oh I don't know, I took a shot figuring that you owed her an apology for something. It seemed to do the trick. I tested the number in front of her, explaining that I wanted to make sure she'd given me the real thing, and while she looked rather horrified, her sister seemed to get a kick out of the interaction. It checks. There you have it. You are welcome."

"This is ridiculous. I'm not calling someone who does not want anything to do with me."

Victoria cocks her head to the side. "Then why are you becoming such a frequent gym goer, huh?"

Simon rubs his eyes in frustration. This was the problem with a small gym. Here he thought the peace would offer escape. Instead he's accidentally landed in a small town in the heart of London.

"Just ring her. Perhaps she's the type that appreciates the chase."

"I have no patience for chasing."

"'Course you do, love." Victoria turns to walk back out the door, with one final statement. "You already started."

IT WAS POSSIBLE THIS WAS considered stalking, he was aware. Simon had knocked on several doors in the building where he knew Lila lived, asking as harmlessly as he could if Lila was home. When people would say no, he made an attempt to look innocent, saying, "Oh no? Apologies. Must have written the wrong number down. Might you know which one the tall American girl lives in?"

Eventually someone caved and directed him one flight up.

And so here he is now, in front of the door, knocking in hopes to see her. Yes, he had skipped the far more reasonable option of taking advantage of her telephone number. No, he did not care that his showing up here like this might not be received well. Lila Ray was going to come around to him, because he was a man who knew what he wanted. And he knew Lila felt the same about him. If she'd get out of her own way, and he was going to see to it that she did.

The door opens, and Simon briefly sees Lila's face before she instantly decides to slam the door. Simon juts out a hand to stop the door from closing, forcing himself through and into the flat.

"Hey! You can't just barge in here. I could scream for help, you know." Her lovely face is twisted in a scowl. "Strange man entering my apartment!" she says just a hair too loud for normal conversation, and he slams the door behind him to prevent any fallout from her proclamation.

Once inside, he scans the small flat. Two brunettes are sitting in the living area, eyebrows raised looking as if they are unsure if they truly are about to be in trouble.

He nods. "Hello, ladies. Lila and I just need a moment to talk."

"No, we do not," Lila says to him. "I thought I made that clear when I blocked you, remember?"

The brunette with the olive complexion rises with a smile. Simon does a quick scan and decides it must be Lucy, Lila's sister.

"Oh, so you're the mean photographer, yes of course." Lucy walks over to him and extends a hand. "We just met your aunt, what a coincidence," she says like she understands his arrival here now is no coincidence at all. "Si, right? I've heard so many wonderful things about you. In fact, Lila's phone is flooded with tabs open of your website and your work. Beautiful, by the way."

"You little sneaky—" Lila glares at her sister.

Simon gives the slightest of smiles and takes Lucy's hand. "Lucy, then, right? Lila's sister?"

Lucy looks with sarcastic shock to her sister. "You've mentioned me, well I'm flattered!"

The brunette on the couch clears her throat, laying her forearms across the back of the couch and resting her chin on her wrists, as if enjoying the scene before her. "Hi. Yes, hello. I'm Penny."

Lila rolls her eyes. "Please, Penny. Don't fall for this guy's innocent look." She turns back to face Simon. "See you got the Dr. Jekyll look today. Glasses and long sleeves, though we can see those tattoos poking out on your neck." She extends a finger along what he knows to be the maze tattoo beneath his ear. "No hiding that without a turtleneck or scarf, now. Ought to be more careful than that." She drops her hand and steps closer to him, inches from his face, whispering, "People might find out who you really are."

For a brief moment Simon worries Grayson got a hold of her. But he decides to ignore that possibility, choosing instead to snatch her arm and lead them back out of the flat, into the landing area of the stairwell.

"Hey!" Lila cries out, but Simon ignores her.

He closes the door, just as a quiet "he's yummy" escapes from the mouth of one of the girls inside.

Once in the hallway, he takes a moment to look Lila up and down. She's in black leggings, with a black long-sleeved top, tight fitting and exposing about an inch of the skin of her stomach. The ensemble leaves little to the imagination. "Do you always dress like that?"

"Oh, fuck you. I'm about to go for an audition, and yes, they like to see our bodies," she says with that signature sarcasm of hers and a brief annoyed widening of her eyes.

"An audition?"

"Yeah. Apparently at my old age, my agency thinks acting is a safe backup."

"For what? What's the part?"

"What do you care?" she asks, hand on a hip and overall look of impatience.

"Are you sure it's nothing...nefarious?"

"You know if I want to do fucking porn to make a living, that's my right, Simon."

He raises his eyebrows in silence, refusing to indulge in her bait.

"Fine" she concedes. "No, it's nothing *nefarious*. Freak. It's just a small part in a mini series of some sort."

"Good."

She sighs impatiently. "Well? Is that it? You've successfully tracked me down just to discuss my career? You know I'll be giving Roger a piece of my mind for disclosing my address to you."

Simon shakes his head. "It wasn't him, he wouldn't do that. I knocked on a few doors until someone told me which flat was yours. Too easy, really. I just asked for the bitchy American."

She huffs out a breath of disbelief, but he sees the drop of her eyes to his mouth. It's fast, but he sees it. Her sage eyes meet his again, and he can see the desire.

It's quiet in the hallway, the only sound he registers is the faint chatter of voices from inside Lila's flat.

"Why are you here, Simon?" Lila asks. "I thought I made it clear I wasn't interested in dinner or being someone's girlfriend. Not yours anyway." Her eyes roam up and down his body, and his mouth twitches in a smile.

"You're full of shit."

"Huh? How so?"

He places a hand on the wall beside her head, partially casing her in. "You like me. And I think you like *you* with me."

"Oh really?" she asks. "Just like that, you know that you like me? You mean all, I don't know, five hours we've spent together between a photo shoot, a picnic, and a seriously bizarre and awkward afternoon in your apartment?" There's genuine disbelief in her voice, and he has a feeling it's not disbelief directed at time frames, but at the ability of him genuinely liking her.

"Generally, we know within a few minutes whether or not we like someone. Doesn't take long. First impressions happen quickly, and they plant a seed."

A bit of her fringe is stuck in her lashes, and he gently moves it aside. "And besides," he says, "it was more like five hours and five minutes. Don't forget the party where we first met."

"Where you turned me down."

"You weren't yourself. I turned down the false Lila. The one you pretend to be." He drops the hand that's on the wall. "The Mr. Hyde, if you will." He takes a step back to lean against the banister of the staircase.

He watches her eyes to see how she takes this. It's the truth, and she knows it, but is she ready to hear that from him? Capable?

She bites her lip and looks at him in question. "Everyone pretends, Si. It's called the game of life."

Si. She called him Si. It gives him hope. "Yes, I agree," he says. "But the glimpses of you I've seen, the *real* you, I like." He sees something move across her face, something he can't quite read. Pain, almost. She doesn't like hearing positive statements, he gathers. Not without the comforting shield of her mask.

He leaves his perch on the banister to step closer to her, taking in the scent of her perfume. Instantly he remembers it from the night she first approached him. Something expensive. Floral and earthy and intoxicating. He notices not for the first time the way her top lip dips in in the middle, creating two arches on either side. She's so beautiful, so painfully and exotically beautiful with features that are anything but conventional. It amazes him how much she draws him in.

He closes the gap between them and pushes her body against the wall, bringing his nose down just below her ear to inhale. "I hate this perfume," he says before dotting a gentle kiss on her neck. He lowers down to the ridge of her collar bone and kisses there as well. Then one more kiss on her throat. "But I like it on you."

Lila lets out a small whimper, but remains surprisingly mute, no comeback for him. His fingertips slowly graze along the exposed skin of her stomach before wrapping around her side and reaching for her wrist. He clasps his hands around both her wrists and raises them up above her head, locking them against the wall with one hand. He looks down to see her face, to look for resistance on her part, but there's none.

Instead, her eyes closed, she lets out a little hum followed by "Just fuck me, Simon," in a whisper. "Come on, take me back to your place and fuck me." She's raising her chin toward the ceiling, offering her neck to him and he runs his tongue along her throat. He presses his erection against her, and she arches her hips responsively. "Please just fuck me."

"No," he says, and then presses his mouth to hers before she can say anything else. He's consumed with heat and desire for her, something he's very much wanting to indulge in, but not like this, not so fast. What he has planned for her will be so much better, and he tells her so between kisses. She just needs to wait and see. To learn.

The jumbling sound of a door unlocking interrupts them. Simon bolts free of Lila just as the door to the flat across the hall opens. A man looking to be about in his sixties exits with a brief nod to the two of them before excusing himself to pass, making his way down the stairs. Lila and Simon exchange looks, and as soon as they hear the building door open for the man's exit, they are back on one another, kissing and pulling hair and pressing against one another with force.

Simon yanks Lila's wrists behind her, once again clasping them in his grasp. He steps behind her and pushes her to the stairs leading up to the next level. With a gentle push he presses his knee into the back of each of hers, forcing her to drop down in a kneel on the stairs. He takes his free hand and grabs hold of her hair, pulling her head back as he presses slow kisses to her neck and shoulder. She moans in response, wriggling her ass against his erection.

With a release of her hair, grasp still held firm on her wrists, he wraps his hand around to the front of her waistband and inches his hand along her smooth skin, under her panties.

"Simon, someone might see, what are you doing?"

"So?" he asks, finding the space he wants. With two fingers he spreads her apart. "Based on how soaked you are, you don't seem to mind."

"You're fucking crazy," she says with a satisfied gasp as he slips his fingers inside her.

"Tell me to stop then."

He smiles at her silence and continues his work. He decides he'll give her this. He'll give her the climax she wants, a small taste, a little teaser so she understands a bit of what's to come. To help her push past her own resistance. He's patient with his strokes, rhythmic and allows her to build to near orgasm, before slowing down again.

"Please don't stop," she breathes out. He pauses his movements completely and bites her shoulder, loving the feel of her jolt against him. "Please, Si, please." A beautiful sound to his ears. "Fuck. Please finish me," she says, the lovely side of her face revealing lashes fluttering in strained ecstasy.

He kisses her shoulder gently and glides his tongue along her neck for one last taste of her before speeding up his movements once again. This time he doesn't stop, and the gape of her mouth and moan of her voice as she comes leaves him with devilish hope for this woman.

So easy. She came so easily for him. No shame in her pleasure, no resistance. Just raw reaction to his touch. It was a beautiful thing, watching Lila Ray fall apart in his grasp.

He frees his hand from her pants and places his fingers in her mouth. She turns her head back towards him and pops open her eyes and looks at him in surprise. "Suck," he says as he releases her wrists and crouches down beside her. She's frozen for a moment, but then closes her mouth around his fingers, and he suppresses his own groan, not wanting to distract in any way from Lila tasting herself. He's eager to taste her himself, but knows that will come soon enough.

Lila closes her eyes, and he feels the smooth and warm wetness of her tongue as she circles his fingers, sucking as if enjoying a popsicle. Her cheeks are hallowed in, and he allows his mind for just a brief flash to imagine her face as he fucks her mouth with his cock.

He can hardly wait.

They barely even register the sound of Lila's door open, with Lucy standing in the doorway. Lila's back is to her sister, but Simon makes eye contact with Lucy and watches as Lucy's jaw drops open. "Oh. What the? What are you doing?" Simon removes his fingers from Lila's mouth, thankful it's out of Lucy's view, and brings his other hand up to cup her cheek.

"We're working some things out." Simon drops his gaze down to Lila, a silent command for her to confirm, and Lila turns to face her sister with a head nod and guilty grin.

"You sure you're okay?" Lucy asks with suspicion, eyes narrowed and zeroing in on her sister.

"One thousand percent, yes," Lila says with amusing enthusiasm. "Go back inside, I'll be right in."

"Okay," Lucy says as she slowly backs into the flat and closes the door. They hear a muffled "I swear they were out there fucking," and Lila looks back at Simon and smiles, biting her lip.

"You're crazy," she says.

"You hardly seem to mind."

Simon rises to a stand, taking the fingers that were just in Lila's mouth and briefly tasting them for himself. "Break a leg," he says before strolling down the stairs, leaving Lila.

"I think I will take that dinner," he hears her shout down the stairwell, and he can't help but smile as he walks out of the building, thinking how royally fucked he is under her spell, and how he's going to enjoy making her pay for it.

twelve

. . .

lila

I CAN'T SAY I'm entirely disappointed I didn't get the part in the mini series, but I must admit I'm struggling to find much hopeful confidence after the rejection. I'm in a bit of a rut with far too few jobs and horribly low cash flow.

"They liked you, they really did. It was the height that was the issue," my agent Mila had said. "You would tower over the rest of the cast, and it wasn't really the right look."

"Isn't that your job to let them know my height?" I fired back, hurt and frustrated that something I have zero control over was being thrown in my face.

Mila's kindness came to a halt. "It's my job to point you in the right direction, and their job to make the decisions. Yes, they knew your height. Yes, they considered you anyway, as they liked your reel. No, they did not choose you in the end. That's how it works sometimes."

I had muttered a thanks and hung up, feeling defeated.

"You're awfully quiet," Lucy says, licking her ice cream cone, the tiniest bit of chocolate on the corner of her mouth. She licks it away and my stomach growls. "You sure you don't want any?" Lucy asks, pointing the cone toward me. "One taste won't kill you."

I groan and cave, allowing just one small lick of the creamy chocolate deliciousness. It's smooth and velvety I can't help but moan with appreciation. "Goddamn, that's good."

"See? Worth every calorie and pound."

I seriously wonder if Lucy's breasts are what absorb her calories, since my sister is slim despite indulging in whatever she wants. "How do you do it? How do you eat like that?"

Lucy knits her brows together. "Seriously?"

I nod. "Yeah. Don't you get scared of getting fat?" We're walking along a path in Holland Park, the place Simon had taken me to. Lucy pauses and turns toward me.

"Lila. It's one ice cream cone. Not five. I workout, I focus on healthy fuel for my meals. And yes, I indulge in ice cream now and then. Pretty straightforward." She shakes her head like I'm stupid, and I bite my lip and try and push down the shame.

We resume our walking and I think back to that one and only relationship I've had. The one I shudder to think about and try my very absolute hardest to forget. I had been my heaviest weight at the time, which I know to most is still slim, but I can still remember all too clearly the small pudge of my belly. The pokes from my boyfriend—(ew, I really hate even referring to him as that)—Royce. The comments of "You sure you want to eat that?" I would feel disgusting, unattractive, disastrously uncomfortable in my own skin to the point of feeling like a foreigner in my own body. Yes, he was an asshole, I know that now. Yes, he was emotionally abusive. Therapy taught me that. But the fucker's words still creep in now and then. He knew very well how to take my insecurities of childhood and exploit them for all he could.

I decide to shake the thoughts away and focus on Lucy. "So, as fun as this has been and all, how long do you plan on staying?" It's been almost two weeks since Lucy's unexpected arrival, and I can definitely sense something's off with her.

"Stop taking me to beautiful places like this and maybe I'll go home," Lucy jokes. The leaves are starting to turn, yellow tinged with some orange, and the air has that crispness in its scent that feels cleansing, in a way.

"Seriously, what's up with you? Is it work? Did you get fired or something?"

Lucy laughs, shaking her head. "No. Work loves me. So much so that they're allowing me to be here, no questions asked, even rearranging meetings to accommodate the time difference."

I see a bench and motion over to it for us to sit. Lucy's got something on her mind, and I'm hopeful she'll share it. Never once can I remember ever being a confidante to her. It's always been the other way around, me confiding in her, or as much as I would allow myself to, anyway.

Lucy has a best friend, Reggie, and the two of them have been attached by the damn hip since they were little girls, before I was even born. I'm guessing Reggie's the one Lucy would usually talk to. I'm far from being a little kid anymore though and for some reason, I kind of want to be that source for Lucy as well. Might be nice for a change.

We take our seats. There's a small pond of water in front of us with an arrangement of boulders and stone features surrounding. Some teens that look like they're on a school trip wander around, back packs and bouncy energy giving the vibe of carefree bliss that only teens can have.

"Alright. Justin then? Something up there?" I ask with a little disbelief. Justin and Lucy have always been calm perfection for one another. I had never even seen them fight, they fit so well. Justin is chill and laid back, perfect for Lucy's high maintenance, slightly overbearing control type. Not that I would say those things to her face, but it's true.

"Yeah. We've been out of sync I guess lately," she says.

"How so?"

Lucy sighs and pulls the chunky wool of her sweater tighter across her chest. "Maybe it's my work. Or his work, I don't know. Work has always been a relatively small piece of his life, but then this new app has all the buzz of being the next big thing, and suddenly he's like...really into it." I see the frown on Lucy's face, as if she's trying to figure it all out herself.

"What's the app?" I ask.

"It's going to be called 'It's Going Around,' and it's specifically for kids. School nurses and pediatricians submit info so that parents can look and see what illnesses are going around in an area at any given time, and the symptoms. Like if strep is going around, only the predominant symptom is stomach issues instead of throat pain, that kind of thing."

"Sounds cool," I say, genuinely impressed. I think about my own job and how utterly uninspiring it can be at times. I wear cool clothes and don't get me wrong, I love showcasing an artist's work like that, but what the hell am I contributing to this world?

"It is, and he's crazy enthusiastic about the whole thing in a way I've never really seen before." Her expression is flat. Bitter, almost, not at all proud wife like I would think.

"And? Is that bad? You're like that too, you know," I point out. Lucy's basically describing her very own level of passion for work.

"I guess that was kind of the thing. It bothered me for some reason. I suppose I think of work as being my thing. You know, being obsessed with the career. It's as though I felt it couldn't be his too."

I give her a little shove with my shoulder, laughing. "Lucy, you're such a hypocrite! What, only you can be career obsessed?"

She covers her forehead with her hand, rubbing with tension. "I know, I know. I feel like a bitch saying it out loud. I don't think I've said that to anyone, or admitted that to myself, for that matter."

I can't deny that I'm super proud of myself for being the one to get that kind of self awareness out of my otherwise perfect, flaw-free big sister. "What bothers you about it exactly? Him also being so passionate about career?"

"That's a really good question, and probably important to think about if I want to figure out how we got here." I'm curious what exactly "here" is. It seems like there's more on her mind than basic career passion. I watch as she scrunches her nose. "Don't judge me, but I think it's that I like when I know I'm the main focus in his world. I like being his priority. And lately it started feeling like I wasn't. Shit, I *know* I wasn't."

"Just because he's really into a project he's working on doesn't mean you're not his priority, Lucy. The man fucking worships you, I'd love to be loved like that." I'm a little startled at my own confession, but I try and ignore that. "You're still his number one I'm sure. The man would set himself on fire for you. It's like he's never felt truly worthy of you and he's always amazed by it and trying to prove it."

We both look at each other, my words hitting pretty hard on something. Again, I can't help my little victory dance at my own insights. Me! The fuckup little sister!

"Holy shit, you're right," she says, eyes wide. "He does always roam around like he's not worthy. And I love that, I eat it up, don't I?"

I suck in air through my teeth. "Oof."

"Except that now, I'm really not sure I'm a priority."

My heart flutters a little. "Uh-oh, how so? What do you mean?"

"He's been talking to this woman that was a consultant on the project. A pediatrician, Dr. Gabby," she says the woman's name in a mocking high-pitched tone that is so catty, so out of character for my sister, I nearly laugh out loud. I stop myself, thankfully. It's definitely not the time for that. "At first he would just come home and share some new idea they had, and I could tell he had a kind of admiring crush on her. I legit thought it was cute. So cute how my little man had this little crush on nerdy Dr.

Gabby. He respected her brain, sort of like he always respected my drive. I felt *that* confident, would you believe that? Like that he loved me so much, I had nothing to worry about. And I still don't believe he'd ever allow anything physical to happen with her. I don't think."

I'm a bit confused and worried as to where she's going with this. I twist to face her and raise a leg up, tucking it in toward my body, waiting for her to continue.

"Naturally I googled her. She's cute. A year younger than me. Super sweet smile and clearly she loves kids, for Christ's sake. Justin's been so eager to have babies, especially with Reggie and Xavier now having two kids. And I've considered it, always knew we would, I just never seem to feel like the time is right. But then here's Miss Perfect—"

"Funny, that's what I call you," I interrupt. I can't help myself, but she snickers in a laugh, thankfully.

"Well, this particular Miss Perfect has apparently been enjoying texting my husband," she says, dropping a bomb in a way that I wonder for a minute if I heard her correctly.

"Wait, she what? Like, what kind of texts are we talking?"

Lucy is staring blankly ahead. "Not great ones. I went through his phone. It started as work stuff, then grew from there. Little questions like 'How do I know if I need to replace a fuse?' or 'What's that Italian place you mentioned that you like?' Or even better, 'What's the difference between a guy flirting with you, and talking to you like he might be ready to chop you up in small pieces?'" She blinks, then rolls her eyes. "Things like that. Lots of them, too many to be normal and friendly. At least, that's how I feel. I wouldn't reach out so often to a married man."

"Oh, that little bitch. Oh I've got some ideas for her, she's going to regret the day she decided to cross that line." I'm fuming now, and I drop my leg back down to the ground, agitation fueling a furious fidgeting of my foot. I hate the little bitch Dr. Gabby. I don't need to know her to know I hate her. "Let's make some phone calls, send someone to egg her car. Or blast her practice on Google, maybe."

"I love you, Lila." Lucy places a hand on my leg and gives it a pat. "You are amazing and the best person to have in your corner. But I don't even think I'm mad at her."

"What?!" I look at my sister likes she's insane. She must be. That's it, she's stunned and temporarily *fucking insane*, because there's not an ounce of me that wouldn't be mad at this conniving beast if I were in Lucy's shoes.

Lucy shrugs. "She didn't take any vows. She doesn't owe me anything. Justin's a sweet guy, he's fun and light hearted, I get it. Can't blame her too much."

I scoff. "I can! She's a fucking cow."

"No, I imagine she's a lonely woman who couldn't help but find comfort and a connection in the guy she's been working closely with. Fine, whatever. Again, she didn't take any vows."

"Well he sure as fuck did. What's his responses been?"

"Actually, he was super chill at first. One word answers, not responding if she continued. And then...not so chill. Lots more back and forth." She shakes her head, and I finally see some real emotion on her face. There's a shift in her gaze, her whole body. "It was fucking awful, Lila," Lucy finally says, emotion thick in her voice. She dabs at the corners of her eyes and I'm surprised at the random tears I feel blooming as well, just watching my sister feel so hurt. *So this thing is bigger than just some random texts,* I think with alarm.

"I scrolled through his phone for like, an hour straight one day. He was doing yard work and I couldn't help it. I just had to know. I knew I wasn't going to like what I'd see, but I had to know. And it was this out of body experience, you could see the whole thing, how it built up and grew. It got more flirtatious over time." Lucy wipes a fallen tear, blinking up at the sky, then huffs out a laugh. "He got her this freaking birthday card with a duck wearing a hat, apparently some inside joke. She put it on her mantle and sent him a pic with some comment like 'Guess the stick really is upside down' and he responded with some gif of a stick flipping through the air. Like, *what the fuck is that*? They have inside jokes?! For some reason that shit hurt so badly. So fucking badly, Lila. I didn't know I could hurt that badly." She's slamming a fist into her chest, near her heart as she speaks.

"I will chop off his dick. Oh my God, Lucy, I seriously can't believe he would do this." Justin??? I'm fuming. Justin was always so nice, easy-going. I had a soft spot for him because he treated me like he and I were in on something when Lucy would be all know-it-all and going off on some lecture. We were kind of alike in a way.

"Lila," she says, turning to face me, eyes locked to mine. "He told her in another life, he could see himself with her." Her lip starts quivering. "He admitted to that, and to wondering what that would be like," she says in a whisper. "And she said she felt like that too. And they went into this whole fucking existential bit on the universe and timing and what's meant to be, and the house they'd live in on some island, and if they exist on another planet some-where and that's the life another version of 'Justin and Gabby' are living."

Lucy covers her face with her hands, silent sobs escaping, her shoulders heaving with them. I wrap my arm around her and run my fingers through her silky hair, my chest tight for her and this pain. How in the world could this have happened? Justin talking existential "what if" shit with another woman? I hardly hear him have a serious conversation as it is, it's like my sister's talking about a completely different person.

After a moment Lucy reaches in her bag, finds a tissue and cleans herself up. I wait for her to speak again, not sure what to possibly say in response to all this. "There's absolutely nothing in the world that can prepare you for finding out your husband has a whole other side you never once knew existed." She nods, the blank stare returning on her face. Robotic. "He did put an end to it though. Before anything got physical—they alluded to feeling attraction, temptation and needing to 'keep their heads on straight.' By the end of the massive amount of texts, there was this point where she had sent a couple unanswered in a row, then asked him if everything was okay. And he said he was feeling guilty. He admitted that they had a connection that was confusing and hard to resist, which hurt like fuck to read, let me tell you." I watch as Lucy wipes more tears, and I give her shoulders another squeeze. "And then he said that he wouldn't like it if his wife was talking so much to someone, and that they should go back to keeping texts to only being about the project. And that was that."

"Asshole." I'm not sure what else to say. Is it normal to have a flirtation like that when you're married? I mean, I guess having a connection with someone is natural, but where's the line of cheating if there's no physical contact? "It's emotional cheating, isn't it?" I ask Lucy.

She nods. "Yeah. And it hurts so badly, I can't even explain. It's like everything I thought I knew is now in question. I feel naive, I can't believe I was ever dumb enough to think my marriage was somehow above ever worrying about anything like that."

"Well you're not wrong, he did put a stop to it." *I hope. Please let that be true and not more of Lucy being naive.*

"Sort of. For a bit. It slowly started to escalate again a couple weeks later. When I first found out, I wasn't going to say anything to him. Because of the clear end point."

"What? How could you keep that in?" I ask, alarmed.

She shrugs. "I think because confronting it meant admitting in the open I had lost the upper hand. At least if I kept quiet, went along with the charade then I could save face, I guess." She looks at me. "Twisted, right?"

I'm kind of speechless, so I just shrug dramatically. "Fuck if I know. Holy hell, Luce."

The corner of her mouth raises in a little sad side smile. "But then once again, I noticed him on his phone a lot, and I finally confronted him."

I look up to see a couple taking a selfie by the water, the guy kissing the girl's cheek as he stretches his arm out holding the phone for the shot, and I get the sudden urge to push them in. "Want me to just take it for you?" I shout over to them, zero attempt to get up and zero warmth on my face or in my tone. "Might make more sense since he's not even looking at the camera to see what he's taking! Looks like you're struggling a little." Hopefully my scowl makes it clear they look ridiculous.

Lucy tenses and shoots a wide eyed look at me. The couple both nervously smile and shake their heads no before walking away, the guy looking back at me like he's unsure if I'm rabid.

I look back down at Lucy and she breaks into a sad laugh. "Oh my God, you are something else."

"They were annoying the shit out of me. They'd been standing there like that for like, ninety-seven and a half minutes! Enough is enough." I pull my arm back from her shoulders and laugh, my irritation quickly shifting as I realize how maniacal I probably seemed. "We probably looked like lesbian lovers that were annoyed with the heterosexual couple comfortably showing so much PDA."

At this, Lucy really starts laughing, and I'm happy I could make her happy for a minute, despite all she's just shared with me. "So what happened then? When you confronted Justin?"

Her smile drops and she lets out a big sigh. "He broke down crying. Apologizing, down on his knees, swearing up and down that nothing happened, which I believe. He's never home late, we know each other's locations at all times, I mean it would be pretty hard to pull off an affair."

"Credit card purchases? Unexplained hotels or restaurants or gifts?" I hate to have to ask, but I want to be sure.

"Nothing, no. I mean I suppose there could be some hot and heavy quickies at the office that I'd never know about. I don't know though, she doesn't seem like the type. Their texts weren't necessarily steamy like that either. And besides, I'm really hurt by the emotional affair of it all more than anything. That's the piece that hurts so fucking much. Sex is just lust. Don't get me wrong, I'd be pissed and tempted to take a golf club to his car, but the emotional connection he had with this woman is so much more hurtful than I could have imagined."

I nod, trying to imagine it for myself. I've never been in love, not really. Royce was a farce, not the real thing. But I can bet it hurts with a fiery pain so intense to have your heart broken like that. To feel like you're not enough if the person you love is capable of having feelings for someone else.

I never want to know pain like that. If Lucy, my strong and amazing sister is capable of hurting like this, I can't even guess what that would do to me.

I never want to find out.

My mind flashes to Simon and I find myself wondering if he'd ever do something like that, emotionally cheat. I doubt it, he's so stony as it is, I can't ever see him having innocent flirtations with someone he wasn't invested in. He seems like an all or nothing kind of guy. Not that it matters, I'm far from being in a relationship with him. He's taken me to dinner once, a surprisingly formal affair, the whole thing.

He picked me up on that beautiful bike of his—a 2003 Triumph Bonneville T100, as I've now learned—and we cruised around London. We made our way to a charming garden cafe along the water in Little Venice. I was nervous, actually nervous for the whole thing. I seriously couldn't remember the last time I'd been on a proper date. It just isn't something I ever do.

Simon was all gentlemanly with me that night. He wore his glasses, but he did wear a basic t-shirt, exposing the mess of tattoos that I was growing quite the habit of masturbating to while imagining those tattooed arms doing all kinds of lovely things to me.

We talked about his work, his favorite places he's photographed, some he said he'd like to take me to if I was interested. I found myself nodding, and meaning it. I'd always liked history, even if there was no real job in it for me. There's something magical about the wisdoms held in the walls and sacred grounds of places left untouched by the modern world. Like those spaces know significant things, hold wisdom. It's part of why I wanted to move overseas. So much more history far beyond the comparative baby-ness of couple hundred year old America.

Growing up we traveled to Europe a lot, usually for my mom's work. I always loved old cathedrals, the cool dampness of them offering a cleansing feeling. The stories captured in stained glass. I would think how sad the people in those windows looked, like a photograph capturing the raw emotion of their pain. I'd wonder who they were, why they were so miserable, my kid brain imagining them shattering the glass and breaking free. I found myself sharing these thoughts with Simon, and realized I really never talked like that to anyone else before.

"*Now* who is the Hot Nerd?" he teased, and I gave him a shove with my foot under the table.

I shook my head and laughed. "I'm not a nerd, I just have a vivid imagination. I got terrible grades, trust me, I'm not smart like that. That would be my sister."

"School isn't designed to cater to all learning abilities. It's not a fair measurement of how smart a person is."

The waitress had come up before I could answer. I ordered a salad, no dressing, and Simon gave me one quick "Lila" glance, and I dropped my eyes to my lap, my heart pounding in mild panic. "And a side of chips," he told the waitress, and I groaned in annoy-ance, but didn't protest. Fine. I'd eat one fry. No big deal.

I ended up eating seven. Seven freaking fries. (Yes, I know I shouldn't have counted them. But look, I ate them, let's take the win, right?) They were crispy and warm and salty and Simon watched me with this *look* the whole time. Admiring. He murmured how sexy I was, how he wanted to watch me eat fries all day, his voice all deep and strained like I was torturing him. I told him he was a freak with a potato fetish.

But I got a little bold, and I licked the salt off my fingers when I was done, one at a time, and he let out this low rumble of appreciation, and I couldn't help but laugh. The desire was so clear, all over his face. It felt unbelievable. I liked being admired while eating. It was a completely foreign feeling to me. My usual self consciousness to eat in front of people had apparently been left outside the restaurant, an unwelcome customer being refused service.

I've heard countless times from men their appreciation over my body. For all Royce's fucked up comments, I'd had a hundred times more comments of admiration from other men. How in shape I was or how my long legs were the stuff of dreams. My sexiness was always wrapped up in the perfection of my body. My desirability contained to my looks.

But sitting there, under the twinkle of lights and surrounded by lush greenery and the encasing warmth of the heat lamps, I felt cozy and sexy. Eating french fries. With an audience.

With an audience that I actually liked.

Except at the end of the night, Simon gave me a hug and chaste kiss in front of my door, and left me hanging. I had texted him, teasing him that he was like Icy Hot, because I know I felt a boner during that hug, and he said he didn't trust himself to do more just yet. I'm dying for us to finally have sex, but Lucy's situation is reminding me that I need to be careful with this guy. I'm slipping into feelings for him, which is confusing and sort of comical too. How can you feel something for someone so bizarre? Maybe it's the forbidden aspect of it, given Grayson's warning for me to stay away. But it's strange, because while Si definitely has an ability to make me feel nervous flutters and a little intimidation, it's not necessarily in an unsafe way. It's hard to explain.

I pause my train of thought, return my attention to Lucy and give her a long hug, rubbing her back in comfort. I joke that we'll burn all Justin's favorite sports equipment, then buy season tickets to the Phillies and never invite him. She assures me that's not necessary, but she'll keep it in mind.

"How are things with hot and wild Simon, by the way?" she

asks, as we stand and abandon our bench to head out. I adore that she's still thinking about me and how I'm doing.

"I think he like, actually wants to be with me."

"The photographer and the model, how romantic."

I shake my head. "No. No thank you. I'm not trying to get attached." The last guy I started to have feelings for, I realized it too late. By then he had moved on—to a freaking famous musician, of all people—and I shut the door on those feelings as quickly as possible by sleeping with the next guy that so much as looked at me.

Lucy slips her arm into mine and we both stumble a little in our steps. "Don't let my situation act as a cautionary tale for you, alright? Based on the way the hot Brit looks at you, he seems to feel pretty intensely. And with how flustered *you* seem to be in his presence, something I've not seen in you in quite some time, I think he might just be getting to you."

"Even if I did actually like him, there's no freakin' way. He looks at beautiful people all day, first through a lens, then through hours of edits on a screen. I'm not trying to compete with that."

A peacock roams past us and Lucy pauses to take a picture. "This place is gorgeous." She pulls me in for a selfie with the peacock in the background, and I bare my teeth in my best attempt at a grin that looks awkward and wide eyed. Lucy laughs and goes, "You know you're a good model when you can even fake being bad at taking pictures." It's a sweet compliment, strange as it is.

"But look, Lila. Beauty is all around us," she says with a hand sweep indicating the gardens and gorgeous bird in our company. "There's never really any knowing when temptation might strike, but I can tell you that the problem for me and Justin wasn't Dr. Gabby being some babe he couldn't resist. She's cute and all, but mousy and nondescript, I'd say."

"So what's the problem, then?"

"Me and Justin, I guess. Not paying enough attention to our own relationship. A big part of that is on me, I can admit. And him too for not talking to me about it, but I know he had been unhappy with me. We put too much focus on everything else, not enough on one another.

"I've made some mistakes too," she says quietly, and a gust of wind blows her long, caramel hair across her face. She reaches a hand up to tuck it back behind her ear. "But ultimately, nothing beats the good stuff with your man. It feels so good to be loved, I wish I had paid better attention to that instead of taking it for granted."

"Ugh, you're too good for words, I don't get it. I'd be all rage and blame."

"That's a waste of energy, sister," Lucy says brightly.

We exit the park and walk onto the street. The change in scenery from peaceful and serene earthiness to the hustle and bustle of cars and shops feels productive, in a way. There's a corner restaurant with a black awning and an inviting chalkboard sign, and we make our way towards it, me thinking about Lucy's words. How it feels good to be loved, and her ability to say that even with the obvious pain she's going through. I can't decide if she's delusional or brilliant. Maybe her time away has made her realize she misses Justin, who knows. I ask her if she thinks they can fix things, but she only says she hopes so.

"You'll take him back? Even after what he did?"

And then I nearly fall over in shock as she mutters her next words. "Actually, I'm just hoping he'll take me back. I'm the one who for real cheated on him. But he doesn't know that yet."

I gasp and look at my sister, into her beautiful eyes framed by her naturally long and dark lashes. I look at her as if I'm seeing her for the first time in my life.

thirteen

. . .

lucy

THERE WAS SOMETHING curious about hearing Lila point out that I call Dr. Gabby "Little Miss Perfect" when that's exactly what Lila calls me. Of course I've heard her say it to my face countless times over the years, usually in a mocking tone when mad at our parents over something.

But I hadn't even recognized the connection. And here's why it's weird.

I distinctly remember the first time Justin came home and told me about his new work gal. He referred to the new pediatrician on the project, the brilliance and how this is going to really help set things in the perfect direction. I remember asking "What's his name?" and Justin got a bit flustered, going "Her name, actually," and I felt some feminist shame recognizing the long ingrained social conditioning that had me automatically assume it was a man.

That was my first tiny little flare up of potential jealousy for Dr. Gabby. Hearing my husband speak so highly with such respect for another woman was a little jarring, I have to admit. So I asked some more questions, wondering what my competition might possibly be.

Except he didn't say she worked in some amazing surgery department at one of the two potential top hospitals near us. He didn't say she was doing any cutting edge care or research somewhere fabulous, or even that she was in her own private practice. No, Dr. Gabby was a basic physician employed by some big old corporate practice. She probably made less than me, which is saying something considering I work for a non-profit. One that offers me a whole lot of community respect, mind you.

So I actually laughed at myself for the smidge of jealousy I had initially felt. She was a nobody! Yeah okay, a doctor was impressive. But not like she was plowing through her career with any major drive. I had nothing to worry about, she was a sweet little small town doc checking kids' growth charts and making referrals to the big wigs somewhere. Basic. No threat. Justin liked strong women. Driven women. She was nothing.

Except that apparently sweet Gabby *was* something for Justin. Something I couldn't be.

Soft.

Gentle.

Patient and compassionate.

Quiet, maybe. (I wouldn't really know any of this, but I assumed.)

When he shut down their texts initially, she was so incredibly apologetic and remorseful. Sweet about it. I wanted to hate her, but I really couldn't. You could just tell that neither one of them meant to let things get to the level of inappropriateness that it had. Justin's an immature joker, and even his jokes held a certain sense of innocence for a decent amount of time.

But they had apparently shared a moment at work. There was some dispute and he raised an opinion on something, it got shot down, and she had chimed in with all her expertness and said how great of an idea Justin's plan was. How she could see how it would funnel out on the user end to be streamlined and practical, and worth the little extra it might cost upfront.

He thanked her privately in text. Talked about how he's usually a "back seat, let the others make all the difficult decisions" guy, and he'll execute on the technical side, but that he felt uncharacteristically excited about this. And how much her sticking up for him meant to him.

I could have thrown up right then and there. I was so mad at myself for being so naive. Who knew, a little softness from a woman and Justin was all insightful and introspective like I'd never seen before.

It almost felt like he'd outgrown me.

I smile at Lila from across the table, determined to try and enjoy our little street side cafe lunch moment with her. I'm thankful she was courteous enough to not probe when I finally confessed to her my brief affair, saying I didn't want to talk about it, that the guy wasn't worth mentioning. It was liberating to admit it to someone—not even my best friend Reggie knows. A small weight is definitely lifted in sharing my big, dark secret. Well, part of it, anyhow.

I know that I can't stay in London forever. I need to get back soon, if for no other reason than to go do responsible things like get blood work ordered and figure out this whole carrying-a-child thing. It's so funny, this odd little role reversal Lila and I have here. Maybe it's an England thing; maybe in a land different from our own hometown, I'm allowed to be the along-for-the-ride one, and she can be the one leading *me* around, showing me the ropes. I wonder if I'd feel as comfortable with this dynamic back home; I don't think I would. It's been nice having Lila show me her spots and tagging along to her random jobs, seeing her in action. It's good to see her doing her thing. I can see why she moved here.

But I realize bitterly how much I'd rather have her home with me if I'm going to be having a baby.

Lila orders us a bottle of wine, saying we need to get horribly drunk today, and I debate whether or not to confess my condition. I also calculate how bad it would be to have a glass. It's early days, I could easily have no clue I was even pregnant, right? One glass can't be too bad. I decide I'm not going to tell her just yet. I'm going to eat lots of pasta to absorb the alcohol, and allow myself to enjoy this one last little glimpse of my past life.

The one where I had it all figured out and was on top of the world. The one where I wasn't a total fuckup, crashing down and ruining my own life and everyone's around me.

fourteen

. . .

lila

I'M AMAZINGLY DEPRESSED as I air kiss my sister goodbye and watch her drive away, off to the airport, on a plane, across an ocean. I know she needs to get back to her real life and work on cleaning up her marriage, but it feels so weird to be the one standing here telling *her* she's got this, telling *her* people mess up sometimes and it's alright.

It feels weird, but also comfortable.

"I think I'm going to miss your sister," Penny says, standing beside me and I look down at her and grin.

"Thanks to her, you and I became friends, not just roommates, huh?"

Penny opens the door to our building and holds it for me. "What do you mean? We were always friends."

I swallow with guilt, thankful that she seems blissfully unaware that I had early on decided I wasn't going to like her when I first moved in. She seemed bubbly and annoying, and not remotely anyone I wanted to hang out with. I guess I was better at faking it than I thought, probably for Grayson's sake as they are friends. But had she heard any of the inner judgment I had passed on her in my mind in those first couple months, she'd go running for the hills.

Interesting to me that Penny never even registered me not liking her. Like the thought hadn't crossed her mind at all.

I follow her up the stairs, explaining that we've had more time to hang out since my sister had been in town.

"And you mean you no longer could pretend you were studying instead of hiding out in your room?" she says with a smile as she opens our door.

"You knew I wasn't studying?"

She shrugs. "Grayson says you take some time to warm up to people, that's all. Figured I'd let you do that in whatever way you needed."

"Oh," I say dumbly.

"And I knew anyone as rude as you were to someone you literally knew nothing about," she says, pointing her index finger to her own smiling face, "just had a tough exterior to try and protect themselves from perceived harm."

"You thought all that?"

Penny reaches in the fridge and pulls out her signature drink pitcher, this time with something flashy orange in it. "I'm a secondary school counselor, I know a surly look of self-preservation when I see it." She raises the pitcher toward me. "Drink?"

I'm pretty sure I've gained five pounds with all the fun and games with Lucy being here. And I'm certain Penny has made another sugary drink that will not help matters.

But I nod and tell her I'd love one.

"SO, ANY UPDATES ON YOUR daughter?" I ask Adrian, my makeup artist once again for a commercial for a nail polish brand. It's a punk-rock purple look with dramatic eyes that I'm kind of loving.

"The fashionista?" he asks. I nod. "I'm amazed you remember."

I shrug. "You saved me from a hangover. The least I could do was feign interest."

He laughs at this and reaches in his pocket. He pulls out his phone and scrolls through for a moment before showing me a picture of two girls. One is tall and curvy and looks far older than the young teen he said she was, the other is all awkward and uncomfortable looking in that about-to-hit-puberty phase that we all hated and suffered through.

"They're gorgeous," I tell him.

"The older one is finding her stride, which is a relief. Now it's the younger one I have to worry about."

"Oh yeah? How so?"

Adrian puffs out his cheeks and returns his phone to his pocket. He grabs a beauty blender and starts dabbing away at various points on my face. He's silent for a moment and I wonder if he's dropping the conversation and regretting saying anything. Eventually though he speaks. "She's been cutting herself. School informed. I had no idea."

The words hit me with an ache, and I wince. "Ah, yes," I nod glumly. "I briefly went through that around her age."

He pauses his movements. "You did? What did you do, how did you stop it?" His eyes are pained in asking me this. I feel the pain straight down to my soul. I think about all I put my own parents through as a kid, how much I must have pained them, though I never thought too much about it at the time. As a kid, I only knew I was hurting.

"And why, if you don't mind me asking?" he asks gently.

I answer as best as I can. "Because I had a whole lot of big feelings, I felt like no one would want to listen or care about my feelings, and cutting was my fun little secret to let out things I couldn't otherwise express. A way to distract from my hurt."

"That's similar to what the therapist has said. I'm trying to understand it, I really am. I feel as though I do listen, though. I tell her I love her daily and I have my sister stop in when she can to offer a female role model." That's right—his wife passed away a few years ago.

Adrian is patting my face with more pressure now, and I grab his wrist to stop him. "Ouch. My face is not the cutting, okay?" I give him a little side smile to let him know I'm not really hurt.

"Apologies. This is why you should maintain professional boundaries." He continues though and softens his movements.

"Look, my parents told me they loved me too. And I had both of them, so don't blame your wife's passing, kay? For me it was more just that I didn't always believe in their love. Saying the words isn't always enough, you know? It was other stuff that made me doubt they cared. The praises my sister constantly got, the way her life dominated conversations. Affection wasn't always something my parents were great at. They were very career driven. Still not always great at affection, really." I have to be careful not to say too much here, being as my mom's name is very well known in the industry. While I like Adrian, you just never know what the gossip mill might accidentally pick up. I have to tread lightly with this, but I want him to hear it from the grown-up version's perspective of someone that formerly dabbled in cutting. Maybe it will help him. Help his daughter.

I continue. "Try and just be present more with your daughter. Pop into her room now and then, ask what she's doing. Just, you know," I shrug, "listen with genuine interest, don't offer advice or God forbid, mock her interests thinking it's all in good fun. It's a sensitive age for that kind of thing."

He nods. "I can't remember the last I've sat in her room to talk to her. Not sure she'd like it."

I wave a dismissive hand. "Kids test their parents' love when they themselves are unsure of who they are or whether or not they're lovable. Pushing them away is part of that process." I'm amazed at how uncomfortable it is to think about that time of my life, my childhood and the depression I struggled with. I haven't thought much about it in so long.

"So how did you stop? The cutting, how did you put an end to it?"

I answer honestly. "I found that not eating was a much easier way to channel the pain." I shrug. "It's the truth, that became my control thing. It got a bit easier as I got older, had a stint doing inpatient at a mental health hospital for my depression, and learned to look around me and see how hard life is for so many. Much harder than for me. Kids way more sick with far less support. Gave me some semblance of perspective, I guess. But also guilt, too. Like, I knew then that I was a selfish brat, you know? I felt sort of ashamed, hospitalized with kids that obviously were far worse off than me."

I feel tears prick behind my eyes as I continue. "I used to think, 'What's wrong with me that I can't even be happy when I have so much more than everyone else?'" A tear seeps its way past my bottom lashes, and Adrian swiftly grabs a tissue to catch it. I feel jot of guilt at potentially screwing up his work.

"Depression doesn't care what external comforts you have, Lila."

I nod, grateful for his kindness and take the tissue from his hand. "No, I know. I do. I was a kid, I didn't know how to deal with the emotions. And my parents had a 'get over it, you're fine' mentality that I know was meant to be tough love, but it just didn't land well with me. My sister Lucy responded better with that kind of thing, but not me."

I drop the tissue on Adrian's table of beauty products and straighten my spine in my chair. "At the hospital I'd listen in group to these kids' stories, horrible things they'd been through." I snort. "I remember even wondering if they were lying, thinking maybe they made it all up."

"I imagine hearing those things was hard, especially as a kid.

Indulging in disbelief was easier than facing that those stories were true."

I nod and close my eyes while he taps some glitter on my lids. "Cutting or controlling my eating was sort of like a way to tell myself that I was broken, and see the brokenness in real time. Like I could cut, and me and that little slash had a relationship of understanding one another. Just two broken pieces, allowed to shine in the bubbles of blood that would pop out. Me and my not good enough self, the shame swapped out for gorgeous crimson." My words are raw in hopes to switch sadness out for gory, but I still feel myself wanting to cry at this. I need to get my shit together so I don't mess up Adrian's hard work, though. "Sorry," I say. "I realize this might be hard to hear."

"No, this is helpful to me. I have been at such a loss and not sure if I should chalk it up to a phase or downplay it so I don't indulge in the attention. But then I think maybe I should make a big fuss so I get through to her. I want to understand it so I can help her."

"Well good, because I don't even think I've gotten this in depth about it with therapists. Definitely don't downplay it, you need to take it seriously. Validate that she's hurting, but help her figure out other ways to navigate her suffering."

"I'd rather her not suffer at all," he says with a pained expression on his face.

"Unrealistic. Suffering is a part of life. Teach her she can handle it, help her feel her strength instead of trying to shield her from suffering, because that can send a message like you think she's incapable."

He nods. "That's hard."

"Yes."

"But I see your point."

I smile genuinely. "Leave it to the person masking me up to help me expose my raw internal thoughts and unleash all these random wisdoms."

"Perhaps it's the essence of my being the catalyst for transformation," Adrian offers.

"Maybe.."

"And the eating? I do recall my forcing a snack on you once upon a time."

I sigh. "Eating is always the hardest, because it's something we have to do daily. I stopped cutting, focused on my looks and eating. Of course growing up in a world surrounded by diet pills and measuring tape and everything beauty, it's even harder. As I got a bit older, and I started realizing people thought I was pretty, I clung to the power of that. I was a very awkward ugly duckling child, so I wrapped up a *lot* in banking on looking a certain way." *I still do,* I think bitterly. "She says while sitting here getting her makeup done," I joke. Adrian remains silent though. "Anyway, my focus became all about being skinny enough. Or later on, doing what I could to be sexy. I felt like I could control that, and at least then I'd have something to offer the world."

Adrian drops the brush in his hand, leans against the small vanity and crosses one foot in front of the other. "I hope I don't have to tell you how wrong that thinking is, right?"

I nod. "I know that, I do. For the most part. My demons raise their little heads now and then, but I'm too much of a bitch to let them run me over."

He laughs at this, and I feel a little relief at being able to lighten the mood a little. I'm not sure what's come over me exactly, why I'm talking to him so openly about things only my journals of childhood know about. I guess my heart goes out to his little girl.

"And now? How do you deal with pain now?" he asks me.

"Adrian, when I figure that shit out I'll let you know."

He smiles. "I think you don't give yourself enough credit."

"If I had a dollar for every time someone said that same exact thing to me..." I say, shaking my head. But I smile at him.

"Well there must be a reason you hear it so often, then." Adrian rises up and grabs the brush again. "Come on. Let's finish getting you dolled up so you can go inspire little girls and boys on camera."

"That's fucking depressing, Adrian."

"No. Because you," he does that pop the brush on my nose thing that he loves to do, "I have a feeling, are going to set the world on fire. Become famous in your own right and speak up about your struggles, and help other kids too, one day."

"Did you just stumble onto my big dreams by accident?" I'm joking slightly, but actually liking the idea of setting something in motion like that.

"God willing, because my daughter needs you, love. So let's make the world fall in love with you, so you can smash that platform and use it for all it's worth."

I smile, then get an idea. I scramble in my purse for a pen and paper, and scribble something down. I ask Adrian what his daughter's name is, and he tells me. I add it in. "Give her this," I say. "Tell her it's from someone very cool and fabulous."

He looks down and reads the note, then smiles. "The world may not understand who you are, but you are the world to someone, Annabelle. Never forget that."

And then later on in the week, I find out I've been selected for a small but steady part in a twelve episode series that is "Destined to be a huge hit!" Playing the part of a struggling model, of all things. Filming to start in two weeks. With a paycheck that is just enough for me to be skipping and swiping to treat myself to a couple new pieces to stuff into my already overflowing wardrobe.

It feels like I'm finally getting a win.

before

· · ·

Dear Simon,

PLEASE READ THIS LETTER.

Please.

I know you're mad at me. I know you are, and yes, you have a right to be. What I did was fucked up, I know. But I had no choice, I had to protect him, you understand that, right? In time, I will make it right, I swear it. I will.

But listen, I do love you. I really do. You were always so good to me when we were kids. I've never forgotten that, you know? You're always in my heart, I hope you know that and feel that. You never forget your first love, even if it was just kids being fools.

I'm happy now though, you need to understand that. He's wonderful to me. And he worships me, and when things aren't quite so complicated we will step out and tell everyone the truth, okay? There are just some things that need to happen, and it takes time to sort these things out.

In the meantime, thank you for doing this for me. I don't want you to worry. I've got it all under control, honest. You know me, I always have the best plans, don't I? Half the fun you, me, and Grayson had were all the Elsie Enlightening Escapades, never a dull moment. I suppose you could think of what I'm doing now as just another Elsie Escapade, and it's just as much, only now it's the grown up variety.

Be well, dear friend. Will be in touch soon.
X
Elsie

fifteen

. . .

simon

I T WAS INTERESTING to him that his aunt had left out the box of small keepsakes, with letters from Elsie on top. He hadn't meant to read any, once had been enough, especially given the aftermath. Had Victoria opened the box and seen the letters? Read them as well? He had been gone while she was there, so he hadn't had a chance to confront her. Although he probably would not have anyways. More than likely it was an afterthought, she must have been vacuuming nooks and crannies and simply forgotten to put it back.

Still. He had in fact read them, and the letters still filled him with hopeless regret.

He gives one final pull on his rowing machine, the lone one here at Roger's Gym, and watches as the water of the machine swirls around with the final force. All of its devastation at the hands of Simon's pulls, now nicely slowing and settling as if it had never happened. It's how his own life feels sometimes. Extreme waves followed by quiet settling. Life goes on.

Only never quite the same, no. Each little abrupt force of

momentum leaves a small mark on your brain, an imprint never to be the same again. Those marks impact how others see you, how you see yourself, the choices you make, the autopilot you set yourself in when making those choices. It had been an autopilot Simon had become good at. It seemed the more numb he became, the more good things life threw at him, as though his own fights had wreaked havoc, and when he eventually gave up, it's when things finally settled.

The problem was, in his state of numbness, the success never really broke through to him in a way that gave him any real joy. Instead he cared less and less, like he'd sold his soul to the devil and ceased to give a fuck anymore.

Ensuring Victoria was taken care of is his only concern now. Each advance in his photography career was just another way he could repay Victoria for her years of giving up her life to raise him. He had to be creative about it, she wouldn't accept money from him for nothing. Stopping over for cooking and housekeeping became the way, and Simon had the feeling she felt better being able to keep tabs on him, so there you had it. It worked for them.

Simon slips past the gym front desk, giving a silent nod to the kid working today, popping her gum and scrolling on her phone. He hadn't seen Roger, which was fine as Simon was in no mood for questions regarding Lila.

Lila, the little fox that had been driving him mad. She had seeped her way into his bones, and it was impossible to stop it. The obnoxious American, it was everything he wanted to hate, but couldn't. She was a wild creature with a spark that was igniting something in him, and he had no choice but to pursue it. He had taken her out twice now—once for a dinner as promised, the next time to a gallery followed by coffee. Both times he was reserved. Restrained. He half expected her to try to block him again, but had been surprised by her continued responses to his daily texts.

She fights her own demons, as we all do, he supposes. Hers appear to be a fondness for emotional swings, though he had been starting to find them more entertaining than irritating, something he would not have expected. Ultimately Simon has accepted that no matter her mercurial tendencies, he has conceded to being unable to keep his distance from her.

He cruises his bike around the street, taking a roundabout way to enjoy a quick ride before making his way down toward his building. He parks and slips off his helmet, thankful the air has been getting cooler, and makes his way up to his flat.

Once at the door, he hears muffled voices coming from inside. He tries the handle and realizes it's open.

"Victoria?" he calls as he steps in.

But he finds not his aunt in her usual place cooking in his kitchen, or dusting down surfaces, or sweeping, or mopping, or doing any of the expected things Simon is used to.

No. His aunt is nearly naked, wearing nothing but a shirt, unbuttoned and draping down her arms and back. She's on the floor of his living room.

And beneath her, between her legs is Roger from the gym.

SIMON WAS TEMPTED TO STAND there, arms crossed as Roger and Victoria scrambled with embarrassment to rearrange themselves. It was his instinct, to make them squirm, a punishment for violating his living room floor so exorbitantly.

But no, Simon was better than that, and frankly not interested in having to avert his eyes in their presence to an amount of skin that he'd rather not have imprinted into his memory. The initial shock of what he'd seen had been enough. He was just thankful the view offered minimal exposure, as they were positioned so that his aunt's back was to the door. The gauzy shirt draping loosely on her arms and hair dangling down her back had at least offered necessary coverage.

So when his aunt shouted, "Simon!" before looking with

complete horror between him and down to Roger's equally panicked face, Simon did the polite thing and stepped back out the door.

Which was where he was now. Jaw tight, fists clenched, attempting to absorb what he had just seen.

The surprise was not in the matchup. Victoria had been singing a lot more lately, upbeat tunes and a lightness to her steps that Simon recognized in the back of his mind somewhere to be the likely new flame of Roger. Which did in fact make Simon happy, mainly because Simon knew Roger to be a good man, and it would be nice to have a break from the nearly codependent relationship Simon and his aunt had.

His anger now is squarely on the misuse of his home. That was the crime.

The door opens and Victoria steps out, hair slightly wild, tucking in her shirt to her jeans. "Hiya," she says with an awkward smile. Simon remains silent. "Right, well I suppose you are wondering what that was all about just there," she says, pointing behind her inside the flat. Through the small opening of the door Simon can just make out the movement of Roger, walking to what he assumes is the bathroom.

"No. I know what it was," Simon says tersely.

Victoria snaps her head up to him, taking Simon by surprise. "Well okay then. Guess that clears that up then, doesn't it? Can you at least be happy for me?"

It's not at all the reaction Simon had expected. His usual passively polite aunt was not one to fight back. It was her soft demeanor that could always get through to Simon, tame him.

"Happy, Victoria? That you are shagging on my floor, in my flat?"

"Don't be crude. You think I don't know of the number of times you and Elsie rolled around in my very bed when you were kids? Huh? Oh yes, I knew about that."

Simon cringes at the memory, having no idea his aunt had any clue of he and Elsie defiling her private room. Stupid teenagers is all they were. Impulsive and wicked and selfish. Elsie always had a penchant for mischief, and Simon would do just about anything she asked of him. Including sullying his aunt's bed, the woman who gave up her life, completely unprepared and unexpectedly, all to raise him.

"It's not very different, then, is it?" Victoria asks. "Only this here was not to be little shites—we would have been in your *bed* if that were the case," she says with a head shake while bringing up her hair to a knot on top of her head.

Simon looks away, a bit stunned at her sharpness. "Fine," he says, gaze held out the window beside them. "What is it then?"

Victoria shrugs. "Sometimes the moment sweeps you away, and we had a moment. No sense in holding back when life is entirely too short," she says like it's the most simple logic in the world.

At that moment Roger steps out, fully clothed now and gives Victoria a quick kiss.

"Hi, Simon. Sorry about that. I promise that wasn't the plan, I brought your aunt some lunch and, well..."

"How kind."

Roger grins at him, zero shame at all in his face. He gives Victoria one last kiss before heading out with a "See you at the gym. Nice flat, by the way."

Victoria and Simon step back into the flat and Simon suddenly feels claustrophobic and wants to abandon the space as quickly as possible. But he needs a shower, so he heads straights back.

"I'll finish up here and then get started on your meals for the weekend," his aunt calls after him.

Simon pauses mid-step and turns back around. "You know what, don't bother."

"But—"

He raises a hand to stop her. "I'm not mad, that's not why. Just think I'd like to head up to the beach for the weekend is all. Get some photos, change of scenery." That and his skin was crawling at what he'd just witnessed, so a little space was feeling necessary.

And he could invite Lila.

"Sounds lovely, if not a bit chilly. Apple cinnamon puffs at least for the road? I have the dough ready, won't take long."

"Fine, thank you." He really needs to find a way to assure his aunt she does not need to cater to him so much. The more he thinks about it, the more relieved he feels with this match with Roger.

"Taking anyone with you? Lila, perhaps?" she asks.

"I'm not sure yet. I haven't asked her."

"Well they'll be plenty for you both, just in case. Fingers crossed."

Fingers crossed indeed. He was already texting her.

sixteen

. . .

lila

FOR A FEW days I couldn't stop thinking about that conversation with Adrian and the thoughts of the ways my depression as a kid would consume me. I never really understood it at the time—my parents were no help—I just knew I felt big feelings. I could be having a blast, rolling from one idea to the next with euphoria, then I'd crash down in a ball of tears feeling like the world was a black hole swallowing me up. I never understood why the happy moods didn't last. Nothing made any sense, I felt like there was some piece of vital information that existed beyond my reach. As if the whole rest of the world understood it all perfectly, but I was in the dark with no one even seeing me or recognizing that I needed anything. The afterthought. I hated school, feared getting called on and not knowing an answer and looking stupid. I would come up with a list of excuses to have prepared to get me out of situations. It was ADHD combined with anxiety and depression, and it was torture. Like my mind did everything it could to work against me, make life harder for me. I was the weird kid and my friendships never lasted long, I'd inevitably do something stupid and my friend of the month would get upset, and I'd explode on them with a temper that was really just me hurting and expressing it all wrong. Still, it earned me a reputation. I was the kid to stay away from, and eventually I learned to keep to myself.

I've stabilized a lot as I've gotten older, thankfully. Therapy and meds have done wonders for me, but man, the depression sucked as a kid. It sneaks in now and then still, but I'm better at managing it. I grew into myself after high school, I guess you could say.

I wish my parents had paid better attention to me though, validated my anxiety. Maybe it wouldn't have lead to moods quite so deep and dark if they had. All the focus was always on Lucy, it was like they didn't even bother with trying to help me figure out my way. Lucy showed promise as having the Lilith Delphi drive that launched the L. Delphi-Ray brand. She had the determination, the brains, charisma, everything my parents wanted. As for me? I was too impulsive, too reckless in my struggles with focus and direction. I was loved, I knew that much, but I often felt I was something my parents would push aside. It was like my family looked at me and thought, "Poor little Lila. That one's a lot of work, we'll just have to figure her out later."

It was the exact kind of thing my ex Royce loved to have a blast with, the prick. He learned pretty quickly my insecurities and knew just how to use them against me.

Not at first, of course, oh no. At first he love bombed the shit out of me, and I was too swept up in his attention and affection to know it wasn't healthy. I know that now. Man, what I wouldn't give to have had someone present that term to me back then—"love bombing." He was one of Lucy's acquaintances and we first met at someone's pool party somewhere. I was seventeen, a week away from graduating high school, and Royce had spotted me in a corner, struck up a conversation. I was feeling buzzy on alcohol and he was sweet to me. Witty. It felt right away like we had a spark. I remember feeling so thankful to have found someone to talk to at a party where I really didn't know anyone well. My sister had dragged me along—probably at my parents' insistence. Having never really formed a steady circle of friends in high school, I think my family worried how I was going to do in my upcoming freshman year at college.

Lucy never did know all the exact details of my struggles as a kid. My parents didn't want her losing her focus while in the midst of pursuing her own education. With our age difference, I often felt more like an only child growing up. But when she was around, it was always understood that she was to look out for me in any way she could. Like I needed a damn babysitter or something. It's funny, though. Now that I think about it, it was really Justin that was the catalyst for the shift of our sisterly relationship. Before him, Lucy acted more like another mom to me. After they got together she started treating me a little more like a sister. Not quite a sister of equals, I'm not sure that'll ever be the case in her eyes, but at the very least not quite her baby anymore.

She first started dating Justin during my senior year of high school, and he had become an unexpected friend to me in a way I didn't know I needed. We'd laugh at how bossy Lucy could be, commiserate together on how it was Lucy's world and we were all just in it. When she'd lecture me on something, it was Justin that would chime in and tell her to give me a break. Justin's not exactly a man of wise words, but he instantly felt like an older brother to me in a way that expressed "I got your back." I felt slightly less lonely when he entered our world, and I prayed Lucy would stick with him.

So I guess you could say that at that pool party, I was at the precipice of change. Everyone there was older than me, more mature, yet I felt a bit more at home than I did with the kids I went to school with. Conversations weren't about who was wearing an ugly outfit or who had been caught by a teacher or admin giving a blowjob in the stairwell, but about actual things happening in the world. With high school coming to an end I was starting to realize there was a life beyond the kids you've spent your whole life with, trapped in a prison called school, like the same painful record playing over and over again. It felt wonderfully liberating to realize I'd soon be free from those chains of preconceived notions of who I was.

I was determined to reinvent myself, and that party seemed like a good starting place. Lucy had loaned me a cute dress for the party (I was usually a leggings and hoodie kind of girl back then), and she did my makeup. She had bleached my hair to platinum, saying I had just the right complexion to pull it off. I felt like a different person, and I remember trying so hard to act older than I was. I was hoping this sweet and cool guy named Royce didn't realize I was only seventeen, worrying that if he did he wouldn't be flirting with me like he was.

That was the other thing—someone was actually *flirting* with me. It was my first real taste of my potential prowess of the art of seduction, the first taste of men actually finding me sexy. In school I was always gangly and awkward, I hadn't even kissed anyone yet. And now suddenly, a cute guy in his twenties was touching my arm, tucking hair behind my ear, telling me my eyes were beautiful. It sparked something in me. We joked around with each other and played a game of "let's try and figure out what each group of people is talking about," and he laughed at the things I came up with like he truly found me funny. I remember Lucy coming up to us at one point, checking in on me and I was worried she was going to blow my cover, but she just smiled, saying, "Oh good, you've met my little sister!" and then eventually left us alone again.

High off of margaritas and a couple hits of Royce's vape pen, I let him lead me inside to the laundry room, the only unoccupied space we could find. He kissed me and I remember hoping he couldn't tell it was my first time (he later told me it was obvious, the jackass), and I let him put his hand down the neckline of my dress, fondling my tiny mosquito bites for boobs, grinding into me in a way I was completely dizzy for. He kept breathing out, "You're so sexy. Lila, you're so damn sexy," and it was the most incredible thing to hear a guy talk about me like that, see him fall apart over me.

I didn't stop him when his hands moved lower. It felt so good to feel someone touch me, his hand slipping right up my dress and between my legs, moving aside my panties with expertise. I remember being embarrassed at how wet I was, and him just telling me how hot I was, like he was powerless under my spell or something.

So when Royce pushed my head down and whipped out his dick, I did what I knew I was supposed to do, and I opened wide and sucked. I wondered briefly, there on the hard linoleum floor, swollen cock in my mouth of a man I knew was twenty-something years old, I wondered if I should reveal my age, if he could get in trouble for this. But I decided since I'd be turning eighteen in a couple months, it wasn't a big deal. I was enjoying this fast train into adulthood entirely too much to risk anything that might put a stop to it.

When he came in my mouth I remember gagging, trying hard to hurry up and swallow, drool spilling down my mouth and me being surprised that the taste of semen wasn't more salty or something. But holy hell, I loved the way he shuddered like that. It was amazing to me that *I* caused that. That little old hot-mess Lila could bring a guy to a state of convulsions, all with my mouth and my apparently "hot" and "sexy" self.

So that was that. The beginning. And when later that evening he brought me to an empty bedroom, once the sun had gone down and the party was really going, it felt like the most natural thing in the world for him to push between my shoulder blades, bending me over on the dresser while he hiked up my dress once more, sliding down my underwear and sticking his dick inside me in one swift push. I remember looking in the mirror at myself, watching while he pulsed behind me, hazy with booze and thankful for its dulling effect on the pain of this new experience of a man inside me. I looked at the platinum blonde staring back at me, bringing a man to this state of ecstasy and I thought, "This is it. This is my power. This is what's been brewing inside you all this time, waiting to come out." Just like that, in one night, I went from never been kissed to sultry temptress, bringing a guy named Royce to his knees in his craving of me.

I remember going the next day to get the morning after pill, just in case.

In many ways I think I used Royce just as much as he used me. I wasn't in love with him, even if I thought I was at the time. I was just in love with the thoughts of what I could do to him, the way I could make him weak. It was addicting. He would call and text me constantly. When I told him my age, he said he was screwed, he was in too deep, so in love with me that there was no turning back.

That was a mere two weeks after we met. Somewhere deep down I knew it was fucked up, knew that love after two weeks and a six year age gap when I was still a minor wasn't exactly right. But I didn't care.

I'd sneak off and spend the night at his place, my parents thinking I had found some new friend group and being more than happy to see me out and about. When I finally turned eighteen at the end of that summer, I wondered if he'd start taking me out or if he'd introduce me to his friends or let me tell Lucy. He never did though, saying people wouldn't understand and that what we had was so much better because it was just for us. I tried convincing him that eighteen and twenty-four was no big deal, but really he just had a convenient way of isolating me so I had no one to talk to when shit did get bad.

And bad they definitely got. All that fun "We're so connected, we're so meant to be" from the beginning fairly quickly fizzled out. Eventually our pattern became him using my insecurities to blow me up just enough to crash me back down again, and I got so used to it I barely even recognized the dysfunction. I just craved the good days like a proper addict, and drowned in depression when it stopped being fun, desperate to have his affection back. I was tense and walking on eggshells around him constantly. I felt like shit—not even because of him, but because of me trying to *fight* him on snapping out of it. Like, see what the hell kind of dick you're being, where did my fun man who adored me go! If he would just wake up and stop with those weird moods, it'd be great! The frustration of it all was so hard, so painful. He'd twist things all around on me, and I'd second guess everything. *Everything.* I'd apologize constantly for who knows what, I'd replay conversations in my head, question if I really had said what he claimed I did, or if I'd mistaken something he'd said. I started relying on text messages just so I'd have proof. I felt like I was losing my mind. He knew my biggest fear was that I was a dumb, selfish, undeserving brat, and he'd use that to his full advantage, making me feel like I was never going to be happy. That I ask too much.

By the third time he had laid hands on me, he did me the favor of leaving a mark. An accident, of course, I just drove him so crazy sometimes but he didn't *mean* for me to get hurt, he didn't expect me to step forward like that right as he was simply trying to push me away. But there it was, a small scar just below my eyebrow, and it woke something in me. It sparked a fire of hatred for him, for marking my face, the face that was my only good thing I had in the world. As much as he'd try to tell me I was unattractive with sneaky comments—"Makeup on you makes you look like a drag queen," or "Bigfoot wants his shoes back,"—I knew he was full of shit. Even at my young age, I knew what he was doing. College had been teaching me a lot, I suddenly liked school thanks to the nature of class discussion and the opportunity to write papers or essays instead of my dreaded multiple choice exams. I learned to sweet talk professors so that I could get alternate test formats when possible, and the subject matter actually interested me. I took as many psychology classes as I could, even asked my parents if I could switch my major to it, but they said business made more sense. Still, I drank up all I could learn in an attempt to better understand myself.

Basically, I was gaining a confidence I never knew possible. I stopped blindly riding the cycle of ups and downs with Royce, the whirlwind of craving his love after he'd be an ass to me. I found myself disgusted by him instead, and managed to put an end to the whole thing. I cut him off, blocked him, and by some grace of God, he left me alone, probably because at that point I knew his weakness—his beloved reputation—and I threatened to tell everyone about us if he didn't leave me alone.

To this day it's one of my proudest moments, me giving him a piece of my mind and closing the door on him. I guess I've always been just self-absorbed enough to know when to walk away. My ego mania got me into the situation in the first place—I loved the initial attention from him. But yeah, it got old. I'm still embarrassed it took me nearly two years to get there, but I did. I got there.

I think he always knew I was too good for him and that the only reason he had been able to manipulate me like he did was because I was young. I can thank Royce for one thing though—he definitely taught me that it's possible for someone to be obsessed with me. I can't be all too awful if someone can go nuts like that over me, right? I'll give him that. It felt good to be toxically loved. I just like to have a little more control than that.

Now I'm almost toxically independent. Finally out of the shadows cast by my mom and sister, and unwilling to share the light with anyone.

And yet? Here I am now, you'll never believe where.

I'm strapped to the back of Simon's bike. To spend a weekend away with him. Go figure.

I THINK THE RECENT UPTICK in my career has me in a "fuck-it, live and let live" mentality. When Simon suggested this little beach getaway (more like demanded), I agreed. What the hell, why not? I'm not overthinking it, I'm just going to let loose and have a little fun. Nothing to lose.

It's a three hour trek and he didn't think I could make it in one go on the bike so we're stopping in a small town called Ely, about two hours north of London. While I tried to tell him I'd be fine, I have to say, I'm more than a little relieved when we finally pull over. I stretch out my back, free my head from the boulder of a helmet, feeling like I've lost a hundred pounds.

It's a chilly day for early fall but something about being tense on a bike for all this time has me warm and grateful for a breeze. Simon grabs my hand, a small gesture I'm honestly not very used to, and we wander along a quaint little street. It's all the things I love about England, cobblestone streets and brown brick with windows encased in crisp white, creating cottage vibes that scream cozy. The street lamps are slim and black, with curved tops like a faucet, bottomed off with the curved domes encasing the bulb. There's a rotund woman watering flowers outside her shop and chatting with an equally rotund man with hairy arms and a toothy smile. It's like everyone in England is just happier. Content. Maybe being surrounded by so much charm will do that to you.

We're heading toward a massive cathedral, and I get the feeling Simon's trying to sell me on it. "A few films have been shot here," he says to me as we make our way in through the arched doorway.

I gasp in awe once we're through, the space opening up in a way that feels like we've stepped into another world entirely. It's massive in here, there's a gothic feel thanks to the architecture that reminds me of an old castle, but instead of being eerie, it's welcoming in a way that feels like sanctuary. Which I guess makes sense, of course. But I'm amazed at the transcendent feel of it all.

We wander further in and I look up to take in the building's anatomy, the rows of arches, multiple levels of them. My beloved stained glass windows, some with intricate mosaic patterns. The ceiling is a quilt-like entity, a work of art, paintings and designs in dizzying patterns. It's beautiful.

But the best part is up ahead, further down the sanctuary hall. I'm basically giddy, even with my neck in pain at holding my head up while I stare at the sight towering easily over a hundred feet above.

"An octagon tower?" I ask like an idiot, even though I can clearly see that it is.

"Yes. Built after the original central tower collapsed."

"Way to create beauty out of tragedy," I murmur. The sunlight shines through the glass in a colorful glow, giving off a gem-like sparkle that feels like a spiritual experience in and of itself.

"You like it?" Simon asks, my hand still in his, and I instinctively raise our clasped hands up and plant a kiss on his.

"My God, Si. This is pretty amazing. I mean, very cool." I'm just bobbing my head in a nod, scanning the space, not sure where to look next but wanting to take it all in. I meet his eyes finally and he looks at me a bit skeptically. "I'm being serious, I mean it," I say a little too loudly, my voice echoing about in the the colossal hallowed halls. I'm annoyed that he thinks I might not be able to appreciate this.

"Alright, simmer down, no need to shout." He considers me for a moment. "Did you think I doubted you?"

"Maybe," I shrug. "You had a weird look on your face." He did, he was smiling a little, it was weird.

He shakes his head and smirks. "So on guard, all the time."

"What's that supposed to mean?"

"I had a weird look on my face? I swear, Lila, you look for a fight, don't you. Ready to roll at any given moment."

"You're an ass," I say and stick my tongue out at him.

He raises a finger to my lips. "Shh, put that thing away, are you twelve? We're in a church," he whispers, dropping his finger but holding his gaze on my mouth. "Show some grace."

"I think you like fighting with me," I say, licking my lips with his eyes still watching them.

"I think you're an instigator," he says, eyes back up to meet mine, that intense green looking ravenous for me.

I start taking steps backward, pulling him with me past one of the massive support columns from an arch. We round the corner, this space offering a smaller, cozy hall that runs alongside the main worship space, and I lean against the column. He responds immediately, cupping my face and swiftly leaning down to kiss me. His hands feel wonderfully rough on my cheeks, the stone behind me hard on the back of my head, but his mouth is all soft warmth, such a welcomed sensation. I love his mouth on mine, I can't help it. There's an excitement in his kisses, maybe because they're always unexpected and slightly inappropriate. I realize we've never actually kissed in total privacy, and I'm hoping I'll still like it as much when the thrill of being caught is off the table.

Though I have a feeling I absolutely will.

We stop to catch our breath and I take the moment to stare at the scars on Simon's face. I reach up to touch the one on his eyebrow, noting that it's like an exaggerated form of my own eyebrow marking. I like knowing that I can touch him without him saying anything. No dumb comment of "You should see the other guy," or even a rushed explanation. He just remains quiet and lets me explore the scar, smooth in that way that only scarred skin can be, and I replace my finger with my lips, kissing it gently with two soft presses.

"So," I say, stepping aside and turning back toward the main hall. "Have you been to this cathedral before?"

He joins me by my side and we continue our self guided tour.

"I have, Victoria took me as a child. I think I had been having a particularly bad day. Or bad week, more likely. She said a little escape was all I needed, and I remember driving up and seeing the cathedral sitting high on the hill in the distance like a castle."

"I thought the same thing," I say. "That it looked like a castle. Only I was clinging for dear life on your bike," I add with a laugh.

It was actually a pretty magical sight, and on the bike was an incredible way to experience it. I tell him so, feeling like I want him to know how much I appreciated it. That I'm not, like he said, looking to start a fight.

"I'm glad our getaway is off to a good start," he says. We continue wandering and he tells me about his attempts to draw the cathedral, looking at photos and using charcoal and creating these haunting images.

"Do you still draw?" I ask.

"Yeah, sometimes." He raises the camera that's dangling from the strap around his neck. "I'm better with photos."

I have this sudden curiosity to know what the space looks like through a lens. "Could I look? Zoom in up to the tower?" I ask. For a moment I'm worried he'll say no and be protective over his beloved tool, but then he releases my hand and reaches into the camera case. I watch with curiosity as he swaps out the lenses, putting a different one on that I assume will be better to zoom in with. He grabs the strap to pull over his head and hands me the camera. I'm nervous, like it's a delicate piece of porcelain and I've got butter on my hands.

He must see my apprehension because he drapes the strap over my head and positions the camera in my hand. "Here," he says, maneuvering my hold to get it right, situating the camera in my palm. "Like this, then you have a steady base."

I stare at the camera in my hand and feel like it's a sacred gift I've been given. This thing that makes Simon a "genius," apparently, now in my grasp. He makes a few adjustments while I hold it, telling me I'll just need to point and shoot now. Zoom in as I like.

I raise it up to my eye and peer through the viewfinder. I twist the lens to zoom in as much as possible, out of sorts at first with everything suddenly close up as if right in front of me. I twist and turn and finagle my way around until I find the tower and the incredible starburst pattern within the center. I'm torn between wanting to center and snap away, or do something more creative, more unexpected. I feel very exposed, knowing that a true artist will be the one downloading these photos. My finger remains on the trigger, but I don't press. I just look and explore, not feeling like any angle I have is quite right or worthy of capture.

"Take a photo, Lila," Simon commands.

I drop the camera from my eye. "No," I say, firing a look at him like he just commanded me to flash the group of people wandering up ahead. "I don't want to, I just wanted to look closer."

"Then why was your finger on the shutter button?" He crosses his arms over his chest, waiting for my answer.

"Habit," I say.

He juts his chin up in a head nod, prompting me. "Go on. Take some photos."

"No."

"Why not?" he says with a twitch of his mouth.

"Because." I bite my lip, contemplating what to say next. I opt for the truth since he seems to know exactly my hesitation. I sigh. "Fine. Because I'm not trying to have my photos judged by Simon the Genius Photographer."

He unwinds his arms and steps behind me, his chest to my back. His arms encase me as he guides my hands up, returning the camera to my face. His movements are gentle and slow, and I feel his breath on my neck as he whispers, "Look through and slowly move, scan around." I do as he says, the starburst filling the frame once again. "Find what speaks to you. Find whatever feels interesting. Don't overthink it. Just try to feel." His voice is so soothing in my ear, so intimate as he calmly coaches me. It's completely different from the condescending directions he gave me in the studio the day of our photo shoot.

I find a spot that I like where the center of the tower is in the corner of my frame, the bit of the starburst pattern shooting out like a firework pattern. "Good," he says. "Pause where you like, focus in where you want." I focus in, loving the way the spray of the curves move across the frame. "Now snap away," he says, and I feel the scratchiness of his facial hair on my neck as he places a kiss just along my jawline. It gives me a chill.

"You're distracting me," I say with a dramatic shudder.

"I should be saying that to you, Ms. Lila Ray. You are very distracting."

He places one final kiss on my shoulder before stepping back and giving me my space. And I do what he says.

I snap away.

seventeen

. . .

simon

THE SUN IS dropping lower in the sky as they make their way up to their final destination, a cozy Victorian cottage near the village of Old Hunstanton. The privacy appealed to him as opposed to a hotel with shared walls. The cottage boasted seclusion, a garden and patio, and Simon could hardly wait to finally do with Lila all the things he had been imagining these past few weeks.

She had been exquisite, absolutely exquisite holding his camera and doing her work. He liked watching and seeing that side of her. Her movements and mannerisms while photographing had been different than usual—a bit timid, almost. Patient and unrushed as she navigated her way exploring the octagon tower. Already he is looking forward to going through her photos with her, showing her what he looks for when selecting images, the composition and the way the eye moves from various points. Any emotion elicited in the captured picture.

Her agreement to join him this weekend had been a relief to him. It's clear they find one another attractive, that was evident right from the start. But it amazed him her initial reluctance when presented with the idea of getting to know one another. As if anything more than casual was a freakish request. It occurs to Simon that she may still feel that way, but at least she was here with him now. Simon was not one to share, and he had a feeling that once they had sex, he was not going to be nearly satisfied of her.

It had been interesting to see her get more comfortable when taking her photos. She quickly seemed to get a feel for the work, her eyebrows would furrow together between shots, the concentration on her face evident as she'd flip through the screen to view what she just captured. He noticed the way she mindlessly teased at the fringe on her forehead as she would think, or bite her lip and release a subtle "hmm" before raising the camera back up to her face. Something about her holding his camera, her delicate hands such a contrast to his own, as if she were cradling a baby bird—it was mesmerizing.

He could watch her all day.

They had wandered over to the stained glass museum and he once again was surprised at just how much she enjoyed the displays. He asked what she liked about it, and she said she liked the ones with people in them, describing them as "trapped souls, beautifully haunting."

Simon's mind had flashed to what Elsie would look like depicted in a stained glass window. His eyes played tricks on him with one piece in particular, a depiction of Virgin Mary. He suddenly felt as though it could be Elsie. Elsie's warm, sandy hair, wide eyes and rounded brows. The piece was the Assumption of the Virgin Mary, and Simon had looked at the Virgin's hands held out wide beside her, imagining Elsie's voice saying, "See there? I'm alright."

It was oddly comforting.

He pulls up to the cottage and parks, pleased with the site. There are overgrown trees framing the small building, a white stone wall providing privacy, tidy pockets of garden. They remove their helmets, he detaches the travel bag and they walk up to the small red door.

"Well, Si. I sure didn't expect all this," Lila says with a wave of her hand around as they find the hidden key and walk in. The place is cozy and clean, with white walls and cream colored carpet, dark wood furnishings, beige sofa and chairs. There's a fireplace equipped with wood and a small cake sitting on the table off to the side.

"What did you expect?" he asks as he sets down their things in the bedroom. She follows behind him, scanning and looking all around.

"First off, not a cute cottage. Back home when someone asks you for a beach getaway, it's straight to some very modern beach house or hotel room, then a quickie to commence the weekend, happy hour followed by bar hopping, bathing in the sun the next day while sweating out your hangover. That kind of thing."

"That sounds dreadful. And hot—temperature-wise, that is."

Lila nods. "You're kinda right, it is." She loops her arm into his with a squeeze. "I guess this will do," she teases.

"You don't mind the cold?"

"No, I actually love fall and winter the best. Bathing suit season used to horrify me—no one wants to see a boy's body in a bikini."

"And yet, you're keen on minding your calorie intake."

Lila gives his shoulder a little shove. "I ate French fries with you, remember that?"

"Vividly. I'd like to feed you more just to have the chance to watch."

"Mmm, would you now? I would let you. You should be flattered, you know. I don't usually like eating in front of anyone. Doesn't seem to bother me with you, though."

Simon's flattered by this. And curious. "Why do you think that is?"

Lila sits down on the edge of the bed, covered with a bleach white blanket. She bounces a little on it, smiling and nodding with appreciation. "Comfy," she says, and he's glad she finds it so. He plans to spend quite a bit of time with her in it. She looks back up to him and he leans against the doorframe, crossing one ankle over the other.

"You're surprisingly easy to be around, I think," she says with a sly smile. "With other people I'm in performance mode, what can I say? Just wired that way." She pauses. "And eating is just so terribly *human*." Lila's tone shifts as she says this, going from charming and flirty to cautious. Confessional, perhaps. "I end up stressing over how big of a bite to take to not make a mess and have food all over my face. It's dumb, I know, but I can't help it. I blame my parents, you know. They're very into being proper and used to tell me I chew too loudly or I wasn't using my fork and knife correctly or to sit up straight or all these other things presented as 'table manners' but it all just gave me anxiety. So I'd go and sneak snacks in my room, hide the trash under my bed until I got a chance to collect it and take it out to the trash bins. That was the start of my dysfunctional relationship with food, I later learned in counseling. A control tactic."

"You've been to therapy then?" he asks, pleased to hear this. He wonders how things might have been different if his own mother had tried to get help. Or Elsie, for that matter.

Lila nods. "Yeah, you got a problem with that?"

He smiles and shakes his head. "See? Always ready for a fight."

She smirks. "Mainly just with you. I'm nicer to other people." She pauses and pinches her eyebrows together. "Actually that's a lie. Maybe not always. I'm working on it."

"But you feel comfortable with me?" He wants to hear her say that she is. "Even when picking a fight?" He steps away from the doorframe and closer to her spot on the bed.

"Yeah." A shift in her expression and she's staring at him, dragging her hand seductively over her chest. Her flirtatious side returned. "Though I must admit," she says breathily, "it's probably because you can be such a dick." A wicked smile. "There's just no pretending with you."

"I'm not good at pleasantries."

"No shit, Sherlock," she teases with a raised eyebrow. "It's refreshing. Besides, I see through you just as you see through me."

"Yeah? How so?"

Her cat eyes stare into his with intensity as she reaches for his arm and pushes up his sleeve, exposing the black ink. "See? You wear a mask too. You cover your tattoos when in work mode, or even at that party where I'm guessing you wanted to have a certain conservative look."

"People too quickly judge a book by its cover," he says. Her fingers explore the art on his forearm, tender caresses on his skin as her fingertips trace along the curves of black ink.

"True. But you're well respected in the industry. And it's a creative world, no one would care about a man covered in ink like this."

"That's not why I tend to cover them." Lila's eyebrows shoot up with skepticism. "Really, judgment or not, I don't care about that. I cover them more out of privacy. What I don't like are the questions. What's this one for, why did you get it? What does it mean, that kind of thing. Tattoos are personal. It's bothersome when people want to know about them. I prefer to avoid the conversation all together."

"Why cover so much of your body in tattoos, then?"

He kneels down in front of her, pulling her in for a kiss before answering. "I was young and not thinking that far ahead." He kisses her again, no longer wanting to talk. It had been torture having her hang on to him for hours on end on the bike. Torture watching her during their stop, a stolen moment in the shadows of the cathedral not nearly enough for him. His patience has suddenly evaporated, and he's eager to touch her, for her to touch him, to do all the things to one another they have both been refraining from.

He breaks their kiss and rises up, walking over to the chair in the corner. He takes a seat and she looks at him with confusion.

"What are you doing?" she asks, puzzled by his retreat.

A smile slithers across his face. "Do you like to pleasure yourself, Lila?"

It's a beautiful sight to him, the startled look she reacts with. He gets himself comfortable in the chair, the cushion molding to his body.

"I'm human, so yes. Why?" she asks.

"Lean back then and show me," he says, nodding to prompt her.

"So I guess that's a no to the quickie, then?"

"That's a no to the quickie, correct."

He watches her face as she thinks about it. He enjoys seeing her out of her comfort zone. "And what do I get in return? If I let you watch me 'pleasure myself' as you say." She says the words with slow and seductive emphasis, and he's already hard at the husky sound of her voice.

"Believe you me, I'll make it very worth your while."

The room is quiet and thick with his proposition. There's a rustling of the trees outside the window, the hum of the heater, but aside from that, minimal noise to distract. Just the scent of fresh linens and the cozy quiet of the space.

Lila scoots herself back on the bed, removing her shoes and socks and placing them on the floor. The bed moans and squeaks as she shimmies herself and her eyes look down at the mattress, then back up to him. "You're serious? You really want me to just lay here and touch myself?"

"Yes."

"And you're just going to sit there and watch?"

He nods, watching her chest rise with heavy breathing.

"You're not going to photograph me or anything, are you?"

Simon places his elbow on the arm rest, resting his face in the L of his index finger and thumb. "I would never photograph you without your permission, Lila." Though he absolutely plans to get her permission for some in the future. He imagines her naked in the shower, skin slick with floral scented soap, steam wrapping around her body.

That will come later.

Lila nods, scooting all the way to the back of the bed, by the headboard. She peels the blankets back and settles herself in. Her movements remind him of the way she was earlier at the cathedral, taking photos. A little slow and unsure, but she progresses with a steady determination. He wonders if she's ever touched herself in front of anyone before, or if this is a new experience for her. She's a willing participant, but her attitude is a far cry from the vixen he first met, suggesting he be her boy toy.

"Are you going to give me instructions or anything?" she asks, pausing what looks to be the intention of removing her shirt.

He likes her asking questions, a turn from her usual demanding demeanor. "I can if you like," he offers.

She releases the hem of her shirt and rests her palms down on the mattress beside her hips. "Can we have some music or something? It's so quiet."

"No. No distractions."

"Are you into like, sub and Dom stuff? Is that what this is?"

He can't help but smile at her, his little fox that looks so uncertain, yet curious. Her cat eyes are narrowed at him. Daring, even in her questioning.

"I don't define anything so specifically, Lila. But yes, I prefer to be in charge." He drops the hand that had been holding up his head and clasps his hands together in his lap. "And I have a feeling that *you* will find far more power in allowing that, much more than you do when you attempt to take control." She nods, looking away, and he can see her wheels turning. "Don't over think it," he says. "Try and just relax and enjoy yourself. That's all this is, it's very simple."

She scoffs in a huff of disbelief, but says okay.

"Why don't you start by removing your shirt?" Simon instructs, and she returns her hands to the hem of her shirt, squeezing the fabric and pulling it over her torso, over her head. Once free from it, she surprises him by tossing it to him, and he catches the messy ball of cotton. He raises it to his nose and inhales the scent of Lila mixed with that perfume she likes. The one he told her he usually hates, but enjoys on her. He likes that she consistently wears it.

Her bra is blood red, with satin-smooth cups that he sees are likely heavily padded. He makes a note to suggest she go braless. "Unclasp your bra," he says.

She stretches behind her and does so, allowing the straps to fall down her arms, revealing two perfectly round breasts, nipples pink and perky as they meet the air. He wants very badly to put his mouth on them, to taste her and feel the beads of her erect nipples on his tongue.

"Beautiful," he breathes out mindlessly.

"Beautiful, yet you won't touch?" Her tone is teasing. "Such incredible restraint, our mastermind has."

"I'd rather watch you touch for now," he responds. "Go on," and he's pleased to see her oblige, grazing her own nipples with her fingertips, then circling around with a manicured nail. First one side, then slowly she drags her fingertips over her skin to the other side, circling once again. She rocks her hips slightly, likely without realizing it, and he's pleased to see her feeling arousal at her own hands. Ease even with his presence.

With eyes closed, Lila drops her head back, exposing the curve of her throat. "Fuck, this is so strangely hot, who knew," she says quietly, almost to herself. She opens her eyes and glances to the side, meeting his gaze. "Are you enjoying yourself?"

"Very much."

"Well what now, master oh master?"

"You may remove your jeans, but leave on your panties," he instructs.

"What if I'm not wearing any?"

Simon takes her shirt, still in his hands, and shakes it out before neatly folding it. He places it on the table beside him and leans forward, resting his arms on his thighs. "Then we'll improvise," he says, but he already knows she has some on, as the line had revealed itself to him on more than one occasion.

She swings her legs over the side of the bed, rises and unbuttons her jeans. Slowly, she moves the zipper down, then expands the fabric to reveal matching blood red panties, silk and lace. "Just kidding," she says, eyes held on his as she slides the jeans down her thighs, her calves, and steps out of them. The room is small and she's only inches in front of him now.

But he stays put.

"Good," he says. "Now sit down on the edge of the bed." She does. "Spread out your legs." Lila straightens her spine and presses her palms into her knees, moving them out wide with the confident expertise of someone doing a strip dance, feet arched and toes perched on the carpet.

"How's this, Genius Mastermind Si?" she says with a head tilt to the side. The triangle of red fabric between her legs is exposed to him perfectly.

"Now slip a finger beneath the fabric, from the side, not the top. By your inner thigh, that's good, yes. Like that. Now move it over, and you're going to graze over those lips, then back again." She does as he says, closing her eyes and sucking in a breath. "Back and forth, let the fabric touch you."

"Oh wow," she breathes out.

"And? How does that feel?" he asks, seeing how she's clearly enjoying herself.

"Like I've been underutilizing my panties," she says with a lazy smile.

"And to think you tried to block me. How much you would have missed."

With that she pauses her movements and opens her eyes to look at him. "I had my reasons," she says with seriousness.

"And where are those reasons now?"

She laughs and closes her eyes again. "Out the fucking window. Don't make me regret it."

She pulls her panties to the side completely, exposing her beautiful self to him, the area clean shaven, swollen and ripe. "I can't believe I'm doing this," she says, eyes still closed, but she maneuvers her fingers along herself, sliding down before dipping a finger in. He groans as he watches her, and she smiles, saying, "Hearing your tortured growl sure is fun, though."

"See? Power in relinquishing control." He leans back in his chair, unsure if he can stop himself from reaching out to touch her if he remains so close. His dick is throbbing, his pulse fast as he watches Lila touch herself. Her hips rock along with her movements, and Simon bites his fist as he sees her movements quicken, knowing she's getting close.

He considers if he should let her finish, or if he should put a stop to it. He was unsure if she would in fact be comfortable enough to reach an orgasm in this way, with him watching, and so decides she should get the reward for her hard work.

"Oh God," she says, dipping her head back further and grinding her hips. Her small breasts bounce in the air beautifully as she rocks into herself, and he groans again as he watches her orgasm, listens as she cries out "Fuck yes, oh my God, holy shit!" It's a sound that's beautiful.

But the sound of his own name from her lips will be even better.

eighteen

. . .

lucy

IT'S TIME TO face reality and I have absolutely zero desire for it. But ready or not, here it is.

"Do you want me to leave the room for any of this?" my best friend Reggie asks. She's all genuine concern and business, not asking from a place of discomfort. Her wild, strawberry blonde hair is tucked up in a ponytail, swinging around as she examines the room.

"No! Stay in the room, please. It's why you're here. It's not like I'm asking you to hold the wand. I'm already basically naked," I say, lifting the papery fabric of my disposable gown.

I'm not entirely sure of how far along I am so my doctor sent me for an ultrasound. Apparently this early on that involves a wand going up on a submarine search mission, not the sweet belly ultra-sounds I can expect further along.

Reggie is the only person I've told about being pregnant. Actually, my exact words were, "I took a pregnancy test and it came out positive."

I know I can trust her. Naturally, she asked why I wasn't telling

Justin yet or having him go with me, and this is exactly why I love Reggie. Because when I said, "Long story. I'm taking it one step at a time at this point and not really ready to get into it," she simply nodded and said, "Alright, then." We understand one another like that, and I'm not sure I've ever been more grateful to have her in my corner than I am right now.

The tech steps in, turns off the overhead lights and tells me to lay back and relax. I laugh, like relaxing will be at all easy to do in this situation. Reggie grabs my hand and I feel the press of the wand go on up and do it its thing, the pressure and unnaturalness of the whole experience so odd. Women really do deserve a medal for their contribution to the species. We may not be perfect, but fuck do we go through hell sometimes.

It's strange to say, but I miss Justin in this moment. I hate so much that he's not here, and I'm not sure how to feel about that reaction. It surprises me to say the least. He'd be so adorably awkward with the whole thing, cracking stupid jokes while I'd be scolding him, but secretly grateful for his comic relief. Ten bucks says he'd ask how the wand compares in size to him, I can just hear it now.

And then I think about the words from that screen, a sight I had seen a little over three months ago, but still the emotion is raw like it was yesterday.

"I had another dream about you last night. We lived on that island and had just gotten married."

My husband. Saying these tender words to a woman that wasn't me. It still hurts so incredibly much.

I look over to Reggie, and see the profile of her face as she's staring at the screen. She's smiling with fondness and her face tells me everything. "Well?" I ask. She blinks a few times and looks back down at me.

"Looks like James and Ronnie will have a Harris playmate," she says brightly, referring to her own two little ones. She kisses my hand a bunch of times, giddy for me, and returns her gaze back to the screen. I still can't bring myself to look.

I'm amazed when small tears form in the corner of my eyes. I'm unable to look yet, I'm still stuck on staring at the ceiling tiles and switched off fluorescent light. Nose scrunched at the stench of the clinical surroundings.

But I hear it. The little heartbeat. Bum-da-dum da-dum da-dum. A little life-force, beating proudly from right inside my body. I press my eyes closed and the tears fall down my temples, into my hair, dampness on my skin and ear. I release Reggie's hand to wipe them away, instinctively holding my breath to near dizziness.

"Ten weeks, three days, it looks like," the tech says. "Strong heartbeat already, that's good."

"How fast?" Reggie asks, and I'm so thankful she's here to be the voice for me. I'm frozen solid and just trying to remember to breathe.

"One fifty-two."

I see Reggie's ponytail swing as she nods. She looks back down at me, then the cloud of concern passes her eyes. "You going to look?" Her tone is soft and nurturing—she's been that nurturing type her whole life, long before kids—but it's odd to hear her use that tone with me.

I inhale sharply, slowly release and exhale while counting backwards from five. I don't know what I'm so nervous for. Hearing the heartbeat was more surreal than anything, what more can a grainy image on a screen do?

"Tell me a joke or something," I say to Reggie, once again wishing Justin were here, despite myself.

"Ahh, umm," she says, face in mock panic. "Got it. If corn oil comes from corn, where does baby oil come from?" she asks with less humor, more tentativeness.

I half laugh, half cry all at once. "My God, Reggie," I wail.

"What? I panicked!"

I shake my head, wiping my eyes and the strange tears cascading down like young, untrained soldiers having no idea where to go or why they're here. She pops up from her seat. I hear the rip of a tissue from its box, then she pops next to me and dabs at my face. I feel utterly pathetic and helpless.

"That was exactly the kind of joke Justin would make," I mutter. I take the tissue and dab my eyes again, and in the middle of my attempt to clean my face up, my eyes go to the screen.

There it is. My little blurb, dots for limbs kicking and punching already. A firecracker.

I swear to God, in that moment, the rest of the room freezes and blurs out, and it's just me and the screen. Right before my eyes, there it is. My little baby. A girl, I think. I just have a feeling, I just know it. And my heart grows about a thousand times bigger. My mind flashes through a cycle of memories to come—a healthy cry at birth, the scent of downy soft baby hair beneath my nose, a messy first birthday cupcake, a bike ride with a little girl and a massive helmet, a skinned knee, a soft hug, toothless grin, tear-stained face from a moment of hurt feelings from a friend.

I see it all flash before my eyes.

"Holy shit, I'm pregnant," I say out loud to the room.

It's the first time I've actually allowed the words to escape my mouth.

AS A KID I HAD all the Barbie dolls and Polly Pockets and goodies every little girl loves. But I also had a dress up suit jacket and sensible heels, imagining one day I'd be a lawyer, maybe later a judge, and I'd make the world a better place one sensible idea at a time. Ruth Bader Ginsberg was my personal hero, even if I did eventually realize I wasn't quite a selfless as her.

I've been known to be a combination of serious in my determination, but I also get the random desire to let my hair down and have a little fun now and then. It's all about balance, I figure. I work hard, I deserve to let loose when I can, though truth be told in recent months, years maybe—I hadn't been working so much on the fun part. Reggie and her husband were busy having babies, Justin and I were in a comfortable marriage routine, and work slipped in and took over.

I guess that's a little bit of the problem of how we ended up exactly here. How simple and beautiful life had been when I knew the balance between Barbie time and Suit Jacket time. How had I faltered and messed it all up?

I'm clutching my roll of ultrasound photos, walking into our house and dreading what I have to do now. Tell Justin. I'd kill for a glass of wine to take the edge off, but since that day at the cafe with Lila I've been forcing myself to face this truth and be the responsible adult I know I need to be. It's all seltzer waters and folic acid and decaf coffee for me. I told Justin I had a high blood pressure reading at a recent doctor's appointment when he questioned my change in morning habits. He only nodded, saying "cool," and poured himself his now decaf cup like it was no big deal.

I walk into the family room and see Justin sitting there on the couch, game controller in hand and screen filled with some car racing thing.

"Hi," I say, popping my purse in its spot on a hook by the side door, and he looks up guilty-like, instantly switching off the game. "It's okay, keep playing your game," I say, and he shakes his head and hops up like he's afraid he'll get in trouble.

"No no, I swore I was gonna be finished like ten minutes ago. I lost track of time." He presses a kiss to my cheek and I try not to tense. "How was happy hour?"

I had told him that's what Reggie and I were doing, that we were sneaking out of work a little early to grab some drinks and catch up.

More lies. So many I'm struggling to keep up. It's gotta stop.

I rub my temples and attempt to start the process to dig myself out. "Actually, Justin, I had her take me to a doctor's appointment."

"For what?" he asks. I instantly realize the mistake of those words. Now he thinks something's wrong and his concern is just making this whole thing ten times worse.

"Because I'm pregnant," I blurt out, unable to stand to wait a second longer. Amazing—just hours ago I was full fledged in denial and tip-toeing around anything that might even accidentally steer any conversation into a kid or baby field. Now here I am word vomiting like I can't hold it in. "I'm pregnant," I repeat with a sigh. I meet Justin's gaze to read his reaction.

It's a little bit tortuous to see the joy sweep across my husband's face as I tell him this news. All I can think about is how often I've seen that kind of joy on his face in the past.

Like when he first asked me out, and I told him no—but then I had a stupid relationship with a narcissistic lawyer, followed by a nasty break-up, (far too nasty for something that had only lasted a couple months). Then a run-in with Justin at the bar a few months later, and this time when Justin asked me again I told him yes. That look on his face said everything that I needed to know. It was filled with such pure, unfiltered joy. He didn't even try and hold it back or play it cool, he just announced to the bar that I said yes, and then people started asking me to see the ring, thinking he had proposed. He joked and said, "Give me one more week!" in that stupid, immature way of his and I think a part of me chose him right then and there. To see that kind of joy on a man's face, all because I agreed to go out with him, it felt downright exhilarating.

Then there was the joy when he really did propose (a year later, not a week), and I said yes. He knew I was going to say yes, I had basically made it clear to him that we'd be getting married soon, so he was far from surprised. But still—the joy on his face.

Then again on our wedding day, when I walked down the aisle and saw him at the other end. Looking so handsome and so genuinely happy. Justin's not really a sentimental kind of guy, he follows my lead on all things thoughtful and meaningful and what not. Presents and birthdays, how to word the perfect text and that kind of thing all fall on me. But his absolute happiness and joy when he saw me walking down the aisle—it was the best kind of look. Like he was still pinching himself that I chose him.

I think that's why it hurt so goddamn much when I first figured out the wicked emotional affair he was having. That he could feel something, a spark like that for a woman that wasn't me when I thought so firmly that I was his world—there are no words capable of describing that kind of hurt.

You see, I loved Justin so much. I still do, believe it or not. With him things had always been easy and sweet. He was the perfect companion for when I wanted to let my hair down, but always let me call the shots and have the final say on what and how or where.

And I thought his love for me was a guarantee. I felt secure with him, felt we had a little connection no one else did. Yin and yang, perfectly complementary and in sync. How stupid I was.

"I feel a connection with you, I can't help it."

I shudder away the image of those texts.

Still. The pain I'm about to cause him is not a punishment that matches his crime. But there's nothing I can do about that.

"You're pregnant?" He blinks at me through his grin. I nod and he rushes at me and wraps me in a bear hug that has me falling over, then he lifts me up off the floor and into a spin. When I land on my feet again, I can't even look into his eyes. I just think about how *that's* how this moment is supposed to go. That is what this magical thing is supposed to be like. I think about what a horrible, selfish person I am for being able to have this miracle in me, yet ruining the way it was all supposed to happen.

Justin drops down to his knees, pressing his lips to my belly and hugging my waist. "My boys can swim!" he says, and I bury my face in my hands, no longer able to contain the tears. I let out a sob and he rises back up. He tries to pry my hands from my face but I don't let him.

"Hey, Luce, hey. I know my jokes are dumb, but the tears? Really?" he says, trying to tease and lighten my mood, but he has no clue why I'm crying. I'm sobbing too heavily to form words, but I try anyway.

"It's not...It's just that..." and my face is back in my hands again, heavy sobs tumbling out, raining down. How I wish they were magic tears capable of cleansing sins. How I wish they were tears with a healing power, or a power to turn back time.

But they aren't.

Justin attempts to hold me and soothe. "This is a good thing, okay? It's exactly what we've needed, something to help us remember what we are, focus on this," he says with a squeeze. "This right here. Fuck everything else, it's you and me, baby. And this baby between us...You know, it's a fresh start." He's trying so hard to find the right words here, it's painfully sweet. My little optimist.

I nod my head automatically, but I don't know why. It's not a fresh start, and I know that. It's a fresh wound, that's what this is. I just don't know how to tell him.

I guess a thought pops in his mind and he releases his embrace, grabbing my shoulders instead. "Hey, is everything okay with it? With the baby?" he asks.

I wipe my tears from my face, attempt to collect my breath and stop my sobs, but all I can do is nod. "Yeah," I manage to eke out. "Everything's healthy so far," I say with a fresh flood of tears, and I squeeze my eyes shut and focus on taking a few deep breaths in.

Justin wipes my tears with the sleeve of his shirt, then drops his hands down to grab mine. "How far along are you?"

This is the moment where it's all going to crash for him.

Because the math won't add up.

This is it, right here.

I'll tell him how far, he'll be excited for a moment, mind probably going to when the due date must be.

But then he'll take a moment to realize that...wait. Something's off, that can't be right. That I can't be just ten weeks, because he and I hadn't had sex in months. Since a beach getaway in July, to be precise, that had ended in a massive fight that now seems so stupid, I barely even remember what the fight was about. Drinks were involved, far too many. *That* I remember. But the context? Who knows. Actually scratch that, I can pretty much guarantee it was work related.

And if that's the last time we had sex, and it's now October, and I'm ten weeks, then that sure is a dangerously close call.

He'll be confused, unsure of his calculations, of when exactly conception would have happened for a woman that is currently ten weeks. He might raise his head in a scratch, a little shy at having to even ask, but now having an awful, nagging feeling that something's not quite right. But he'll be consumed with his own guilt of his own indiscretions and therefore unsure how to even approach me with his doubt or questioning. He may even keep it to himself, then silently sneak off and do some Google searches on his phone to check.

What a unique kind of torture it will be when he's *still* not entirely sure. I can just see him scrolling through the calendar on his phone, counting backwards from now, landing to the ten weeks, but then minus two, having learned on Google that a pregnancy is calculated as a start date on the first day of a woman's last period, two weeks *before* conception. Meaning it's really more like I'm only eight weeks, and that for sure isn't math he wants to learn. He'll scroll and count those weeks, and drop his phone in horror. Because he'll know at that point. He'll know what I did.

Yes, what a God awful torture that would be.

I decide to save him from it, even though the alternative isn't a whole lot better.

"Justin," I say. "I'm ten weeks, and it's not your baby."

nineteen

. . .

lila

I DON'T KNOW about you, but I've definitely never full fledged masturbated with someone watching. And I mean, I'm no stranger to fun sex. I've fucked in beds, I've fucked on dressers (or beside them, as you've now learned), I've fucked in restaurant hallways and fucked in cars with my long limbs working against me but still enjoying the immediacy of it.

But I've never done what I just did with Simon. I've never played with myself with someone watching like that.

There was something wonderfully intimate about the whole thing, it's wild. I'm pretty sure I've had a guy ask me to before (hell, maybe even Royce, but I shudder to think about that). But I can say with absolute certainty I never went for it, instead probably choosing to take matters into my own hands and direct the course of what me and the flavor of the month guy were going to do that was most certainly not me spread out and touching myself for their enjoyment.

And I'm trying to figure out why, exactly. I guess the idea of it prior to today was just entirely too vulnerable, if I'm being honest.

Me time has always been just that—*me* time. Not to be shared. I've never really cared to share that with anyone else.

Yet when he asked, when Simon made it clear that was his plan for me, I had this little spark of curiosity come to life. I *wanted* to do this thing in front of him. Almost to prove that I could, not just for him, but for myself. I wanted to prove that I could be that comfortable in my own skin to do all the things that I needed to reach the coveted pot of gold at the end of the orgasm rainbow. It is such an open and out there thing, for some reason. To get into the pleasure of it you absolutely have to get out of your head, which means not thinking about how your body is positioned and if you're carrying yourself in a way that highlights all your best angles. It's exposing the hungry way you move your hands on yourself, the moans that accompany it, all of it. Now that I'm on the other side of the experience, I highly recommend it. Find someone you feel some semblance of trust and comfort with, and go for it.

Because I gotta say, I've never felt more sexy, more *connected* with my body in my entire life.

Maybe it's the "fuck-it" mentality I've been embracing more and more, this new relinquishing of control that I'm kind of all about. I mean shit, if Lucy's marriage can be in trouble, and with my whole life plan of modeling quickly rising and morphing to acting, then what the hell am I clinging onto anyway? Why not let Simon the Hot Nerd watch me fuck myself? Saying no almost felt like a loss, and I wanted to win.

So I did.

I'm not really sure exactly what it is about him that's got me so off kilter, all my usual tactics with men totally out the window. I think it's just that he's so different from any other man I've known. He's not the polite but boring type, or the sales charm that quickly gets old and annoying type. He's not the asshole that says dumb shit like "It's not cocky, it's confident" or the lost puppy dog that wants to follow you around everywhere type. (Those you need to drop right away, just a heads up. They fall in love way too easily.)

Simon's in a class of his own, and it feels different. Like a challenge. One I'm not backing down from.

I fully expected him to rip off my panties after my little performance and do all the fun dirty things to me, but he didn't.

Instead, he fed me the cake that the cottage hosts left. And yes, I ate it, a whole damn slice because it was really, really good. This classic vanilla sponge cake with maybe a touch of lemon in it, and that shit melted in my mouth and I was moaning all over again. I didn't even count my bites. I give that credit all to myself, by the way, not Simon. He may be challenging me in new ways, may be helping hold me accountable on healthy calorie intake, but it's me all the way that's pulling the trigger. He doesn't get an ounce of credit for that.

And now we're all bundled up, the sun low and the breeze kicking in, and we're hiking along the beach. Holding hands. Looking like any old sweet little couple, I bet.

There was an adorably quaint light house, we snapped a few photos there. Now we're making our way down a sandy path flanked by scraggly greenery, and Simon tells me the best is yet to come.

He's right. We make it down to the beach and I look ahead to see these cliffs towering above like a majestic wall of a statue. It's a slice that's cut just right into the land, exposing a raw edge of layers, the base a vibrant fiery orange, then a near perfect line where the orange stops and the rest is topped with white. It's a crazy beautiful look. I inhale deeply and take in the salty scent combined with mineral and sea. No matter where you are in the world—no matter how different this particular beach looks with its insane sunset-orange cliffs that are so entirely different from the easy sands and boardwalks of beaches I grew up on—that sea smell is familiar and comforting.

"What makes the color change?" I ask him. "On the cliffs?" I assume he knows, of course he must know.

"The red comes from staining by iron, but both the red and

white of the rock are limestone. Which means once upon a time the climate here was much warmer, as limestone is generally formed in tropical regions."

I nod, intrigued and trying to imagine this chilly day feeling as warm as a palm tree filled area might feel. Which seems all wrong, I can't imagine it. I much prefer this climate instead. It's like a cleanse took place, leaving just these cliffs, the very best left behind.

"A shedding of the unfitting," I say, and Simon looks at me quizzically. "The cliffs," I explain. "The best part of the beach kept here, but the stifling heat long gone. I like that. It feels like what I'm doing."

"Not losing your heat, I hope."

"Oh please, I think you see all my heat just fine."

"Yes, I very much do," he says, pushing his sunglasses further back on his face. "I'm kidding, go on. What you're doing?"

I nod and he releases my hand to pick up his camera. He zeros in on me and I turn my head to the side, knowing my profile will run along parallel with the cliffs. I continue talking as he photographs. "I'm shedding in my own way. It's what your twenties are all about, right?" I hear the snaps of the shutter and I imagine my face in the circle of Simon's lens, surrounded by the wall of rock behind me.

"What are you shedding?"

I turn my face to look directly into the camera. "Why the old mask, Si. A protective layer that I'm learning to leave behind." A gust of wind blows and I know my hair is looking wildly insane, but I don't care. I pull only the pieces that are sticking to my lipgloss, no attempt to control the rest, and I grin into the camera. Not the goofy grin I did with Lucy and the peacock, but a real one that amazingly seems to elevate my already good mood that much more.

Simon snaps, then drops the camera. He marches a couple long strides over to me, shoves my hair back from my face and kisses me, his tongue invasive in my mouth. I laugh into his kiss, teeth clanging, my cold nose against his warm cheek feeling so right.

We pause our kiss and I laugh again. "You're not a man of many words, but you sure know how to express the right things."

His gorgeous emerald eyes look at me, scarred eyebrow arching. "I'm happy you can hear those things, Lila."

MY BELLY IS THIS STRANGE ball of flutter as we get back to the cottage, him finishing a cigarette and me finding that I very much love the smell of his curious tobacco habit. He smokes pretty minimally, I've learned, just two or three a day. When I asked him why he rolls his own, he said it started back when he was broke, and this option was cheaper. Now he simply appreciates the quality and the ritual of smoking his own "Rollies," as they are apparently called. He has zero plans to stop, which is interesting to me.

"Don't you fear lung cancer?" I had asked, and he had shaken his head no.

"I ride a motorcycle. A freak accident on that is far more risky. What's a little smoke?" I loved his straight-forward answer, so unapologetic in his vice.

We step inside our temporary lodging and remove jackets and boots, shake out the sand, do all these very domestic things. I head to the bathroom, go pee and take a glance at myself in the mirror. I'm a windblown mess but aside from a quick finger-comb of my hair and a dab of lipgloss, I let it be. It is what it is. I suck in a big old breath and exhale before heading back out and to the kitchen.

My bare feet pad across the carpet of the bedroom, then out to the cool floors of the kitchen, my belly flipping right along with each step. I've never felt so oddly nervous like this, and it's all because I'm pretty sure Simon and I are finally, finally going to have sex. Enough with the build up, already. I need to see this man's penis (oh my God, I haven't even seen it yet?), and now I'm freaking out because what if it's super small or crooked or something and that's why he's taken all this time?

No. I've seen him in gym shorts. It's not small. Like, at all.

Maybe he's worried I won't be able to take it?

Oh my, I'm losing my mind.

I mindlessly wander up to Simon and he grabs my hand, startling me out of my thoughts. "Hey, you alright?" he asks. I look at him in his black long sleeve shirt, dark jeans, bare feet, maze tattoo on his neck screaming to let me do delicious things to it.

"Um, yes! Yes. What now?" I smile in a way I hope is flirtatious, but I fear might be more maniacal.

Simon drops my hand, smiling mischievously but backing away from me. "Why don't you pour us a drink?" he says, nodding toward the kitchen counter.

I laugh nervously. "We should have brought tequila."

"Ask and you shall receive. Open the cupboard."

I step forward, passing him to do so. I open one door, see glasses and pull two down. I open another and sure enough, a delicious looking bottle glimmering invitingly looks back at me. "How would you like—" I start to ask, turning around to question him, but Simon's disappeared. I hear him shuffling around in the room so I decide to look for some ice in the small freezer, thankful when I open and see a tray with little blobs of frozen cubes. I pull it out and drop it on the counter. My hands are still freezing so I rub them together before resuming my work.

I'm tempted, like really tempted, to take a quick shot to calm my nerves. Why am I so nervous for this? It's far from my first time.

But I decide against it. I want to be present for this, so I pop the cubes in the glasses, hearing a delightful *ting* as they drop in, and then pour a conservative amount of the tequila in each glass. I vaguely remember telling him at some point that it was my drink of choice, and I'm flattered he remembered. I see a couple green limes as well (he thought of everything!) so I shuffle around to find a cutting board. After slicing and squeezing the juice in the glasses, I lick the tart juice off my fingers.

I hear his footsteps behind me, but before I have the chance to turn around I feel fabric on my eyes.

Oh my.

I gasp a little, then hum and instinctively reach up for the blindfold covering my face. He's behind me, securing a tight knot and I can smell the masculine pine and tobacco scent on him. I feel his fingers on my hair by my neck, pulling strands aside. I hear his low voice whisper in my ear, "Come up with a safe word, Lila," and fuck if my belly doesn't do a thousand more cartwheels at that. My heart's pounding in my chest with anticipation, and a throb pulses between my legs.

I laugh out loud, though. I can't help it. "You're kidding. A safe word? For real?" I bite my lip, fighting the urge to say something smart.

"Yes."

"Why, because you're going to cause me so much pain? Are you planning on whipping me?"

"No. It's because I'm going to cause you so much pleasure, you'll need a safe word to tell me to stop." I feel his lips on my neck, the gentle scratch of his scruff and a flush of heat passes over my entire body. "I was thinking about you touching yourself that whole time on the beach." Another kiss. "And now." A kiss. "I can no longer keep myself from you, Lila. I've imagined being inside you a hundred different times."

"Only a hundred?" I breathe out.

He growls a low grumble and I feel a small bite on my side, just above my hip. "A safe word," he repeats.

I whimper out and grip my hands so tightly on the edge of this counter I think I might bleed. "Why don't I just say 'stop'?" I whisper.

He grazes his nose up my back, along the back of my neck, through my hair, moving his face from one side to the other. Once again I feel his fingers move aside my hair to expose the skin of my neck, and he kisses again. I press my back into him, against his chest, wanting so much more than this tease he's giving me.

"Safe. Word. Lila."

"I..." I can barely concentrate, all because of a damn blindfold that's igniting the rest of my senses and the simple act of his lips on my neck. "I'll just say stop."

With an abruptness he presses his body more firmly into mine, pinning me against the counter, my hipbones digging in. "No. That's not enough. Sometimes when pleasure is so good, we can say 'stop' because the word is right there. But we don't really want to stop. If we can push through, we can reach pleasure of levels we'd never imagined." He grabs both my wrists and pins them behind me, a thing I'm gathering he really likes to do, and I really like him doing it. My wrists pinned in his one hand, I feel his other on my throat, his touch firm and so incredibly erotic. He whispers in my ear. "And I plan to give you pleasure of that level. So...Your safe word," he commands.

I can't even think straight because I'm already dizzy just in this compromising position here in this darling little cottage kitchen. I imagine the sweet little old couple that must be our hosts, baking us that lovely cake, leaving us lovely teas.

And here we are, defiling the place with blindfolds and tequila I haven't even sipped yet and safe words. "October," I blurt out. It's all I can think of. The goddamn month we're currently in. I'm sure there's something more clever or sexy, "red" or whatever the standard is, but it's all I got.

"Good. October, then," he says. He removes his hand from my throat but leaves my wrists in his grasp. I feel his body lean over to the side for a moment, then back again directly behind me. Then something cool on my lips. "Open," he commands, and I do. I taste the lime slice on my tongue, laced with...the tequila, I realize. He must have dipped it in the drink before placing it on my lips.

It's fucking delicious. I'm amazed at just how heightened all the rest of my senses are, having now lost the sense of sight. I suck and moan in appreciation, loving everything happening in my body right now, at the hands of this man. I don't have to do a single thing, it's like there's no work involved at all. Just let go and experience, feel all these sensations, and it's magical. A sense of ease and relief like no other sexual encounter I've ever had before.

He removes the lime from my mouth and then moments later I feel his finger in my mouth, the taste of lime and tequila on it. I swirl my tongue around, then he replaces his finger with his thumb, and I repeat.

I hear a bird tweet outside the window and smile at the sweetness of it. Can this bird see what's happening in here? Does it sense the thick air of sexual tension? I smile and ask Simon his thoughts on it.

"A bird is the farthest thing from my mind," he grumbles out, and I laugh in appreciation.

He reaches a hand up my shirt, straight up to my bare breast and grazes my nipple ever so softly. "Well done, you took my advice," he says.

"The bra was uncomfortable, that's all. I did it for me, not you," I say, and he squeezes hard on my nipple. I cry out, loving the sensation. I drop my head back into the crook of his shoulder, wanting to melt my whole body right into his.

"Sly little fox, you are," he says, releasing my nipple to fully cup his hand over my breast, pressing me into him. He walks us backward and out of the kitchen. I'm disoriented but completely devoid of resolve to attempt any control, just blindly allowing him to guide us wherever. I feel the floor on my feet change to the cushion of the carpet, my indication that we're now in the bedroom.

He releases me and I hear the sounds of fabric, then a strong whiff of his scent within the tiniest gust of air consumes me. I think he's in front of me now, but I'm not sure. I feel him reach for my hands and he presses them up against his chest. There's bare skin and a sprinkle of chest hair beneath my palms. He drops his own hands, leaving mine on his torso, and I tentatively explore his skin, his shoulders, his biceps. I imagine the black ink on them and smile.

"I like your skin," I tell him, not even caring that that's a funny sounding line.

He says nothing, just kisses me briefly before pulling my shirt over my head, careful not to disturb my blindfold. He unbuttons and unzips my jeans and pulls them down along with my panties. I'm completely naked now, and I feel him gently guide me backwards. The back of my legs hit the bed.

"Sit," he instructs, and I do. My bare ass feels the smooth fabric of sheets. The original blanket top must be off the bed. "Further back," he says, and I scoot my body back a bit, then more until he tells me to stop. "Now lie down," he says, and I do.

For a brief moment I wonder how I must look, naked and blindfolded on this bed like a mannequin in a box waiting for its next assignment. Generally I'd be trying to find my just-right sexy position to lay in, trying to make wicked eye contact, all flirtatious body language in my role. But not here. I'm just lying here, totally at Simon's mercy.

He pulls one hand up and over my head, and I feel the scratchy fabric of some sort on my wrist, then a tight wrap around it. I reach up and can feel the same fabric on my knuckles, and I realize it's some sort of industrial strap. I wrap my hand around it and pull, wondering where it's attached as there weren't any poles or rails on the headboard.

He wraps up my other wrist, then I feel his hands on my ankles, all callused and warm. With a jerk, he yanks my ankles apart, spreading me out like a starfish and I feel a flood of warmth between my legs. I realize I must be soaked, completely soaked already. I feel the same wraps around each of my ankles, now completely confused as to how he's doing this, but loving every single minute of this chance to let go and just let him take the lead.

It's exhilarating.

"You remember your safe word?" Simon asks, and I nod,

bracing myself for what might be coming next. A slap? A tickle of leather whip tassels on my belly? Or will he just slide up on me, enter me and fuck me just like this? I have absolutely no idea.

I hear him rustle around and the anticipation is killing me. I can't wait to feel whatever he has in store for me next. I'm ninety-nine percent sure I'm never again going to enjoy sex as much as I'm about to.

He turns on some music, a soft instrumental of some sort. Then I feel his hands on my shins, sliding up to my thighs, and I moan in appreciation of the contact.

He climbs onto the bed and slides up next to me and by the feel of skin, I think he's naked now. I feel his fingers on my jaw as he turns my head toward him.

"Open your mouth, Lila. You're going to suck my cock," and my toes instantly curl because I am *giddy* with excitement to feel him in my mouth. He's British, which means he's likely not circumcised, a first for me. I do as he says and feel the massive cylinder of skin in my mouth—

And metal.

I instinctively grasp onto the straps by my hands, alarmed at the newness of the feeling in my mouth and on my tongue. It's not just the size that has my head spinning, it's the small, hard dots, four in total, two on either side. I run my tongue in between and feel the skin, raised in ridges at the two bars that run beneath the surface.

A Jacob's ladder? Two piercings is what I'm feeling, one right on top of the other and just below the head of his penis. Yes, that's exactly what this is. I've seen pictures, never the real thing, but in the photos those were spaced out like actual rungs of a ladder. These aren't quite that, but the concept is there.

Simon's patient with me as I let my tongue and mouth do all the exploring for me. It's wild to learn of this little hidden gem of his cock in this way, with only my mouth, no visuals to aid me. Wild, and yet so tender at the same time. It's the way it is with Simon. My icy hot—sturdy and nerdy one minute, wild fire the next. Here's this man with his cock in my mouth, two piercings that threw me for such a loop, and he's all calm patience as he lets me get comfortable with the newness of it all.

Naturally, it doesn't last. He slowly starts rocking deeper into my mouth. With me strapped down and blind like this, there's not much I can do except take him in as deeply as possible, sucking and moaning as I go. I think briefly how I'd even be able to say "October" right now. I mumble it out without even thinking, the word basically a bumpy road of a gurgle, completely indiscernible I'm sure, but immediately Simon stops and pulls his cock out of my mouth.

I miss it. I feel horribly empty and vacant. "I didn't mean it," I say, opening my mouth like a hungry and helpless creature desperate for food. "I was just testing it, I didn't mean it. How did you even understand?" I ask to the darkness.

"I told you to name your safe word. You did, so I stopped. That's how this works, Lila."

I wriggle my limbs in their traps, my body so fucking eager for more action, more play, more *anything*.

But he moves away from my head.

And down. In one swift move, I feel his mouth on me between my legs, hot and frantic and immediate, and within thirty seconds of his greedy pursuit I'm coming apart in red hot waves. Just like that, so instantaneous. This orgasm has been building for what feels like hours, though really it's probably only been about fifteen minutes. Since he first put the blindfold on me and ignited all my other senses. But it's ripping through my body now in exquisite torment.

"Fuck, stop, I can't. Fuck!" I scream out, squeezing my thighs together the tiniest bit that I can with the minimal slack of the straps around my ankles, willing him to stop because it's too much. I'm blind with the intensity of this orgasm, but he doesn't stop. If anything, he further pushes his mouth into me with relentless force between each and every on fire spot of that oh so sensitive spot between my legs, and I'm fucking dying at the intensity of this feeling. "Stop!" I shout out again, trying to squeeze my thighs on his head, the sensation too much to handle. I feel it deep in my belly, and I grip the straps by my hands, my body writhing.

October. That's what I'm supposed to say, it occurs to me. Say October and he'll stop. October, that stupid word I blurted out, laughing at the ridiculousness of it, that's my ticket out of this fucking unbearable sensation of his mouth riding between my legs, gorgeously torturing me.

But I don't. Instead I writhe my body and attempt to withstand this dagger hot sensation, accept the challenge of this cresting tsunami of a wave. I writhe in attempt to expel the energy bursting within, my body exploding with pleasure so intense it's torture. I cry out a thousand obscenities over and over and over again, before finally screaming out "*Simon*" in a moan so loud, any other time I'd be embarrassed. But there's no room for it here, it's the only thing I can do, my only tool to handle this orgasm that's beyond any climax I've formerly thought I've experienced. It might as well be named something completely different.

I take it, screaming out uncontrollably, powerless to stop it as screaming is the only way to withstand. Just like he wanted me to, like he knew I could if just given the little reminder to go one step beyond a basic "stop" command. I take it and ride this impossible thing the absolute best I can.

Until I finally shout out, "Simon! Fucking October!" gasping for air like I just finished a marathon.

He stops.

But I'm already shattering into a million beautiful glittering pieces, never to be the same again.

twenty

. . .

lucy

JUSTIN AND I have been in a limbo of existence since my confession. I feel a sense of relief at no longer holding it in, but now there's other questions up in the air. All on pause for right now as neither one of us seem to know what to do. So like I always do, I've avoided by focusing on work.

And find that I secretly hope Justin will just go and fuck Dr. Gabby, if he hasn't already, so that we're even. So that I'm not the only monster.

That's how completely fucked up everything is right now. I'm wishing my husband would sleep with another woman.

Except that I really don't, given how much he actually *cares* about her. That much is clear. Them fucking wouldn't just be fucking, would it? No. It might even be making love, and I'm fooling myself if I think I could actually be okay with that. Him touching her, slowly undressing her, exploring her body. Him relishing in the softness of her skin. Him looking into her eyes as he pushes himself into her, joining bodies with the intensity of all their pent up emotions for one another. My Justin. Another woman.

I'm nearly sick with the thought.

And I realize that's nothing like the quick and dirty fucking I allowed with Carter.

I sigh heavily and walk out of the meeting, having avoided eye contact with Carter the entire time. I've ignored his texts and his calls, and he got the picture, finally ceasing to reach out. I'm so incredibly thankful that this week is apparently his last one here. He's moving onto some big shot corporate company somewhere. He sure didn't last long here, I think bitterly. Funny how just a couple months ago he was the new guy everyone was excited to be working with, and pretty quickly people began to slowly find him unnerving.

I blame myself for bringing him on.

At some point I know I have to tell him. It's his baby, he's the father, and he has a right to know. Will he want to be in the baby's life? Will he take me to court for joint custody? I wonder how that would even work, I can't imagine he'd want to take care of a baby on his own. I barely do and I'm its mother—it's growing inside me. But what about later, when the kid is older, will Carter want to have a constant fatherly role then?

Fuck, fuck, fuck, I hate that I have hitched my wagon to this epic mistake in this way.

I walk into my office, close the door behind me and sink into my chair, slipping off my heels as I do. My lip is trembling, yet another goddamn round of tears threatening to cascade down, but I'm hell bent on holding it in. I just need to focus on work and on the zillion tasks that I've been slipping on. One step at a time. I can handle this.

A knock on the door interrupts me. "Come in," I say and to my surprise, in walks my husband. His auburn hair is trimmed, face clean shaven, professional in his slacks and polo shirt, but he looks like shit. His eyes have a dullness to them accompanied by a greenish tinge of shadow beneath. He's been sleeping in the guest room and we've barely spoken to one another since I broke the news to him a few days ago.

He steps in with a bag of food, and the smell instantly has me fighting down a gag. I catch a corner stain of grease seeping through the brown paper and I'm done for. I rise up, barefoot and all and rush past him, down the hall to the ladies room. I throw open the door and just barely make it into the trashcan, unable to get to an actual stall. All I can think is that now the poor custodian is added to the list of casualties of my mistakes by having to clean out this bin. Actually no, scratch that. I'll take it out myself, I decide. Yup, I will.

I finish up, rinse cold water on my face and wash out my mouth, and I make my way back to the trash bin. With a wet paper towel I wipe around the sides where chunks of this morning's banana and oatmeal made their way, then toss the towel in before pulling with a tug on the bag. It's heavy, so freaking heavy and my little bird arms haven't lifted a weight in far too long.

I need leverage to pull this thing out, so I lift my wrap dress up, lift a leg and plant a bare foot on the wall and finally free the damn thing, praying no one walks in on me doing this. I tie it up and head back out into the hall, bumping into Justin.

"Are you okay?" he asks, looking first at me, then down to the bag in my hands. "What are you doing?"

"I'm taking out the trash."

"Why? And where are you shoes?"

"At my desk," I say, chin held high like this is all very natural. It feels odd to have my husband see me like this, here in my office with my very respectful job, barefoot holding a clear, industrial looking trash bag you only see in bathrooms with fluorescent lights, about to walk out and roam around to find the dumpster. "Would you mind grabbing them for me? My shoes, you know so I can take this outside?"

He pinches his eyebrows together in confusion and maybe even a little concern. In our house, Justin is generally the trash removal person, not me. Not that I *never* do it, it's just that I'm the type to push it down as best I can, hoping he'll be the one to take out the trash, and generally speaking it pisses him off enough so that I never have to. That sort of morphed into trash being a Justin Job. So this must be quite the sight.

Justin nods, turning around down the hall and towards my office, and I'm standing there holding the bag. A co-worker walks by, looks at me a little startled and I smile and nod like there's nothing weird about me standing here.

Justin returns with my shoes and drops them to the floor for me. I wobble a little slipping them on and he offers out his hand for support.

"Do you want me to take that out for you?" he asks.

"Nope, I got it," I insist, now strangely hell bent on doing this task on my own. "I'll be right back."

A few minutes later, hands washed vigorously, mint in mouth and some composure regained, I walk back into my office. Justin is sitting on one of the club chairs, no sight of the food anywhere. I smell my perfume and realize he must have found it in my purse and sprayed.

I close the door and take a seat not in my usual chair behind the desk, but at the club chair beside him. Once again I slip off my shoes and I curl my legs up under me. He scans the look of me, probably wondering if I've gone mad, sitting in my office like this.

"I uh, I put the food in the break room. Didn't seem like you reacted too well," he says with a side smile. "Unless that was because of me."

"Thank you. And no, it wasn't because of you." I smile too at my husband, sitting here in my office, looking so out of place. "So," I say with a sigh. "What brings you in?" It sounds stupid, even to me, but I'm too tired to think about anything better to say. My energy has been nonexistent.

Justin shrugs. "I'm not really sure, actually. I just figured we could start with sharing a meal in a public space where you're less likely to kill me. Or me you," he snorts.

"I don't know, I think you've missed a key piece. Domestic homicides often happen with angry husbands or exes storming into work. Statistically it's right on track."

He stares at me unblinking, like he's not sure what to say. I prompt him with a "What, go on?"

He clears his throat nervously. "I ugh…I really want to crack a joke about heading back outside and then storming back in here, looking all disheveled and on a rampage to play the part, but I'm scared you're going to get pissed at me if I do."

I sigh, thinking about what he just said. He's right. Once upon a time I loved his idiotic and wildly inappropriate jokes. I'd laugh and scold him, playfully giving him a shove or something like that. It was almost a bit that we did I guess. He says something dumb, I scold him, we share a little affectionate smile.

These days I'm far more serious and annoyed with him. Never even noticed the change.

"You're right. I would have given you a hard time."

We both just kind of nod at each other, so much said in that little observation. The shift between us from fun and foolish to stony serious.

"I miss you, Justin," I finally say, filling our silence.

"You do?" There's so much surprise in his face, at the idea of me missing him that I'm filled with even more guilt.

"Yeah. I really really do. When Reggie took me to the ultrasound, I asked her to say a stupid joke. Like you would have done."

"And? Did she deliver?"

I give a half-hearted shrug. "She did actually, she asked if corn oil comes from corn, where does baby oil come from; it was very on brand for you."

The tiniest little light flickers in his eyes. "I didn't know she had it in her, huh. I'm proud."

"I knew you would be."

I'm tempted to grab his hand, to reach for him and connect in some way, but I'm not sure I should. He's the one who came here, though. Was it to try and make amends?

"So you've seen the baby?" he asks.

I nod.

He looks away and out my office window, through the slats of cheap blinds and out to the parking lot. "I just thought it was a normal doctor's appointment. I guess I didn't realize you had an ultrasound."

"I wasn't exactly sure of the timing so my doctor ordered me one." I try and read his face, but it's hard to. He doesn't look angry or sad or hopeful or anything. He's just staring blankly.

I take a chance and reach for his hand. "Justin, do you think we can survive this?" I ask, attempting to find a courage in my voice that I'm not entirely sure exists. "Try for counseling, work on things and save the marriage?"

Still, nothing from him. He's not even looking at me. His hand lays flat in my palm, no attempt to curl around mine. I continue on anyway. "Because I want to, I want to try. I love you, Justin, and this is worth fixing. Right? We got caught up in the wrong things, lost track of us. *I* lost track of us," I add, attempting to take ownership as the one who crossed the ultimate line.

He nods. "I know that, and I agree. I do."

Relief washes over me at that spark of hope he just extended.

"I just don't think I can do it though, Luce. I mean, I can't raise someone else's kid." He turns his head back my way and looks me directly in the eyes.

I suck in my lips to attempt to hide the quiver, but my chin gives me away. The tears well up and I hold in a breath, knowing I'm one blink away from them falling.

"I'm sorry," he says with a look so tender I can't even be angry. I wish I could be angry. What a wonderful relief anger would be from the anguish I feel instead. But there's none.

Justin pulls his hand from mine. "I'm so sorry, but I just don't see myself doing that, trying to be a — a dad to it. Raise someone else's kid, it's just…" Justin's handsome face is crumpled up in his own kind of agony, and I realize I never even considered what exactly I'd be asking him in giving us another chance. That I'd be asking him to raise the baby that was the product of my abominable actions. I only thought about his forgiveness, of trying to put it all behind us. But it can't be put behind us, can it? It's impossible when proof of it, the reminder of it is growing inside me as we speak.

I can't say I blame Justin for feeling this way. Could I if the roles were reversed? Help raise a kid that was his with someone else, someone he cheated on me with? If he and Dr. Gabby had slept together and she got pregnant, would I be able to openly have the kid over and bake it cookies and do tuck ins and what not? I want to say I could, but I guess that's the kind of thing easier said when it's only in theory.

And when you have a clear bias.

Justin sniffs his nose loudly and wipes at his face from a tear that managed to escape. I watch him pinch his nose and look up for a moment—at what, I don't know.

I try and scoot closer to him, gently touching his arm. "And if I terminated?" He looks back over to me, eyes narrowed. "The pregnancy. What if…what if I terminated, and we just tried to move past all of it. Start fresh and start again. It's not too late, I'd have to decide as soon as possible, but it's not too late." Even as I speak, I hate the words so much because I know I'm a monster for saying them.

But I have to know. I have to know if that would change things for him. For us. "Would you be willing to try then?"

Justin rubs his nose once more before dropping his head down with a shake. "I don't know, Luce. You can't put something like that on me. That's not my choice to make."

"I know it's not," I say, my voice pleading. "That's not what I'm asking. I'm just trying to see if you even see another chance with me. That's all I mean. I'm not saying I would even do it, I'm not sure that I could, but what I want to know is if this wasn't a thing," I mindlessly place my hand on my belly, "if this wasn't part of the equation, would you be willing to give me a second chance? Could you forgive me?"

The air is thick with his silence. There's phones ringing outside the office and car traffic beyond the window, but ultimately it's a dooming silence that I hear.

Eventually he breaks it, whispering his answer. "Maybe. Yes." It's as if he himself hates that that's his truth, his gut feeling on it. "If this weren't a result of it, I mean, then yes. We both fucked up, I know that." I watch as he bends at the waist, putting his head between his legs and running his hands through his hair.

All I can think now is what was the point of me even asking him that. It was unfair, so unfair. Of course I can't put that on him.

Still, it was the only way to know if he thinks I'm worthy of forgiveness. Which apparently I might have been.

If it weren't for this.

I nod. "Okay."

twenty-one

. . .

simon

THEY WALK UP the stairs to Lila's apartment and Simon watches the sway of her hips the entire time. He dragged out their next day at the beach for as long as possible, lazily laying in bed, bringing her breakfast in bed (which she greedily ate), then more exploring before the real world eventually beckoned. He needed to get back to work, edits and contracts waiting for him back in London.

She pauses before opening her door and turns to him.

"You know, Si. The first orgasm you gave me happened right here in this little stairwell."

He tries not to look in her eyes, knowing she'll have a wicked glint in them that will draw him in, and he needs to get back home. Instead he looks at her neck, but that does no good. All he sees is the small hickey he left there last night, just above her collar bone. Looking lower to her body won't work either, as he'll imagine the many more marks he knows he's left on her.

So he looks above her head to the wall behind her. "I remember it well. And?"

She turns back to the door with her hand on the knob to open it. She twists and pushes the door forward, but stops and turns back to him before fully entering the flat. "And I guess that makes you my boy toy after all," she says with that sly little smile as she steps in. "Bye, now. Thanks for the weekend." She starts to close the door on him, but with a jolt, he follows in behind her.

He grabs her arms and pushes her backwards into the flat, kicking the door closed behind him. In the small kitchen off to the side are two people—the roommate Penny that he recognizes, and a man. The fiancé, he assumes. Simon gives them a nod, but the two look over to Simon and Lila with startled looks. Simon spins Lila around so she can face them, wrapping an arm tightly over her chest.

The man steps forward with a look like he's about to intervene. "Everything okay there, Lila?"

"You know actually, I could use a little help," she says through a giggle, and Simon gives her a tighter squeeze.

"Lila, tell your friends that you're fine," he says through gritted teeth.

"Am I though? I'm just not sure that I am, Master oh Master."

The fiancé takes another step forward, but Penny reaches an arm to pull him back. "Relax, Charles. I think Lila here is just fine," she says with a smile, and the fiancé looks at her.

"Have you gone mad? He's hurting her," Charles says with a gesture toward the two of them.

Lila, still in Simon's grasp, lets out a laugh. "I assure you, Charles. He's most definitely not hurting me. I think it might be more the other way around." She raises her free arm up, places her hand by her mouth as if to shield from lip reading, and whispers dramatically, "I called him my Boy Toy, and he didn't like that."

With that Simon pushes them both towards her bedroom, drops her bag on the floor and throws the laughing Lila onto her bed. She scoots back quickly, out of his grasp.

"You," he starts to say with a finger to her face, but then pauses.

He walks out of the room and into the kitchen where the still confused looking fiancé stands next to a grinning Penny as she holds an electric green drink of some sort.

"Apologies," he says as he reaches in his back pocket for his wallet. He opens it, pulls out a few bills and holds them up between his fingers. "This here, my treat for tonight's dinner, yeah? Dinner *out*," Simon adds, tossing the bills toward the counter. He turns back around but hears Penny call behind him.

"We'll want dessert as well. And it's a bit early for dinner yet, maybe some drinks first to start?"

Simon spins on his heels, marches back towards the couple, Charles now beet red with eyes wide, and he pulls out his wallet again. He grabs a credit card and holds it up. "Can I trust you with this?" he asks Penny.

She nods emphatically. "I'm very trustworthy I assure you, yes." She snatches up the card, grabbing her fiancé's hand. "Come on, we're going out. *Now*," and they scurry off and out the door.

The flat now empty, Simon makes his way back to Lila's room, but it's also empty. Or appears to be. "Lila oh Lila, where might you be?" There's no real places to hide, but he looks anyway. A peer behind the bed, beside the chest of drawers. A quick peek in the wardrobe, but all he finds is a neat lineup of clothing, a whiff of Lila's perfume consuming him as he rifles through.

He feels a tap on his shoulder and turns around to find her standing there, cat eyes narrowed. "Looking for me?" she asks, her tone feigning innocence.

He spins her around and presses his knees into the backs of hers, forcing her to kneel to the floor. With a shove he pushes her torso down onto her bed, her stomach pressed to the mattress as he pins both her arms up above her head. He pulls her pants down to her knees, exposing her bare ass.

Palm on one cheek, Simon softly rubs and massages her, leaning over to whisper in her ear. "Tell me, Lila. Tell me what you think I am."

She bites her lip and contains a giggle, shaking her head no.

"You take it back then?" he asks, palm still making its circles and gentle presses on her ass. He moves his hand between her legs and feels the slickness. She closes her eyes and moans out in response.

His own cock is throbbing in his jeans, and he pulls away from her to work to unbutton them, cursing as he struggles with just one hand. He releases her wrists to work his jeans down, freeing his cock, and Lila tries to wriggle out away from him, climbing up onto the bed.

He lets her free herself just a little before slamming one hand on her thighs, pulling her back as his other lands with a smack on her ass. She cries out with a "Fuck!" and Simon once again presses his torso against her back, pressing her into the mattress.

"Does that sting?" he asks. He knows the answer based on his own stinging palm. It was a good smack.

His little fox grins and shakes her head. "Nope. Not at all."

"A lie," he says, slipping his cock between her thighs and rubbing against her, teasing. She responds, closing her eyes and releasing a "Please," despite herself.

"That's not so difficult then, is it?" He continues his thrusts against her, still teasing. She's deliciously soaked, and he tells her she's making a mess on his cock.

He puts a hand up her shirt, feeling the smoothness of her back, her skin. His hand moves around to her front and he lifts her slightly to squeeze in between their bodies and her mattress. Her chest fills with a vibration as she hums an appreciative purr. Simon pulls back slightly to take in the sight of Lila—the gorgeous messy spray of blonde hair on her face, on her pale orange comforter. Like rays of a sunset. It's amazing to him how quickly she has moved into his mind with no real signs of leaving. This spoiled American, Lila Ray, a sly little fox that he can't seem to get enough of.

"But you like when I make a mess on you, my Boy Toy," she says with a grin he can barely make out through the mess of hair spilling on the side of her face. Simon finds her nipple and pinches, hard, leaning forward again and pressing his torso more firmly into her.

"What was that?" he asks through her cries and curses. He pinches again, then slowly strokes a finger between her breasts, dragging down to her stomach, her belly button. He frees his hand from beneath her shirt and reaches for her throat, wrapping his hand around her slender neck.

"My Boy Toy," she whispers again with closed eyes and a dreamy look on her face.

Simon tightens his grasp on her neck and pulses his hips into her once more, watching her face for her reaction. Eyes still closed, she pinches her eyebrows together and he worries he's going too rough on her. He releases some pressure both from his weight on her back and the grasp on her throat, scanning her face to assess, but all he sees is the smile creep back up again.

"So you did hear me," she murmurs, wicked music to his ears.

He kisses her shoulder, smiling despite himself. It's against the unspoken rules of the play, she should be given another slap or squeeze or something for that line, but he's momentarily caught up in affection for her. It catches him by surprise. All his interactions with Lila Ray have been out of sorts—from the first encounter when he recognized her as the model he'd be working with, then heard her obnoxious pick-up line, a line that now sends him twitching with anticipation. To the moment he saw the softness in her when he reached to touch her at the photo shoot. Then the jealousy that pinched at him when seeing her flirt with another man at the gym. His overall inability to keep his hands off her, consumed with wanting to touch her, hold her, have her wicked mouth on him and his on her. This woman that has most unexpectedly worked her way under his skin with her mischievous sage eyes and teasing flirtations, all hiding a beautifully complex soul. One that apparently loves history, stained glass windows, is seeking to find her place in the world with bravery in a new country. The spoiled

American he once saw in her is so far removed from the woman he's getting to know her to be.

Simon's realizing he has no intentions of letting her go. Not anytime soon, anyway.

Lila breaks through his thoughts with a wiggle of her ass up against his cock. "My Boy Toy's awfully quiet," she says with a laugh, and then turns her head to press her face in the bed. "I'm sorry, I can't, it's too funny." Her voice is muffled, and Simon watches her curiously. "I can't believe I called you my Boy Toy that night!" Her body convulses with laughter, and once again Simon can't help but smile too. "That's so embarrassing," she says through her muffled laughs. He can barely make out what she's saying, but he's aware that he's quickly losing all the glorious tension they had built up. Instead of being annoyed or disappointed by it though, he's amused. Another surprising fact.

"Lila, Lila, why are you laughing?" he says. "No laughing, Lila Ray."

She frees her face from the mattress and turns her head back on its side, sucking her lips in and out. "I'm sorry. I'm very serious again, I promise. Mastermind Photographer."

"Good," he says with a firm grab of her hair in a tight fist. He yanks her head back. He's determined to get back on track. To get *her* back on track.

"You know, Lila. We haven't fucked like this, yet. With me entering your cunt from behind."

"Yeah? So?"

"You should know, you have yet to fully experience the pleasure of those piercings you like so much." He leans down and lowers his face to her neck, feeling the tickle of her hair on his nose. She smells so good, so feminine and sexy. "This angle can bring a whole other level of sensation," he says with a slip of his finger inside of her, finding the spot he's referring to. Lila moans responsively and rocks her hips in rhythm with his movements.

"Feels so good," she murmurs.

"Good. Now imagine this with my cock." He slips his fingers out to grab himself, rubbing around her in continued teasing strokes. "My cock inside you in this way."

Lila shrugs. "The piercings are just okay."

"Just okay?" He pulls his hand back to deliver another slap to her cheek. She startles, then opens her eyes and smiles.

Simon scans her face. There's something off about the look in her eye—it's like she's staring off into space and no longer in the moment.

"What's wrong?" he asks. Silence, no response.

"Lila, hey, what's wrong? Where'd you go?" He leans to the side to face her better.

Lila blinks rapidly and squeezes her eyes shut. "Fuck, um...I'm good, I'm fine. It's just..." He waits patiently for her to speak, caught off guard by her sudden shift.

She pops herself up and pushes against him. She rests her forearms on the bed. Her mood has shifted, the playfulness gone, even the humor has evaporated. She bites her lip in concentration and Simon pushes the hair from out of her eyes, caressing her cheek with his thumb.

"Si, I really, really love fucking you. I think we figured that out yesterday pretty clearly. And this morning," she adds with a half-hearted smile.

His mind flashes back to last night, climbing on top of her when she was still strapped to the bed. Lifting her blindfold to look in her eyes, wanting to see them, watch her expression as he entered her for the first time. Her sage eyes were more hazel then, glossy with desire for him. Then later them both dozing off, only to wake in the middle of the night, her climbing on top of him, tugging at his hair, his mouth tugging at her breasts, bouncing in front of his face as she fucked him.

Then this morning, pressing her against the shower wall, her legs wrapped around him, steam and sweat enveloping them in a dizzying effect. It had been ecstasy.

He opts for simplicity in his response. "Yes, alright," he says.

"I've literally never had so many orgasms in such a short span, you should know. I mean like, hats off to you, you very clearly have a commitment to bringing women pleasure."

"Only ones I very clearly like and want a commitment with, Lila. There's shagging for a shag, and then there's what I like to do with you." He needs her to hear that—that the level of passion and play he's engaged in with her is not something he does with every woman he's brought in his bed. "I like you, Lila. Beyond the physical attraction."

She smiles and nods. "I gathered as much." It's a teasing tone, but there's still a distance in her eyes. "And I'm really fucking glad, let me make that clear."

"What is it, Lila? What are you trying to tell me?"

"I just...I don't come in this position, okay?" she says, glancing behind them. It occurs to him they must look a sight, both still dressed, only with pants shoved carelessly down to their knees. Kneeling on the floor beside her bed, as if saying their nightly prayers.

Lila continues. "Like, doggie style, I guess. You from the back, it doesn't work for me, is what I'm saying. It's uncomfortable and I just don't want you to have expectations and be disappointed if I don't have an orgasm. Especially with, you know. The piercings promise."

"That's what you're worried about?"

She nods. "Usually I would just fake it, but..."

"But?" he asks, his heart skipping a tiny beat at her honesty, her concern at disappointing him.

"I don't want to fake anything with you. So just, don't take it personally if I don't come, okay?"

It seems so very un-Lila, to be so candid, worrying about hurting feelings and sharing this openly. All because she fears she won't have an orgasm this way. Because of a position she doesn't like, one that he's initiated. There's a soft sweetness to it, a far cry from the temper-laden fighter role Lila often slips into.

His cock, which had been slowly softening, suddenly springs right back to life again at the unexpected intimacy of this moment with her.

Simon presses a kiss onto her forehead. "We don't have to do this position at all, you know."

She glances down between them at his erection. "It seems like you want to," she says with a grin. "And I want to, I want to at least try."

Simon kisses her again, then returns to kneeling up behind her, gently pushing her back down on the bed. He rubs her back, moves her hair from her neck and places a few tender kisses on her, feeling her relax beneath him.

"We'll go slow then, yeah?" he says. "You tell me when to stop, no need for a safe word." He studies her face for signs of resistance. Thankfully he sees none.

Which is good, because he wants this for her. He wants to give her pleasure in this position, especially if it's something never given to her before.

A first.

That could be his.

An idea comes to mind. "Where's your vibrator, Lila?"

"How do you know I have one?"

He shifts himself back, bends down to playfully bite her left ass cheek, the right one still red from his slaps. "Is this like the panties? You going to try and tell me there's none when we both know there is?"

"You knew I was bluffing about the panties?" He hears the grin in her voice even without looking at her. He's shuffling around the drawer beside her bed.

"I had been staring at your ass at every chance I had, Lila, thankful your jacket was short. Yes. I knew you were bluffing about the panties." Bingo, he finds what he's looking for. "And this, you sly little fox," he says, turning toward her and holding up the purple bullet.

"Guilty."

He scoots back to her and resumes his position, pushing her back down again. He pushes two fingers inside her, confirming she's still wet, then slips them back out to pop into her mouth. "Seems we don't need your little assistant just yet."

She obligingly sucks his fingers and shakes her head no, humming. He loves the sound of her satisfied hums, a habit of hers he's quickly becoming addicted to.

He removes his fingers from her mouth, pushes her pants further down, lifts her knees one at a time to move the fabric under, down to her ankles, then off completely. With his knees he spreads her legs out wide and wraps his hand around his cock. "Now, in the future I'd like your legs kept nice and tight together, and I think you will too. But for now we're going to have you open wide."

"Yes doctor."

"Are you quite comfortable, Lila?" he asks. He presses the tip of his cock at her opening.

"Quite comfortable," she says through a small gasp.

"Good." He struggles to concentrate with his own blinding arousal, but he's committed to ensuring she's okay with this. He pushes himself in a little further, then back out again, then in. A little further once more, a gentle rocking rhythm of subtle thrusts. He watches her face, her eyes squeezed shut, her expression one of concentration, but she's humming. He presses himself in further, nearly fully in, but not quite. Lila grips her comforter in tight fists. "How is this?" he asks, reaching around to her front and stroking her in rhythm with his thrusts.

"It's good. It's really good," she says with a nod. She opens her eyes and glances behind her shoulder. "Go all the way, it's okay."

"Are you in any pain?" His question is meant to be serious, but she grins.

"Oh, just the right amount, doctor."

With a shake of his head he eases himself fully into her, her ass pressing against him and a groan escapes his mouth. "Fucking bloody hell, Lila. You feel…" he says, dropping the line as his own pleasure builds with his thrusts. He's careful with them, and it takes every ounce of strength in him to be.

"So very unprofessional," she says through small gasps. Her fingers are still gripping her blanket, but she arches her back up, leaning herself further into him, joining him in his movements.

He's pleased to see she's enjoying this, her own arousal evident in her body's ability to take in all of him, but he wants to make sure she's fully present.

Because he's not stopping until she's screaming out his name and he feels her pulsing around his cock.

He continues his thrusts combined with the stimulation through her folds, watching as her back continues to arch with what he hopes to be her building pleasure.

He stops.

Pulls himself out halfway. Moves his fingers to the side to tease and caress the soft skin at the very top of her inner thigh. He pulses slightly, knowing the extra stimulation his piercings will have as long as he has the spot just right.

"Tell me, Lila. Tell me when you feel it."

"I fucking feel it, oh my God, Si."

"What do you feel?"

"I feel it. The fucking piercings, *fuck*."

"And?"

"It's wild. Holy shit, that feels…" her voice trails off in a desperate whimper. "Oh my God," she says, reaching her hand back and squeezing at his thigh, nails scratching through his skin.

It's torture for him to slow down and pulse like this, but her pleasure is the only thing that matters. He just needs to keep her present in everything she's feeling. Present, and begging for more.

He stills completely.

Her eyes pop open. "Oh my God, I will fucking kill you, Si. Please don't stop. Please."

"Close your eyes," he commands. She does. "Now tell me what you want. And tell me nicely."

"I need you to move again. Please."

"Why?"

"Because..." she gasps. "Because it feels...I'm close," she says with a shimmy of her ass.

He obliges and resumes his pulses, faster this time. He studies her face and notes the quickness of her breaths, short gasps combined with bites to her lip. This is the time to get just right. He knows she's close, and he doesn't want her to lose it.

He pauses again.

Lila slams a fist down onto her mattress. "Fucking Christ, Simon please, *please* fuck me! Touch me and fuck me or I'm going to scream!"

"Are you sure?"

"Yes! Please, please, fuck I'm sure!"

He bites inside his own cheek to keep himself from coming and ruining the entire experience, the sound of her pleads nearly too much. Her insides are clenched around him so tightly he's seconds away from exploding. She shimmies her ass again and he has to back himself almost fully out of her, slapping hard down on her ass, three consecutive times. "Don't. Fucking. Move, Lila." His breaths are hard in his chest as he bites his cheek again, his mind rolling to any benign subject he can think of.

He feels Lila grab his hand, maneuvering it back to resume touching her, her hand kept over his to guide him. They work together for a few moments, him still frozen just barely inside her. She speeds up the movements and he knows she's once again getting close. He pushes in a bit further, now knowing her spot, and pulses again.

Unable to hold back any longer Simon slams himself into her, and Lila lets out a cry. But she doesn't stay stop, instead crying out

"Yes, harder!" and Simon continues, unsure he could stop if he tried. She drops her head down, removes her hand from his, clawing at her blankets with moans and curses as he continues with faster thrusts and strokes to her front.

Then the words he'd been holding out for. "Simon, fuck yes, I'm coming...I'm coming..." she cries out, clenching around his cock, and there's no holding back now. He explodes inside her, grabbing her hips and pressing deeper.

Deeper than he's ever been able to go with another woman.

In a beautifully timed joint orgasm.

And they both collapse on her bed.

twenty-two

· · ·

lila

S O I GUESS I have a boyfriend now. It feels weird to say, especially because the only other "boyfriend" I ever had was one that was always kept secret. Really that one doesn't even count.

Simon had asked me about that first relationship that I had mentioned, and I ended up telling him the truth. I swear, he's got this whole truth serum thing. It's like the lies I so neatly used to craft, small omissions I have left out for a large part of my adult life —they all spill out in confessions of the heart with him. He's like a damn reporter or something. He knows just the right questions to ask, tenderness to convey combined with that whole stony "I command you, Lila" thing that's my unraveling.

We had been looking at the photos I took with his camera on our mini trip. He said I have a good eye, pointed out things that I managed to capture, little patterns or small details that I may not have even realized, but that made all the difference in the mood of the end result.

"I like when you compliment me," I had said. It was kind of a mindless observation I had made. My therapist once told me I struggle with "positive affect tolerance," meaning that praise or appreciation can be hard for me to accept thanks to a somewhat emotionally cold upbringing and, well—that fucker Royce. So when I didn't immediately jolt with discomfort when Simon told me I had a good eye, it felt significant.

Simon wrapped his arm around me, pulling me in closer to him. "I noticed it's been easier for you," and my heart skipped a beat at hearing him pay attention to that.

Royce was good at observing too, but only so that he could later use that shit against me. Simon and I have been dating for a few weeks now. Long enough that I can solidly say he's not showing any of those red flags. No backhanded compliments or jabs that pretend to be teasing. I hate to compare the two of them like this, but I guess at the very least I should use the Royce experience as a measurement tool of what's fucked up, so I can learn to see what's not.

It's about trusting the patterns a man shows you and never fooling yourself into falling for potential. Potential is too easily a broken promise. I'm here to tell you, you want patterns. Simon has all the right patterns. And I deserve them.

So yeah, I shared with Simon my fucked up little piece of history. In broad strokes. (No need for every detail, oh no.) But I was completely open about the beginning, that party and how it all started. And let me just tell you, if you're locking up something dark and shameful like that, let it out. Yeah, the conversation was hard at first, but worth it—it's like it built a connection between us that I hadn't expected, and that feels really good.

Sure, my therapist knows my stuff. It took me a while to get to that point with her, but it was good when I finally did. But as for anyone personal in my life? Simon would be the first. I'd prefer to keep it with just him, no need to resurrect the whole thing to any listening ear, but it feels really good to share with someone I'm real quick-like catching feelings for.

And it feels really good to be able to catch real feelings for someone. I think I'm growing. Call the press.

Simon had listened so carefully, so calmly, but I could see the anger in his eyes as I shared. His body was all tense. He asked me where the fucker was now, and I said I had no idea, didn't care, good riddance. I have a sneaky feeling though that if the dude weren't an ocean away, Simon would be paying him a little visit.

"He took advantage of you, Lila. You understand that, right? That wasn't just a bad relationship, that was rape. Followed by calculated manipulation."

His cat Basil was on my lap at the time, purring sweetly while I pet him. A little ball of comfort. I scrunched up my nose, not liking the term "rape" to describe it. "Yeah, I know," I assured Simon. "But he didn't know my age at first."

He slammed a fist down on his desk, startling me and causing Basil to jump out of my lap. "He should have asked! He knew you were Lucy's younger sister! And you had been drinking, there's no excuse for his actions!"

I put a hand on my chest, startled. "Jesus! Look, I realize this is all fresh for you, but fucking hell, Si! I don't need to relive it just so you can feel like the big and bad protector here." I got up and walked over to the window, looked down to the street to the people walking by. On their way to some errand or adventure. I thought how now I'm the one captured in a window, looking out at the free. I inhaled a big breath, counted to four, then slowly exhaled for eight beats. Repeated until I was re-regulated.

I heard Simon come up behind me. Felt him wrap his arms around me and I allowed myself to melt into his body. He kissed my cheek, and then we stood there like that for a while, saying nothing.

And then he made love to me. Like, real slow and without any play or games, kind of love. I may have cried a little afterwards, yup. And then there he was kissing my tears, concerned, and me telling him he better watch out because I'm clearly crazy if I'm crying happy tears after sex. And I told him I've realized I never had sex before him, not really. I have a body count that's probably higher than your average twenty-five year old woman, some experiences fun, some regrettable, but ultimately I've never experienced the act in the beautiful way that it is with him. It was a seriously vulnerable moment for me, you should be proud.

Get this—I think I may have caught a little glimpse of wetness from his eyes too as I shared this all with him. Big and scary neck tattoos, Simon, teary eyed. I know, it's all so wild.

Then he told me he thinks he might love me.

"You think you might?" I said with a pinch to his nipple.

"I'm warning you...I pinch much harder."

"I know," I said with a shimmy of my naked breasts.

He looked at me all seriously though. "Yes, I think I might love you, Lila. It's only been a few weeks, it's early still, and I don't make this confession lightly. I don't expect you to say anything in return either, I just want you to know that I am developing very strong feelings for you, ones that I think may be turning into love."

And I ate that shit up for all I could, let me tell you. I didn't say anything back, just kissed him, wondering at what point "think" and "may" turn into "definitely and I'm never letting go."

"What's got you so smiley?" Penny asks me now, wiping pasta sauce from her mouth and sipping her wine. We're enjoying yet another little dinner together, something we've built a habit of whenever we're both home and free. No more me hiding in my room pretending to study while really taking solo shots of tequila and scrolling through my phone.

"Nothing. I'm not smiling," I say, shoving a forkful of pasta in my mouth. I've gained a solid five or six pounds in the past two months. I remind myself that it's a good thing, that it's healthy. And it's good and healthy to not feel hungry all the time. (I've been known to obsess over the need to feel hungry once upon a time. Dark times.) My boobs actually seemed to have filled in a bit with it, so I'm focusing on that as opposed to any belly softness. Trying to anyways. Wardrobe fittings for my new show were a bit uneasy for me, but I looked in the mirror and reminded myself that I'm here, I earned this because I'm a talented badass and belly softness has nothing to do with that. It felt good, babes—real good.

"You *are* smiling, my dear," Penny insists. "But I can take a guess as to who is on your mind."

I dab my napkin at my mouth, stifling a smile.

"You know," she says, whispering as if there were anyone around. "I bought those straps you told me about. The ones that go under the mattress."

I look at her, confused for a moment, then vaguely recall another wine infused night with Penny when I apparently bragged all about my fun sexual escapades to her. It was quite the girls night in. I think we actually did braid each other's hair.

"Well? Have you used them yet?" I ask. Penny really is adorable, maybe it's those dimples.

"I absofuckinglutely have. Magnificent," she says with a pinch of her thumb and index finger. "Only I strapped *him* to the bed. I never thought a blow job could happen that fast. I felt very power-ful," she says matter of factly.

"That sounds like a me move, good for you, Pen," I say and clink her wine glass.

"So...how's your sister and the pregnancy?" she asks.

I laugh. "Well I think you have some facts wrong, because Lucy is most definitely not pregnant."

Penny freezes her forkful of pasta mid air. I look at her, then second guess myself. "Wait, what makes you say that?" I ask.

She drops the fork on her plate and sits back. "I heard her getting sick a couple times when she was here. You were either asleep maybe or on a job, I'm not sure. But I had a hunch. And then at one point I caught her pouring a bit of a drink down the sink, very clearly trying to hide it. She was always so tired, lots of hand-on-the-belly moments. I put two and two together."

"Did you say anything to her? Ask her?"

Penny shakes her head. "No, it didn't feel like my place to. But I figured she'd tell you at some point." She contorts her forehead. "I'm sorry, I don't know why I didn't say anything sooner. And I could be wrong!" she says brightly. "I certainly don't have any confirmation."

I think about this, and I have the sneaking suspicion Penny might be right. In all my Simon-high glory, I've barely spoken to my family beyond a few texts or the occasional "How do I?" phone calls with my mom. Could Lucy be pregnant? And if so, why wouldn't she tell me?

I rest my elbows on the chair armrests. "It's possible, actually. I caught her do the drink down the drain thing too, and she said her stomach was feeling off. Huh."

"You two are close, just try asking her maybe?" Penny says, eyebrows raised, tone a little mocking as if to say the simplest solution is usually the best.

"It's a brilliant plan," I say.

AFTER DINNER I RESOLVE TO call in to see how Lucy's doing. Simon's out of town on a job, and no matter what, I really should be a better sister knowing the struggles she's been having with Justin.

Justin, my God. I feel like such a brat, I can't believe I haven't been better about this whole thing. I've sent zero check in texts or calls or anything, of course Lucy wouldn't tell me if she was freakin' pregnant. It's like if something's not right in front of my face, I forget it exists. Even my very own sister. It's an ADHD thing, but it still feels really shitty, especially because we did have a pretty awesome time while she was here. Probably the most consecutive days together in our entire adult lives.

I lay down on my bed on my stomach, phone in hand. I

prompt the call but get no answer. She's probably in a meeting or something, I figure, so I decide I'll try again later.

A text comes in from her though telling me she can't talk right now. Something about the tone of it feels off, like it's flat and lifeless or something. I tell her that it's an emergency, and then try her again.

She answers this time and I feel a teeny bit guilty for the extremes, so I get right to the point. "Are you pregnant?" I blurt out, and she groans with a sound like she just stubbed her toe.

"Lila, I'm in my office with my door open, and you're on speaker phone."

"Well when someone calls you and says it's an emergency, assume they would want *privacy*!"

I hear her door latch closed, then hear her take a deep breath. "Fine, you're right. My mistake. It's fine, I don't think anyone heard," she says quietly.

I note that that sounds like confirmation. "Well? Is it true? Penny asked how you were feeling, and imagine my shock when she shared her suspicions on your delicate state."

Lucy scoffs, then starts up with her typical big sister lecture packaged in mockery. "Hi, Lucy. How is your life going, Lucy? Thought I'd be a good little sister and check in given that I know it must have been hard for you to confess all about your marriage woes to me, *Lucy*!"

I fire right back. "Hi, Lila. How is *your* life going, Lila? Given that you're all the way across an ocean doing big and scary modeling and acting career things, terrifying table read rehearsals in your new role, finding your way in life?"

"Real fucking mature."

"You started it," I say. Then I sigh, bite back a nasty comment, because I know she's right. I have been a shit sister, and what she has going on is a little more important than my London adventures. Well, given a possible pregnancy, maybe a lot more important.

"Okay, re-do," I start again. "That's not how I wanted this to go. I'm sorry I haven't checked in." I debate sharing my Simon updates, it feels trite to in a way with all she has going on, but then again, I'm amping up my honesty attempts in life. "I'm officially together with Simon the Hot Nerd Photographer." It feels like a confession to say it. "And it's caused me to be a little wrapped up and painfully ignorant to things that aren't right in front of me. Though you will be happy to hear I've formed quite the friendship with Penny. But yeah, Simon and I are a thing. A really good thing, he's—" I try and search for the right words, "—he's smart and treats me like a star, but doesn't let me get away with my bullshit. You'd love him," I add with a laugh.

"That's awesome, Lila. His aunt seemed really sweet too." Her voice has this distance to it. Like the life has been sucked out of her and now she's just a robot, making this oddly simple and serious statement. Normal Lucy I would have expected a little more from, a firing of questions or some spark of excitement, not this flat and tired tone.

I try and lighten the mood. "Well get this—apparently Aunt Victoria and Roger from the gym have started quite the hot and wild relationship of their own. It's all the town gossip."

"Love is in the air, I guess," she says sadly, and my heart squeezes for my sister. Miss Perfect, apparently with her own struggles.

"So you are, then? Pregnant?" I ask quietly.

"Yes. Fourteen weeks now," she says with a long and dramatic exhale.

"Does Justin know yet?"

"Yes, and Reggie too, but they're the only ones. I haven't told work or Mom and Dad yet."

"But this is a good thing, right?" I try and have the most gentle yet enthusiastic tone possible. "Maybe help you and Justin get back on track?"

I hear a sniffle on the other end of the line, and I'm on edge.

I'm not great at this kind of thing, at offering up emotional support. I'm no good at finding the right words to comfort someone, let alone my big sister where the task seems that much more daunting. My sister who is carrying a baby right in the midst of the rockiest point in her marriage.

"No, Lila," she says, her voice a mixture of sadness and irritation, and I brace myself. "It's the exact opposite of the thing to help us get back on track. Because it's not Justin's baby. It's the fuck-face affair guy's baby. And Justin wants nothing to do with raising someone else's baby. And while I considered an abortion, it turns out I actually do have some semblance of a soul because I just couldn't move forward with it, and now it's too late to anyway. So no, it's not a good thing."

Oh *fuck*. Fuck, fuck, fuck is all I can think as I let that bomb of a revelation seep into my body.

Not Justin's baby.

Holy shit.

I gulp, my head spinning a little. "And the guy?" I ask, not sure how to form the words or what I'm even asking.

"The guy is a nobody, just a big mistake. He doesn't know yet, that's next on my fabulous to-do list."

I have absolutely no words of wisdom for my poor, amazing sister that deserves a much better sibling than me. When I was younger I would have thought seeing Lucy fail now and then would be a sick kind of blessing for me. Let Lucy be painfully human, just for once, so that I had a fighting chance to shine. But hearing her tone now, so horribly sad and dejected and so un-Lucy-like, it actually makes the world feel completely upside down. As if she had been a North Star for me all these years, even if I had resented her for it. And without that bright and shiny guiding point to show the way, even if I only stumbled awkwardly in its direction, I suddenly feel off kilter and out of whack.

I say the only words I can think to say. "What can I do, Lucy?"

And she gives me an impossible answer. "Drop your budding

London career, your amazing new boyfriend, and move back home to help your sister raise her baby as a single mom?"

Double fuck.

Because while my sister's words are wrapped in a joke, I know she means them.

twenty-three

. . .

lucy

I HANG UP with Lila and fall back with a thump into my office chair. A whole new bag of emotions are now hanging out with me. I guess there's relief at letting her know, not that there's anything my baby sister can do. I really would love if she could drop everything and come help me do this because I feel so utterly alone, it's crippling.

I'm just starting my second trimester and already I'm looking into the best day care/pre-schools because I'll be damned if I'm unprepared on that front. This baby may have been far from planned, but it'll get the best of the best from here on out. And thanks to my job, I know all too well the lack of adequate care, the demand far outweighing the supply, the waitlists on these places, etc.

With the thoughts of these day care decisions comes another wave of emotion—sadness or grief or something along those lines, because here I am, already thinking about how quickly I'll be able to get back to work after the baby's born. And that feels painful in and of itself. I have a whole new level of respect for working moms of the world. It's one thing to hear about the struggles, but to think about being part of that group is surreal. And I'm lucky, I have the income and resources to find support. What in the world would I do if my circumstances were different? How much more bleak would my outlook be?

Our non-profit does wonderful things for the kids in our programs, but what about the mothers that have found themselves in the positions to have their kids in foster care in the first place? I suddenly feel like we've treated them as lost causes, all because it's all too easy to see the kids and want to focus in on their needs, but more needs to be done without a doubt to support our mamas as they get back on their feet.

Thankfully, I work somewhere and have the kind of respect here where I can actually do things to potentially shift the needle.

My silver lining in all this, I suppose. It will be my next mission. Nothing like a glimpse in someone else's shoes to teach you a thing or two.

I hear the creak of my door open and my stomach drops at the sight of Carter, all cocky smile, just waltzing right in my space without even knocking. What the fuck is wrong with me for ever allowing this guy's penis inside my body? I'm disgusted with myself. And then I feel a little bad that I'm so harsh—it's not like he took the vows. Just like I said about Dr. Gabby.

"Hey," he says with a grin. I start to speak but he throws his hands up in surrender. "I can take the hint, you're done with me, I get it."

I lean back in my chair again, exhausted, suddenly. "I just woke up and realized I was using you in my own avoidance, that's all. We both knew it was never anything more than that, right?" I'm eager to close up shop on any potential feelings here. I don't plan on telling him about the baby for a little while longer, until he's long gone from here, in his new job, and there's been a bit of distance between us. But in the meantime I need to at least ensure there isn't some lingering hope or thoughts that whatever it was we were doing could ever be resumed.

"Oh yeah, of course. We had fun," he says with a grin that's far too shiny.

"Yeah. But anyhow, you feel ready for the new job? I hear it's a great place to work." Even I can hear how fake my tone sounds.

"Lucy," he says, stepping forward and leaning two hands on my desk. He looks me dead in the eyes. "I overheard your phone call just now."

My stomach drops. *Oh my God, no, no.* I am not ready for this. Not ready to announce to the world and suddenly be treated like a delicate woman in a delicate condition, and certainly not ready to tell him he's the father. There's no way I can face any of that just yet. I fight a wave a nausea.

He continues. "I see now why you stopped talking to me, what with the pregnancy and all. Just came to say congratulations." He pushes up off my desk and puts a hand on his hip. "I like to think I helped get something out of your system, maybe helped you and Justin fire up the old flame."

His smile is sickening, and for some reason I *hate* hearing him say my husband's name. Like they're old friends or something. And the *audacity*—helped me get something out of my system! Wow, just wow. I sure know how to pick 'em.

But it occurs to me—Carter has no idea the baby is his. For all he knows I could be just a few weeks, meaning not within the window of our brief fling. He's leaving the company soon, relocating to DC, a solid two hour drive away. By the time the baby's born it'll have been months since we'd even seen one another. I'll be hunkered down with the new baby, chances of him hearing about the birth are slim.

Maybe, just maybe, Carter never even has to know.

before

. . .

Simon, Simon. I hope you read this, please do. Please please...

You're disgusted with me I know and you think I'm making a mistake by staying, but you see right now I need to stay and help him, you know? It's most important. I love him. And besides, if I leave him he'll only get worse and I can't do that to him. I'm less worried about myself and more about him doing something to harm himself, you see? You can understand that, can't you? He's very talented it makes him a bit mad at times is all, and he's been working so hard on his music, we both know it's only a matter of time before he gets all he deserves. When Mum and Dad first hired him for the shop they loved him and believed in him. You remember that, right? He was always a good employee and I just KNOW that there's a good person in him and they got it all wrong.

Enough about me. How is Grayson? I can't believe he's nearly fifteen now. I don't get to talk to him as often as I'd like, please keep an eye on him for me. As best you can, anyhow, hopefully he's not mad at you too.

I hear you've taken your photography to the next level, that school has been a success for you? I wish at times I hadn't dropped out but there's always the future! For now I need to focus on helping him.

Just a little while longer, alright? Keep covering for me just a little bit longer, and I promise I'll make it all clear to my family. Everyone will understand and you will no longer be the bad guy, you'll be the hero, yeah? Once he finishes this album and gets it sent out he'll certainly get the deal he so desperately deserves, he'll climb out of this dark place that he's in.

He loves me Simon. He really does.

X

Elsie

twenty-four

. . .

simon

VICTORIA HAD BEEN around to cook and clean for Simon less and less, what with her newfound love interest consuming much of her time. She pops in now and then to leave him food or clean still, but it's to the point where the last time Simon tried to give her money, she waved him off.

At some point he had finally shared his intention to help her get her teeth straightened out, but she only laughed at him, saying she loved her crooked teeth and crooked smile, and Simon actually had felt a twinge of shame in the suggestion. They were in a strange new space, moving apart, but in a way they both knew was a good sign of changing times.

"No Lila tonight?" Victoria asks, gathering her things to head out.

Simon looks at his watch. "She should be here any minute. Today was her first day of filming."

"Oh how exciting! You know I like her for you, Simon," Victoria beams. "I think she's a keeper."

Simon walks over to the kitchen counter, leans against it and crosses his ankles. "She is."

"Don't look too excited, now."

"There's one problem, unfortunately."

Victoria scans his face, then walks over to his kitchen table, pulling out a chair to sit. "Alright, nothing we can't solve I'm sure. What is it?"

"Grayson." The name hangs in the air for a moment. A kind of sacred set of letters, creating the word.

"What about him?" Victoria finally asks.

"They're friends. Grayson and Lila. Very good friends, particularly with Lila's friends and family back in the states. She revealed that when she first moved here, he warned her that if she ever ended up working with me to steer clear."

"Oh boy," Victoria says with a knowing nod. "What are the odds?"

"Apparently quite good. Or bad, rather. For me. Grayson's in town right now and having a small holiday get together this coming weekend. Invited Lila. She wants me to come along to try and make amends."

"Does she know what happened between you two?"

"A little. I said I used to date his sister years back, when Elsie and I were young teens, and Grayson was just twelve or so. And that he believes I treated her poorly."

Victoria tilts her head to the side. "Simon, that's what you told her? Why not tell her the rest? The truth?"

Simon shrugs, considering his aunt's proposition. He had considered telling Lila the whole story, but their relationship feels too new and delicate still. An incubator needing just the right temperature, or else suffer detrimental consequences. And the story sounds wrong, even to Simon.

He attempts to try and answer Victoria. "I need to make things right with Grayson first, I think it would be far more effective. Better if I can make Grayson understand. Perhaps enough time has passed. Maybe he could be open to listening, hearing more clearly without his grief being the massive wall preventing any attempts to understand. Maybe he's healed enough past the anger."

"Oh, Simon." Victoria rises up and walks over to him, perching next to him against the counter and releasing a heavy sigh. "You know, when your mum died, I had no idea what I was doing with you," she says to his surprise. "Me, with a child! I was young and broke, in and out of one bad relationship after another.

"But you, my dear, sweet boy. You saved me in a way, you know that? And ever since you were old enough to hold a job, you do all you can to continue saving and supporting me, I can see that. Even pretending to need me to keep house for you just so you can ensure I have a little extra cash. I do know that half the time you clean right after me when I leave," she says with a sardonic smile.

Simon flinches at this. "No idea what you mean."

Victoria gives him a little shove. "I tested the theory. I purposely skipped wiping down one of the cupboards and didn't dust the top of a picture frame. And yet, next time I was here, it was magically dust free! Now how do you suppose that happens?"

"How did you—why did you test that in the first place?" Simon wonders exactly how long she's realized this truth, that he cleans with meticulous detail the minute Victoria's out the door.

"Because we both know I've never loved the job, it's just the one that offered the most flexibility when you came into my care. Couldn't wait tables at night with a little one at home now, could I? And you've always been an absurdly tidy person, even as a child. But actually it was Roger that told me. He said you mentioned it once to him, before he and I met."

"What? I did?" Simon's in disbelief, having no recollection of that.

"Yep, you came in smelling like pine and lemon, and he made a comment, and you grumbled that your aunt had been cleaning, which meant you needed to go in and clean after her." She grins.

"Careful who you share things with. You never know what might circle back around."

Simon scoffs. "I will be, without a doubt. Traitor, that Roger," he says with a head shake. "Your cooking, however, I absolutely do appreciate. I'm a shit cook."

"I know. And that's rather good, actually. Because I've decided to quit cleaning and open up a bakery. Which means I officially resign as your housekeeper. You can still have my scones and goodies, you'll just have to head to the shop for them."

"What?" he says with both surprise and relief. "That's...that's wonderful, when did this all come about?"

Victoria shrugs. "Roger helped me get things started, he talked me through the steps I'd need to take, helped me get a loan, and here we are!"

Simon squeezes his aunt in an embrace, something he doesn't often do, but his heart swells for her and this plan. When he releases her, she looks into his face with sincerity. "You're a good man, Simon. I hope you know that. And what happened with Elsie was not your fault. It wasn't," she emphasizes as Simon shakes his head and turns his back to her. "You can't avoid one another forever, you know. Maybe this is a sign that it's time to heal this rift with my family."

Simon looks back at her, aware that she called them "my family." "Not our family" or "your aunt and uncle and Grayson," but "*my*."

Because they weren't ever really his family, of course. Not by blood.

But they were Victoria's—her sister and brother-in-law and niece and nephew. And Simon's actions have kept her from them too, all these years. Nine years of being shut out by them, all because of Simon. He realizes the hope Victoria might have in this chance, this push to try and make amends.

Victoria approaches him, looks up at him with motherly tenderness on her face. "Hey...this could be good," she says softly.

"Take the opportunity to see him, finally. It's been years, he's no longer a child. He'll understand better."

Simon shakes his head. "I fucked up, I should have helped her."

Victoria places a hand on his cheek. "You can't help someone that's not ready to accept it, love. There was nothing you could do for her, Simon. Just like there was nothing I could do for your own mum. And believe me, I tried. I may not have known the whole story when it came to Elsie, but even if I had, even if you had told us, it wouldn't have changed anything. She would have either resented us for keeping her from him, or she would have snuck out and run away like she did anyways. Doubt there ever would have been any stopping her. Trust me."

"You can't know that."

"Yes. I can. Because the only thing that ever stopped me from choosing the wrong men was you." An affectionate smile spreads across her face. "Having a new little man in my life that mattered more than anything else."

"And Roger? He treats you right?"

Victoria grins. "More than alright, as you got quite the glimpse of."

Simon turns away, grimacing. "Alright, that's enough then. Go on, get out of here and have fun with your own American. Your shop."

"Oh I very much will. Nothing to worry about there."

Simon wished he could say the same. He had a feeling revisiting the Grayson chapter of his life would not go as smoothly as both Victoria and Lila seemed to hope. But Victoria deserved the chance, he could see how much she wanted it.

He had to try, both for the woman who gave up everything to step in as a mother figure to him, and for Lila, the woman he's quite certain he loves.

twenty-five

. . .

lila

I KNOCK ON Simon's door with a whirlwind of emotions floating around me, and I'm in need of a good distraction.

First, let me tell you about this show I'm doing. The one where I'm playing a model.

It's pretty incredible. As in, my dream job…The director is a woman and she's known for some kickass female empowerment tales, so of course I'm all for that. The show is loosely based on a swimwear line that launched in the 70s, and the story is all about the early pitfalls of that brand, the dismissiveness the innovative designer faced. She was behind the new lightweight fabric that she was sure was destined to be the future of swimwear material (she was right), but she had been met with all kinds of barriers because of her inconvenience of being, well—a woman.

Basically, it's all the things I love. It's history, it's fashion, it's badass women paving the way forward. But get this—that swimwear brand the show is loosely based off of? Well my mom, good old L. Delphi-Ray, is the brand's most recent collaboration. You get what I'm saying here?

Let me spell it out for you—my "good luck" and "talent" in landing this job was in fact 100% because of my mom.

I mean, that's how the world works I guess, right? But fuck, it's such a goddamn blow to my self-esteem. Did I earn the job in my own right? Do I deserve it? I'm finding it really hard to tell myself that yes, I do deserve it when I've got the big fat shiny star L. Delphi-Ray looming over it, blinding me.

And this director! She's amazing, I've been studying up on her work as she's still somewhat new to the industry and earning her bragging rights. But I can see the creative vision—think Sofia Coppola or Gina Prince Bythewood's gifts for closely observed female characters, all combined with Emerald Fennell's visual maximalism.

Basically, this chick is the real deal, and she's going places, and I'm a part of it.

The cast and crew as a whole are a hodgepodge of creative souls that have a "fuck it, we do us" mentality too. None of it screams an operation that falls in line with nepotism, but there's no denying that my reel would not have landed on anyone's laptop screen had it not been for that connection with my mom. They're already talking about how that will be a fantastic angle to roll out when the time comes—that L. Delphi-Ray's daughter has a supporting role in the show. My chest gets cripplingly tight, my face hot just thinking about it.

My mom had been in full business mode when I tried to ask her about it. Can't turn on a damn TV, such an *airhead* at times, it's wild. I swear she thinks mundane tasks are beneath her. But she's the genius business woman and creative queen when it comes to her design world, and she had meticulously calculated all of this, naturally.

"Lila, take the win, it's a fantastic step for you," she had said when I called, ready to scream. I didn't want her help. I needed to prove to her, to my family, to *myself* that I could be someone on my own. I know it's stupid, it seems trivial I'm sure to anyone else.

Landed a great role that's sure to bump your career, not to mention deliver a guaranteed, steady paycheck for the next several months, and you're complaining because you had a little help?

Here's the thing though—where does your self confidence lay, your critical piece of feeling worthy and deserving and good enough —where is it when everything you've accomplished is basically all because of someone else? And that's the shit that hurts.

So of course I used my good old anger to channel that pain. It felt better to yell. "Why, why just once can't I do something on my own, mother?! I had been making progress! I didn't need your goddamn help!"

"Enough with the tantrum, Lila. Don't be so dramatic."

I wanted to throw the phone across the room. But I had already done that back within my first week here in London, lost a phone to my temper, and I really couldn't afford a new one. Instead I pulled the phone away from my ear while she babbled on and I attempted to take some deep breaths. I could hear more lecturing, I think something about "control your emotions," all the usual shit that only sent my blood boiling even more. When I heard the, "Lila?" I put the phone back to my ear, trying to keep my cool.

"I'm here, just listening," I lied, heart pounding in my chest.

"Look, you need to see the big picture," she was saying. I could hear her annoyance with me. The child she was trying to make understand. "This was a wonderful case of the stars lining up, that's all. It's a win-win for all involved. It helps me out to have your youth pull the interest in my new role for the brand with the younger demographics, and helps you as an added bonus!"

Ah, there it is. The truth. I'm being used.

"Look," she says, voice calm and soothing. "They wouldn't have cast you if they didn't think you were right for it."

I scoff. "Sure, how hard is it to cast a blonde model role anyways? Sure must be difficult to find those girls." I rolled my eyes, glad she couldn't see that.

We eventually hung up, but I still haven't been able to shake off my complete and utter disappointment and hurt at the whole thing. It stole the zest right out from me all while the wool was being pulled over me. The initial buzzing energy of the win in landing this part now vaporized. All a lie.

See, I had been falling into this growing feeling that Simon was right—modeling *wasn't* really in my heart, but acting was. What started out as a suggestion from my agency to help broaden my horizons turned into me feeling a much stronger passion. Growing up in the fashion world and being just a hair shy of six feet, modeling just seemed like the obvious route. But shit, I've been acting my whole life in many ways. I thought maybe I was actually good at it as a result. Maybe I could convey emotion and bring to life characters and be able to do this thing that's been such a long-standing piece of storytelling since the days of Ancient Greece.

Just kidding. It's all just because of my mom.

But I try and push that all down, down, down as I walk into Simon's apartment. Instead I wrap my arms around him in a kiss so deep, so passionate, biting and tugging and pulling at his mouth so that when we eventually stop, he asks me if I've been drinking.

And when I slap him across the face in response, he snatches my arms up, pins me against his kitchen counter, the edges digging into the top of my ass, and says, "Easy, now."

"Don't ask insulting questions," I pant.

He pins me harder, running his face along my neck and down to my chest, biting my collar bone. It's everything I need right now. I need to feel his power over me. I need to be able to let go. I need to defy it with a fight so that he exerts just the right pressure on me so that I'm actually able to release. He's the only one who can do it, who can get me there.

I lift my knee up, shimmy my leg between his legs and stroke through his pants, feeling his erection building. "Play with me, Si. Don't hold back." I'm staring at his neck, the black maze of tattoos calling me in to get lost in there.

"Oh little fox," he says with a small smile and cinnamon on his breath. I see all the fire in his delicious absinthe green eyes. "I make the commands."

He still has me pinned, but I lean my face forward towards his ear. "Boy…Toy," I taunt.

To my surprise he shoves up my dress, lifts me up onto the counter and spreads my legs out wide. He pulls me forward to the edge, completely rips my panties, halfway pulling them off, the only parts remaining are the ones trapped under my ass. His tongue is on my clit so fast and furious, I'm trembling within seconds, it feels like, gripping the edges of the counter and crying out for him to keep going, don't stop.

But of course he does. "You think I'm going to let you come after slapping me?" he says, rising up and grabbing my chin in his grasp. He turns around and starts walking to his room, stating "Come" as his only command.

"Oh I plan to," I say as I jump down and follow him. I walk past Basil, the cat sitting defiantly on the kitchen table, not a care in the world that he's on off-limits property.

In Simon's room, he lights a candle, the smells of teakwood quickly filling the space. He turns on some soft music, turns down the lights, and I'm already buzzing at the sudden shift in slow and methodical energy.

"You say you want to play?" he asks.

I nod my head, a little heady with what he might have in store for me. There's a twinge of something in my belly, excitement mixed with apprehension. I somehow know he'd never hurt me, but there's still the bit of fear of what's to come.

"Lie down," he commands nodding to the bed. My dress is still hiked up around my waist, my torn panties left behind on his kitchen counter, and I start to pull my dress back down.

"Leave it," he says, lighting another candle, this one maroon.

I pull the dress down anyways, sit down on his bed and feel the subtle fuzz of his dark blanket beneath my legs.

He yanks off his t-shirt, leaving me with a glorious view of his bare torso and arms and all that charcoal ink. I can't help myself, I reach over and place my hands on his forearms, run them up and over his biceps, feel the ripple of muscles of his arms, his shoulders, his chest as I explore.

Until he snatches my wrists like I knew he would, holding them there between our bodies. "Safe word, Lila."

"Why? What do you have in store for me?"

His eyes dart over to the maroon candle. "See that candle there?" I nod yes. "It's meant to be poured. On skin."

I tingle at the thought of hot wax on me, at Simon dotting little bits along my skin, the initial sting of the burn, tempered by his mouth. I let out a little pant of breath in anticipation.

"And where will you be pouring it?" I ask, imagining just the right soft crook of skin where thigh and pelvis meet. The stinging burns. How enticing that would be.

"Ahh, the fun is in not knowing," he murmurs. "Safe word."

Should I come up with something new? The standard "red" or something more sexy?

I decide I like our ridiculous little word I came up with back at the beach cottage, back when I had no idea if he was serious and blurted out whatever came to mind. Because after that, there was no denying I was going to let Simon into my soul.

"October," I whisper, peering up at him beneath my lashes.

I'm hoping I get the chance to use it.

He nods once, tells me he can only trust me if I use it, and I promise him I will.

Make me cry, Simon. I need to cry, help me get there, I silently pray to him.

He releases my hands and slowly grazes a finger down my throat, then my chest, sending chills up and down my skin. "I should slap you for slapping me," he says, and I flinch instinctively. He leans down closer to me, resting one hand on either side of my hips, his shoulders and face in front of my own. "But I don't hit women, Lila. Not like that. And I expect you to never hit me like that again either, understand?" His eyes are like glowing rings of green surrounded by black pupils, eerie in this candlelight.

I reach up and slap him again, harder this time, heart beating in my chest at what he'll do in return.

He closes his eyes, jaw clenched, barely a reaction on his face, then opens his eyes again, staring so intensely in mine that I have a little flutter of fear in my chest.

He keeps his eyes on me and slowly rises up, backing away from the bed and me. I reach up to grab at the waist of his jeans, a silent plea to come back closer to me, but he pushes my arm away and continues his retreat, walking slowly backwards to the wall, eyes held firmly on me. He crosses his arms over his chest and I scan the sight of him. If you didn't know better, you'd think he was a bouncer at a seedy nightclub that does shady tattoo work for gangs in the secret back room. Intimidating and risky looking, yet I know better.

I know that if I slap a man twice, with zero violence given in return, then there's nothing but safe warmth and protection under all that fierce and intimidating facade.

"What are you doing, Lila?" Simon asks to my surprise. My eyes adjust in having to find his eyes in the darkness.

"I'm playing," I say.

"No. You're not. I told you we won't be doing that, hits to the face, and you did it again anyways. That's testing me. Not playing." His body is immobile against the wall.

I shrug like I haven't a care in the world. Like I'm not hot and eager for him, all at just the mere sight of him and sound of his baritone voice. "So? What if I was?" I ask.

He unwinds his arms and steps back to me, kneeling down in front of me, spreading out my legs. I press my calves against his torso, feeling the warmth of his skin.

He grabs my hips gently and pulls me closer to him. "Is that how he would fuck you, Lila?"

A lightening crash. That's what happens to me with his question. Like a blinding lightening crash right in front of my face.

His question feels like its own slap to the face, and I try and pull back from him, but he tightens his grasp on my hips. "Is that how it was? Your temper would flare in a fight and you'd slap him, and then he'd slap you and then what, he'd hurt you more, and then fuck you and make you think that was love?"

I have the urge to throw up.

I don't know why I do it, it's exactly what not to do, but I reach up to try and slap Si again, only he snatches my arm before I get the chance. I try and wriggle free from his grasp, amazed at how much easier that seems. So instinctive and easy for me to pick a fight that builds to violence and ends in fucking.

Only Simon lets go completely of his grasp on me, then swiftly gets up and backs away again before I get the chance to hit him. I rise up off the bed, going after him, shoving him backwards. But he only steps back with my force, then leans against the wall again.

"Fight me, come on!" I say, tears stinging behind my eyes. The tears I wanted, only I thought they'd come from slaps to my ass, or a crash of a paddle on my bare skin, a whip, something like that. Toys I hadn't ever used before, but toys I craved to bring on my tears.

Not this. Not his complete disarming, his brick wall becoming a cloud, leaving nothing for me to fight against but empty air. Why is that so terrifying to me?

I pound my fists onto his chest, so much energy exploding out of me, and for a moment he lets me. Just the cloud, nothing to fight back. Eventually he grabs my arms, twisting me around and locking me in, my back against his chest, my arms locked under his. I try and buck and flail out my legs in kicks, but he only keeps his embrace, twisting his own leg against both of mine to keep me from kicking, letting me fight and flail uselessly in his grasp until eventually the fatigue sets in and I'm deflated with no fight left in me anymore. How long it takes is hard to say. Seconds? Minutes maybe? Me flailing in a temper tantrum like a toddler, with emotions too big to know how to regulate. Except I'm not a kid, I'm a twenty-five year old woman who should know better. Who does know better.

It should be embarrassing. I should be consumed with shame, but somehow that's only a tiny flicker of what I feel. Shame is a card I carry with me all around. Shame of my past, my depression, my lack of skills, my wavering sense of worth—it's all so familiar. It should be here with me now as I had just been flailing in my man's arms, letting him fully see the real me, my final mask shed.

But it's barely there, the shame. I don't know why or how it all shrunk down. Maybe it's the way I've learned to have pride in my temper, the one thing I know is very much *me*. Something my therapist has taught me to learn to love, explaining that self worth isn't based on accomplishments, but understanding and loving the pieces of us that are inherently us, no matter the accomplishments we can put on paper.

Wish I had remembered that earlier today, when I was spiraling in my own self doubt and hatred.

Or maybe I just needed to kick the shame all away right along with the demon energy fueling the kicks of my tantrum. Maybe that's just how I work.

That energy is gone now though, exerted out and I feel tired, I realize. Defeated, but in a beautifully freeing way, as if I defeated my own shadowy self.

Simon's arms remain around me, but he loosens his grip slightly, unwraps his leg that had been on mine, and I still my body against him. He kisses my temple, my wet cheeks. He whispers "I'm here, Lila" and "I love you" over and over again in my ear, kisses mixed in with his words.

And I realize something. This moment right here, feeling a man's arms around me, so tender and soft after all that intensity, hearing him tell me he loves me—it's similar to the high I used to feel with Royce, post-big fights that would get horribly scary, right up until he left that scar. Only this time, there was no messy crash and burn to rock bottom before reaching the high. None whatsoever, and yet, I feel the high nonetheless.

I never before believed I ever could feel that high again. But I do.

No, actually—this high is even better. Different. Because it's pure, it's not built off a stolen soul. It's just pure and good and clean. A runner's high as opposed to a heroin one.

I spin myself around in Simon's arms, wrap my arms around his neck and kiss him and cry and tell him I love him too, that I'm sorry and I love him too. He kisses my mouth so gently with such tenderness, my soft sobs slowing down in his kisses, ceasing altogether.

A scary thought reaches the depths of my mind. I debate shoving it aside, but decide I'm not doing that anymore. I've come all the way here, this far, no sense in hiding myself anymore now that Simon has seen this ugliest side of me. The darkest places my mind and behaviors will go, on full display. So I share my scary thought.

"Am I the abuser now?" I whisper into the crook of his neck, my head laying on his shoulder.

"Oh Lila," he sighs. "No, Lila, you're not." I feel his hand on my back, rubbing up and down in comfort.

"How do you know?" I ask. "How can you be sure?" I'm desperate for an answer here, scared of it being true, that I am the monster now. "I did all the things, Simon. I pushed you, I picked a fight, I lashed out, I *hit* you. And now I'm crying my apologies, all of it." It's sickening to hear my own words, see the similarities between my own pathetic behavior and that abuse cycle. "So how can you be sure?" I repeat. "What's the difference between a basic human meltdown and a violent episode?"

And Simon, the beautiful, wise, incredible human soul that he is...he rocks my world with his answer.

He looks down at me, kisses me softly on the lips before speaking.

"Power, Lila. It's power, that's the difference."

Power.

Just that simple little thing. It all makes sense, of course, he's right. It's so much easier to feel all the things that feed the cycle—fear, feeling threatened, out of control, guilty and shamed, confused—so much easier when there's the almighty Holy Grail of a power imbalance.

It's why it's so effective when you're dating a man in secret, who's six years older than you and you're just a teen.

So much more effective when that man isolates you and puts you in a position where he holds all the cards.

And you're just along for the ride with no one to talk to or sort through the confusion and torment. Telling yourself the age difference is no big deal. Him taking your virginity was only technically wrong by mere weeks, really.

Besides, the good times are *so good*.

But it all comes back to power. It's why my mom always presses on me and Lucy to have good jobs, to make our own good money, to never rely solely on a man. I wonder for the first time if my mom had once experienced a similar cycle? Not with my dad, he doesn't have a mean bone in his body. But maybe someone before him.

And it's why since that power imbalance I endured, I had somewhere in the back of my mind resolved to never give that power to someone again. Instead I chose one night stands and casual relationships that meant nothing, keeping everyone at arm's length.

Dating down.

Dating someone I thought was easy to manipulate, to control. Someone less attractive than me or who had even less money than I had, or someone I didn't take seriously.

Or someone cripplingly *nice*, like Joey Conti—Lucy's childhood friend from our neighborhood. And now Joey is engaged to

Grayson's best friend, fellow musician Ruby Francesca. Joey was nice and safe. Easy.

That's how I've done it, I'd date down, so that I could be safe and always feel a notch above.

Until now. With Simon. My Hot Nerd Photographer Mastermind that challenges me in ways I've never let anyone before. He broke me. In the best way possible.

"Do you understand, Lila?" he asks, eyes so tender looking into mine.

I nod. "Yes. No power imbalance because you never felt like the situation was out of your control."

"Precisely, that's right," he says with a kiss on the ridges of knuckles on each of my hands.

I bite my lip, another thought on my mind that I have to ask. "And what if I lose my temper and slap you again? I'm not always the best with that kind of thing." It feels odd to admit that out loud to someone. I try and wear my temper with pride. I've worked hard to learn to like that about myself, see it as an endearing flaw, but I can admit it's not always pleasant, my temper. Even now with how far I've come in being able to regulate my emotions, flare ups happen.

Simon takes my hand and walks me over to his bed. He lifts up my dress and removes it so that I stand before him naked with just my heels on. I watch as he unbuttons and removes his own jeans and boxers, and I start to think he's ignoring my question, but then he speaks, standing naked before me. "If that happens, I'll ask that you try to recognize when your temper is flaring, and breathe through it and see your own power in being able to control, and to get to the bottom of what is really beneath the anger." He cups my cheeks in his hands. "You can do that, if you choose to, Lila. I believe that. But if you can't," he leans down to my breast, the warm heat of his mouth like the inviting escape in those first moments when you sink into a hot tub. Hot relief, and I moan in a similar ecstasy until he pauses to speak again. "If you can't, and you mess up as we all do," he says, tongue slipping back out to circle around my nipple.

"Yes?" I half whisper, half moan. I feel the tightness in my lower belly, slickness between my legs.

"Know that I'll help calm you down. And I will never, ever, *ever*, hit you back."

"Uh-huh," I whimper out, rolling my head back, feeling a dizzying mix of emotion at his promise, mixed with loving pleasure.

He kneels down in front of me. "I'll never hurt you, Lila." I whimper again, feeling a finger slip inside me. "Say you understand."

"I understand," I gasp, my pleasure rising.

And then a *thwack* on my ass, hot and stinging. I look down at him, startled.

"Unless we're playing," he says with a wolfish grin, and fuck if I don't spin myself right around, drop to the floor on all fours, offering up my ass to him free and clear and say, "Let's play."

I GUESS I OWE YOU an explanation. I may have lied a little and downplayed the number of times Royce put his hands on me. I'm pretty good at twisting up my own stories, a little tweak here or there to make them sound better, but I'm working on it.

It was true that I finally ended it when he left his first scar on me, that was honest. But yeah, I guess it wasn't quite as high and mighty and fabulous as me walking away after just three little incidents. Sounds nicer that way though.

After Simon and I had our little fun time playing, and then fun time making love, and then fun time laying sweaty and panting in each other's arms, I asked him how he knew. I had downplayed it all to him too, so how did he know what was happening when I slapped him, trying to mask it as foreplay?

And listen to this—he said he saw it in my eyes, and my body language. He could tell something wasn't right, and that when you engage in the kind of kinks he likes (and me too, I'm very quickly finding; highly recommend the candle), that you need to have full trust and be able to know one another well. That's it, that's all. Apparently we're only just getting started, and there's a lot more to come in the way of fulfilling sexual fantasies.

He asked me what had been on my mind that brought on my meltdown (my word choice, not his), and I told him about work. Finding out my mom was the one that got me the job and how it sent me in a spiral of embarrassment in stupidly thinking that the entire crew, everyone involved in the project that I was so excited about, that they actually chose me for me. It felt humiliating, standing there reciting my lines, playing my part, hoping it sounded natural, paranoid and wondering who knew and who didn't. It sent me down into a self-doubt realizing I never actually earned it, this project I've been so excited to be a part of.

"Lila, quit trying to prove so much to everyone. You may have had a nudge to help get you in front of them, and that's how the industry works. It's a good project though. They would not have chosen you if they felt you weren't going to be a good fit."

"I hope you're right."

"I am," he said with a squeeze. "Just know who you are, the amazing fierceness that rests inside of you, and live your life. What in bloody hell are you trying to prove anyways, how do you even know if you're proving the *right* thing? It's impossible to know, nothing in life is as steady and static as that. And if we try and live by those standards, we box ourselves in and then we're left empty and alone when the world inevitably changes."

"So what do you do instead?" I asked, genuinely trusting his guidance.

"Listen to your instincts. Pay attention to what you feel here," he said, hand on my belly.

"Trust my gut?"

"Yes. Very simple."

I had nodded, laughing internally at how Simon had a bizarre way of simplifying intense situations. Maybe that's just what happens when you've been orphaned like he had, raised by a faux aunt put up to the challenge to be his stand in mother-figure. Big, traumatic problem, loving solution.

"So," he asked, "what do your instincts tell you? About this job, I mean."

"That I'm exactly where I'm supposed to be, and I should embrace it."

I felt those words, too. Just a gut feeling I have, that this role *is* meant for me. Maybe that in and of itself was the scariest part of all, thus sending me finding all the ways to not trust it. Determined to call its bluff.

But I'm going to push past.

It's a little scary how much this man has been able to help me in such a short time.

But now it's my turn to help him, because there's one little piece between us that still needs to be figured out. Grayson.

It seems to me like a whole lot of past stuff that should be water under the bridge, but what do I know. It's hard to explain Grayson and Ruby and my sister and this whole pseudo family we are, but we're a tight knit group, and so with me very much in love with Simon, they need to get over their issues.

It's my next mission.

twenty-six

. . .

lucy

IT'S TIME FOR me and Justin to figure out our next steps. We've been co-existing in our house for weeks now, and at this four month mark I'm definitely starting to show, even with my height offering a bit of forgiveness. There's only so far my loose sweaters can go. I can't hide this from my parents forever, and of course the truth will spill its way out and everywhere once the excitement of "I'm pregnant!" quickly turns to "But it's not Justin's and he's leaving me because even though we both agree there's still love here, he can't bring himself to raise someone else's baby."

Never did I ever think I'd be a divorcee and single mother.

Justin and I are sitting out on our back porch, the evening November air chilly but crisp, just right to sit out here with the blanket I have snuggled around me. A neighbor somewhere must have a bonfire going, the smell of wood and little distant rumbles of laughter floating their way in to our space. I push myself on our porch swing, thinking how little we ever used our own gorgeous outdoor fireplace that came with the house. How little we've done of anything really fun lately. Work took center stage.

"Do you want to keep the house?" Justin asks me. He's sitting in an Adirondack chair across from me, sipping a beer and looking relaxed and casual. To an outsider you'd think we were just a happy couple, enjoying a Friday evening together.

The porch swing creaks rhythmically with each little push I give it. *Creak.*

Creak.

Creak.

Like a ticking time bomb.

"I'm not sure. It's too big, I just don't know that I'd want to maintain all of this on my own, but if you..." I don't say the next words. That if he wants to keep it he can. He'd have to buy me out, but if he wants to, he can.

But why would he want all this for just himself?

"I don't," he says, staring out at the woods beyond our porch, our patio, the massive stone fireplace that we've used exactly once in two years.

"When do you think it all started slipping for us?" I ask, a feverish need building in me as I look around at the lavishness of this home we expected to fulfill all our dreams, but now feels absolutely absurd as we both talk about how neither one wants it in the divorce. "Do you think it was this house?"

"Maybe, actually. Yeah," he snorts, raising his bottle for a sip.

"You never wanted this house," I mutter out with sadness. "But you always go along with whatever I say, don't you?"

"Fuck, you make me sound like a damn dog, Luce. Or a bee buzzing around to fulfill the queen's needs." His tone is bitter.

I dig my toe into the floor, pausing my rocking. "Did you ever feel that way?"

He rests his hand down on his armrest and turns to me. "Sometimes, actually. Yeah."

Don't ask questions you don't want to know the answers to.

"Why did you do it? Why let me boss you around like that?"

"For real?" He frowns at me like I'm crazy for asking.

"Yeah, for real. I'm trying to figure out what happened, I need to understand and get to the bottom of it."

He snickers. "That's exactly it, Luce. You approach life like it's a problem to be solved. Actually no—*conquered*. Yeah. You have this need to conquer any problem you can. I always just figured, let her. She's good at that. It's definitely not the way I operate, and I mostly admired you for the way you could do that. It was confidence, it was sexy." He looks away again, shaking his head and taking another long pull on his beer. His leg starts fidgeting, a maniacal little bounce. The conversation is getting to him.

It's not the way we talk, the two of us. Never. We never have these big "What are we, what is us?" type talks. Is that what couples are supposed to do? I think about Reggie and her husband Xavier —I can absolutely see them having those kinds of talks. My parents? Doubtful, I can't see it. They'd be all business. Guess that's where I learned it from.

I resume my swinging, the creaking picking up again.

"I'm sorry I was so controlling, Justin. I'm sorry my need to conquer and control stopped being sexy for you." It's passive aggressive of me to say, but it's all I have in me.

"Are you fucking kidding me?" he asks, looking at me. We hold eye contact for a split second, then he turns away again, back out to the forest with a "huh" kind of sarcastic huff. He's shaking his head, his leg fidgeting like a rocket, ready to burst and take off. He takes another swig of beer, this one emptying the bottle. He looks at it, tosses it into the corner recycle bin where the bottle hits the rim and it momentarily looks like it might not make it in, but then does, disappearing with a clanging crash to join the other empty bottles.

He gets up to the mini fridge we keep out here, pulls open the door, then pauses for a sec, looking at me saying, "You know what?" But then he thinks better of it and shakes his head again, grabs another beer. He goes to pop off the top with his wedding ring, usually on his left hand, and realizes it's not there. I watch Justin's body in a sort of sick fascination. It's as if he's an exploding bottle of soda someone shook up and then ever so slightly twisted the top off, just enough to send it spinning and fizzing chaotically, ready to burst. He's muttering under his breath sarcastically while he searches around the porch for a bottle opener. I point over to the armrest of his chair where he left it, and he lets out a "Of course you know where it is," shaking and agitated as he finally frees his beer.

He stops and looks at me. "You think that's what it is, huh? That I just magically stopped finding the person that you are sexy?" He shakes his head yet again, takes another sip, paces up and down in frantic little bursts. Three steps. Then a pause, two steps. A clench and unclench of a fist. Scattered energy.

"You said you *admired* it, my conquer and control. Admired. Past tense," I spit out.

"Dammit, Lucy! I *love* that you love control, present fucking tense! I do, I really do!" He looks away from me, despondent. Wipes his cheeks and his tears. "What I don't love is the...is the... robot of a wife I suddenly got! Yeah," he nods frantically, "all right around when we got this house, when you got the promotion, yup. Then you turned into a robot of a wife. I mean..." he turns and looks at me, arms wide out to his side. "Do you think it feels *good* to be shrugged away from when I try and go in for a hug? Like I'm an inconvenience to you? Or to feel like you think fucking me is a chore? When you dropped the laugh and eye roll I used to get at my jokes, but just stuck with the eye roll. No more laugh, no smile or any sense of appreciation. *Just the eye roll,* Lucy. It's *that,* that's what I didn't like. That change. Excuse me if I struggled to find your obvious disgust with me *sexy.*"

He looks away and paces again. My heart is pounding as I listen, but my face remains stoic. "I used to love making you laugh," he says, almost more to himself than to me. He wipes his face again, and I wonder what the hell is wrong with me that I'm not crying.

"It didn't mean you should go flirting with another woman, all but planning your dream life with her," I say.

"Fine, you're right. You win, I started this spiral, I know that. I should not have let that happen, and I've told you time and time again I'm sorry for that. So incredibly sorry, it was wrong and I know I hurt you, I do.

"But you know what?" He slips a hand in his pocket, his agitated energy needing to be contained. He huffs out a sarcastic laugh. "It's a little bit like your need for control had gone so far, you were thriving off of it *so much*, that you needed to control how lovable you'd allow yourself to be."

Ouch.

That you needed to control how lovable you'd allow yourself to be. Why does that feel painfully in the vicinity of—accurate?

"Do you see that?" he asks, his voice almost pleading. "Like your control turned inward and you locked up the warm person you used to be. And I think you did it because otherwise, otherwise —you might be loved by me too much, and you might love *me* too much in return, and then you'd fall and lose control completely, lost in that. Lost in me. Imagine that. Losing yourself in hopeless love to me." His voice catches on his last words.

There's the lump in my throat. I can feel the sting of tears behind my eyes. My simple Justin throwing out a truth that cuts right to my core with how right he is.

"But the problem is, Lucy," he says softly, barely above a whisper. "I had already lost myself to you. I just wish you had been there with me."

And with that he walks past me, into our home, the whiff of his shaving lotion, his musky cologne hitting me in his wake. Once alone, I finally allow myself to burst into tears.

twenty-seven

. . .

lila

I GIVE SIMON'S hand a squeeze and smile at him as he looks around the luxurious lobby of Grayson's building. It's glittering with garland dipped in silver sparkle, twinkle lights, and a faux fir tree fit for the White House. I can see that Simon's nervous as we give our names to the doorman, his palm sweaty in mine. The doorman scans through a screen, says Simon's not on the list, and I smile and say he's my date. I ask him to call up and see if Lila Ray can have a plus one.

A few minutes later and we're walking into the flat, at what is definitely not a small holiday get together as promised, but a pulsing party of maybe fifty or so beautifully dressed guests. It's dark and offers speakeasy vibes, save for the music. Not Christmas tunes, but the Dog Tags & Lace album is thumping through the speakers. It's Ruby Francesca's album she released right before the one that earned her her multiple music awards. All her albums have skyrocketed along with her continued fame and success, and I wonder briefly if she and Joey are here.

I look over to Simon, his face serious as he scans the room, the modern luxury and high ceilings. He has on his glasses, a long-sleeved black button-down, black jeans. It's nearly the professor-look I first recognized in him, only with the neck tattoos now on display beneath his trim shadow of facial hair.

We wander around, mingle and smile and grab some drinks, still yet to run into anyone we know beyond casual acquaintance. I feel someone grab my arm and spin around to see Penny and Charles, looking awkward and nervous.

"So many fancy people here, it's wild! I still think of Grayson as this gangly boy who kindly let me do his makeup now and then when we were in primary school. I forget that he's got a whole famous life now!" Penny's beaming. "And I finally got to meet Ruby!" she says, leaning into me so I can hear over the music.

I follow Penny's eyes across the crowd and over to a small cluster of high back armchairs, Ruby perched on the edge of one, legs crossed and long dark curls dangling to one side. Joey's standing behind her, hands on her shoulders as they talk with another couple in similar positions beside them. I make eye contact with Joey, and he flashes his dimples in a smile and head nod. To my relief, I feel none of the longing for him I once had. The longing that crept in unexpectedly just last year, right as he and Ruby had once again gotten back together after three years apart.

Joey whispers something in Ruby's ear, points in our direction and she looks up, giving me a little nod and fake smile.

I may not have always been very nice to Ruby in the past. I'll work on it.

Charles and Simon are chatting about something, but I can clearly see Simon is uncomfortable. I ask Penny where Grayson is and then slink off to find him, figuring I'll give him the heads up on who my plus one is.

I wander into a room with a massive projector screen filled with the green grass of some soccer (fine, football) game that's playing. I see Grayson in all his gorgeous charm, looking sharp in a maroon suit with a luxurious sheen to it, black t-shirt beneath the jacket with some graphic design pattern. He rises up to me and kisses me on either cheek before taking my hand and prompting me to spin while he appraises my outfit.

"Let's see it, who are we wearing tonight?"

"Oh, just a little vintage shop find," I say, waving the flared sleeves of chiffon like dark fairy wings.

"Embracing your new 70s vibes, I see. I love it," he says with a kiss to my hand. "Congrats on the show, by the way." And I thank him sincerely, which feels nice. "Where is this date of yours, then?"

"Right. So, I wanted to talk to you about that," I say, grabbing his arm and pulling him out of the room and into a quieter hallway.

"Oh, Lila, my oh my, is he hideous? Do you need to hide him, prep me or something?"

"No he's very handsome. Smoldering, even."

"Do you mind sharing, then? Or wait! Is he married and you're indulging in a sordid affair that must be kept under wraps?" he says, his eyes dancing with mischief.

I laugh. "Hardly. No."

"Shame," Grayson pouts.

I go for ripping off the Band-Aid. "Actually, it's your old friend. Faux cousin. Simon Sharp. The photographer. And we're very much in love and so you have to get over this whole past thing with him and try and forgive and heal together," I ramble on, aware that it's a loaded statement given the delicate nature. Elsie, Simon's ex, was Grayson's big sister, so I'm sure any mention of her in any capacity comes laced with heavy emotion.

A look crosses over Grayson's eyes and he grabs my arm, pulling me into the butler's pantry corridor, then around the side to a bedroom door. He pulls me into the room, where there's a bed and two night tables, each with a small lamp on, providing a warm glow of light. The music and crowd beyond are muffled as he pushes the door nearly to a close.

I'm nervous as I look at him.

"Lila," he says to me with this jaw clench that is so uncharacteristically Grayson, I'm a little shaken by it. "You...are not to continue seeing him anymore."

I laugh, I can't help myself.

But his ominous gray eyes reach mine with seriousness that can only be described as deadly. It's like daggers are shooting from them, as opposed to the care that I think—I *think* he's trying to convey.

"Grayson. With all due respect, you're not my father, okay?" I'm trying to keep my tone light, breezy. Breezy! Because he's got to be kidding me.

Except that he's definitely not. Grayson charges towards me, grabbing my arms just beneath the shoulders and giving me a firm shake. "This is not a joke, Lila. Don't pull the classic 'I don't Give a Shit about Anyone but Myself' Lila Show on this! Not this!"

Fuck, his words hurt. "What the hell is that supposed to mean, Grayson?" I ask, reaching a hand up to hold one of the spots where he's aggressively grabbing.

It's so far from the Grayson I know, and it's kind of scaring me. "That's really what you think? That I don't give a shit about anyone?" I have tears in my eyes, but I refuse to let them out. I cried enough this past week over things far more worthy than Grayson's hurtful words.

"Get the fuck off her," I hear the all too familiar baritone voice behind me.

Simon.

All at once Grayson releases me and I stumble back into Simon's chest. With a quickness, his hands jut out and he catches me. I'm nearly lifeless, cradled in his embrace, my legs wanting to give out and my heart pounding.

I feel torn. Everything about Simon's arms around me feels so good, so right, that's it's disarming. But Grayson is a trusted friend. One that has been a part of my extended friend group for a couple years now. One that I know in my heart to be a decent human being and the token gay best friend every girl wants to have, there to offer a man's accolades without feeling unsafe and objectified. The man that helped me get on my feet when I first moved to London. The Best Man to Ruby in Joey and Ruby's upcoming wedding, the officiant in countless others because he's too nice to say no, even with his rocker status and star fame soaring by the minute. That's Grayson.

And yet? I want to listen to Simon, not Grayson in this moment. I want to turn my head and nuzzle in the smell of Simon's pine and tobacco scented neck, feel the scratchiness of it on my nose.

Grayson lets out a little "huff" and wipes something off his nose, and I realize he too is fighting his emotions. He puts his hands on his hips, looking like he's contemplating what to say next. "You think he's good people, huh?" he says to me, his tone basically accusatory.

I ignore him. I'm still mad and not ready to let his last comment slide. "What the hell did you mean when you said I don't give a shit about anyone, Grayson?" I'm trying to stay calm and collected when I say it, I guess fall into my usual "carefree calm and cool and selfish" Lila tone Grayson's currently accusing me of, but I'm struggling. My voice is faltering, and I hate it.

Grayson's face softens, ever so slightly. I can see it, he feels badly.

Still, that doesn't erase the words.

"Ignore him, Lila," Simon says, his arms tight around me.

I feel like I'm caught in the middle of some rivalry, and I'm not sure where to go or what to do.

"Ask him where he got his scars," Grayson says. "Go on, then. See if you know the real Simon. If this tidied up version is the real him," he says with a hand wave up and down towards us, "or if there's a darker monster beneath all this."

"Don't you dare call him a monster!" I scream, attempting to step forward, fully planning on using the sudden surge of energy bursting through my veins to shove Grayson.

But I'm locked up tight in Simon's arms. "Let me go," I say, turning my head up towards Simon. "He has no right, no right! To talk to you like that." Tears are streaming down my face, but I have no idea why. My stomach is doing flips, my pulse is racing red hot. I hate so much that my anger is coming out, *again*, all in tears in this moment. I hate that I'm an angry crier.

I feel Simon's grasp loosen though. "Yes he does," he says in a whisper.

"No. He doesn't. You're far from a monster," I scoff, attempting to come off sarcastic, not desperate.

The alarm on my face must be a glaring spray of lights, but no one in the room seems to notice. I turn back to Grayson. "What the hell are you talking about, why would you say that?"

"He knows why," Grayson says, nodding toward Simon. "Elsie."

The word fills the room like a spell. I see its power and its eminence, I can feel it all around me. *Elsie*. A spell of a word that sits and hangs in the air.

Simon releases me completely and takes a step back. "He's right. You should stay away from me, Lila. He's right."

"What?" I say, trying to step closer to him, but Simon only steps further back, out of the room and into the hall. "Si? What are you saying, don't let that fucker talk like that." I look back at Grayson, and now his face is the one with all the soft concern as he looks back and forth between the two of us.

"Lila, come on," Grayson says, stepping towards me to put a hand on my elbow. I let him, only because I'm not sure what else to do. Simon's face has completely turned to ice and his body is slowly being swallowed up by the dark depths of the butler's pantry corridor—reminding me of when I watched him walk away from me in the dark that very first night we met. He turns and walks towards the door at the end of the corridor, a side service exit to the flat.

"I fucking love you, you bastard!" I shout out to the shadowy dark of the hall. "I don't care what you did, I love you! You made me do that!" My voice echoes wildly down the hall. The murmuring voices of the party behind us start to quiet, the party getting wind of something going down.

I reach for the closest thing next to me, a vase on a table, and I grab it getting ready to throw it. But then pause. I look over to Grayson, and he gently grabs the vase from my grasp, putting it back down. No anger on his face anymore, just sadness.

"Carry on, now!" Simon says brightly to the guests that have started to crowd around the entrance of the hallway. "Just a little lover's quarrel, move along, I've got it." His voice has such easy charm to it, the familiar Grayson I know and have come to love, and I wonder how often he's had to slide into the charm when there was something far darker weighing on his mind.

"Come on, Lila," Grayson says to me, pulling me back into the room and towards its en-suite. "Let's get you cleaned up."

I lifelessly follow, seeing nothing but red hot rage through my tears, not even sure what in the world is happening or what's going on. I only know I'm getting my heart broken into a million horrifying pieces, and I have no strength for it. Slowly, I feel myself calming, my tears stopping altogether, the life-force in me slowly leaving my body. Like a body bag is being zipped up over me, and last to lock up is my face.

"I'm sorry for what I said, that was uncalled for," Grayson whispers as he sets me down on a small padded bench. He grabs tissues and gently dabs my face.

I only nod dumbly, staring off at nothing, no emotion left in me. I'm in such disbelief at what just happened back there. The reaction from Grayson, the confrontation of him and Simon, the shift in Simon as he acquiesced to everything Grayson spat at him.

As if Simon believes he really is a monster. Like the word "Elsie" unlocked something in him.

What is he hiding? What's he not telling me? Because clearly this is more than just a bad break-up with Grayson's big sister that Grayson never got over. This was something more. Something I missed.

Is this for real? Is this really happening? Am I once again the fuckup that trusted the wrong person and made all the wrong decisions, and now I'm being punished for it? That's how I feel, that I'm being so horribly punished for it.

"You see," Grayson says, stepping back from me and looking at my face with pain in his eyes. "Simon is the very reason my sister is dead."

twenty-eight

. . .

lila

I T'S FUNNY TO me how I can feel like I've come so far, yet suddenly feel lost all over again.

I remember being younger, back when I had first come back from my inpatient hospital stay, depression a word my parents had reluctantly been forced to let into the household, hush hush as they demanded it all be kept. Can't worry Lucy! Can't let the world know that L. Delphi-Ray's daughter is suffering!

I had walked back into my childhood bedroom, exactly the same as I had left it with its random Disney posters (we teens thought we were so cute and ironic). My hoodies were neatly stacked as if far fancier, looking the way my mom's collection of Hermes scarves might be assembled.

It was around the time "Keep Calm and Carry on" was big, and I thought that shit was so simple and genius that I even my own little painting of it that sat propped up on my nightstand. It wasn't until later that I learned this darling little British phrase was actually created in 1939 as—get this—war propaganda.

My room felt different though, somehow. Hanging for a few

days with beige walls and no shoelaces, no pens or pencils, no freedom or anything because God forbid you get creative and try and harm yourself—let's make you feel like you're in prison instead!—after being there, then walking into the colors of my room, it felt completely different.

Because I was no longer the same. As much as I hated that time in my life, it was a good step for me, finally opening up about thoughts in my head and working to figure out some things. I met so many other kids with their own horror stories, far worse than anything my spoiled self was going through. But coming out I felt like there was the tiniest bit of hope. That maybe this darkness wouldn't last forever.

I had come far, but felt loss in the sense of needing to figure out a new direction, convinced now that my old one was no longer for me. There was something scary but exhilarating about it. I never cut again after that inpatient stay, even if my eating habits were still problematic at that time. I was determined to find some way to get a grip on things, some comforting control.

That's how I feel right now. Like I've crossed some goal point but I need to figure out the new task, because I'm at a loss. Everything I've mastered has come with a setback. I have a great job in my new role (yeah!) but it wasn't entirely earned (ouch). I have allowed myself to get close to someone and fall in love (awww!) but oh yeah, he apparently has a real dark past and kinda, sorta, is the reason my friend's big sister in now dead (fuck, fuck, fuck).

Even Penny, my awesome first real girlfriend that I made completely on my own—she's getting married soon and I doubt they're looking for a grown-up child living with them.

So here I am, sitting and staring at my laptop for a long overdue Telehealth session with Caroline, my therapist. I lied and told her I'm still in Pennsylvania so that she can legally see me since that's where she's licensed. I know she's going to give me a hard time about where I've been, why I've been MIA from sessions, and sure enough, within minutes she confronts me on that.

"Well, partially because I'm living in London now, though totally in PA at the moment visiting home, wink, wink," I say. She raises her eyebrows, knowing I'm lying, but she doesn't end the call.

I give her a rundown of all that's been going on, my wins and their tainted stipulations, Lucy and the baby and her upcoming divorce, my confusion because of how much I really feel in my heart Simon is a good guy, but I haven't heard from him and I haven't reached out to him, so there's that.

"What did Grayson say happened, exactly?" she asks. I look at her screen, a blank dark wall behind her, and a shelf with what I'm guessing are strategically placed books and some knick-knacks. One of the items is this large crystal rock—and amethyst. The crystal for serenity, healing, mental clarity. I could use that shit right about now.

I cringe. Caroline is not going to like this answer. But it's why I have to talk to her, because it doesn't seem right.

"Listen first, don't jump to conclusions, okay?"

She raises a scolding eyebrow to me. "Lila, love. What the hell do you think I do, exactly?"

I roll my eyes, sure she judges all kinds of things, who wouldn't? But I dive in anyway. "According to Grayson, Simon and Grayson's sister Elsie dated on and off for years. First as kids, young teens, then something went down a few years later when they were like eighteen or nineteen, and Grayson was fifteen. Apparently Elsie started getting shady, and then showing up with bruises on her arms, a busted lip, that kind of thing."

I furrow my eyebrows, because Caroline knows about my own history and similar markings, but she gracefully doesn't mention this parallel. It's not the time.

"She had moved out and said she was living with friends, but Grayson's parents figured she had secretly moved in with Simon, who was going to art school in London by then. They were worried about her, so they confronted Simon and his aunt...oh right, you don't know this," I say, and I go on to explain how Simon was an orphan, his late mom's best friend Victoria took him in, and how Victoria's sister Daisy is Grayson and Elsie's mom.

I see Caroline scribbling down her notes, the pad just off screen, probably trying to wrap her head around the odd family tree. I continue while she writes. "Then a little while later, Elsie kills herself. Swallowed up a whole bunch of pills, and that was that. Grayson and his family blamed Simon, said he had gotten her into drugs, had been beating her, all these really terrible things. A few days after Elsie's death, Simon gets into some massive fight, nearly kills a guy...at least, the family is pretty sure Simon's the one involved, and now Simon's on the run and in hiding, and Victoria begs her family not to turn him in. They agree, but only if Victoria and Simon never see them again."

Caroline nods, and lets out a deep breath. "Alright, well then."

"Yeah." I sit and wait for her to say something, but apparently she's got nothing to offer up just yet.

So I keep talking. "Here's the thing, though...I just don't really believe Simon is capable of any of that. Beating a girl. Drugs, nearly killing a man out of nowhere, any of it."

"His mom died of an overdose you said, right?"

Bitch. I hate that Caroline said that. "Yes, but that doesn't automatically make Simon a fucking addict!"

Caroline shakes her head. "No no, of course not, easy now, Lila. That's not what I'm saying. I'm saying that for the parents of Elsie and Grayson, they're of course going to look for the most obvious answer. Grief, in its torment, seeks blame as its way to heal. So it's not surprising that they'd blame Simon for getting their daughter into drugs if that's what they know is a part of his past, even if it was his mother and not him."

I nod, thinking about that. It makes sense, but I still hate it.

"What has Simon told you about his past?"

I shrug. "I mean, it looks bad, yeah. Addict mom, no dad, really. He says he got into fights a lot as a kid and that it took him a while to get on his feet. But never drugs or anything like that. Even his smoking habits are painfully controlled, he rolls his own cigarettes for less toxins, and honestly barely even smokes them, he's very disciplined. He's got this amazing career as a very well respected photographer." I sigh. "I don't know. He's amazing."

Caroline smiles, like she knows I got it bad. "How does he treat you?"

There it is, I figured this question was coming. I try my best to speak my next words as clearly and firmly as I possibly can. "Like the best I've ever been treated by anyone in my life. Ever."

"How do you know, what does 'best' mean? What does that look like?"

I contemplate the right way to explain this and finally land on, "Best means consistency. No ups and horrible crashes down, just steady and smooth and consistent."

"A pattern."

"Yes, a pattern. Trust patterns, not potential you say, right?" I smile at her, sip my water next to me to collect my thoughts before I continue. "Even with my parents' unconditional love, I still never felt the warmth and support that I feel with Simon. Oh!" I say, excited at this new thing I'm about to share. "And get this shit—I slapped him! Twice!"

She looks all startled and babbles on about how she's going to need to hear more on that.

I laugh. "I was all in my anger, not my greatest moment. He said I was testing him."

"Were you?" she asks, head slightly turned to the side like she finds this intriguing.

"Yeah, I guess I was, though it's not like I consciously was doing it in the moment."

"Our tests we put on people hardly ever are conscious," she agrees. "So what happened, how did he react?"

"Caroline—he backed away. He tried to talk to me, then I slapped him again, and he just kept his distance from me."

I leave out the whole tantrum that ensued. Best leave some things out of this.

"I just don't believe he could hit a woman, not when he's had plenty of time with me to show me his true colors. Not when I prompted a physical fight and he only worked really fucking hard to deescalate."

She sips her coffee, it's morning her time, afternoon here, then rests her face in her hands, elbow on her desk. "Lila, based on what you're telling me,"—(her disclaimer, no doubt. I'm onto her)—"it does in fact sound like you have seen nothing but good with Simon so far. But his past violence, this potential man he almost killed—"

"Maybe," I say, cutting her off. "That's not confirmed that they knew for sure it was Simon, they just suspected it for some reason. It may not have been him at all."

She nods, "Okay, yes. Just keep all of those things in mind, that's all."

"It doesn't even matter," I say with a defeated sigh. "He hasn't contacted me since the night when this all blew up. At Grayson's." I wonder momentarily how many stories Caroline hears about famous people. Must be hard to keep that all in, knowing juicy secrets.

"I'm guessing you haven't tried to contact him either?" she asks.

"No. I want to, I'm just not sure how to proceed yet."

"How are you feeling in all of this?" she asks.

"Well obviously a fucking mess, Caroline, that's why I called you," I say, rolling my eyes. I feel a little guilty for snapping. But whatever, that's her job, right? To deal with people when they're at their worst?

"A mess, what does that mean? What makes you a mess exactly?" It's a tactic of Caroline's that she's explained to me, where she asks seemingly dumb questions like what does "best" mean or "mess" mean.

It's annoyingly helpful when I take it seriously.

I sigh heavily. "A mess means I can't sleep, I can't stop crying any chance I'm able to, I miss him so much it physically hurts. The amazing director I'm working with had to have a pep talk with me after a scene I'm pretty sure I bombed, though she was too nice to put it that way. My sister needs me but I can't throw away my career and be there for her. I feel like nothing in my life is *right*, you know what I mean?"

She nods. "Aright, so how do you make it right?"

"How the fuck am I supposed to know, that's what you're here for."

She smiles, and I have to admit I kinda missed Caroline. "No no, my dear. I'm here to help *you* figure out *you*. By asking the right questions that unlock parts of your mind that have been hidden."

"Well go ahead," I say. "Work your magic, ask me the right questions so I can figure out what to do."

"You sure? It may take a little noodling on, so don't try and immediately answer. Can you do that?"

I nod. "Yes, fine, whatever. I'll let it sit for a sec." I'm dying for her amazing question that's going to magically help me solve for myself the complex puzzle of what to do.

"Alright. Lila...what exactly do you need right now?"

I open my mouth to shout out "To not feel like shit!" but then remember my promise, and I let it sit.

And think.

And then I feel. *What do I need right now?*

But I'm stuck. I dart my eyes over to her, silently telling her I'm stuck.

"Get into your body," she instructs me. "Close your eyes. What do you feel in your body, where do you feel something? Our bodies are often far more in tune, and can be the driving force of our minds, not the other way around like we often think."

I nod, close my eyes and try and feel what's in my body. I feel the fuzzy blanket beneath my bare ankles as I sit on my bed, legs tucked under me like a pretzel. I feel the tension in my shoulders and I shake them out and drop them.

And then I feel something in my throat. Like a lump. Like a communication I'm wanting. And I notice a tingle near my temples. I sit with the feelings, exaggerate them in my mind and let my mind wander like Caroline has guided me to do in the past. There's a boulder in my throat. Heavy and burdensome. In my temples the tingle is accompanied by a flaring light, blinking like a distress signal.

"What do you notice?" she quietly prompts.

"A boulder. Here," I say, signaling my throat. "And tingles and flashing distress signal lights in my temples."

"Good," she says. "Keep going."

But I don't even need to. Because I realize what I need.

I open my eyes. "Answers," I say.

"Answers. What kind?"

"Yes answers. I need to know the truth about this man they think Simon almost beat to death. I need to know who he was, if Simon really was involved, or if he's being wrongfully accused." I smile. "I have the feeling that Simon's being wrongfully accused, that he had nothing to do with this guy at all."

She smiles back. "Good. You look lighter. And how do you feel now?"

"Better than I've felt all week," I answer honestly.

It's time to start digging.

after

. . .

My dearest Simon,

I will keep this short. You never were much for talking.

You reading this means I am dead. My choice. I'm too tired, Simon. I'm just so tired, and it hurts. I hurt, and I don't want to hurt anymore. I can't continue.

I just wanted to say...

You were right. About everything.

Please forgive me.

X

Elsie

twenty-nine

. . .

lucy

YOU KNOW, JUSTIN has never once asked me who the father of the baby is. Isn't that strange? It occurs to me as we're walking back in the door, the two strange roommates, post mediation meeting, to figure out logistics as we proceed with the D word. Divorce. In December. The month of our anniversary.

I've been numb through this whole process, just functioning like a zombie robot. I go to work, come home, clean, maybe Google baby things, (the baby is a lima bean! An avocado! Pick your food of choice and we'll figure out how to make it weird!)—doing everything I can to avoid the emotions of it all. I think I'm in a frozen zone or something. I can't seem to really *move* emotionally. As though I'm waiting for something, but I don't know what. I think I learned that emotional coldness from my mother.

Speaking of, her response to the news had been as expected. She's constantly on the move and hard to nail down, but I ripped off the Band-Aid during one of her brief moments of being home and actually available. She did the usual Lilith Delphi-Ray things— a weighted sigh. A pursing of the lips. A comment on how she warned me that Justin was never going to be a "mover or shaker" and how of course I got bored with him.

I could have leapt over and throttled her. I bet Lila would have.

But not me. I'm the "yes, ma'am" daughter. I just let her lecture me and that was that. My father eventually rose from his chair with a quick but loving pat on my shoulder before he exited the room. That's it, that's all the support you get in the Ray household. Just an "I told you so" and a sad little pat on the shoulder from a man who probably had more to say, just never any space to actually say it.

I shake away the bitterness and look over to Justin. He's getting ready to head up the stairs, (presumably to retreat to his room and avoid me), and I blurt out my question.

"Why don't you want to know who the father is?" I ask. It comes out like an accusation more than anything.

Justin pauses, mid climb, one leg bent on the stair ahead of him. He turns his head and looks at me, then drops his gaze down to the floor and my heart pinches with guilt. He shifts position, turning completely to retreat back down the stairs. Puts his hands in the pockets of his gray slacks. He looks professional and poised, standing there in a polo shirt, shoulders back. It's only his eyes that give him away. To an outsider, you might think he was talking to a business associate, not his wife about the product of her affair.

"I'm sorry," I say, "that came out kind of abrupt." I grab my hair in my hands behind my neck, fiddle with it as if about to put it in a ponytail, eager to be doing something. I drop my hands down and repeat my question. "Why?"

"Because I already know who the father is, Luce."

I take a step back, heart skipping a beat. Then I laugh, "I'm sorry, but what?"

He shrugs. "Your watch. It lit up with Snapchats from him a few times, and I pretty much knew that if you were talking on there that something was off. I thought maybe you were doing the same kind of thing I had been. Until you told me you were pregnant, that is." He drops his head down and stares back down at the floor.

I feel exposed, blindsided, even deluded in a sense as I listen to him. Here I am thinking Justin was just avoiding knowing, and all this time he had already figured it out? I'm surprised by his air of calm as he casually confesses this.

"Why didn't you say anything?" I ask, putting my hand on my belly. "Not just now, but before the pregnancy?" *Before I had a chance to sleep with him.*

All I can think is *why, why, why didn't you say anything*?

Is that all I ever really wanted in the first place? For Justin to notice me with that little secret flirtation going on? See me with that same warm look on my face, all while paying attention to something that wasn't him? Because maybe if he had said something, if he fought for me, or tried to present his suspicions back when it *was* just the texting and flirting, back before it crossed that line, maybe I wouldn't have taken it any further.

It all dawns on me—maybe that's exactly what I had been hoping for. To be caught. To stir up anger. To feel my husband's fight in not wanting to lose me.

I think ever since I confronted him on the Dr. Gabby thing, he and I have been stuck. Frozen on a lake of ice and avoidance, not sure of where to go or how we ever even got there. We had never said we were splitting up. As hurt as I was through it all, I didn't feel it was worth giving up on us. I couldn't, not when Justin was begging for my forgiveness and I was caught between my confusion and my love for him. My own hurt and anger were suffocating, but part of it was anger at myself for being naive in thinking he and I were untouchable from such a destructible force.

But marriage isn't like that, is it? It's not quite so simple. When you're with someone for years, you'll inevitably be met with obstacles. The stresses of life and pressures you put on yourself to meet the next goal—they can take center stage at some point if you're not careful. You stop prioritizing your spouse, and suddenly that little switch turns from them being the love of your life and focal point, to them being a nuisance in the way of what you're trying to do. That's it, that's the danger zone when you let that happen. Marriage is like a hallway with lots of doors. When the hallway is pretty, tidy, well decorated, those doors remain firmly closed.

But when the hallway starts to get a little messy, the doors open, just a little. And you have a choice then—you can either roll up your sleeves, clean up the hallway, or not. And cleaning it is hard work, there's piles and boxes and you're scared to move them and see a spider crawl out unexpectedly. It's a dirty job, and one we can easily ignore. So you start to look out one of those doors instead. Just a peek, just to get a breath of fresh air, see what's there.

Well, I went ahead and took it a step further in my little peek out the door. Because when this convenient little flirtation struck up, offering the perfect way to sidestep everything, I went for it. I had been too hurt by Justin to accept any love from him, and this thing felt so wonderfully naughty, a thing just for me. I had been so sick of always being the responsible one, the one to figure everything out, to take care of everything. The one always there to initiate cleaning of the fucking hallway. Why should I have to be the one to fix things with my marriage, why couldn't my husband take the reins for once? Call up a marriage counselor, offer up solutions, *anything*?! I hated that the cheerleader role, the fix it role, the responsibilities and planning and organizing—it all always fell on me.

I guess I had finally decided I was tired, and ready to give up control.

Here's the thing though. When I tried to do that, I subconsciously set out an expectation for Justin to take the reins, but I never once told him. I just dropped the test on him, and that was that. Which left us stuck on that frozen lake. Until I found a convenient distraction and a new door popped open.

In fact, I remember wondering if my watch or my phone would ever give me away. I remember thinking maybe then it could be a tit for tat. We could be even. Justin would catch me in this flirtation and then we'd have the big blow up fight all over again, and then maybe he'd fight for me and we'd actually get something moving.

But he never did.

I shake my head. "You know, Justin? As sick as it is, I think I wanted you to catch me. So that we could be even."

I glance up at him, waiting for a response or reaction, but I get none. Once again, zero fight for me.

I sigh, trying to explain it to him. "I just don't understand why you never said anything." My voice is calm and steady. Mournful, maybe, but there are no tears. "Maybe if you had tried to fight for me, I wouldn't have ever crossed the line and slept with him at all."

My soon to be ex husband breaks my heart a little more when he looks at me. "Because, Lucy. After what I had done to you, I didn't think I had any right to."

thirty

. . .

lila

"J UST CHECK IN on her from time to time, that's all I'm asking," Reggie says to me on the other end of the line, and I squeeze the bridge of my nose in annoyance.

"I will, I've sent some texts but I've been slammed since filming started." It's an excuse, we both know it, but emotionally I'm vexed. It's hard to be front and center for my sister when I myself feel like I'm hanging on by a thread.

"Lila, Lila," Reggie scolds teasingly. "Alright, I get it. Congratulations, by the way."

"Thank you," I say, though my heart's not in it. As much as I love the project and the role and all of it, I still can't help but feel like I'm a sham.

"When does it air?"

"First episode premiers in April. Right around Lucy's due date." I groan at the reminder. I want to be there for the birth, but of course there's a million promo events around then that I'm contracted to attend.

"Ooo. Rough timing, kid," Reggie says in her no-nonsense way.

"I'll figure it out."

"Well in the meantime, Lucy could use you for some moral support in general, okay? I can feel her unraveling. And you know she's hopeless when it comes to asking for help, so don't expect some banner flying across the sky with the request."

I'm irritated at Reggie pinning this on me for some reason. It's like I'm being guilted into a check-in-on-Lucy schedule. Like I don't have enough shit going on as it is, now I'm being called out for not being a better sister? Not meeting some imaginary quota of phone calls? Which is really fucking irritating considering I *have* actually ramped up my contact attempts with my sister, not that I can get any gold stars for that. No one sees those efforts, they only see where I'm falling short.

"What the hell am I supposed to do across an ocean, Reggie? You're right there at least!" I snap. "With two kids of your own, aren't you the better one to help support the soon-to-be mom?"

"Yes, that's true," she says with annoying calm like she's trying not to wake a bear. "But I am also aware that those two kids come with a doting husband, and a grandma and great-grandma that live on my property and can help out. I'm not exactly the most relatable person right now. Of course I'm going to be there as much as possible, Xavier and I both are, but Lucy holds back with me. I can feel it. I think she's struggling to be in a situation where shit's not all perfectly figured out, and she needs her sister, I'm telling you..."

I roll my eyes, blow out a big breath while Reggie rambles on. "...Phone calls to her so she can vent or cry or whatever," she continues. "Check ins where you ask her if she's okay, then push your way past the bullshit answer you'll initially get of 'Fine!' and make sure she really talks. You know your mom's not doing that," she says with irritation. We all know that my mom is strained when it comes to emotional support. For her it's more about "I told you so" or "Here's what you're going to to do."

I drop myself down on my desk chair, nodding. "You're right, I hear ya." I pick up a pen and spin it around in my fingers, changing the subject. "Has Justin moved out yet?"

"He has. Joey is back out in LA getting ready to open his new restaurant there, so Justin's crashing at Joey's Philly apartment for now. It's hitting Lucy pretty hard, I think she feels like it's all real now that Justin's out."

I hate hearing this. I'm sad for them both. Obviously I love my sister, but truth be told, I love Justin too. He's the brother I was always supposed to have. I find myself wondering how he's doing in all this just as much as I'm worrying about my own sister.

Eventually I hang up with Reggie, promising her I'll step it up, check in with Lucy more, and also promising to myself that I'll reach out to Justin. He has an older brother but I think they're more brothers in name, two polar opposite souls that aren't particularly close. For some reason, I feel more of a pull to reach out to Justin than anything else. I still want to cut off his dick for what he did with his little texting affair, but I also know my sister, and know how cold she can be to him without realizing it. And now with her infidelity, my rage towards Justin has lowered and made space for some empathy.

I sigh and open up my laptop, ready to distract myself with more amateur investigating on anything Simon and Elsie related. My screen is flooded with various tabs as I've been searching for any information I can get on the two of them as well as the guy Simon apparently beat to within an inch of his life. I'm convinced it wasn't Simon, that he's being wrongfully accused here, but I don't even know the victim's name.

There's been one article in particular that I keep coming back to. It's a recounting of an incident of a man being nearly beaten to death on the street outside a pub in Cambridge. There's a few different witness perspectives. The man who was beaten was named Harvey T. Smithson, and he was a wannabe musician with very little success. Simon's name is nowhere in the article, but I found him after stumbling across another article, one about Elsie and Grayson's parents' music store. This article was a plea for help on the theft issues they were having, which they believed were at the hands of a former employee, you guessed it—none other than our boy Harvey. It's just an interesting coincidence. Not only did this guy formerly work for Grayson and Elsie's family, but he was thought to be a thief that apparently escaped any kind of consequence. Then suddenly, a year later, he turns up not far from where Grayson and Elsie and Simon all grew up, battered and clinging for life, with no suspect ever caught? Truth be told, this doesn't exactly look great for my Clear Simon's Name mission, but it still feels like I'm getting somewhere.

I search around some more, determined to find a link here as I just can't shake the feeling that Harvey is significant in this. I find him on Facebook, now fully healed and still plugging away hopelessly at his music (which is bad, I find after listening to his YouTube videos). I scroll and scroll, quickly becoming irked with the guy, and then stumble across something—a post with Elsie. I feel a flush of heat as I scroll back, having nearly zipped right past it. The post was from five years ago, which would have been three years after her death, and it's the two of them, Harvey and Elsie. His arm is around her, and the caption says, "This song's for you," with just about the dumbest tune about lost but never forgotten, always in my heart. It is so unoriginal I want to punch this guy's face.

This has me convinced Harvey is the right guy, though nowhere have I found anything linking Simon to this case. More searching yields another article on the beating, this one with a grainy surveillance photo of what is believed to be the suspect, and my heart skips a little beat.

I try and zoom in, willing the graininess to magically become clear. There's something about it that's jumping out at me. I lean in closer, squinting in my efforts.

I don't even hear Penny come up behind me, saying, "Detective work now?" and I jump in my seat, startled.

"Lord, woman! You scared me half to death," I say with a hand over my heart.

"Sorry, love. Drink?" she says, offering up a pitcher of pink.

I shake my head no. "Nope, gotta be a good little girl while filming," I say.

"I figured, you have been very responsible, I must say," she says with an approving nod. "I can't wait to tell everyone my flatmate is on TV! Between you and Grayson I'm feeling very fancy."

I smile, Penny is just so bright and shiny and lovable. I adore her. "Not that you need us to be fancy, but happy to assist," I say.

"Well, good luck studying tattoo guy over there," she says, nodding to my laptop screen before waltzing out the door.

"Tattoo guy?" I mutter out, then look at the screen again. I zoom back out and then see it.

Sure enough, the man's arm is covered. At first it just looks like a textured long sleeve shirt with a pattern on it. You can't see the man's face, just this one little clip of the side of him, but I can see it now.

Tattoos on the arm. You can't possibly make out what they are, but it's clear.

But does that mean it's Simon?

I POUND ON THE DOOR with determination, my hand nearly in pain from the action. I pause and scan around me, worried I'm about to get kicked out of the building by a neighbor or something given the late hour. But I couldn't sleep, just tossed and turned as my wheels were spinning on this potential link, and next thing you know, I was walking up to Simon's door.

I'm just about to give up when I finally hear some movement on the other side.

Simon opens the door, looking exhausted. My walking canvas is shirtless and his hair is a mess. I fight the urge to throw myself in his arms. I've missed him so much, I realize, and now I'm struggling to breathe as the intensity of emotion I've been blocking out comes piling up in me at the sight of my sleepy love, all confusion on his face behind his glasses as he registers my unexpected visit.

"Lila, bloody hell, what are you doing here?"

I push past him, into his kitchen and lean against the counter. Basil pops up on the floor beside me and snakes his way between my ankles. I reach down and pick him up, welcoming his snuggles. In an awkward juggle of trying to keep Basil in my arms, I reach into my purse and pull out the grainy photo I had printed out, thrusting it at Simon. "This is you, isn't it? In the photo there, and those are your tattoos."

He reaches over for the paper, looks at it, then curses and drops it down, raising a hand up and rubbing it over his jaw.

Confirming my suspicion.

"That's why you walk around all covered up, right?" Basil stretches himself out of my grasp, jumping down onto the floor. I rub off the cat hair left behind and continue. "You hide your tattoos, just in case you get photographed and then risk potentially being caught. Not because you don't want people to be nosy or whatever, not because that's the professional look you want, but because of this one and only photo that's still floating around online."

"How did you find this?" Simon asks, hands on his hips, his voice soft.

"Where there's a will, there's a way, Si." I walk over to him and grab his face in my hands. "Is that where you got those scars?" I say, rubbing the one over his mouth with my thumb. "In the fight?"

He allows the subtlest of confirming nods, and I notice a soft sadness in his emerald eyes. I think he's about to kiss me, but then he surprises me and takes my wrists, dropping my hands from his face. He walks back to his front door and opens it. "You should leave, Lila." Basil saunters over to the door, about to make his escape, and Simon pushes the cat away with his foot.

"What?!" I shout, surprised. "Fuck no, you're going to explain this to me." There's no way he's kicking me out now. I'm not leaving without answers. Not when the mere sight of my man in nothing but boxer briefs and his glasses has me both begging for his body on mine but also eager to get to the bottom of this thing.

Simon closes the door, more to keep Basil in I'm guessing and not because of wanting to keep me here. "Lila, what's there to explain? It seems you've figured it all out perfectly. I'm no good, running from a crime committed nearly a decade ago, and you should stay away from me."

I cross my arms over my chest, smiling. "No, babe. I'm not going anywhere."

"This isn't a joke, Lila!" he snaps, slamming a fist into his door. The neighbors must love him. That or they're all deaf. We stare at each other for a moment, a silent game of chicken.

"You see, Simon," I say, walking over to him again, this time locking his door before reaching up to wrap my arms around his neck. He's tense but doesn't resist. "I've had way too many people size me up incorrectly before giving up on me or my potential. I comfort myself by thinking of all they missed out on in not giving me a chance." I kiss him on the corner of his mouth, on his scar. "I'm not giving up on you, because I know I'd be missing out on so much. And I'm too greedy to deprive myself." I kiss him again, not even caring that he's got sleep breath and that I should most definitely be getting my beauty rest right now instead of standing here, forcing this man to explain himself, to not give up on us.

"You're insane," he whispers, arms wrapped around my waist. "You have a death wish or something? Don't you see, I'm a fugitive. I'm very dangerous."

I shake my head at him. "No you're not. There's always more to the story. You just need a chance to tell it."

after

. . .

> **To: Grayson Atkinson**
> **From: Simon Sharp**

Grayson,

You are hurting in a most undeserving and unimaginable way, and for that I am so very sorry. We all are hurting. Elsie was a force in her own right and a light that will forever be missed.

This will be very difficult to understand and believe, I know. But none of it was me. Please, give me a chance to explain.

I'm sure you remember Harvey from your parents' music shop. Elsie had been dating Harvey for a little while. Apparently they had run into one another not too long after he was let go from your parents' store. Naturally, she didn't feel she could tell anyone about their relationship, though she was convinced Harvey was innocent as far as the stolen money went.

I myself had barely spoken with her at the time. I was busy in my own escape at school and had no idea any of this was even happening. One day she had reached out to me, asking if she could come visit with me in London, and I agreed, thinking nothing of it.

Something was off with her on that visit, but I wasn't entirely sure what. She was cagey, almost. On the surface she was her usual bubbly self, but I could tell she was hiding something.

She said she was seeing someone new, someone she was in love with, and asked if I could cover for her. I didn't know at the time it was Harvey, but apparently she had already been telling your family that she was with me, that she and I had gotten back together. She explained to me she was living with him now, but not ready to tell the family just yet.

I don't know why I agreed to go along with it, but that was my first mistake. I believe I just wanted to appease her and then send her back on her way. I thought not much of it, told her "Yeah, fine," closing the door on her and getting back on with my life. I dismissed her and in doing so ignored the signs of her trouble in favor of my own avoidance.

Then the day came when your parents accused me of hurting her. Imagine my surprise, I hadn't so much as seen her since that one and only visit. I tried to explain that no, it wasn't me, that Elsie had been seeing someone else. Victoria tried to stand up for me as well, but your parents weren't hearing it.

I reached out to Elsie, and I'll admit my priority here was to tear her down for throwing me under the bus. That was my second mistake. I focused on the wrong thing, my own rage at the accusations, and not nearly enough on the fact that Elsie was in her own trouble.

She eventually explained to me who it was she had been seeing and why it had to be kept secret, apologizing profusely and assuring me she was okay.

Mistake three. I should have told your parents straightaway and stopped it. I wish very much that I had. I wonder how things would have been different today. If she would still be alive.

Instead I once again ignored it. I wanted nothing to do with any of it. I was consumed with my own anger at anyone thinking so poorly of me.

When she turned up dead after taking her own life, and your parents decided I was to blame for getting her mixed up in all the wrong things, I couldn't deny my own guilt.

I wish I could bring her back, Grayson. I wish I could, and I'll never forgive myself for not doing something, anything to prevent what happened.

I will do one thing, though. I'll make sure Harvey pays.

-Simon

thirty-one

. . .

simon

LILA FOLDS UP the letter with serene calm as she silently nods. He watches her curiously and wonders what she's thinking.

"Well?" he asks, unable to wait for a response.

"He should see this. Grayson, I mean," she says. She's holding the letter up as if it were a white flag of surrender and peace.

"He has already, Lila."

She frowns. "But it says return to sender."

Simon sits down on the edge of his bed, taking the letter and putting it back in the box where he's kept it all these years. "Victoria had taken it to him some time later, after I had found Harvey and there was a search out for the man that had beaten him. He was in a coma, we weren't sure if he'd make it at that point. I was considering turning myself in."

Lila raises a hand to her mouth. "Were you trying to kill him?"

He shakes his head, "I don't know what I meant to do. I was only seeing through hurt and rage and felt that he deserved some consequence. When I found him, I was struggling to keep control.

And then he pulled a knife on me, and that was it. I unleashed on him, beating him with bare hands and then left him to rot on the street."

"Do you regret it?" she asks, stepping closer to him as she does.

"No," he answers softly. "I'm relieved he didn't die, but admittedly more for my own sake. It made it easier for the case to turn cold."

Lila sits down on the bed next to him and takes his hand. "So then what? You're on the run, Victoria shows her sister and family this letter, hoping they'll what, cover for you too?"

"Yes. Cover for me and convince them it wasn't me that had gotten her to such a bad place. Only, all it did was make them blame me further, because if that were true then it meant I had known what Elsie was getting into and I hadn't done more to intervene. I was the enemy no matter which way they saw it."

"So Grayson already knows."

"Yes."

"Then why did he make it sound like he still thought it was you? That you had been with Elsie and hurting her?"

It hurts Simon to hear that that's the story in Grayson's mind, even still. He tries to think what it must be like to live in Grayson's shoes, with the pain of losing his big sister. And with Simon having been aware that she was in trouble. "I imagine I am as good as guilty no matter what in his eyes. He probably was hoping that would keep you away from me."

She crosses her arms over her chest, pinching together her eyebrows. "And here I thought I was trying to clear your name from this assault thing with Harvey to try and make Grayson see he had pegged you all wrong."

Simon wraps an arm around Lila and pulls her close on his body, inhaling the scent of her perfume that he had missed so much. He hates to see the disappointment on her face, her original mission misguided. "So why did you show up tonight then?" he asks. "Once you figured it out and knew it was me after all?"

"Elsie," she mutters out to his surprise.

"Elsie?"

"Yeah, I think so. I heard this little voice in my head that said this Harvey guy was somehow at fault. It just felt familiar. I know how easy it is to find yourself in a bad situation, carrying around a bag of secrets and lies and coverups. And I knew that if you had put a target on this guy's head, then there was a good reason for it. That he had been bad to her. I could just feel it."

Simon closes his eyes, the pain of those truths still pulsing in his veins. "So now what?" he asks.

"What do you mean, now what?"

"Grayson. Me."

"And?" she asks, confusion in her voice.

He hates to remind her of that rift, but it has to be addressed. She needs to understand that. "Lila, I had held onto hope for a brief moment that maybe enough time had passed. That when we showed up to his place that night, Grayson would be open to... something. Perhaps not quite forgiveness, but at the very least, he'd moved beyond hatred toward me. But clearly that's not the case."

Lila pulls away from him, and for a moment he worries she's going to leave. Instead, she studies him, her eyes curious as they move across his face. "You miss him, don't you?" she says finally.

"He's the only family I have, really. Had. And Victoria, she chose me in all of it, thereby losing her own family."

"They didn't have to shut you both out like that, you know. Especially not Victoria. Hold the grudge against you—fine. But not her."

"It's her that keeps the distance, I think. I believe she worries that if she reconnects with them, I'll feel she's abandoning me in choosing them. She hasn't said it, but I know she misses them."

Lila extends an arm out to Simon and pulls his face to turn towards her, then pulls to lay them both down on his bed. He adjusts himself, turning on his side to look at her. She does the same, propping her head in her hand as she smiles. "Hi," she says.

"Hi." He studies her face, her hazel-sage cat eyes, the slope of her cheekbones, the pout of her bottom lip. The room is quiet, the world beyond the windows all asleep, the only noise to accompany them is the gentle hum of the fan above.

She puts a hand on his chest, tracing a tattoo. "I choose you, Simon, okay?" She continues her movements, leaving chills with her gentle caresses, dragging her hand up to his neck to examine the maze tattoo below his stubble. "Just letting you know. That I'm here, through and through. I'll be your family."

Her words are effortless. Casual, even. He reaches out to feel her skin, still struggling to believe she's really here. "You trust me already? Just like that, when you've only known me a few months?"

"I do, yes."

"How?"

She grins. "You can get a feel for someone within five minutes, remember?" she says with an eyebrow raise, reminding him of what he once said to her. "And besides, we're all a little bit of a monster now and then, aren't we?" Simon recalls the way Grayson had referred to him that night. "Me especially. We've all got a history and mistakes and flaws. I mean come on now...you saw the monster in me right here in this room not too long ago," and her eyes dart over to the wall where Simon had held her tight until her fury had calmed. "I never thought someone could love that ugly side of me."

"You have no ugly side," he whispers. "I love all of you, Lila." He kisses her, his heart bursting and body hungry at this beautiful and wicked woman in his bed. Choosing him, even knowing what he's done. And knowing they'll never have Grayson's approval. "And Grayson? You're okay with that never being mended?"

She shrugs. "He's got a right to make his choice, and I mine. And you know what, he'll always be Ruby's best friend first and foremost, and Ruby and I never really clicked, you might say. So be it." A grin works her way across her face. "And Si, the things you do to me are far more worthwhile to have in my life."

He reaches forward for Lila's hips and pulls her body in closer to his, no longer able to resist the lure of her skin, her hair, her mouth. He kisses her, long and slowly, and she wraps a leg around him. They greedily consume one another and he works to lift her shirt over her head, groaning at the hot relief of having her that much closer to naked beside him.

"I thought I told you to stop wearing this," he says as he reaches up her back, fumbling to undo the clasp of her bra.

"Why, not a fan of false advertising?"

"Not a fan of an unnecessary layer to bypass." He frees her of the bra, then reaches his mouth down to the underside of her breast, sucking gently and loving the sweet taste of her skin. He pulls away momentarily, his thumb grazing over the hard ridge of her nipple. "And your breasts are perfect as is, Lila."

She throws her head back, purring soft moans as he continues teasing her, soft kisses combined with gentle flicks of his tongue.

"So bossy," she pants, her hands in his hair, tugging.

After far too short of a time like this, Lila pauses them mid frantic kiss, mid undressing, mid all of the things Simon does not want her to be pausing. He feels her hand on his chest as she gently shoves him away, chest rising steadily as she catches her breath.

"Do you forgive yourself?" she asks, panting, and for a moment he thinks he misheard her.

"Do I...what?"

"For those mistakes there in the letter. Do you forgive your-self?" she repeats.

Simon tries to blink away his lust and arousal, struggling to focus. "Must we discuss this right now?"

"Yes, we must," she says with another shove to his chest, this one harder. "I need to know."

He sighs, knowing there's no way out of this. He lays back on his pillow to attempt to compose himself. Finally, he answers her. "I don't think I ever will, not entirely," he admits. His mind goes to Grayson, realizing how impossible it would be for him to move past this if Simon himself can never find his own forgiveness.

Lila nods. "Fair enough."

"Why do you ask?" He hates to probe, much preferring to resume their attack on one another, but it's clear she has something on her mind.

"Because," she starts. "I needed to know why you pushed me out so easily. Instead of fighting for me, I mean. But you couldn't fight, I realize, because you still blame yourself. Right?" She stares at him, looking for an answer, perhaps, but he has none to give her. She pulls his face towards her. "You figured you deserved to lose me. So you gave up, you gave in and let me go." She's searching his face, her eyes looking back and forth to both of his.

He considers her words. It wasn't a conscious choice, but he realizes her assessment. That he did in fact give up on her thinking it was better this way and that she deserved better than him. "I think so," he whispers.

"Okay," she says with one firm nod, like she's solved a puzzle. Or accepts his answer, he's not sure.

He leans in to kiss her, but she starts up again, saying, "We all have our baggage," her words mumble halfway in his mouth, and he concedes and pulls back groaning in frustration.

"You have more to say, I take it?" he asks, laying his head back on his pillow in defeat.

"I do, actually, yeah. So listen carefully." She props up on her elbow, her hair falling over her face as she leans over him. He reaches out and tucks some behind her ear.

"I'm listening, go on, then." The door creaks slightly and Basil saunters in, hopping up on the windowsill to settle himself in the peek of moonlight.

And Simon smirks, bracing himself for the wrath of Lila.

"Don't fuck up like that again. You hear me?" Her voice is firm. Low. Demanding.

"I hear you."

"I'm serious. That was your one chance. Don't let your shit get in the way of this," she says, gesturing back and forth between the two of them. "Don't avoid and shut down and walk away on us. I won't have it. I came back to you this time, and that took a whole lot of putting my own pride aside."

"I imagine it did."

"I'd rather not do that again."

"I'd rather not lose you again."

"You lost me by choice," she says, plopping herself down beside him. Simon hates hearing her accusation, accurate as it is. It means he hurt her. Something he had no plans of doing, though empty assurances of not doing so again seem trivial.

Lila turns her head to look over to Basil who is purring quietly. She seems to have more to say, but keeps quiet. Basil startles at the sound of a car alarm out on the street, a steady beeping sound from somewhere nearby, and Simon smiles in amusement before noticing Lila's face remains serious.

"Is Elsie the love of your life?" Lila whispers into the darkness above them.

Ah. So there it is, Lila's fear.

Simon grabs her hand and laces his fingers through hers, realizing now what she's been worried about. He tries to find the right words to reassure her. "No Lila, she is not."

"I don't want to be the second choice."

He reaches for her and pulls her on top of him, naked skin on naked skin as she steadies herself on his body. "We were just kids when we were together. It was convenient more than anything, we spent so much time together as it was. I loved her, yes. But not as the love of my life. I think we both knew that was not what we were to one another."

Lila overlaps her forearms on his chest and lowers her chin to her wrists. "When Grayson said her name that night, I saw the shift in you."

"Only because of my guilt in not stopping her or saving her. That's all that was." He runs a finger down the slope of her nose, down to her lips. She parts them, and playfully bites his finger. "I'm sorry I walked out that night," he whispers.

She shrugs. "You didn't have much of a choice, I don't think. No need to make a scene."

"Do you forgive me for that?"

She rolls back off of him, then slips her hands into the waistband of her leggings, slipping them and her underwear down her legs. "I forgive you for that, yes." The beeping car alarm outside the window finally stops.

"Now," she says, stripping him of his boxers before straddling him. "Make it up to me. Fuck my brains out so we can have the best makeup sex of our lives."

"Don't you have work tomorrow?"

"That's what makeup's for."

thirty-two

. . .

lila

I WAKE UP in Simon's bed feeling sore and deliciously satisfied. It was a wild night. I'm exhausted, yet in heaven.

I sneak out, trying not to wake him, and he sleepily pulls me in for a kiss and pat on my ass. He starts to get up to walk me out and I push him back down, not sure I can face the temptation of blowing off work and responsibilities all in favor of spending the day with him.

Does that mean I'm anxiously attached? Who knows.

I startle when I slip into the kitchen and find Victoria, leaning into the fridge and putting something inside.

"Oh, hi," I say, hoping the annoyance isn't too obvious in my voice. How long has she been here for? What if Simon and I were just fucking, which very easily could have been the case? I'm a little uneasy at their closeness, I have to admit.

She pops up, smiles a crooked teeth grin at me, then looks momentarily horrified. "I didn't wake you when I came in, did I? I meant to be quick and quiet as a mouse!"

I kind of want to get out of here as quickly as possible, but I also can't deny my very real concern at her presence. "I'm sorry but, what exactly are you doing here?" Maybe it's not my right to say, but I don't really care.

"You're back! I thought you and Simon had broken up, I'm mortified, oh my."

A red hot flush creeps up her fair skin. At least she has the social awareness to look embarrassed. Still, I'm not convinced her being here is exactly healthy. I cross my arms, eyebrow raised waiting for a response.

"Right," she says, awkwardly rummaging in a bag on the counter. "I just wanted to pop in and leave some things for Si to eat, I didn't realize he had company."

Great. I'm dating a mama's boy. Only the mama in question isn't even really Simon's mother, and she gave up her own family to stand up for Simon, and now I'm thinking I'm fucked.

Victoria must see the horror on my face because she awkwardly rushes to try and explain. "I'm opening a new bakery, and I need taste testers! Critiques for my new recipes, that sort of thing."

"Victoria?" Simon walks into the kitchen wearing sweatpants and in the midst of pulling a T-shirt over his head. I'm feeling very confused between lusting after those abs, and the alarming presence of a motherly figure mere feet away.

"What in the bloody hell are you doing here?" he asks as he adjusts the glasses on his face.

Oh, thank God. He's annoyed at her presence too. At least there's that.

The three of us all stand there in the kitchen. An awkward little tripod.

And suddenly I feel badly for poor Victoria, clearly uncomfortable in her most unwelcome presence here this morning, just trying to feed the man. So call me crazy, but I find myself explaining for her. "Victoria has some new recipes she wants you to taste test. For her new bakery."

"Key," is all Simon responds, holding out his hand, palm up.

I snort out a laugh, I can't help myself. He looks ridiculous standing there like that, hair a mess, sweats put on in an obvious rush, probably after the alarm at hearing his aunt's voice in the flat. He's trying for that whole tough-as-nails commanding thing he does so well, but I can't help but giggle.

Victoria fumbles in the pocket of her tattered and torn jeans, pulling out the item of request, mumbling out apologies as she does. Okay, so clearly this was her stepping out of line a bit. I'm starting to get the feeling our Victoria here has something causing her distress.

"Simon," I say, voice smooth and sweet, "why don't you go get in the shower, I'll skip my coffee stop in favor of coffee here and let me have a little chat with Victoria."

His green eyes dart to me in concern. "I'll handle this, Lila. No need to."

"I really am sorry—" Victoria starts to say.

I laugh. "Relax, I'm not going to give your aunt a hard time. Promise," I say, crossing my heart. I look back over to the perplexed Victoria. "I have a feeling there's something on Victoria's mind, though."

She looks over to me, startled. And then Victoria blurts out, "Roger asked me to marry him."

Ha! Well I'll be damned, I do know a thing or two when I pause to pay attention.

I peer out of the side of my eyes to Simon, feeling smug and vindicated.

Simon simply turns on his heels and starts to walk out, muttering a "Congratulations to the happy couple" with an air kiss as he goes. A moment later we hear the shower turn on and I look back to Victoria as she exhales a sigh of relief.

"I think that's him happy," I say, pointing a finger in the direction of the bathroom.

She nods, relief clear on her face. "It is. I don't know why I was worried about that." She slinks down into a chair by the kitchen table and I join her. As quickly as she sits, she pops back up again with a bright, "Oh right! Your coffee!"

I nod and thank her, figuring the darling thing likes to bustle around and keep busy.

"So, congratulations are in order it seems," I say to her back. The woman really does have the nervous energy of a scurrying little field mouse.

"Thank you, I don't know why I was so very nervous to tell Simon! Although now that you're back, I suppose I don't need to worry so much about him at all!" She turns her head and smiles brightly at me, haphazardly wiping down a spill on the counter as my coffee brews. "You are here to stay, I hope? I did hear about Grayson," she says, her voice now about ten notches down from the previous revved up high pitch of anxiety.

My senses spike up a bit at the opportunity to discuss this with her. I can't imagine being stuck in between something like that. First given a child to raise that isn't yours, then that child and your niece have this teenage fling, then the niece throws herself into a bad situation, blaming your adopted son to cover her own ass, then more trouble, a tragic death, more blame of your not-blood-kid but totally your kid, and now you're estranged from your own flesh and blood.

It's a sacrifice I don't think I could in a million years make. The woman is a saint and I want to understand. Maybe I'll never be as good a person as all that, (I was raised in a family that prides themselves on selfishness, I've come to realize), but a girl can strive, right?

"I'm sorry," I say. "I guess I didn't understand the whole story. I really hoped I could swoop in and magically fix that."

Victoria shakes her head. "I never was the pride and joy of our family, I'm afraid. My sister has always had the smarts, you know?"

I nod. "Oh, do I. Yes, I get that. Got a little of the same thing with my sister." Though I can never imagine Lucy straight up abandoning me, but I don't share that out loud.

"Elsie was a lot like me in many ways. A bit of the wild child, like I was. I think in some ways my sister resented me for Elsie being more like me than them."

Ouch. That has to hurt. I'm starting to feel some real admiration and empathy for our Victoria. "So you were a wild child, huh?" I say.

She nods vigorously, pouring my coffee. I get up to add some cream in it, then we both take our seats at the table, Victoria across from me, sipping tea.

"I was a stupid wild child. Before Simon came into my care, I was in one bad relationship after another. I had such low self-respect, really. Men would use and abuse me and I fell for it each and every time. I was the black sheep of the family, and that was that. I was not nearly as charismatic as Elsie could be, but we were similar in our destructive tendencies."

I try and imagine Victoria as a young woman. She is pretty, a little sprinkle of freckles accompany the lines on her face. Slim with muscular arms that are evident in her short sleeves. Arms sculpted not by a gym, but by hard work. I can imagine her lifting buckets of water for mopping up and down stairs with ease. Lifting couches, no chore or task beyond her capabilities.

"So, what changed? I mean the destructive tendencies?" I ask, sipping my coffee. It's the perfect temperature, hot but drinkable, with vanilla undertones.

"Simon changed that for me, honestly. I saw the broken little boy in him and knew I needed to do right by him. So I did. At twenty-nine, I had no idea what I was doing," she says with that nervous laugh of hers, "but I knew I could do right by him, yeah? And in turn, he saved me."

I nod knowingly, though I really have no idea at all. "I choose men that I feel I can manipulate," I mutter with a sad little sigh. The words slip out unexpectedly, a confession I didn't know I needed to blurt out and send into the universe.

"Oh?"

"I used to, at least." I think we both know there's no manipulating Simon. "Does that make me a bad person?"

"A little bit, yes."

I look up at her, startled. I was definitely fishing for a little pseudo support, there. Not "Yes, you're a shithead."

She sets down her mug and stretches an arm across the table, hand grabbing mine. She smiles. "Doesn't mean you can't change, though. Sometimes we tell ourselves we're bad and broken, all so that we can sidestep the trouble of accountability and responsibility. It's the easy way out, we fool ourselves to believe. But it harms us in the long run."

My oh my. This Victoria knows a thing or two.

"So how do you get out of it?" I'm asking seriously. Because blowing up the ship and chalking it up to the "Oh well, that's just Lila!" mentality feels like all I know. But I'm trying. I want to do better. I'm here now, right? But I'm scared of myself and of my own tendency to want to fuck it all up and run away, just to not get hurt.

Sometimes it's harder to trust what feels good than it is to suffer through what feels bad.

Victoria squeezes my hands in hers. "You get your shit together, that's how. Be honest with yourself and think about what you really, truly want, and get your shit together to chase it. Make it yours. Don't let fear take hold so you make those mistakes. Just make what you want yours."

"Make it mine." I nod. "I guess I can do that."

I ROLL ONTO SET WITH just two minutes to spare, panting as I make my way over to the dressing area. I've been rehearsing my lines, practicing various inflections and trying to find the right balance for this scene. It's a small clip on my end for today's filming, but has some big moments because my character drops a line that in many ways says a similar kind of thing Victoria had said earlier. The designer in the show gets yet another "Quit your little dream, doll, you ain't gonna make this happen" type message from a potential investor, and one of her models (me) tells her "You think he can manifest a lasting failure in you? He'd like to, that's for damn sure. But it's up to you, babe ("babe" being my own ad-lib). Up to you to fail and fail, all without fear as many times as it takes. All so that the one time you don't, the gorgeous one time you succeed, you can do so with grace and rise above it all. And the failing is the exact thing that will make the success so beautifully earned. Success can only feel bland without failures, remember that. It's the failures that give success its worth."

I'm nervous, I'll admit. The scene needs to pack an emotional punch. It's my best scene in the whole show.

"My, what a lucky day it is, I get to paint the lovely Lila Ray," says Adrian, his arms out wide as I step into the makeup chair.

"What are you doing here?" I gush in surprise, immediately rising back up for his hug.

"I've been trying to get in here for weeks now, love. The project is creating quite a stir already, I told anyone and everyone who would listen to have me first on the list for backup should they ever need. And today is that day!"

Is it possible to miss the fatherly warmth of someone you hardly know? Because I realize now that I do, and I tell Adrian so.

"Family dinner is always available to you, you know," he scolds with an eyebrow raise.

Guilt. I make a silent promise to actually take him up on that. Soon. "How are your daughters?" I ask. "Annabelle and…"

"Holly."

"Right. Did Annabelle like my note?" I'm scrambling to remember what I even said in it. Something about you are the world to someone.

"She did, in fact. I told her I'd see you today and she was very impressed."

Poor girl—if she only knew. I try and squash down the thought. I'm here. I'm going to own it.

Adrian continues. "There are many long mirror glances still, but no more cutting, at least." I watch him unroll his brushes and think about how excited I still get at being made up. It's long ingrained in me—I have to fight myself to leave the house without makeup—and I'm sad thinking about Adrian's girls potentially feeling that.

"Well watch for that," I warn. "The mirror can be a funny thing. I still catch myself now and then looking at my reflection like I'm outside of my body and looking in. Think she'd be okay with another note from me?"

"Annabelle? Oh she'd be thrilled. She might even question if it was really from you." Adrian starts to swipe concealer on my eyes, asking not unkindly about the dark circles, but I stop him.

"Wait a sec. I'm going to write Annabelle another little something and you take a pic of me holding the note."

"Ahhh, good proof," he says through a smile.

"But *without* my makeup on." I scramble for pen and paper and think about what to say. I want to tell her that the reflection in the mirror is beautiful because it's her, and no matter what the reflection shows, it's exactly as it should be. I want to tell her every strand of hair is falling just as it should, every curve is healthy and beautiful. I feel a surge of adrenaline mixed with panic to get this note just right.

I start writing, and decide to add in that every time she looks in the mirror she needs to name out at least three things she sees that she loves, no matter how she looks that day. And one thing that's something she can't see.

I look in the mirror beside me, see the circles due to last night's shenanigans, and try the exercise on myself. *You look beautiful, your cheekbones are strong. Your circles are signs of being fiercely loved, and fighting for your love.*

You are a strong fighter who deserves the world.

I look back at the note, sign "with love, Lila" and hold it up for Adrian to take a picture. He snaps and then hands his phone to me to see.

I look happy. I look a little tired. My smile is genuine. My face has the normal color variation and blemishes any un-made-up face should. *You look beautiful.*

I hope so much Adrian's little girl can feel her own beauty too.

I hand Adrian back his phone, heart feeling pretty damn full, and briefly give him the cliff notes on how mastermind Simon Sharp and I are an item. I share the little scuffle we'd had (I spare the real details), and the late night reconnect that are the cause of said tired circles. Adrian tells me all about how when he heard I would be on this show, he had a feeling it was going to be a fantastic role for me. I mutter out the real reason I got the part—the connection with my mom.

He makes a dramatic slow turn from his arsenal on the table to now facing me. "Is that what you think, love? That your mum is the reason you're here?"

I nod. "I don't think, I know. She confirmed it."

Adrian shakes his head. "You little fool. No, no. In fact," he says, raising his index finger up to emphasize his point, "I happen to know from the most reputable of sources that your fabulous director Meredith Saunders wanted nothing to do with you at first, all *because* of the connection."

I scoff. "Right, sure. Why wouldn't she want that?"

"Think about it. It takes away the credibility of her as an artist. She feared the L. Delphi-Ray name would overshadow, especially given that she's known to be designer of choice for the very famous Ruby Francesca. Meredith didn't want the exploitation of her daughter," he says, waving the handle of a powder brush in front of my face, "in the show to become this hot and trendy thing, cheapening the real story she wants to tell—the one of a brilliant science mind utilizing her feminine force to combine new age performance design and fashion in a man's world."

I sink back into my chair, incredulous as I absorb this information. "I really want to believe that."

"Well then believe it. Because it's true, I wouldn't lie, love. Meredith figured she'd play along, watch the reel just to be able to give solid reasons why you weren't cast, but then she fell in love. Whoops," he says with a wink. "Apparently you had the right raw fierceness combined with transitional adaptability to pull off the role exactly right."

"I don't even know what that means, Adrian."

"No need. They do, and I have no doubt that you're completely brilliant. So come on, let's fix up those circles so I can go scurry you onto set and see all this buzzed about magic come to life."

<hr>

I'M FLOATING, ABSOLUTELY FLOATING, AS I hear the final "Cut!" and "That's a wrap!" after countless hours on set.

Meredith approaches me as I slip out of the dressing area, back in my own clothes. As a mere side part, she doesn't talk to me nearly as much as the other actors, so I'm a little taken aback when she pulls me aside.

"Lila!" she says with a no-nonsense smile that's more business than friendly.

"Hi, yes?" I say tentatively. I'm scared for some reason that I'm in trouble. Or about to get fired. I went from feeling like I didn't earn this role, to being terrified that I actually *did* and that now I'll let everyone down.

Insecurities fucking suck.

"Exceptional job today. Truly. The emotion was palpable, I wish you could see it from our vantage point, the crew were all dabbing at tears."

"Oh, wow. Thank you. Great directing," I add, feeling stupid for having no better response. I should say something more brilliant. Anything. But my mind is blank.

"Cool. See you tomorrow," she says, walking away.

"Wait!" I call after her. She stops, turning her head back to me waiting for what else I have to say. "That suggestion you made, the one about pausing in the middle and imagining momentarily someone pushing me in a cage..." There's a question in there somewhere. How did she come up with that? In a line where I'm supposed to be empowering? I mumble out some semblance of those questions.

"Our greatest power in motivational words comes from the pain we've experienced to get there. Otherwise the words can feel too—" she snaps her fingers repeatedly to accentuate her next word, "—gimmicky. The flicker of pain in your gaze brought the authenticity."

"Right," I nod. "Well I felt it. It helped, thank you."

She mumbles another accolade and wanders off, probably far too busy to keep talking to little old me. But I'm thankful for the chance to chat.

My phone buzzes in my pocket and I see a text from Lucy. And my heart sinks.

Come home, please. I need you.

thirty-three

. . .

lucy

JUSTIN LEAVING HAPPENED in this very surprising way.

It was in the middle of the night one night, and I woke up crying. I had been having a bad dream and I guess that dream was fairly consuming because when I woke up my cheeks were damp and I was curled in the fetal position.

I heard a knock on the door, followed by Justin slipping in.

"Luce? You okay?" he had said. His voice was thick and scratchy with sleep, but I could hear genuine concern.

I said nothing, just popped myself up, extending an arm out to him, still half asleep to even register what exactly I was doing. But he came to me in our bed, wrapped his own arms around me and let me weep, my belly round between us. I remember apologizing over and over, and him brushing the hair from my face and telling me "It's okay."

He eventually climbed into bed behind me, and I curled my back against his chest, cocooned in his embrace just like old times. Very old times I guess because truth be told it had been a long time since we had actually held one another like that. Lesson to be learned here, folks. I firmly believe our human bodies need physical touch like that. It centers us and helps our systems regulate, all in the warm flow of intimacy offered by the other person's body. Never discount that or forget how beautifully fulfilling simple touch can be.

I'm not sure who initiated kisses, then undressing, then him slipping himself inside me as we lay like that, me reaching behind me to fist his hair, him kissing my neck with each tender thrust. When I eventually turned myself, my belly so bizarre and heavy with the move, I pushed him back and straddled him, the feeling of his penis inside me so foreign, so full in a way I hadn't yet experienced given the new bundle that was sharing this moment with us. I felt surprisingly feminine as I was riding my husband in this pregnant state, my breasts swollen and tender, relishing in the feel of his mouth on each of them.

When I came, I came so hard and so intense that I thought the orgasm might never end. His shudder beneath me felt just as drawn out. A crest of a wave neither one of us thought we could ride for so long. Our middle of the night sex always had been our best in many ways. In fact, now that I think about it, the last time we had sex it was middle of the night like that as well.

We fell asleep, never even getting up to use the bathroom, me just letting the juices of him float around inside me, a practice I never previously did. Him sticky with our sex next to me. It was the best night's sleep I'd had in months.

When I woke up, he was gone. He had slipped out, packed up and left with a text saying he'd be staying at Joey's.

I didn't make it into work that day. Or the next. By the third day in bed, soaking in hormonal sweat and tears and depression, no shower in 72 hours and barely a thing to eat, I knew I needed help.

So I texted my sister. It was the only thing I could think to do, even as impossible as reaching out to her was given the demands of her show.

And yet? She showed up anyways. And saved me.

HERE I AM SOBBING NOW, really sobbing into my baby sister's shoulder, and she soothes me with gentle rocking. I had barely even registered her coming in, no idea how she even got into the house, for that matter. These are questions I would normally ask. The old Lucy would want to know, would ask how her flight was, who picked her up from the airport, how long is she planning on staying.

And how on earth did she get in the house.

But I don't say any of those things. Instead I just cry into her sweet smelling hair as I unfold as a debilitating basket case.

"I hate myself, Lila. I hate myself so much for doing this to my kid," I cry, and she rocks me and listens. "I hate that I'm starting off its life this way, with a dad that doesn't want it and a mom that's a complete and fucking mess!"

"He doesn't want it?" she asks. "What do you mean, like its bio dad? Your affair?"

I sniffle in, attempting to control the mess of snot running down my nose. I nod and explain that I debated even telling him, but then eventually did and that he was only horrified, saying he couldn't be a dad, this was not part of his plan. He all but erased me in that moment, I think. He couldn't hang up the phone fast enough.

Here I thought he had the right to know. Turns out he would have rather never known at all. That's what he said to me.

"Did you love him?" Lila asks.

I shake my head. "Not even the slightest bit, no. His absence is a relief in that way."

"Well good, fuck him then." She pulls me back into the crook of her neck.

My face is pounding with the pressure of my tears and I feel like my head is going to burst. "I just feel badly for the baby," I cry again, unable to stop. "Why? Why did I have to be so *stupid*? Why?

I wish I could go back, take it all back. FUUUCKKK why oh why can't I take it all back?" I wail again into her shoulder. And Lila rocks me back and forth, and back and forth, soothing me with gentle shushes and telling me it's okay, that she's here and it's going to be okay.

When I finally settle down, I pull back from her and look out the window, unable to so much as look at her face. I feel the dab of a tissue on my cheeks, my nose as Lila pinches and wipes the snot from it. Her movements are so tender and gentle that my lip quivers again at the feeling of love. In my sister wiping snot from my face. At least one of us will make a good mother figure. Who knew it would be my baby sister?

I finally look at her with a sigh. "I wish I could undo it all."

She tilts her head to one side and places a hand on my belly. "But then you wouldn't have this. And this right here is a gift that has been bestowed upon you, for whatever reason, babe. You might not understand the reason yet, but there's one for it, I'm sure of it."

I smile sadly at her. "Since when are you so wise, little sis?"

She laughs. "I'm probably the dumbest person on the planet," she says, eyebrow raised as though in concern. "I just walked away from the career of a lifetime, breaking my contract, and left the love of my life an ocean away with no idea how or when we'll be reunited."

I start to speak up, to protest that she doesn't have to do all that, that I got this. But the words are stuck in my throat.

Because I don't have this. I can feel that. She can feel that.

Lila smiles forcibly. "But it's all good, right? Because you and me, sis, are having a baby."

Her hands are on my belly and I put mine over top of hers. "Let's hope it's a fucking girl," I mutter.

"Amen," Lila agrees.

thirty-four

. . .

lila

"WHO'S THE FATHER, Lucy?" I finally ask my big sister (in a very literal sense) one day. We're sitting on the floor in her gorgeous living room. In all my charm and glory I managed to convince her to hold onto the house for now. Why sell a home she loved so much? Thankfully she agreed, probably more out of lack of energy to make any big move than anything else.

We're both sitting with legs crossed like kids in elementary school during morning circle. We're facing one another, her belly between us. The air is crisp and chilly this March morning as winter is in full swing, and the crackle of the fireplace provides us the sweet kind of ambiance where if we were lovers would be highly romantic.

"Actually, before you answer that, remember when we were in that park in London when you were visiting, and I yelled at that couple doing selfies?" It's a fond memory for me, even as unsteady as things had been at that time. Funny to I think about that now.

"Where you thought they thought we were gay and jealous of

their heterosexual PDA?" Lucy has her eyes closed in concentration as she practices her breathing exercises, but she's smiling.

I run my hands along her belly and laugh as her eyes pop open with a little alien kick. "Does it hurt?" I look in wonder at the gentle glide of a lump that swiftly disappears back in the mysteries of its cocoon.

She shakes her head, her glossy caramel hair (so gorgeously full which I guess is a weird pregnancy thing) sending whiffs of coconut my way. "No, not right now. Maybe ticklish I'd say? It's when I'm standing and get a bladder punch that I don't love as much. Or a rib kick."

I continue my soothing belly strokes, waiting to watch for another kick of a surprise jack-in-the-box. You just never know when one will come.

"You ever think society is doing it all wrong?" I ask her. "Like maybe women are supposed to be raising children together, and men out doing the hunting and fishing and..." I'm not sure what else the men would be doing, actually.

"And returning for the fucking?" Lucy offers.

I laugh. "Yeah, exactly."

"It is kind of nice having my sister here in this stage. Certain things only a woman can understand or appreciate," she says with a sweet and soft little side smile. She's happier than she's looked since the day I arrived several weeks ago. I no longer have to remind her to shower.

"Appreciate or stomach, you mean?" I'm speaking from experience. You haven't really lived until you've examined a woman's fluids, wondering whether or not it's a "mucus plug" alerting you of impending labor and all that jazz. She's three weeks out from her due date but apparently has started dilating already.

"Stomach, yes, exactly. Justin would be dry heaving, I'm pretty sure."

It's good to hear Lucy be able to say Justin's name with dry eyes. It's progress.

"That settles it, then. We're inventing a new way of life. Women at the center. Supporting and loving and checking underwear for signs of new life to come, it's perfect." I retract my hands and rearrange my legs to tuck into my chest.

"Do we have to only raise the kids though?" she whines. "I like my work."

"You can work, I'll stay home to raise the baby. We'll make mom watch the kid on nights we want to go out and find prospects for all the fucking." I'm supposed to be comic relief here and I think I'm doing a good job of it, but at the mention of that last bit my heart squeezes for Simon. We still talk consistently, the phone sex is as good as it can be, but I haven't physically been in his presence since I left. And now that baby arrival is a ticking time bomb, I have no clue when I'll be able to see him. Maybe when Victoria and Roger get married in a few weeks, I'm hoping.

But that all depends on Lucy and how she's doing.

Figures. I finally grow up and have a real, healthy, adult relationship, but circumstances mean there's an ocean between us. A part of me wants to be a self-pitying brat about it, but amazingly that part is small. Because ultimately, I'm right where I'm supposed to be, and I know that. My sister needs me and it feels really good to be the one to help her. I'm back to bartending and catching the occasional photo shoot gig or hopping into New York for a commercial audition, that kind of thing. I've obliterated my reputation in London by leaving my agency to clean up the mess of my breach of contract, but I did so with the best integrity possible. I wrote the director and crew an email explaining my dilemma, the difficulty in the decision to walk away from a project I had felt so passionately about, but that ultimately, my family came first. I felt really good about it, it's far more than the efforts I would have taken in the past where I'd have just dropped the ball without a second thought.

Unfortunately, I heard nothing back. So be it. Can't say I blame them.

"You mean mom will hire a babysitter to watch the kid," Lucy jokes. "It's hard to imagine her being very grandmotherly. But I do really miss fucking."

"Can't help you there, sorry, babe. I draw the line at incest."

She nods with mock seriousness. "It's a good line."

"I mean, I bet Justin would come over for a favor?"

Confession—this is totally a test line on my part. Lucy told me about the last night he was here. I've also been in contact with Justin, first as a friendly "how are you" check in text (see how I've grown!), which slowly has led to me planting seeds for potentially giving him and Lucy another chance. There's so much love that is one hundred percent still there for both of them. In one text (I'm pretty sure he'd been drinking because he was awfully candid with me), he admitted to sleeping with a woman he met on Tinder and pretending it was Lucy the whole time. And when Lucy wakes up in the middle of the night with a Charlie horse, screaming and I go rushing in to massage it out, eventually falling asleep next to her in bed, I sometimes hear her muttering Justin's name in her sleep.

Can love overcome a mistake like this? I hope so. As beautiful as our little sister commune is, I do want to try and get back to my own life at some point. Back to Simon. Specifically, back to Simon before he falls in love with a gorgeous somebody and forgets all about me.

"Remember Royce Carter?" Lucy asks, interrupting my thoughts with a mic drop. Why is she mentioning *Royce*? Oh, right.

Because I caved after weeks of trying to be cool and respectful and finally asked her *who the father is.*

She continues on while I slowly feel the wind knocked out of me and my blood thickens in my neck, hot under my ears. "The guy you had that little crush on back in the day?" she clarifies as if I need any reminders of who Royce is.

I gulp. Omg, please please oh please tell me that's not what's happening. It can't be. This can't be Royce Carter's baby that I had just been feeling under the palm of my hands, kicking at me and pulling on my heart strings before it's even born.

"Uh-huh," I say. My body has got to be completely frozen and tense. Does she notice? A million thoughts swirl in my mind as I struggle to make sense of this. *Why would he do this?* But of course he would. He's sick and twisted and selfish and disgusting. Thank *God* he said he wanted nothing to do with the baby. I'm making Lucy put Justin down as the father on the birth certificate, just to cover her ass. I can do that, right?

Fuck.

"So I don't think you ever met him," Lucy continues, "but Royce has a little brother. Devin is his name. That's who, Devin is the father. I had run into him, he was looking for a job, I got him in with my HR people, and he was grateful in that whole 'what do I owe you' kind of hinting flirtatious way." She bites her lip to stop the quiver, her eyes welling. "I had been so hurt by Justin and it felt good to be flirted with and admired like that. I didn't mean for it to go so far."

I feel my whole body start to tingle like a wave of shock and relief and "what the fuck" all mixed together. I'm stunned into silence.

"Lila? You alive, did you hear me? Devin Carter. Or Carter, as he goes by." She looks down at her belly. "It's his, he's the bio dad."

"Oh, thank God," I breathe, folding myself forward, my forehead resting on her belly. I start laughing. "Oh lord you have no idea what a relief that is."

"You're not going to make fun of me for sleeping with a guy four years younger than me?" she asks, fingers twirling through my hair.

"You cougar you." I say, rising back up, a little light-headed.

"There it is."

But I'm just laughing and laughing at the absurdity of it all. I'm laughing far too much for what makes sense for the situation.

She cocks her head to the side to examine me, dabbing at her eyes. Her swollen belly is all cumbersome as she shimmies with incredible effort to lay on her side on the floor, her head propped on her elbow.

"What's so funny?" she asks, a little out of breath. She looks highly uncomfortable so I grab a pillow from the couch, slip it under her elbow, then another under her belly in an attempt to support some of the weight.

And I look at my sister in preparation to tell her my truth. My big and dark mistake of my past. I realize it's time I say it all out loud to her. Why not? Right here and now, confessions on Lucy's living room floor.

I start to talk, my body trembling a little to my surprise. I tell her that yes, yes I do remember Royce and even Devin, who I had met exactly twice and had seemed to be the lesser of the two evils, though definitely a douche. And I tell her about big brother Royce Carter. How I didn't just have a crush on him that started at that party she took me to several years ago, but how I had my first kiss with him right there at that party. And how that later turned into him taking my virginity, knowing I was still in high school. When the look of horror crosses her face, tears in her eyes with a "Oh, Lila," I shake my head and tell her I've been to therapy for this, I'm okay.

Neither one of us talks about the way my body is shaking as I tell this story. She just holds my hand and lets me talk.

I explain how when I eventually told him I had yet to turn eighteen, he was all for the secrecy of it. How I was like his little kept girl, hearing his slurred speech on the phone after a night out drinking, and how he'd tell me I'm not missing anything because I wasn't twenty-one yet and couldn't go out anyways. The hurt and loneliness I'd feel, but I was too hooked to let him go. The loneliness of being with him still felt better than the loneliness of nobody at all.

How eventually my hurt grew to anger, and led to little fights, which led to pushes, that led to real big fights and physical hurt and long sleeves to hide bruises. Then I start to cry.

But these tears aren't for Royce. They're because long sleeves reminds me of Simon's righteous sins covered under his long sleeves. I cry because of the sadness I feel for all the people in this world that have been hurt by people and feel the need to hide it.

I cry too because I miss Simon so, so much it hurts my heart. I cry to Lucy and tell her how heartbroken I am, even though it's the last thing she needs to hear because she knows it's because of her mistakes that I'm here. That I'll stay for as long as I need in order to help her as she labors this baby. That I'll make sure she doesn't take it home to an empty house, all alone. That I won't leave until I know I can trust her to take regular showers and until the spark in her eye has returned, until I know she's able to show up for work and continue to do all the amazing good things she does in her field, especially with the new maternal aid project she's embarking on.

I leave out the emails Simon and I send that are too short because neither one of us is happy, and that writing too much just ends up being more painful. I don't mention the constant pang of jealousy I have when I know he's doing photo shoots and studying gorgeous women through his lens, sharing an intimate creative space with them, then staring at them again through his screen while editing, or thumbing through portfolios to find the right girl for the next job.

Especially when I was his "right" girl once too.

I leave out how much it scares me to think about the moments Simon and I are missing out on, and whether or not waiting is not enough for him. If I could be replaced, even though he's consistent in his contact to me and his assurances that he loves and misses me and will wait however long it takes. I leave out how scary it is to feel my hope in his patience, and to have faith in trusting it.

These just aren't words Lucy needs to hear. They are the words of a reality that I have chosen, and am courageously staying in, all because Simon is worth the risk of heartbreak.

But my loneliness and fear of losing him is crippling at times.

Lucy cries too for all her sadness for me, for having no idea about any of that horrible time I had gone through with the older Carter brother, definitely the worse of the two assholes.

Lucy cries now for how much she misses Justin, for how much she wishes she had taken the time to recognize and appreciate the goodness in him, despite the mistakes, the stupid jokes, the basic flaws that are really just sweet bits of human-ness he holds in him. She cries with longing for an undoing that is impossible to make happen, because some mistakes are permanent and leave scars that if you're lucky, turn into a tiny human miracle.

I lie down next to her and we just lie there together like that with our limbs curled and a little baby in the ball between us. Two puddles on the floor. Wrapped around like the little yin and yang that we surprisingly are. Control freaks in our own different ways that both have completely lost all control, as life inevitably goes, terrifying us both.

Yet liberating us in a way as well.

thirty-five

. . .

lila

IN THE MIDDLE of the night, a baby wails. Little Noah Ray Harris, a healthy baby boy, just shy of a full ten pounds on a birth date two weeks early. Which was actually rather convenient so that new grandma L. Delphi-Ray was out of town on her zillionth career endeavor, thus leaving Lucy to birth in peace with her dear old little sister. And now baby Noah is home and wreaking havoc on his mother and aunt.

Oh God, I'm delirious. I must be if I'm narrating my life. So incredibly tired and delirious. I roll over and rise to help Lucy by making sure she has water, doing a diaper change, that kind of thing. We're three weeks into this odd co-parenting existence, and we're spent. I brace myself to see what version of my sister I'm going to walk in to—out cold and lifeless as the baby cries next to her? Zombie completely asleep through his hungry tears? Or the glazed over version numbly taking the baby onto her breast, now a faucet as her milk has been pouring in with a vengeance given Noah's newfound strength in suckling?

I hear quiet though as I make my way through the double doors of her bedroom. I see Lucy propped up in bed, smiling as she looks down at Noah. She looks peaceful. Happy. I'm tempted to step back out and leave them, but she mutters out a word before I can, her eyes still held firmly onto the baby.

"Congratulations," she says, and I blink in confusion.

I point to her as I make my way beside her in bed. "I think you're the one that is supposed to receive congratulations, not me."

She grins now, still holding her gaze on the baby. "Your Aunt Lila doesn't know yet, does she!"

Great. Now Lucy's delusional. How the fuck am I supposed to deal with this? I put the back of my hand to her forehead to check for a fever.

She laughs, pushing my hand away. "You should probably check your phone, sis. Apparently there's good things going on."

I furrow my eyebrows but then scramble out of bed, too curious to see what she's referring to. When I get back to my room and unplug my phone from its charger I widen my eyes in disbelief when I see fifty-seven notifications, and my socials basically exploding.

My hand starts shaking as I unlock it. Missed calls, emails, texts. Congratulations and subject headings of "Updated Contract" and "Filming Schedule" and "Upcoming Interview" and a slurry of other things I can't wrap my head around. I open the contract email, my eyes scanning furiously to absorb the information as I scroll.

The release of the show has been happening all this week as we crossed into April, right as Lucy and I have been thrust into the very new and scary world of all things keeping a newborn alive. I mentally blocked it out and used Noah's birth as a convenient avoidance opportunity.

But now it's knocking on my phone screen.

"Lucy!" I scream excitedly, running down the hall. I burst back into her room, about to scream again but then remembering we have a baby now, and I need to learn to contain my oh-so big emotions to not disturb the babe while nursing. "Lucy," I whisper shout.

She looks at me grinning. "I know. They love you. You're apparently stealing the show already. We've been up for two hours, I couldn't wait to tell you but I wanted you to sleep." I'd give her a hard time about not waking me to help, but truth be told, I'm just thankful.

All the emotions are flooding me. It's a really challenging thing to have the best career news of your life, being offered a redemption contract *and* pay increase thanks to your resounding fan fave status, and to have to be quiet through it all.

But then I realize. I can't be excited. I can't have this redemption chance because circumstances haven't changed. I have a sister with a newborn, and she needs me.

Lucy must see my face change because she drops her smile and shakes her head. "Uh-uh. No. No you are not walking away from this because of this one," she says, looking down at Noah, unable to stop herself from smiling again.

"We'll talk about it in the morning," I blurt out.

Lucy reaches out a hand to my wrist. "Hey. No, we will not talk about it in the morning. There's nothing to discuss."

"But you need help—"

"And I'll find help. That's something I'm perfectly capable of doing. And besides, look at me! I smile now! Genuinely smile! Here I thought I'd be dying to get back to work, and now I'm only dreading the day I have to leave this wee one in child care." She beams and looks back down at the sweet babe in her arms, and I'm in awe of how perfectly natural my sister is at this. The mother in her coming to life.

Still, this is only the beginning. There's postpartum anxiety and depression to worry about, late night feedings, our mother trying to push a live in nanny on Lucy and all around driving her crazy. So many things that I can't walk away from.

Lucy looks up at me. Noah has fallen back asleep and she passes him to me to change. I unzip his little sleep sack, smiling at what a tiny little present this little boy seems to be.

"Lila, you are absolutely going back to London ASAP, alright?" I don't respond, I just busy myself with the task of Noah's diaper change. "You got me through the absolute toughest time in my life, and I'm not sure I can ever properly express just what that means to me.

"But I can feel this little shift inside me. I was so worried I'd have a whole fresh wave of depression when he was born, but it was like the minute I held him, he didn't feel foreign to me in the way that I thought he would. Sometimes I catch myself trying to breathe in his little baby breaths, because I love him so much I can't even stand it."

"Freak."

"I know," she says with a sleepy smile. "He just feels so....and I feel..." She trails off, either struggling to find the words, or just too tired to finish her sentence, maybe. I finish my task, tuck in Noah's legs and zip his sleep sack back up, amazed at the milk drunk baby asleep through the whole thing.

"You felt like you were exactly where you were supposed to be?" I offer in a whisper as I gently place Noah in his bassinet. He stirs a little when I put him down so I turn on the vibration, praying it does the trick. I gently rock the bassinet as well and look over to Lucy. Her eyes are closed. She's still propped up in bed, nursing pillow in her lap, but her little snores tell me she's already asleep. Just like that. Exhaustion is funny that way I guess.

Once I feel satisfied that Noah is out for at least a little bit, I quietly tiptoe around the bed and climb in next to Lucy, too tired to even make it down the hall back to my room.

As I fall asleep, I allow my mind to dance in the hope of making this work. I could do this—I could go back to London when needed, do the filming and whatever events I'm needed at, and fly back here for Lucy. I'd be stretched thin and exhausted, sure, but I could do it. I'll call Reggie and have her come for the next few days like she's offered. I bet even Reggie's mom would step in and help out.

And I could see Simon.

I book a ticket the next day for a flight out the following week.

thirty-six

. . .

simon

THEY KNOCK ON the door, holding hands and a basket of Aunt Victoria's famous scones. It's become a bit of a ritual for them the past several weeks, these family dinners and game night here in this quiet neighborhood just outside of London. Once Victoria and Roger had even joined them as well.

Simon looks at Lila and kisses her cheek. "Relax," he says. "Don't be so nervous."

She shrugs. "I'm not nervous, what do you take me for?"

He smirks but lets her comment slide. The door opens and they each step into Adrian's waiting arms.

"Right on time, we were just getting set up for a game of Cluedo."

Simon sees Lila visibly relax as they enter into the small home, overstuffed with piles of papers, school work, scattered shoes and sweaters and books. It's a proper lived in family home, and Adrian and his daughters have welcomed Lila and Simon as most unexpected extensions of their own family within a few short weeks. Lila had been adamant about attending dinner here once she returned to town, having regretted never meeting Adrian's daughters before she left back in February. Simon had missed her too much to be willing to lose an evening together. So here they were, regulars at quaint family dinners. No one was more surprised by it than Simon himself.

The past two months have been a whirlwind for Lila with the success of the show, a tight filming schedule to fill in for critical parts she had missed that they had originally written her character out of, but were going back to refill with Lila's return. And all of this paired with frequent trips back home as often as her schedule would allow. She had been grinding—committed to showing up bigger and better with her own pressures to show complete gratitude for this second chance. Simon tried to reassure her as much as he could, and Adrian tried as well. Apparently the director had admired Lila's sacrifice of the opportunity in favor of her family, and so when her character received such rave reviews after the initial episode was released, Meredith Saunders pushed to find a way to have Lila rejoin the project. She promised flexibility to allow Lila trips stateside as needed. Her popularity made it hard to refuse.

Still, Lila was committed to going above and beyond in every way she could, and it was starting to take a toll on her. Thankfully, she was finally in a much needed quiet break now that filming had been completed. Things were settling, but Lila had begun getting restless, Simon could tell. He knew she was always eager to get back home.

After Cluedo followed by dinner, Simon wanders outside to find Lila in Adrian's garden with the girls. It's a balmy spring evening and Adrian's rosebush garden offers the perfect break from the city. He sees Lila painting nails with Holly and Annabelle, Adrian's daughters and number one Lila Ray fans. He can't help but smile at seeing her with the two girls, she's a natural in her ability to break past their adolescent mood swings, or so Adrian had told Simon.

Dinners here were not Simon's first choice past time, but he enjoyed Adrian's company, and Lila had been adamant once she forged an unlikely friendship with the two girls that she would not let them down.

Except that today she was about to.

Simon clears his throat and places a hand on Lila's back, prompting her to share their news. She looks up at him and he sees the apprehension in her eyes.

Holly, the older daughter picks up on the tension and pauses her painting. "What is it? Something is going on, I can tell."

"How did you...?" Lila starts, but then shakes her head. She sighs. "Fine, yes, we have something to share." She looks over to Simon with a smile. Adrian steps out to join them, passing out Victoria's scones. He already knows the news.

"You're having a baby!" Annabelle gushes.

"Ha! No," Lila says.

"What then?" Holly prompts.

Lila clears her throat and begins to explain. "You know, your dad offered for me to come to family dinner a long time ago, back in like, September or something, and I never did. I was a stubborn idiot because I wish I had the chance to meet you girls sooner."

"You weren't very famous then, we might not have liked you as much," Annabelle blurts out, then pops her hand over her mouth as if shocked by her own words.

Lila laughs. "Fair enough, spitting truths on me, I get it."

Holly crosses her arms in annoyance. "So what is it?"

"Well, Simon and I are going to move back to where I'm from. Near Philadelphia, so I can be closer to my sister."

"We'll still travel back here as often as we can," Simon adds, surprised at his own struggle to see the disappointment on the girls' faces.

"Could we come visit you?" Holly asks.

All three adults exchanged startled looks. But Lila recovers quickly, smiling. "I'm thinking once you're on holiday, we would absolutely love to have you. I'll show you what a proper closet looks like."

"Great, they'll never want to come back," Adrian mutters.

"You can meet my nephew and my sister Lucy, we'll go shopping and eat all the good American pizza we can find. I'll show you all the best spots."

Both girls nod excitedly while gushing out sad "But I'll miss you" and "It's not fair, we've barely got any time with you" sentiments. Lila rattles on about how coming to stay will be so much better anyways, and apparently the promise of American adventures is enough to at least settle the girls' emotions for now.

When it's time to go, they exchange tearful hugs good-bye, ensuring one last visit before Simon and Lila leave town. Simon watches Lila affectionately and notes what a wonderful mother she will one day be. A flash of memories to be made flood his mind of their future together raising a family. A family of his own.

He can hardly wait.

ONCE BACK IN HIS FLAT, Simon turns to Lila, placing an arm around her shoulder.

She looks down at his hand dangling in front of her, holding a ring. It's a square emerald turned at an angle to appear in a diamond shape. "This is for you," he whispers in her ear.

Lila smiles and reaches for the ring. "Absinthe green? To match your eyes?"

Simon removes his arm from her shoulder and steps in front to face her. He lifts her left hand and places the ring on her fourth finger. "Marry me," he whispers.

She laughs. "I was wondering when you were finally going to give this to me. I found it three weeks ago," she says with an eyebrow raise.

Simon shakes his head. "Trouble, you are."

"You've learned to love it."

"That I have." He leans down and kisses her. "I didn't know how to do it. If I should do a grand gesture or wait until I met the rest of your family or what."

Lila shakes her head, to his relief. "No, you would absolutely hate a grand gesture." She laughs with amusement at the absurdity. "What would you have even done?"

"I thought about staging a photo shoot job where I'd be the photographer and you'd be modeling for a jeweler. I would have the stylist trying all these things and saying nothing was right. Eventually once you were good and boiling, your patience dwindling, I'd say maybe the model was the problem. You'd get angry with everyone and annoyed at the mess of a situation, until I'd finally pull out the ring and say 'try this.' The room would gasp and someone would put an image through a lighting projector saying 'Marry me.'" He clenches his jaw, eyes burning into Lila's with seriousness.

"Wow," she breathes out. "I kind of wish you had."

She's kidding. Simon knows she's kidding. He slowly shakes his head at her, the corner of his mouth raising. "Don't lie, now, Lila."

She backs away from him, three slow and methodical steps until she's against the wall. "But Simon. If I don't toy with you and lie now and then, how will you ever become my Boy Toy?" With that, she darts away, out of his reach.

But he finds her. He always does.

thirty-seven

. . .

lucy

I SIGH WITH anxiety as I press in his name and see his handsome and achingly familiar face lighting up my screen. I can't believe I'm doing this. I'm calling my almost ex husband at eleven o'clock at night, completely out of the blue when we haven't spoken in who knows how long.

But I can't stand it anymore.

The blossom of hope that maybe Justin still did love me, or could forgive me all started a couple weeks ago. It was the first real warm day of early spring and I had braved the grocery store on my own. I had Noah strapped to my chest and was praying I could get in and out of there before he woke up. I was frazzled and throwing things into the cart as fast as I could when I heard a male voice say my name.

"Lucy Harris, look at you!" I had been annoyed at the interruption and in no mood for small talk, but I smiled politely when I saw the familiar face. It was a former colleague of Justin's, an older gentleman whose name was escaping me. I hadn't seen him in years and was surprised he even recognized me. I smiled and said the obligatory hello while he congratulated me on the baby saying he didn't know we'd had one. *Why would he?* was all I could think. I didn't bother correcting him on the fact that "we" didn't have a baby as Justin and I were no longer together. The whole thing was just a bothersome interaction, and Noah was starting to stir so my panic was rising.

"Well, good to see you, gotta go before this one wakes up!" I said brightly, eager to escape.

"One more thing," the man said, and I fought the urge to groan out loud. "Tell Justin thank you. Carter has been a great fit for the DC firm. He's got some pretty cutthroat but innovative ideas."

I must have looked confused because the man rushed on to explain. "Forgive me, you probably have no idea what I'm even talking about! Justin will though. Just pass on a thanks to him for sending me this guy's resume and urging me to set up an interview with him. I did it more as a favor, but the guy really proved to be exactly the kind of shark we needed. Justin will know who I'm talking about."

I nodded, dumbfounded and just standing there until the guy finally gave up on me and walked away. I shouted after him. "Hold on, what was the name again? I just want to make sure I pass on the message properly," I said through a smile.

"Oh yeah. Devin Carter. Goes by Carter."

I rushed home to process this information.

Justin is the reason Carter is in DC right now. Two hours away. No longer here, and no longer with my company.

Justin orchestrated it. He attempted to push Carter out and away from me.

It was his crafty way of fighting for me. I never even knew it.

I knew then my ex husband probably had a lot more fight in him than I had realized, I just never allowed myself to see it. Maybe it was easier for me to quit on us than it was to have faith in our ability to overcome this whole thing. That was the control he alluded to in me.

The phone rings now and after a moment I hear Justin's voice, scratchy with sleep on the other end. A pit in my belly forms as it occurs to me he could have another woman in bed with him—maybe even Dr. Gabby—but I try and push that thought aside.

"Hypothetically, if I had a sick baby question, would you be able to hack into your new app system and tell me what's going around?"

"Luce? Are you okay? Is...is the baby okay?"

I close my eyes with guilt. "Sorry, yes. I'm fine, the baby's fine. I just didn't know how to break the ice."

I can hear some shuffling around and imagine him propping himself up in bed, trying to get comfortable. "I guess that's one way. Though the app launched a few days ago, you wouldn't even need my insider access, you can just look yourself, you know."

"Oh, congratulations," I say, disappointed in his response. It was so very ordinary and un-Justin-like.

"Unless you just love a bad boy that thieves and hacks into systems, going against all company policy."

I smile. "Caught me. That's exactly what this is about."

"You're wicked."

"A real rule breaker." Neither of us points out the truth or irony in that.

We talk all night, him staying on the line with me when the baby wakes up, asking me about nursing and what it's like having a newborn. I tell him my boobs are basically out 24/7 and he jokes that he'd love to see that. I tell him how it's horrifically exhausting in a way I never knew possible, but that we're through the worst of it and I wouldn't trade it for a thing. I attempt sugar coating my love for Noah, so as to protect Justin's feelings, but I can't. He needs to know how incredibly happy I am that he's here.

Justin tells me he's happy for me. And that he'd love to meet baby Noah Ray Harris.

WHEN JUSTIN MOVES BACK IN a couple weeks later, I finally hand him the envelope that's been slithering its way in the back of my mind for weeks.

"What's this?" he asks, taking it from me. It's still sealed, never been opened.

"Paternity test results," I say.

He furrows his brows and looks at me. "You saying it's possible Noah is mine?"

I puff out my cheeks in a deep breath. "It's possible, yes. He was born two weeks early and was nearly ten pounds. And the night you left, the last time we...we made love before you moved out—it reminded me of a night over the summer I had..." I'm so awkward, I should have planned this better. I don't want to say that I forgot about a time we made love, that seems wrong.

"You started to wonder," Justin says, saving me.

I shrug and nod and attempt to appear casual in this monumental moment, but my heart is pounding with anxiety. Not even because of wanting to know the paternity. I have a feeling in my gut that it's Justin after all. Then again, I also thought for sure I was carrying a girl and about died when I heard my sister say, "It's a boy!" the day of his birth. So maybe I'm wrong.

But it doesn't matter, because my love for this baby is the same no matter what. Of course I want my husband to be the bio father, but somehow I know that as we raise this baby, and this baby turns into a toddler, then a kid, then a teen and all of that, whether or not Justin is the dad by birth won't make a difference.

No, I hope for Noah's sake he can have the peace of mind to call Justin his flesh and blood. Ultimately though, what is a father? It has nothing to do with a donation made, does it? It's all the things that come afterwards.

"You know what, I don't think it matters," Justin says. "No need to know."

"*What*?!"

"Yeah, let's save it and give it to him on his eighteenth birthday. Let him decide if he wants to know."

"And in the meantime?" My voice is shrill. "What are we supposed to tell him in the meantime, Justin? That we *think* you're his bio dad, but there's a possibility that's not true? Or what, we just drop this potential bomb on him at eighteen?"

Justin stares at me for a beat. But I see it, the flicker in his eyes. He's fucking with me.

"Just kidding," he finally says. "I'm not that cool."

I slink down in the nearest chair in laughter. My immature jokester, even in the most emotionally heightened of conversations.

"Hey," he says gently. "You *laughed* with the eye roll that time. Your laugh is back. I missed it."

I look up at him and see the sincerity in his eyes as he makes this point so succinctly. "I'm sorry," I say. "I'm sorry it went away."

A quiet nod. A shuffling of his feet. Then a quick kiss to my cheek and he returns to the task, greedily ripping open the envelope. He has such assurance, it's nearly startling.

My mind rolls through a million scenarios of how this could possibly play out. What if I'm wrong? Then I guess nothing really changes, Justin came back to me under the impression that Noah was not biologically his.

But if he is? Will there be a new wave of fury at having missed out on so much already? On the last weeks of pregnancy, the birth, being one of the first people to hold his son, the middle of the night feedings that offered up an earthly calm and serenity that had unexpectedly become some of my favorite moments?

Justin pauses before pulling out the paper. "Wait, how did you get a sample?"

I gargle out something that sounds like a laugh. "Right. Well Lila got a little creative on a coffee date with you."

He nods as if that isn't highly questionable, then smiles sadly. "She told me, Luce. She didn't get creative, she straight up told me.

And said Noah had my auburn hair. She also said not to tell you. I was only asking to see if you knew."

I shouldn't be surprised at this. I'm not, in fact. Basically I tasked my baby sister with this and left her to her own devices, not wanting to know the how. I think it was because I was hoping she would pull out all the Lila stops and get this ball rolling for me.

"It was before I knew about Carter and the DC job push, Justin. I wanted you back. I've *always* wanted you back, I just didn't think you wanted me." I shrug. "But at the very least, you deserved to know this. I figured I'd find the right time to open it, but for some reason I just couldn't without you."

"Ten bucks says Lila already knows," he says with an eyebrow raise.

And this is why I love my husband. Here we are, two souls having been through marital hell and back, and he can still keep things light as much as is humanly possible.

Justin finally pulls out the paper and unfolds it. The emotional squeeze of his eyes accompanied by a grin tell me everything I need to know. I do a silent chant to promise myself I'll laugh if he says "My boys really *can* swim!" but thankfully he remains quiet.

He folds back up the paper and stuffs it back in the envelope, his face no longer grinning or full of jokes, but soft and serious. I see his Adam's apple move in a gulp. "It's a good thing you named him..." he starts, then trails off, voice heavy with emotion and unable to speak. He takes a deep breath and tries again.

"I need you to know, Luce—I'd be here no matter what. I mean that, okay?" I nod, blinking away my tears, heart squeezing in my chest as I see the sincerity in my husband's eyes. His love and adoration for me, despite everything. He continues, his voice nearly a whisper. "This outcome doesn't matter to me. Because *you* matter to me, and it's all I've ever wanted. And...and I'm sorry that I gave up at some point in all the things that made us us." He kneels down in front of me and reaches forward. How I love and have missed the feel of his arms wrapped around me like this. Such sweet, simple comfort in his hugs.

"I love you so much, Justin."

"I love you." He kisses me softly. Then kisses my temple. We hold each other and I hear his voice, soft in my ear. "It's a good thing you named him Noah Harris, isn't it? Our son." Another kiss to my temple. "Thanks for making me a father." Justin chokes on those last words and we both let the tears fall between our cheeks, faces pressed together as he collapses into me.

I realize with such pure exhausted relief the meaning of our joined tears—they are the tears of a war finally over. And these tears and this embrace, right here and now, this is our peace. The surrender to one another, the thing I had been avoiding. Sweet surrender was all I ever needed all along.

Because this man will always save me.

I just have to let him.

epilogue

. . .

IN A BEIGE apartment in a beige building in a parking lot littered with sensible cars and yuppies with sensible dreams, one car stands out—the irrepressibly ostentatious Porsche of baby blue. Out of it steps an attractive blond man of medium build with a clean shaven face, and a smile that comes with a perfect tinny "ding" sound at the exact moment said smile is unleashed.

He steps out of his vehicle, does a scan around the parking lot that is intended to look casual, but really is more of a "Did anyone see me in my beautiful car?" type of scan. The residents here already know it, and know him, so no one pays him much mind. But in his head, someone is definitely peering from behind a window curtain, admiring from afar. This brings him immense joy, the sensation of being admired in such a clandestine way.

He had convinced his date to follow him home, a conquest he wasn't entirely sure he'd secure the deal on. But that second bottle of wine—(in the range of $90, which he was sure to point out to her at dinner as he casually turned the menu towards her and asked, "What do you think of this one, have you had it? Oh no? It's delicious, you'll love it.")—that second bottle he was pretty sure sealed the deal. So sweet Emma was due here any moment, and he wants to hurry upstairs to get the lights in the perfect dimmed setting, the music just right. He'll light the candle he knows women go nuts for, the perfect combination of comfort and intoxicating masculinity. It was called "Worn Leather."

He makes his way upstairs, two at a time, a sense of urgency creeping in. He wonders what kind of panties Emma is wearing tonight. Maybe she's the type to surprise you—red lace or nothing at all, when on the outside she looks the type that's white cotton all the way. He was eager to find out.

He slips in the apartment and picks up the mail from the floor. There's a card on top that sticks out to him, and for the briefest moment he considers opening it out of curiosity, but he thinks better of it. He has work to do.

First, the lighting. His apartment isn't much—soon he'll be in one of those bachelor pads with floor to ceiling windows and electronic everything. There won't be a single thing without a remote or voice command of some sort. But for now, just for now, he's here. So yes, dim lights are necessary.

Second, the music. Naturally, he has the latest and greatest of sound systems, no expense spared to be able to achieve the perfect low rumbles of bass, or to be able to feel as if you're in the action when watching a movie, shots fired from directions both left and right, never quite knowing where the hidden speakers are. It was great when it startled a girl, his date of the month, and he could easily slip his arm around her in soft comfort to protect her from the big, bad noises.

Third, the candles. Two single-wicks on the Ikea coffee table and one large three-wick one on his stove, nestled between the rusted coils of the burners. The fourth and final candle on the wobbly table adjacent to the front door. His thumb flicks the lighter one final time for this fourth candle, and he struggles to keep the flame from burning his hand as he tilts to light, the wick just a bit far out of reach for comfort. But alas, victory. The candle is lit.

As he places the candle down, his eyes catch on the pile of mail in front of him. Particularly, the card that's on top. At first glance, it appears to be an invitation, the envelope sleek and dazzling in a metallic gold with thick, black cursive. But there's a peculiar "Thank you" written on the bottom left corner, and the corners of his mouth lift in a smile. Who might this appreciative card be from? His mind rolls through the various interactions he's recently had, small favors he's done or gestures of kindness when attempting to close one deal or another. This card of gratitude could be from anyone.

Or perhaps it's from a girl he recently seduced. Maybe someone looking for seconds. Eagerly he takes his letter opener (gold and silver with his name engraved on the blade), and enters just the tip right into the small sliver of an opening at the otherwise sealed corner of the envelope.

And a light tap on the door momentarily pauses him. Emma. He reaches for the doorknob, twists and pulls back, armed with a toothy grin and "ding" as he readies to greet his guest.

"Hi," he says. "God, you're so hot."

"You said that already tonight. A few times, you know." Emma steps in and he beams at her, loving the way she flirts. He closes the door behind her. Her eyes move to scan the space, and he worries momentarily that she's judging its size.

But then he remembers the card in his hand. "I was going through some mail real quick, I hope you don't mind. Got this card I think might be from a client, look at that beautiful stationary," he says, holding the card up to show her.

She nods twice, eyebrows raised, and does another scan around the place. "Cool, yeah."

"Two seconds, and then I'm all yours," he says with a quick peck on her cheek.

Then one quick slice with the letter opener, and the envelope is open. He pulls out the card, pinches his brow as he reads the lettering on the front.

"Because humanity and apologies are beyond you..." he reads quietly in confusion.

And he opens the card to an explosion.

Of gold glitter.

Dotted with small gold confetti pieces of—

"Are those *dicks*?" exclaims Emma, wide eyed but cautiously smiling. She takes a step back, away from the infectious glitter, but starts full-fledged laughing.

He's stunned, completely stunned. Frozen in place at the horror of this cruel joke.

And Emma is laughing like it might be the most hilarious thing she's ever seen. He watches in terror as she heads back towards the door, opens it and slips out before saying, "Devin Carter—I knew there was something off about you. Tell whoever that gift-giver is 'thank you,' because yeah, I can pretty much guarantee that little gift is from a woman. Have a nice life, *dick*." And with that, Emma slams the door. He's left with the muffled sounds of her taunting laughter all the way down the hall.

Carter looks back at the card still in his hand. Drops it to the floor and watches as another cloud of glitter and confetti penises fluff in one final breath of air before settling into the fine grooves of polyester carpet.

It dawns on him. Who the card's from.

The two sisters he feels one hundred percent certain are the masterminds behind this little act, given the recent "Stay the hell away from my family" phone call lashing Lila gave.

Lila and Lucy.

"Why those *LITTLE MOTHER FUCKING BI—*"

acknowledgments & thoughts

So much to unpack here I'm not entirely sure where to start, other than THANK YOU my amazing readers for being here! How can I ever show my gratitude? I hope so much that you loved these beautifully flawed characters as much as I did!

Speaking of flawed—Justin and Lucy. (Heart squeeze.) The idea to do an emotional affair came because it's not an uncommon tale. If this hit home for you, then I imagine it stirred up some things and my hope is that you could feel a little less alone in reading. Maybe even get an idea of the way all marriages/relationships hit their ups and downs, because for longevity to be achieved, it's not all going to be pretty. It is always my hope with my stories that whatever is relatable can also offer you the healing journey you deserve. It may be difficult to ride through, but when we move through our pain we can find the beautiful spaces on the other side.

I wanted to start off with Lucy's affair in here so that we get to that judgmental place in our minds, only to then learn that wait a sec—*he* has some mistakes of his own. There's always more to the story, more than meets the eye and many layers that impact the outward behavior. That was my mission here, to dissect those very real layers that can often go unrecognized until it's too late. But I *believe*, dear loves! I believe that true love can beat out the toughest of things, as long as there is accountability and genuine remorse from both parties and a willingness to do the work to recognize where things went wrong and how to fix it. I could and want to say more here, but I fear then I'd be creating a whole other novel.

Let's talk about our darling sister duo, Lucy and Lila—

In intake sessions with clients (I am a therapist, by the way), I ask about family history. I explain that while yes, I do enjoy a psychodynamic lens to start that dives into early childhood and caregiver relationships, I promise that's not where we'll stay. It's simply a great place to begin to help unveil early learned aspects of how we handle conflict, birth order, the family constellation and all sorts of other useful things that help inform not only my concepts of treatment for an individual, but FAR more importantly, their own insight.

It's dangerous to categorize as there are exceptions to every rule, so I say this with caution! But often we notice that with birth order, there can be a big sibling/little sibling dynamic where the big sibling is like Lucy—responsible and holding lots of pressure, and the little sibling is like Lila—feels more misunderstood as the wild child. I wanted to emphasize the unique pressures each of these birth orders can have but in a way that allows someone on the other side of it to truly see and feel what the experience is like for their sibling.

In short—I wanted you to love and see Lucy if you related more to Lila, and visa versa.

We get glimpses of the way both sisters grew up with rather emotionally detached parents, yet the effects of that appear in different ways. Lucy is responsible, but her love of control and determination come to a boiling point. (I loved so much the scene where Justin finally identifies this—calling her out on the love for control going so far that it was as though she wouldn't allow too much love between them, lest she fall and lose her cherished grasp.) Lila feels very little control as the "tossed aside" child and therefore grasps it in other ways, namely food and body image. Lucy and Lila both share a bit of toxic independence in their avoidant attachment styles.

It was important to me to show a twist from the traditional "here's what that birth order does." I wanted Lucy the Responsible Rule Follower older child to finally be allowed to mess up. I wanted Lila the Reckless Wild Card younger child to surprise everyone by proving she *does* know what she's doing, if she's only shown a little support and faith. I wanted Lucy to have a happy ending even with her mess ups, and Lila to see for herself and the world that she could in fact matter in big and important ways, even if just to one small human (Adrian's daughter Annabelle.)

I purposely didn't have a massive resolution on Lila's body image struggles. We see her growth in little moments as she slowly inches herself closer to people her previous self would have always kept at arm's length. And we see her find purpose in the opportunity to connect with Annabelle, a fellow little sister with an affinity for grueling mirror sessions. But ultimately for many our body image struggles are a lifelong battle. There's raw truth in that, and it was important to me to honor that in a way that still allowed room for blissful happiness. We can have peace and self love even if it's a lifelong journey to stay in the healthy spaces of our minds.

Finally, Simon—our Bad Boy with a heart of gold. We often hear about codependent relationships in the context of addiction or other toxic dynamics. Generally there's one person that is in need of fixing, and the other that's there to fix, all sprinkled with enabling behaviors and feeling responsible for the other's actions. But rather than show that in a romantic sense, I decided to show it with Victoria and Simon, the makeshift mother/son duo. They both hold guilt for past mistakes and their inability to help when others were suffering. They in turn cling to one another in a pattern of caretaking, with some blurred boundaries evident. There's a sweetness to it, even if we can sense that it's a bit much at times, so much like the codependent relationships we can find ourselves slipping into, all with the best intentions. It's when Victoria and Roger get together that Simon finally allows himself to run full steam ahead with Lila. Would he have done so otherwise, or would he have continued to hold back, torn in his sense of responsibility for Victoria? Just some food for thought.

But onto the people I have to thank for helping get me here.

First, my wise beyond her years and selfless beyond basic

humanity gal Jacqui Muller. You are 100% the reason my stories get to that final place of depth and dimension. That's just the bottom line truth, and I promise you when I'm able to get my dream beach house, you will have a permanent open-door invitation.

My beta readers Carly and Meg! Naturally I had to give little spots in here to you as a model and stylist in Chapter 1, because you are the best cheerleaders a new author like me could ask for, even when I'm painfully behind on the times and have little idea what Goodreads is :)

Penny Lane Girling, my everything British reader! I met Penny many moons ago when my husband and I lived in England, and was so thankful to have her kindly read through this without hesitation, especially when thrillers are her genre, not romance! Penny helped me tweak for authenticity, and naturally Lila's roommate in turn had to be given her name. And Jennie Lecesse! I agree, totally could have spent more time in Ely :)

Another name that is here—Meredith. My girl Meredith Haggerty is my everything movie go-to gal, so when I needed to act like I knew a thing or two about female directors, Meredith gave me a mini lesson with some rather stellar verbiage. Hopefully I did you proud in the end!

Catherine Skeans, my proofreading magician. Seriously, it's magic. (And I'm sorry I made Lucy cheat, but it was necessary.) But WHAT WOULD I DO without you and your witchy talents? I'm amazed every time.

Jen Denver, thank you for reading my stories and cheering me on, even though I struggle with watching certain things and I love the Grinch more than Santa.

Thank you to the real life interior design extraordinaire Beth Diana Smith for allowing me to have her appear in a character role. I had the privilege of briefly meeting her at a design show house, and just like Lila in Chapter 1, I wandered into the glorious Wine Lounge in complete awe of the details and talent surrounding me. In a similar fashion to Lila, I had been babbling on about how it was my favorite room in the house, and heard a "Thank you" from a woman that appeared far too gracious to have created a room like the one we were standing in. (I suppose I'd expected a more aloof and haughty presence.) If anyone is in the market for a transformation—you can thank me later for finding your gal!

Finally, thank you to my four babies and my husband for, as our daughter Gwenna says, allowing me to be a "Girl Boss" which sometimes equals a not-so-perfect domestic goddess. Seriously. The beach house, guys. Just you wait. Oh, and for randomly singing and blasting Hamilton music through the house and making me so proud.

about the author

A believer that life is all about the great stories we live to share, Vanessa Zian loves helping people find the heart and ah-ha moments in their own tales. Her two loves are romance novels and tapping into underlying emotions.

When she's not writing or reading romance, Vanessa works as a therapist, helping clients heal through the powers of introspection. She writes with the same goals in mind—to find value in the conflict and strength of character in beautiful stories, and to celebrate our happy endings.

Vanessa lives in Delaware with her childhood crush-turned-husband, their four kids, and their rescue pup Mikka.

And lots of high heels.

Readers—please consider leaving a rating or review! As someone brand new out here, it's not only so appreciated, but vital to helping me keep writing.

Let's cheer and love and cry and learn together in the fourth and final Dog Tags & Lace book, *March Becomes Dawn,* out October 2024

Join my newsletter where I will randomly ask for character name ideas, offer therapeutic tidbits, share sneak peeks, etc! Visit vanessazian.com

Email: Vanessa@vanessazian.com

Ely Cathedral, 2011

Ely Cathedral, 2011 (Vanessa with her husband and
two children)

facebook.com/VanessaZianWrites

instagram.com/vanessa_zian

tiktok.com/@vanessazian